Other

The Broken World Series:
Broken World
Shattered World
Mad World
Lost World
New World
Forgotten World
Silent World
Broken Stories

The Twisted Series:
Twisted World
Twisted Mind
Twisted Memories
Twisted Fate

The Oklahoma Wastelands:
The Loudest Silence

Zombie Apocalypse Love Story Novellas:
More than Survival
Fighting to Forget
Playing the Odds
Key to Survival
Surviving the Storm
The Things We Cannot Change

The Outliers Saga:
Outliers
Uprising
Retribution

The Blood Will Dry

Collision

The College of Charleston Series:
The List
No Regrets
Moving On
Letting Go

When We Were Human

Alone: A Zombie Novel

The Moonchild Series:
Moonchild
Liberation

Anthologies:
Prep For Doom
Gone with the Dead

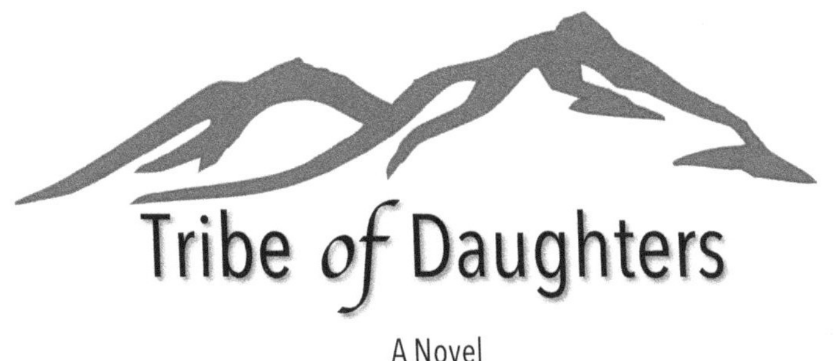

Tribe *of* Daughters

A Novel

KATE L. MARY

Published by Twisted Press, LLC, an independently owned company.

This book is a work of fiction. The names, characters, places, and incidents are fictitious or have been used fictitiously, and are not to be construed as real in any way. Any resemblance to person, living or dead, actual events, locales or organizations is entirely coincidental.

ISBN-13: 978-1727367775
ISBN-10: 1727367774
Cover Art by Kate L. Mary
Edited by Lori Whitwam

For Stacey.

Thanks for the support.

PART I: Husband

CHAPTER ONE

Jameson

THE RAIN OUTSIDE FALLS IN THICK SHEETS THAT MAKE IT seem like it's trying to wash us away, and all I can do is cower in my tent and wonder how the cold sank deep enough inside my body to turn my blood to ice. And how the hell I ended up here to begin with.

Forge A New Frontier!

The company slogan was just upbeat enough to trick me into signing on the dotted line, and the next thing I knew, I was on a train headed west. Now I realize how idiotic I'd been, but at the time it seemed like an adventure. The load of cash they'd promised probably had a little something to do with how blind I'd been as well. It's damn hard to see straight when someone dangles that many dollar signs in front of your face, especially when your life has been a pile of shit for as long as you can remember.

Of course, the asshole who recruited me failed to mention that most of these trips ended with half the crew dying of things like cholera or dysentery.

Illnesses no one should have these days, not even in the cities where the air is thick with pollution and garbage lines the streets. Out here, though, where civilization slipped away decades ago and has stayed extinct, anything goes.

The tent flap gets shoved open, letting in a burst of rain and wind, and Daniel ducks inside a second later. "It's comin' down like a monsoon out there."

He yanks his hat off and shakes it, throwing drops of rain across the tent, and shivers shoot through my body.

"It's wet enough in here, you asshole," I grumble and pull the blanket tighter around my shoulders. "Should have kept my ass where I was."

Daniel drops at my side and flashes me teeth the color of the weak tea my mom used to drink, courtesy of the chewing tobacco he can't go a second without. He's only a little older than my twenty-seven years, but he looks like he has at least a decade on me. A jagged scar runs up one side of his face, from his jaw to the corner of his eye, and poorly drawn tattoos cover most of his arms. He's also missing a front tooth and the little finger on his right hand, almost like he's falling apart one piece at a time.

"Just a little rain," he says in a voice that wheezes its way out of him. "I been through worse."

I don't doubt it—for him, this trip wasn't optional; it was this or jail—but I keep my thoughts about how he probably deserves worse to myself.

"Yeah, well, my life has always been shit, but at least I was usually dry," I say, wondering if jail could possibly be worse than sitting in a mud puddle in the middle of nowhere.

"Everybody's life is shit these days." Daniel's mouth scrunches up like he's about to spit, but he stops when I pin him with a glare icy enough to freeze the devil in hell.

He isn't wrong. Things haven't been good for decades. The plague that killed off most of the population seventy years ago is long gone, but we sure as hell haven't recovered. I've seen movies about the old west and pioneers who braved savage people and wild, untamed lands, and the scenario isn't too far from where we are now. In fact, if it wasn't for the technology left over from the old days, I'm sure we'd be right back there.

Not that it does the average person a lot of good. The cars still running are reserved for the wealthy since oil production is slow and expensive, and electricity comes and goes most of the time. Growing up, a night with no lights and no heat wasn't uncommon, and I should be used to freezing my ass off the way I am, but this trip isn't anything like I expected.

This damn trip.

I shake my head thinking about it. The railroad company promised me a decent chunk of money up front and a shit ton when I returned home, and it had all seemed so simple when I signed up. Even now, hunkered down in a shitty tent while it pours buckets, I'm not sure where I went wrong. We go out in a group and repair the train tracks damaged from years of disuse. No problem, right? Except there's only one working train, so they had no intention of leaving it with us. We could have used trucks, but these days gasoline is more valuable than gold, which means we've been traveling across the country in wagons pulled by horses.

Another detail conveniently left out of the company's sales pitch.

"Should have stayed back in Baltimore," I mutter to myself.

Daniel hoots like it's the best joke he's ever heard, and I stifle an urge to punch him.

I'm in the middle of glaring at him when a shout rises up outside. It's barely audible over the pounding rain, but the whinny of the horses is loud and clear despite the storm, and it has my back stiffening as thoughts of wild animals flip through my mind. I heard a rumor that the last group had an altercation with a pack of lions. The cats aren't indigenous to the area, but before the plague, parks displaying all kinds of exotic animals dotted the country, and a lot of them were released when people realized the end was near. Some species have thrived in the wild, especially out here where there are no humans left.

I've never seen a lion in person, but I've seen pictures, and the last thing I want is to have one of them sink their teeth into me. So I stay where I am and pull my blanket tighter around my shoulders like the thin fabric will keep me safe.

More shouting breaks through the air, this time angry, even violent sounding. There's something distinctly feminine about the voices, which makes no sense because there are no women on this trip, and even though I don't want to get my face eaten off, I find myself getting to my feet.

"What do you think is goin' on out there?" Daniel asks, not bothering to drag himself up off the ground.

"No clue."

Part of me thinks I should go check it out, but the idea of getting soaked again when I've barely gotten dry sounds as unappealing as getting eaten by a lion. Even when more yelling joins in the ruckus, I don't move. My feet stay rooted to the semi-dry floor of my tent while my heart pounds harder and harder with each passing second. Someone lets out an agonizing howl, and the sound raises the hair on my arms even higher than the goose bumps did, but I still don't move.

"What the—"

Daniel's words get cut off when the tent flap bursts open. I stumble back, but it's the sight of the person who leaps inside that knocks me on my ass. It's a woman, all right, but like none I've ever seen. Animal hides wrap around her body, secured by leather strips that crisscross over her chest and waist. They wind around her legs, too, giving off the impression that with a simple tug her clothes will fall to the ground. She towers over me, the muscles in her arms straining against the leather when she raises a bow. She has her dark hair slicked back, not from the rain but with mud, and black paint covers most of her face. Intelligent, pale blue eyes sweep across the inside of the tent, going from Daniel to me and back again, taking in every detail in less than a second before she releases her arrow.

It flies through the air, piercing Daniel in the heart before he has a chance to blink. He opens his mouth, and a wet cry bubbles up, joined a moment later by blood spraying from his lips and running down his face and neck. His body drops to the ground.

Then the woman is on me, her bow somehow gone and in its place a knife carved from bone, its blade long and pointed enough to prick the skin on my neck with little effort, drawing blood. I let out a low hiss of pain but don't move an inch.

"You are healthy?" the woman asks in a dialect as foreign as she is.

She has her knees planted firmly on my chest, her feet on each side of my torso to steady herself. Blue eyes narrow as they take me in, reminding me of the way starving children stare at cakes through bakery windows, and my pulse quickens at the predatory expression.

"Yeah," I whisper, barely moving my lips, terrified she'll slice my throat open.

"Yes?" Her voice goes up in a questioning tone like she doesn't understand.

"Yes," I clarify.

Her head bobs once, and she gets to her feet, pulling me with her. Even standing, I have to strain to look up at her, because she has to be well over six feet, and her firm grip on my arm will most definitely be leaving a purple handprint behind.

"You will come," she says, dragging me toward the flap of the tent.

I do as I'm told, and her grip doesn't loosen as she drags me forward, my feet tripping over blankets and other items. We step outside, leaving the relatively dry tent behind, as well as Daniel's body, and the wind and rain pound against my face. I'm not wearing shoes, and the muddy earth is cold beneath my bare feet. The woman holding me doesn't let go, but she does change positions. She keeps the blade at my throat while moving behind me, her free arm around my chest and the knife still against my throat.

"Walk," she calls over the rain.

Several of the other tents are torn open, their sides now gaping holes that flap in the wind. Most of the lights seem to have been extinguished in the scuffle, but the few still working reveal a bizarre scene where primitive women dressed in leather hold men at their mercy. Through the rain and darkness, I count six other men, all of them kneeling in the mud with their hands tied behind their backs. Four women stand over them, loaded down with homemade bows and spears, while three more gather the horses.

"One more," the woman at my back calls.

When we reach the others, she kicks the back of my knees, and I go down, relieved that the knife seems to have disappeared from my neck. I hit the ground, and mud squishes under my knees, and a second later my arms are yanked behind my back and tied around my wrists and at the elbows, making the muscles in my shoulders ache.

"Do not move," the woman behind me says before releasing my arm.

To say I'm too shocked to do anything is an understatement. I search the darkness, trying to find the men in their group, but there are only women. Eight in all, and every one is muscular and broad, reminding me of the prizefighters I used to go see and how they would dedicate every free second they had to lifting weights, knowing it was the best way to escape the poverty they'd grown up with. But these are women, and this isn't the city, and I doubt they're on their way to a ring to beat the shit out of each other.

The women talk back and forth while they go about gathering things. Their words are slow, overly pronounced, their dialect making them sound simple even though they're clearly intelligent and organized. They dig through tents and wagons, and toss away things like food and money and shoes, but take common items like glass jars. Nothing they do makes sense, but they seem to have a purpose in everything, and they work together like a finely tuned machine or the cogs in a watch, winding around and around, hour after hour in perfect harmony.

The only issue comes when they discuss the wagons. Two of the women, the tall one who grabbed me and another one with skin the color of coffee beans, want to load the supplies onto a wagon, while the other women want to leave it behind.

A woman with gray, stringy hair lifts her hands before the discussion gets too heated. "I am Elder Warrior, and I will choose," she calls. "It cannot make the trip up the mountain, and we do not want anyone coming after it. We will leave the vehicle behind."

The other seven women turn their backs on the wagon like her decision is law.

When they head our way, I stiffen and for the first time wonder what our fate will be. These women kept the seven of us alive for a reason, but what that reason is, I can't even begin to guess. Are they hoping to hold us for ransom? If so, they're going to be disappointed. The men who signed up for this detail did it because they had no money, no family, and no hope. We are worthless in the eyes of the rest of the world.

"Stand," the woman with the dark skin says when she stops in front of us. "We will go now."

I struggle to my feet, finding it difficult to maintain my balance with my arms tied behind my back the way they are. The ground is slick with mud, and two men actually slide and start to lose their footing, but the women are there to brace them before they have a chance to fall. With the heavy rain coming down, it's tough to make out the faces of the men at my side, and the two I can see, I can't put names to. We've been on the road for a couple weeks, but I've been too miserable to take the time to get to know anyone other than Daniel, and that wasn't by choice.

"Move," a woman at my back barks.

She shoves me, but it isn't hard enough to make me fall, just enough to get me moving. I walk, cringing when cold mud squishes between my toes, and follow the other men and women toward the horses. There are half a dozen animals, but eight women and seven men, and I can picture the women riding the horses through the rain as they lead us behind them, tied together by rope. But that isn't what happens, and I watch almost dumbfounded as one by one the men are helped onto the horses.

When it's my turn, one of the women holds me steady while another laces her fingers together and kneels and motions for me to use her hands as a foothold. I slip my mud-covered foot into her hands while the woman at my back gives me a push and the one in front hoists me up, and I find myself sprawled across the horse on my stomach. Some careful maneuvering by the women fixes that, though, and once I'm straddling the animal, the broad woman who killed Daniel climbs on with me.

I sit behind her, my arms still behind my back and my body shivering from the cold. A leather strap is tied around our waists, securing me to the woman, and someone throws a thick blanket of fur over my shoulders.

All around me, the other men are in the same positions, already on horses or being helped onto one. The women are silent, focused on their task. They gather the items they salvaged from our wrecked camp and tie them into bundles, attaching them to the horses. The aroma of wet fur is heavy in my nostrils, along with the salty scent of body odor from the woman in front of me. The smell isn't sweat or filth, which is how the vagrants in the city smell, but earthier. Dirt and rain and pine, with a hint of perspiration. Not pleasant, but nothing to cringe away from.

When everyone is seated, we take off, moving in a line. There are twelve of us on horses, the front horse holding two men instead of one prisoner and a woman, while three women lead the group on foot, carrying bundles of stolen goods and weapons. The woman in front of me rides like a pro, using the horse's mane and a gentle press of her heels to lead it where she wants it to go. The pace is slow, but with the fur around my shoulders, I'm surprisingly warm.

It isn't long before the rain tapers off, but even once the deafening noise of the storm is gone, no one talks, and the only sound is the steady beat of the horses' hooves against the ground as they squish through the mud. There's nothing but darkness upon darkness as far as the eye can see. Even the stars have been blotted out by the thick cover of clouds, and with the never-ending blackness in front of us, I can't help wondering if these women are dragging me to hell.

After an hour or so of riding, my ass already hurts. It'll be numb by the time we make it to wherever these women are taking us. It's still night, but in the distance something has begun to form, pulling itself from the blackness like a rat climbing from a sewer. It's a continuous shape, swallowing up the horizon. A mountain, maybe, or a forest. It's hard to tell with the thick darkness hanging over us.

The woman in front of me is as stoic as she is muscular, so I doubt she'll tell me a thing, but after hours of riding in silent suspense, I find it impossible to stay quiet. "Where are we going?"

"Our village." She doesn't even look back, and she doesn't elaborate.

A million other questions go through my head, but I say nothing because I'm too afraid to hear the answer to most of them.

We go back to riding in silence.

The rain may have stopped, but the air is still wet, and my body is covered in goose bumps, thanks to my damp clothes. Even the fur draped around my shoulders can't block out the chill in my bones, and I bounce back and forth between sweating and freezing as, in the distance, the sky turns orange. In the dawn of a new day, I'm able to see I was right and the massive shape looming in front of us is, in fact, a mountain.

The light also helps me get a better look at our captors. They're wild, the very definition of savage, and their leather clothes homemade, as are their weapons. The fur draped around my shoulders isn't a blanket, but a pelt that looks like it was peeled right from an animal's body. Still, in the light of day, there's something beautiful about these women. About their strength and power and the way they carry themselves with their heads held high. Wherever they're from, it's obvious they've been secluded from the outside world for a very long time. Possibly since the plague.

When I glance over my shoulder, the eyes of the woman on the horse behind me bore into mine. Her skin is the color of coffee beans and her irises only a shade lighter, and she has her hair shaved to the scalp, revealing every follicle on her head, and muscled forearms that flex with each step the horse makes. She'd be beautiful, with defined cheekbones and full lips, if there was anything soft about her at all. But there isn't. She's as hard and unyielding as steel.

In that moment, with her gaze holding mine, a new and terrifying possibility occurs to me, and the shiver that shakes my body has nothing to do with the dampness sinking into my bones. These women could be cannibals. Those groups existed, back in the early days after the plague when food was scarce and life was hard, and though it's believed they all died out years ago, it's possible some still remain. Hidden away from civilization, wild and savage like these women.

When a second shiver moves through me, I pull my gaze from the woman and hunch my shoulders like it will make me invisible. More than ever, I wish I hadn't let that damn railroad company sucker me with promises of good fortune. I should have known shit like that doesn't exist anymore, especially not for a guy like me.

CHAPTER TWO

Wilderness

THE SUN PEEKS THROUGH THE CLOUDS, DESPERATELY trying to win a battle against the spring storm rolling in, while far below me a dense fog hovers above the forest floor. The white haze feels like an omen, although whether it is good or bad, I cannot know for certain. What I do know is my life is about to change. Only whether I am ready for the change remains to be seen.

At my back the walkway creaks, and I turn to find Raven, the High Elder of our village, heading my way. She is cloaked in furs, the coat of a once majestic black bear over her shoulders to protect her from the chilly spring, while a deer pelt covers the lower half of her body. Her feet are bare and her legs long and lean, the freckles and sunspots dotting her skin the only indication that she has reached middle age. Pink blooms across her cheeks from the cold, but her skin, which is pale and wintry, appears almost white in the early light of day.

A cool breeze sweeps across the village, making the walkways leading from tree house to tree house sway, and the wind catches Raven's long, gray hair, blowing it across her face and momentarily blocking her smile from view. I do not need to see her grin to know it is there, though. Like all the Elders in our village, she has looked forward to this day for the past five years, but for her it is particularly special.

"Are you heading out to hunt?" she asks when she stops at my side.

"Soon," I reply, but my eyes are once again trained on the forest floor.

Not long ago, the warriors were gathered there, preparing to head out, but now the earth looks barren, the grass worn thin from dozens of feet trampling the ground. Brown leaves dot the clearing, but it will not be long before they are stomped out, becoming nothing more than dust in the wind. Just like the life I have always known is about to be.

"The warriors will return soon, Wilderness," Raven says, drawing my gaze back to her. The expression of pride and hope in her soft, brown eyes seems at contrast with the uneasiness living inside me. "You are lucky. I had to wait until I was almost thirty to gain a husband. You, though, will have first pick."

She is right, I know she is, but knowing I am first in line for the Gleaning does not give me peace the way it does most women. At twenty-five, I am fortunate to be gaining a husband, but the responsibility of what is to come is not lost on me. With any luck, I will very soon become a mother, and one day an Elder. Until then, I am expected to keep my husband in line and teach him the ways of the village. But it is not an easy task, and I am not sure if I have it in me to do the things my mother and the other Elders have done.

"What is it?" she asks when I say nothing. "What are you feeling?"

I swallow, forcing down words that will paint me as weak, but once they are gone, I come up with nothing else to say. At my side, Raven's smile fades the way sunshine does when the clouds block it out, darkening her face like a storm is on the way. I do my best to straighten my shoulders so she cannot see the uncertainty inside me, but find it is impossible to hide my feelings completely.

"Wilderness—" She grabs my shoulders and turns me to face her, her hands strong and firm on my body. "My daughter, you know this is how we survive. You know the stories of how we came here, of what our ancestors endured. What we have now is better than the old ways. They had women cowering in fear. Had them controlled by men. Women were weak in the old world, and afraid, but here we no longer live in fear. Never again will we let men tell us what to do."

"I know." I try to make my voice steady and my words firm, but the tremor has not disappeared. "I am anxious. That is all. I will be okay."

"Good." When Raven releases my shoulders and steps back, her steady gaze turns me into a small child, and I have to fight the urge to curl into her the way I used to when I was frightened or hurt. "I know you will do what you must. I know you will keep our village strong by bearing daughters and becoming the High Elder you are destined to be."

She nods once before turning away, leaving me to contemplate her words, and I watch as she heads across the walkway, marveling at how tall she stands and how big she seems, even surrounded by the towering trees.

The sky is now thick with clouds, but a few rays of sunshine manage to force their way through, and when my mother's gray is once again caught by the wind, it shimmers under the light. She is everything I am destined to be but so much stronger than I am in every way, and I have no idea how I will ever be able to walk in her footsteps without falling. I can only hope if I pray hard enough and ask the Great Mother for help, I will one day be as good of a leader as Raven.

When my mother has finally disappeared into a distant hut, I grab my bow and head for the ladder on the other side of the platform, knowing that the warriors have gone to do their job, and in turn I must do mine. The Gleaning will come whether or not I have confidence in myself, and when it does, I will take my place in the village as all the other women before me have. It is my duty.

The rope ladder groans when I climb down, a couple rungs wiggling under my grasp. When I reach the ground, I lift my head to the sky and take a deep breath. Moisture clings to the air from the incoming storm, and overhead dozens of huts dot the surrounding trees, suspended high above me.

I have always lived in the air like a bird, never once having slept on the cold, hard ground, but I know it is not like this everywhere. There are other places, far away from the forest and the mountains, where the trees are few and much more spread out. Places I have never been and never plan to go. Places where the old ways have survived and women cower under the thumbs of men. But not here.

I leave the women's village behind, heading deeper into the forest where the brush grows thicker and scratches at me even as I stick to the path long ago worn into the ground by the feet of my ancestors. The foliage thins before long, though, finally giving way to the clearing where the men's village sits. The huts here are not in the trees, but instead rest on stilts, and beneath them sit pens brimming with chickens and goats, pigs and rabbits. A flurry of movement moves through the enclosures at my sudden appearance, and the closer I get, the louder the animals' clamor becomes. As does their stench.

"Wilderness!"

I lift my face toward the sound of my name ringing through the air, knowing who called out before I have even laid eyes on him.

"Hello, Zachariah."

My mother's husband smiles down at me from the platform outside his hut then grabs the rope in front of him and swings to the ground. The soft thud of his feet as they hit the earth is seemingly loud in the quiet village.

We walk toward one another, meeting in the center of the clearing as all around us other men work, feeding and tending the animals, preparing the fields for crops. As Zachariah comes to a stop in front of me, a burst of sunshine breaks through the clouds, shining down and exaggerating his features. His smile is open and warm, his blue eyes friendly, but his face is all hard angles and crests. Cheekbones that are too prominent, a chin too pointed, and a nose that is only a little less so, thanks to the hook at the end.

"Headed out to hunt?" Zachariah nods to the bow in my hand.

"I am," I say, returning his warm smile.

He lifts his face to the sky, and his mouth turns down, but only in one corner, as if he finds it impossible to stop smiling. He runs his hand over his soft brown hair, but the short fibers barely move. At only two fingertip lengths, Zachariah keeps his hair much shorter than the other men in the village.

"A storm is coming," he says, his eyes still focused on the sky.

"Yes."

I follow his gaze, studying the gray clouds currently trying to swallow up the last bit of sunshine. In the distance, the sky is even darker, the deep gray warning of an incoming storm, and even the odor of animal excrement and dirt cannot mask the scent of rain clinging to the air. It is earthy and damp and smells like spring.

The storm is a good omen for the warriors, I tell myself, a blessing from the Great Mother. It will give them cover so they can sweep in unnoticed and return home safely, bringing me a husband.

I exhale and once again focus on Zachariah. "The warriors left yesterday."

He pulls his gaze from the sky. "I heard."

His brows lift, but there is no surprise in his blue eyes. They hold mine, and the uneasiness from earlier creeps back, feeling like something inside me is alive and trying to break out. It has been this way for weeks, growing worse as the day of the Gleaning draws closer, and no matter what I do, I cannot make it go away.

Just as I cannot force my destiny to go away.

"How are the yieldlings?" I ask, looking toward the huts in the distance in hopes of thinking of anything but the Gleaning.

"They are young and stupid, but they will learn." Zachariah shrugs as if this is normal, a smile once again pulling up his lips. "Canyon and Flint work with them the most. I stick with the animals."

Distracting myself is an impossible task, and as I stare at the young boys tending the field, I imagine how different the Gleaning would be if I got matched with a yieldling. Either way, I would have a husband, but at least a yieldling would know what to expect. My husband will be a foundling. An outsider. He will be new to our customs, which can be difficult for everyone, and it will be up to me to show him the way.

"Are you nervous?" Zachariah asks, pulling my gaze back to him.

"No," I lie.

His head bobs, but the way the corners of his lips tilt down says he knows I am not speaking the truth. He reaches out as if to touch my arm but stops himself, his hand frozen in the air as though he cannot bring himself to lower it. It is something he does often.

Zachariah is not a yieldling; he was not born in our village, but brought here by the warriors when he was twenty-two years old. As a foundling, though, he has adjusted well, something I attribute to my mother's strong leadership. Perhaps that is what makes me so nervous. Maybe I do not believe I can live up to Raven.

"You will be okay," Zachariah says when his arm is once again resting at his side. "I will be in charge of the foundlings, and I will make sure your husband understands what is expected of him."

This information is not new, but somehow it brings me peace.

"Thank you, Zachariah."

Something in his expression changes, bringing to mind the way my mother used to look at me when I was a small child. As if she would gladly meet her end to keep me safe. I study Zachariah, trying to figure it out, but he looks away too quickly, almost like he is afraid I will see something he should keep hidden.

"Go hunt, Wilderness," he says, his gaze still on the ground. "Bring in some meat so Ash and Hawk have something to keep them busy."

"I will."

Saying nothing else, I leave Zachariah behind and head deeper into the men's village, past the huts and the field where green sprouts poke through the dark earth in neat rows, their tops a promise of life. Yieldlings kneel in the dirt, picking at weeds before their roots have a chance to choke the life out of the crops, while Canyon and Flint watch over them. The older of the two, Canyon, nods when I go by, and I return the gesture. He is a man, so we interact very little, but there was a time when that was not true, when we were younger and the rules were looser, and I was allowed to run through the forest with the yieldlings. Many seasons have gone by since those days, but time has not been able to completely erase the longing inside me.

When I pass the goat pen, the animals belt out sounds that bring a crying child to mind, and in the next pen the chickens squawk, flapping their wings as if trying to flee. Even when I have stepped out of the village the smell of their waste does not fade, but chases me like a hungry wolf pursuing a rabbit, carried on the wind and teasing my nostrils with its foul stench.

I walk faster, my feet crunching over long-ago fallen leaves and sticks, their cracks cutting through the silence hanging over the forest. Branches reach out to me, their fingers nipping at my skin the way the chill in the air nips at my hope of spring. With each step the wind seems to cool more, but I keep going, my heart pounding with the beat of my feet, the rhythm pushing away my thoughts and fears the way nothing else has been able to. Thoughts of the Gleaning and my husband, and questions about how I will handle it. Things I have no desire to think about because there is nothing I can do to chase away my fears or change what is to come.

When I am far away from the village and the sounds of life have faded to nothing, I stop and lower myself to the ground, my back settled against a trunk. The trees above me sway with the incoming wind, their half-naked branches clicking together. A few of the newly sprouted buds have begun to open, transforming into tiny leaves overnight like a butterfly materializing from a chrysalis. They blot out the little bit of light that has been able to penetrate the clouds, blanketing the surrounding forest in darkness that makes it seem like dusk is setting in.

The storm moves in much faster than I expected, and before long the clouds open up, and fat, icy drops pelt me in the face. The branches above me sway in a violent dance while the same wind that whirls them around throws buckets of rain on my head. Water soon weighs down the fur that had at first kept me warm, but I stay where I am, hoping the Great Mother will choose to bless me, and a deer will venture out to enjoy the spring shower. Going back to the village before I have made a kill is not an option. When the warriors return, we will have the Gleaning, and my duty will be to my husband. Meaning I will be forced to take the day off from hunting.

I pull the fur up over my head to block out the rain. The forest is quiet despite the water pounding against the ground, but before long the crack of a breaking stick catches my attention. I raise my bow on instinct and hold my breath, peering out into the rain, searching the wet forest for the animal. At first there is nothing, but I only have to wait a blink longer for another snap to cut through the roar of the pounding rain.

The sound is barely audible, but my hunter's ears pick it up with no problem, and I ready myself, staring into the trees where I am certain the creature is hiding. A doe steps through the brush only a moment later, stopping as if sensing my presence, her ear twitching. Her eyes huge.

She is too late.

When I release the arrow, it flies through the air, hitting the mark perfectly, and I let out a sigh of relief. Now I can return to the village feeling like I have done my job.

BY THE TIME I HAVE PREPARED MY KILL AND DRAGGED IT BACK to the men's village, the forest floor is soft and wet. My feet slosh in the muck, which tries desperately to suck me in, and I have to work to pry them free of the muddy earth each time I lift my legs. The rain has soaked my hair and furs, but the walk through the woods warmed me enough that I have started to sweat despite the chill in the air. My arms ache from lugging the heavy carcass through the forest, but it is a good feeling. It means we will not go hungry.

I drop the deer when I reach the first hut and climb the ladder, pausing under the overhang. Here the roof blocks out the rain, and I finally feel as if I am sucking in air instead of mouthfuls of water. Through the cracks in the shutters, light flickers like the sun's rays shimmering on water. I watch it as I knock, noting the dark figure passing, momentarily obstructing the light, and the heavy footsteps that pound against the floor of the hut.

Only a couple blinks later, the door opens, and I'm greeted by the amber eyes of Hawk.

"Good eve, Wilderness," he says, smiling like we are old friends. Which we are.

"I have brought a deer for you to butcher," I tell the man in front of me.

His eyes look through me, out into the rainy night. "You must be cold."

The words remind me of the goose bumps on my legs and arms, something the trek through the woods had chased from my thoughts. Now, standing with the wind slamming into me and my fur soaked through, I have to fight off a shiver.

"It is not too bad," I lie and take a step back when Hawk walks out onto the platform, careful to keep space between us. "It is a doe."

He bends over the rail so he can look down at the deer, and the rain pummels him in the back of the head, soaking his blond hair. He rights himself and turns back to face me, and little droplets of water fall from his curls and onto his bare chest and leather pants, and I shiver at the sight.

"I will get Ash to help me," he says. "Thank you, Wilderness."

"Thank you, Hawk."

I pause, wanting to say more. It is an old feeling, left over from our days as children, but unlike with Canyon earlier, I find it difficult to walk away. Hawk is the husband of Dawn, though, and no matter how often he and I played together as children, I have no claim over him now.

The ache in my chest does not lessen as I give him one final nod and turn my back on him. Like Zachariah did earlier, I grab the rope hanging in front of the platform and swing to the ground, my feet sloshing in a puddle, then take off. No longer weighed down by the deer, I move faster than before, preventing the wet earth from sucking me down with every step I take. Branches and leaves slap against my face as I dash through the forest, but in no time I break through the brush. In front of me, the women's village looms, the huts hanging high above my head, ablaze with flickering lights now that the sun is hidden behind the clouds. Even with the rain coming down, I spy a few figures moving across the walkways.

I climb a ladder, eager to make it to my hut so I can get dry, but only make it across one walkway before getting derailed by Dove.

"Good eve, Wilderness," she calls over the rain when she stops in front of me.

She has her dark hair twisted into cords, which are barely concealed by the fur pulled up over her head, and the infant she gave birth to less than three cycles ago strapped to her chest, a thick pelt wrapped around his body to keep the dampness out.

"Hello, Dove." I nod to the baby. "How is River?"

"He is strong. A good yieldling." She pats his back as if trying to soothe him even though the child has not made a noise. "In two years he can join the men, and then I will try for a daughter."

The baby makes a sound muffled by the fur, and Dove once again begins to pat his back. I watch as she soothes the child, awed by how natural it seems. Dove is only two seasons older than I am, but she was fortunate enough to get matched with a yieldling. This child, River, is her first, but already her actions seem practiced, and I find it difficult to imagine myself in the same role, though I know it could happen for me very soon.

"The Gleaning will be here soon," Dove says, as if reading my thoughts.

I tear my gaze from the fur-wrapped bundle and instead focus on the water dripping from the rope railing at my side, watching as it falls and hits the plank beneath my feet, joining the rain already collected on the bridge.

"Are you nervous, old friend?" she asks when I say nothing.

I shrug but say, "It would not be so bad if I were matched with a yieldling like you." *And like Dawn,* I think but do not say it. My longing for Hawk is something I keep to myself. A secret no one must ever know. "Most foundlings do not last. Most are too savage to adapt to our ways."

"You will be fine, Wilderness." I lift my gaze to find a comforting smile on Dove's face. "Focus on the union. Once you have a daughter, your husband will no longer matter."

She is right, I know she is, but I cannot help the nervous tingle moving through me when I think about what will happen after the Gleaning. Foundlings are unpredictable, and it is impossible to know how they will act.

"The medicine will help," Dove says, and her words once again make me feel as if she can see into my head.

I nod, and when a shiver runs down my spine, either from the cold or the uncertainty of the future, I wrap my arms around myself. "Thank you, Dove. It will be fine, I know. For now, I need to go. I have been out hunting, and I want to get dry."

"Good eve, Wilderness," she says, once again smiling. "Pray to the Great Mother for strength, and it will be much easier than you think."

"I will. Good eve, Dove," I reply as I move past her.

I leave her then, winding my way across the pathways as I head to my hut, anxious to get dry and be alone with my thoughts. Halfway there, I pass a hut with its doors and shutters thrown open despite the rain. Inside, a handful of women have gathered, eating and laughing as children toddle at their feet. Most are girls, but I spy a few yieldlings mixed in with the bunch, none of them over the age of three. It is okay for the boys to mingle when they are young like this, but it cannot last. Before long, their evil natures will begin to develop, and then they will be sent to live in the men's village. Like Hawk was all those seasons ago.

My own hut is dark when I slip inside, but it takes only a moment to find my lantern and the two pieces of flint I keep beside it. I strike them together, and sparks break through the blackness, but the flame does not catch, so I do it again. It catches on the third try, and soon the hut is filled with the soft glow of the flickering flame and the scent of burning animal fat. My stomach growls, reminding me that I did not eat before I went hunting. Thinking about the Gleaning had made my insides too uneasy to even consider food. Now, though, I am as hungry as a bear newly awoken from a long winter's nap.

After slinking out of my wet furs and laying them out to dry, I dig through my cache of food. Dried meat and nuts, as well as a handful of dried cranberries left over from last summer. The sight of them makes my mouth water, and my thoughts turn to spring and how the forest will soon be brimming with life and hope, bursting with berries and other savory treats ripe for the picking.

Naked but comfortable in my little hut, I throw myself on my bed, and the soft fur tickles my skin as I take a bite of the tough meat. These things, as well as all the other furs in my hut, are a result of my skill as a hunter. I took these animals out with my bow and dragged them back, and my position in the village gives me pride, because I know I am helping. I provide food and warmth and help keep us alive. But I cannot help wondering if I will take the same pride in teaching my husband. It is new territory for me, but the role is no less important than the one I already have, and I can only hope I have inherited my mother's ability to lead, and my husband is willing to learn.

Out there the world is dark and dangerous, but here we have peace and hope and do not struggle the way they do. Still, most men brought in from the outside are unable to understand that our ways are better, and I can only pray that the Great Mother chooses to bless my union and that my husband will be able to see us for what we really are.

CHAPTER THREE

Jameson

THE MOUNTAINS GROW CLOSER AS WE RIDE, THEIR white caps peeking out of the clouds still hanging in the sky as afternoon turns into evening. They're larger than I originally thought, and the closer we get, the more imposing they seem.

Other than a decrepit town that hasn't seen humans for decades, we don't see a damn thing except rocks and trees, and the silence has started to get to me. I don't even try to start up a conversation with my captors, though. As much as I hate to admit it—even to myself—I don't have the balls. Not after watching the rest of our camp get slaughtered only a few hours ago.

My ass is almost numb by the time the sun has begun to sink behind the mountains, and we've already begun our ascent into the rocky peaks. The ride is bumpy and uneven, and I find myself wishing I could hold onto the woman in front of me, but with my hands tied behind my back, I can't do a damn thing other than pray the leather strip tying us together keeps me seated. The last thing I need is to fall off and knock myself on the head, because I have a strong suspicion any sign of weakness will be met with a knife to my throat, and that sure as hell isn't how I plan to go down. Not now, not ever.

By the time we slow to a stop, I have to work twice as hard to breathe, and around me the other men seem to be having trouble as well. Their shoulders rise higher than usual with each mouthful of air they suck in, but the women don't seem to notice the change in pressure, telling me they're used to being this high up, and we're probably getting pretty close to our destination.

"Stay," the woman in front of me says.

A second later, the leather strap comes free and she slides off the horse, and the other women dismount as well, while like me, the men remain seated. Then we're led forward, each of the women leading the horse she was previously riding like this is some kind of twisted parade and we're the guests of honor. Or the game trophies. The thought makes me shudder, especially when I realize if their plan is to eat me, there's pretty much nothing I can do about it other than pray they kill me fast.

A few minutes later, we break through the trees and enter a different world. It's almost full dark now, but the fire in the large clearing helps illuminate the village and the six huts in front of us. They sit on stilts so they're at least ten feet off the ground, while under them pens have been built, each one holding a different kind of animal—goats, chickens, and pigs to name a few. Pelts, furs, and hides hang from the railings of nearly every hut, and at the other end of the clearing I can make out a field where a couple teenage boys stand, dumping buckets of water on the soil. They look up at our entrance, but only for a second before going back to their work.

Around them, half a dozen dogs mill, as do a handful of people of various ages. A few are so ancient their hair is whiter than snow, while others can't be more than five years old, but with the exception of the women who led us here, everyone in the clearing is male.

The woman with gray hair steps forward and lets out a whoop that reminds me of a battle cry, and it rings through the air, echoing off the huts and trees. Less than two seconds later, a man steps out of the center building. He's shirtless and wearing pants made of animal hides that, like the women's, are woven together and secured with strips of leather, making it seem like they're barely hanging on.

"You have returned early, Lake." He smiles and opens his arms like he's welcoming us.

The old woman doesn't return his smile. "We came upon a camp less than a day's ride from here. We have brought you seven foundlings, Zachariah."

The man grabs a rope hanging from the post in front of him and swings to the ground, his feet hitting the soft earth with a thud. When he turns to face us, his eyes, blue and clear and not the least bit threatening, sweep over the men in my group one by one, making my scalp prickle. His assessment of me is quick, though, and over in a second, and then he's turned his eyes to the next man.

Now that we're in a clearing and lined up side by side, I'm able to get a better look at my companions. We're all a little worse for wear, soaked and muddy and half dressed, thanks to the sudden way we were ripped from our tents, but every person in our group is one of the younger men in the company. Twenties, early thirties. It looks like the women killed or left anyone over the age of thirty-five. We're a healthy lot, too, considering the riffraff that signed up for the detail. Men like Daniel were common, missing teeth or digits and marred by life, but none of those men are here now.

The women were very selective in their choices, and once again I start to worry these people dragged us here to feast on our flesh. It makes sense, as uneasy as it makes me feel, that they wouldn't want to serve up anyone who looked unhealthy, and it also makes me wish I'd turned to drugs or crime when I was younger like so many of the guys I grew up with in the slums of Baltimore.

"Seven is a large number," Zachariah says, drawing my attention back to him.

He's probably in his early fifties, lean but muscular, with a smile that doesn't sit well with me. It looks genuine enough, but that's what makes it *feel* so wrong. No one should be smiling like that while my hands are tied behind my back, which means he's either sadistic or insane. Too bad I'm not sure which one I should be rooting for.

Zachariah looks us over a second time, his gaze stopping on a man two horses down, and a jolt of recognition goes through me. Other than Daniel, my unfortunate tentmate who's now rotting in the middle of nowhere, I hadn't taken the time to get to know many people, but this guy I actually know. Deacon is his name, and he's around my age, late twenties. He's been quiet on the road, keeping to himself most of the time like I have, but the few interactions I've had with him have been decent. Most of the assholes in the company were the type of people I avoided more than the plague, but I got a good vibe from this guy. Too bad I have a really bad feeling about the way Zachariah is eyeing him.

The older man steps closer to Deacon, his eyes narrowing as he studies him. "How old are you?"

Deacon's own eyes grow large, and he looks around, almost like he's begging the rest of us for help. Too bad we're as helpless as he is right now. Not only are we still sitting on the horses with our hands tied behind our backs, but we're also as in the dark about what the hell is going on as he is.

"Twenty-eight," Deacon manages to get out.

"Not old." Zachariah's lips pull down, and as fast as his smile flips, I find it difficult to believe it was there to begin with. "Open your mouth. I want to see your teeth."

Deacon's eyebrows shoot up, and when he doesn't obey immediately, the woman who pulled me from my tent grabs him by the elbow and yanks him off his horse. He drops to the ground with a thud that makes my own bones throb, and in seconds, the woman has her knee pressed into the center of his chest. She grabs his face and squeezes his cheeks, forcing his mouth open, and Zachariah moves closer so he can peer into Deacon's mouth, stepping away only seconds later.

The older man shakes his head. "This one is no good."

"How can you tell?" the woman he called Lake asks.

"He is a drug user. I can tell by the rotten nubs in his mouth and the circles under his eyes. He will start withdrawal soon, and then he will be worthless. We cannot risk using the medicine on someone like him." Zachariah turns his back to the man and with a wave of his hand says, "Six is enough. We should end this man now."

The woman holding Deacon whips out a knife, and I have less than a second to wonder what's going to happen before she slices the blade across his throat. Blood pours from the wound, but she doesn't even give him a second glance before she climbs to her feet.

Deacon writhes on the ground, and his mouth opens and closes in silent screams, and not only is he unable to make a sound, but he can't even cover the gaping wound since his hands are tied behind his back. The life floods out of him and pools under his body, black in the dark night until the firelight flickers off it, highlighting the red hue.

My insides twist when Deacon finally goes still. I'm still on my horse, and a sudden wave of lightheadedness has me wishing I were on the ground, because the last thing I want is to pass out and fall on my face. Especially when I have no doubt what that will get me—a slit throat.

I tear my gaze away from the now lifeless body of Deacon to find Zachariah's blue eyes zeroed in on my face, and the intensity in the look makes me start. For a moment, he stares at me, studying me more than he did before, and my heart thumps harder. Shit. Am I next? Never for a second did I suspect Deacon was using, and I'm not even totally convinced he was, because he didn't seem like the type. Is it possible Zachariah will think I'm on drugs, too? Will he order the Goliath of a woman to pull me from this horse so she can slit my throat?

"Do not worry," he finally says. "We rarely need to end new foundlings."

"What's a foundling?" I ask, barely able to get my voice to work. I'm afraid to ask, but at the same time, I'm desperate to get some answers about what's happening here and what I can expect to happen next.

"You are."

Zachariah smiles, and the shadows playing across his face emphasize the dramatic curve and dip of his features. With Deacon's gruesome death still fresh in my mind, I can't help thinking the expression looks evil. Sadistic or crazy, I don't think it matters, because I'm pretty sure I'm in deep shit.

He's still grinning when he turns away. "It is time to get down from the horses."

I expect some of the men to come over, but instead the women drag us off the animals. The tall woman who rode with me grabs my arm and pulls me down, like she did with Deacon, and I slide to the ground, almost losing my footing. She's there to catch me, but not to keep me up, because less than a second after I'm down, she forces me to my knees just like she did back in the camp.

The same happens with the other men until we're lined up in a row, but I barely notice them because I'm too busy scanning the village, watching the men who don't even notice our presence. Zachariah is the only one who seems at all interested in us. The others are farming, tending animals, or even lounging around.

A woman with fiery orange hair stops in front of me, holding a knife chiseled from bone, and I start to shrink away, but she grabs my arm and pulls me forward until I'm bent over. A part of me wants to struggle, but another part knows there's nothing I can do. If I fight, I make myself a target, but if I cooperate, I might make it through today alive. Then I can figure out how the hell to get out of here.

I hold my breath and work to keep my body still, praying she's only going to cut me free and not slice me open. She saws the knife back and forth, and a second later, the rope falls away, giving my arms a break from the painful twisting. When she releases me, I sit up, rolling my shoulders to get the blood flowing and ease some of the pain. Already she's working on the next man. Zachariah is once again studying us, and it's unnerving how often his gaze moves back to me.

"You are foundlings," he says once the last man has been cut free, repeating the confusing word he said earlier. "You will do as you are told. You will listen. If you do well, you will be rewarded. If you do not…" He shrugs, his smile fading, and nods toward Deacon's body. "We will end you."

I swallow and look around at the other men. Some look as terrified as I feel, but others, like the blond guy at my side, look like they're ready to jump up and rip Zachariah's throat out. If I've learned anything in life, it's that playing it cool until you have the upper hand is the best plan in most situations, so despite the fact that I'd love nothing more than to charge down this mountain, I know I need to take my time.

I just hope to God time is something I have.

CHAPTER FOUR

Wilderness

MY MOTHER STOPS IN THE OPEN DOOR OF MY HUT, her long gray hair flowing down her back and around her shoulders. The skin around her eyes crinkles when she smiles, and I freeze, knowing what she is going to tell me before she has even uttered a word.

"They are back," Raven says, echoing what I already knew. "Zachariah is looking the foundlings over now. We will have the Gleaning tomorrow."

"Good," I say, but nothing about it feels good. It feels as if I am standing on the edge of a cliff about to be pushed off.

The look she gives me is only slightly sympathetic, which is not surprising. Even when I was a small child, Raven was never one to coddle me. I could trip and skin my knee, and all she would do is set me on my feet and look me square in the eye as she told me I needed to be strong. Show no weakness, she would tell me, or someone will swoop in and take advantage of you the way the owl snatches up a mouse. It was not until I got older that I realized she meant one of the men.

"Take heart, Wilderness," she says. "You will have the first pick. This Gleaning will be good for you."

"Most foundlings are nothing like Zachariah," I remind her, finally voicing the worry that has been nagging at me for years. The voice in my head reminds me that some men are like the owl she warned me about all those years ago, waiting for me to show weakness so they can snatch me up. "I should have been paired with Hawk instead of Dawn," I say. "I should have had a yieldling."

My mother's smile fades the way light does at the end of the day. "Hawk is Dawn's husband. It was meant to be. You will be fine, Wilderness. You are strong, and you will have no problem teaching the foundling his place in our tribe."

She turns away, and I watch from my bed until she has crossed the walkway and passed the neighboring hut.

I do not make my move until I am sure she is not going to look back, then I leave my hut and climb from the trees. My mother would never approve of what I am about to do, but I cannot make myself stay in my hut when my stomach is this uneasy. The Gleaning will take place first thing in the morning, but I need to get a look at the foundlings now. Need to know what is in store for me.

I duck low when I reach the edge of our village, moving through the forest at a crouch so no one will catch sight of me. The ground is still damp from the rain, and the soft earth helps mask the sound of my footsteps as I near the men's village. I slow and work on calming my pounding heart as the huts come into view, barely visible through the thick foliage, but it isn't until I reach the edge of the forest that I am finally able to see the men, and I drop to my knees.

They have the foundlings lined up, kneeling in front of Zachariah as he talks, but I am too far away to make out more than a few notes of what he says, carried to me on the wind. He talks about the ceremony, about duty, and about the importance of obedience, but nothing about the speech is comforting. The majority of the burden will rest on my shoulders, and I know it is up to me to teach my husband what is right.

The warriors, having not yet retired to their own village, stand off to the side. They are not a large group, only eight in all, but even from my position they seem as fierce as a pack of wolves. Especially amidst the men. The warriors have replaced their furs with leather, and weapons adorn their backs. Bows, spears, and shivs with long, angry blades as pointed as a bear's tooth. The black stain they smeared across their faces before they left was only partially washed away by the rain, and what is left paints them into different people, making them almost unrecognizable. *Almost* because there are a few who cannot hide their identity no matter what they do. The orange hue of Dawn's hair peeks through the mud and leaves covering her head, and Rain's deep brown skin is impossible to mask. Grove, too, stands out, but only because she towers over everyone the way the mountain towers over the plains.

With their shoulders squared and their backs as straight as the arrow I used to kill the doe, the warriors' bodies look as hard as stone. It comes from hours of climbing trees and throwing rocks and carrying logs as big as I am. They train for this position, do everything they can to ensure they are strong enough to defeat any threat that might come our way, and it has paid off.

Dawn stands at the edge of the group with Hawk, the orange of her hair magnified by the fire. They stand close to one another. Too close. It makes my insides twist like young children do when their mothers try to tame their hair. Hawk is her husband, and I know this intimacy is natural, but I still find it impossible to quiet the longing inside me. I miss the boy I played with as a child, and it makes me feel like the mouse my mother warned me about. Weak and vulnerable as the owl stares down at it from above.

But Hawk and Dawn are not why I came here, so I tear my gaze from them and once again focus on the foundlings, still kneeling in front of Zachariah.

The sun is tucked away for the night, and were it not for the flames crackling through the blackness, I would be unable to see them at all. Leaning forward on my hands and knees, hoping to get a better look, I study the six men. They kneel with their backs to me, their clothes ripped and covered in mud, and like nothing I have ever seen before. No furs, no leather. The pants are made of a strange material, and unlike the men in the village, their chests are covered. Over the years, I have seen many foundlings, but never like this. Never when they are first brought in and still look so out of place.

Zachariah says something I do not catch, and the men get to their feet and begin to move around, some stretching their arms above their heads while others stand still and shuffle their feet.

Without warning, one of them lunges at Grove. She stops him with one blow to the chest, and he flies backward, his body slamming into the ground where he lies on his back, gasping for breath and staring up at the dark sky. Grove hovers over the man, looking as if she is ready to stomp the life out of him, but she does not move. Neither does he.

Zachariah throws his head back and laughs, but I stiffen.

This foundling is much too bold. He will not be my choice tomorrow.

Once the fallen man has climbed to his feet, careful to keep a distance from Grove this time, Zachariah says something else that gets lost in the wind. When the men begin to disrobe, heat that makes it seem like I am standing too close to a fire flames across my cheeks, and I consider looking away, only I can't. I need to watch. Need to know what will happen next. Need to see if any of the other men will try to resist.

The men remove their shirts, and with their torsos bared, they look more like the men I am used to seeing. It helps calm some of my nerves. The foundling closest to me has a picture on his back, below his right shoulder blade. It is a bird in flight, possibly a kind of hawk, and its wings are spread as if soaring through the air. Even from a distance it is breathtakingly beautiful.

When he turns, more pictures come into view, this time on his left arm, and although I can't make them out completely from where I'm kneeling, they look simpler than the bird. Nothing more than thick, black lines wrapping around his bicep. Although why he would have them is a mystery.

I scan the other men in the group and find that a few more also have pictures on their bodies. What could they mean? The images could be some kind of mark given to signify that they are the property of someone, or possibly they are the stories of their lives. Perhaps the man with the bird on his back is also called Hawk?

When the men start dropping their pants, I look away, but I do not leave. Instead, I watch the foundlings out of the corner of my eye, anxious to see if anyone else makes a move as foolish as the man who tried to lunge at Grove. Nothing like that happens, though, and for the most part they listen well. They line up in front of the bucket when Zachariah tells them to, washing the mud from their bodies, and then he gives them leather so they can dress. Most of the foundlings require help to secure the pants, but it does not take long before all six of them once again have their male parts covered.

Now they look like foundlings.

I stay where I am for a little longer, studying each of the men from my hiding spot. They cooperate, which is a good sign, but I know from past Gleanings that it does not always last.

As a whole, the group looks healthy and strong, so I try my best to imagine the daughters they might give me. The shoulders of the man with the bird on his back are broad and strong, but his looks are not as pleasing as the man next to him. That man's hair is the color of wheat, and his features are soft while his body is firm, and though I know it should not affect my decision, I cannot help admitting that I like how this man looks. Very much, actually.

I stay where I am until Zachariah heads for his hut with the men trailing behind him and the warriors turn toward my hiding place. Finally, I slink back into the forest so I can return to my own village and rest up for tomorrow. My mother will arrive early, along with a few other women, and together they will prepare me for the Gleaning. I am the eldest daughter who has not yet chosen a husband, so my match is guaranteed, but there are other girls who have had to wait until the warriors' return to find out if they, too, will get a husband. Six foundlings is a good number, much better than the last trip, which means five other women can be matched tomorrow.

Once I return to my hut, though, sleep does not come. Instead, I lie on my bed, awake and staring into the darkness as I think about who the other women will be. Brooke is not much younger than I am, and then there is Rose and Ivy and Blossom. The sixth woman I am unsure of. The other girls in the village are much younger, and it is not usual to take a husband before your eighteenth season. The elders may choose to keep the final foundling until one of the other girls comes of age, or they may end him tomorrow, but it is unlikely that my mother will allow a girl of seventeen to take a husband. It is much too young, and part of the reason we came here to begin with.

The night does not bless me with restful sleep. I spend most of it tossing on my bed while trying not to think about what lies ahead for me, but morning comes despite my uneasiness, and shortly after the sun's rays have forced their way through the cracks in my shutters, there is a knock at my door.

My legs are stiff and heavy when I head across the hut, and I pull the door open to reveal the smiling face of my mother.

"Raven," I say, doing my best to sound strong and sure.

Her smile grows as she enters my hut, and when she passes me, the fragrant scent of blossoms wafts from the clay bowl in her hands. Willow and Summer, two other Elders, step in behind her. One of them holds a dress made of fox fur, the pelts woven together by strips of leather, while the other carries a garland of purple wildflowers.

"My daughter." Raven sets the bowl down and turns to me, her smile making her look ten seasons younger. "This is a day I have longed for. My only daughter will take a husband."

I try to return her expression of happiness, but what I force out feels as dry and cracked as the leaves in the fall.

"She is nervous," Summer says as she lays the garland next to the bowl.

"No," I protest, but their gentle smiles tell me they do not believe me.

"It is normal." My mother's gaze zeroes in on me, making her look more like Raven, the High Elder of the village, than the woman who raised me. "I was also nervous on the day of my Gleaning, but Zachariah has proven to be a very loyal husband."

"You were nervous?"

I have never pictured my mother as anything other than confident, and learning she was also nervous before her own Gleaning eases some of my worry. Perhaps it is normal. Perhaps all women feel this way before they choose a husband.

"I was." My mother dips a small tuft of fur into the fragrant water and smiles again. "Let us prepare you."

I stand in front of the other women, naked and silent while they wash my body with the scented water. The sweet fragrance fills the hut and has a calming affect even if it does not chase my fears away completely. There are just too many.

When I am clean, I don the fox fur dress and allow Willow to brush out my long hair. Her fingers weave the strands into elaborate coils that flow down my back, and when she is done, she secures my hair with a thin strip of leather. The final touch is to place the wreath of wildflowers on my head.

"Beautiful," my mother whispers, earning a disapproving look from Summer. "She is my daughter. I am allowed to tell my greatest creation how perfect she is."

Willow nods, but I can tell she, too, does not approve of the sentiment.

Despite the other women's displeasure, my mother's mention of physical beauty once again brings the foundlings to mind, specifically the man whose looks called out to me last night. His blond hair shone like the sun, and his skin was as smooth as ice on a pond, but tan like the skin of a deer. He was not as broad as the man with the bird drawing, though, and I know this man's strength should have more of an impression on me than the other's appearance. Perhaps the blond man will not be so pleasing in the light of day. Maybe when I come face to face with him at the Gleaning I will find some flaw in his appearance that changes my mind. Or maybe I will like how he looks even more than I did last night.

Either way, I must be careful not to let looks influence my decision. Finding a good husband in a foundling is not an easy task, and his appearance should have nothing to do with my decision. I need a man who will give me strong daughters, but one who will also be pliable and obedient. These are not easy things to find, and I need to be careful not to let the blond man's appearance confuse me even more.

My mother steps toward the door, and when she pulls it open, my stomach sinks like a rock that has been tossed it into the river.

"You are ready," she says, beaming as she motions for me to step out. "Let the Gleaning begin."

We move down the walkway together, my mother and the other two elders following me as I head for the ladder. Below us, most of the village has already gathered, and the excitement is thick. The Gleaning happens only once every five years and is considered a festival by most of the village even though we do not have a formal celebration after. In the past, I looked forward to the ceremony, but not today. Today I think only of the men I will have to choose from and which one will be a good husband. Today I think only of the mistakes I could make and how my decision will affect my future.

When my group reaches the ground, the other women choosing husbands are already waiting. Blossom, Brooke, Rose, and Ivy each wear a garland on their heads like I do, but if they are as nervous as I am, it does not show. My stomach is full of activity, as if a newly disturbed hornets' nest rests inside.

My mother readies herself for the ceremony while I take slow breaths, trying to ease the swarm inside me. When she places the crown of feathers on her head, the dark quills contrast with her soft, gray hair. She is a regal woman, a born leader, but her confidence must be something learned, not passed on, because I find it impossible to hold myself as straight as she does, and I am never as sure of my decisions as she seems to be. There is even a part of me that is very certain I will make the wrong choice here today.

When my mother turns, she smiles. "You will be fine, Wilderness. You are smart and strong, and I know you will pick the right man."

Her confidence in me is welcome but unfounded, because even when we start moving through the crowd, I find I have no confidence in myself.

CHAPTER FIVE

Jameson

THE PAST TWENTY-FOUR HOURS HAVE BEEN THE MOST bizarre of my life, but at least I'm no longer worried I'm in danger. Not the way I originally thought, anyway. The man who seems to be in charge of us, Zachariah, talks in riddles I don't totally understand, but I've gathered enough information to realize the other men and I are here for some kind of ceremony where we'll be *chosen*. For what, I still don't know, but after a night of restless sleep on the hard floor of a hut, I'm fairly certain we're not going to be someone's dinner. That's something, at least.

"You will do as you are told," Zachariah says, standing over us as we once again kneel in front of him, this time in the hut.

He never stops grinning. Not last night when he led us into this hut or when he woke us up this morning—not that any of us got any real rest—or when he pointed to a bucket of cold water sitting on a table and told us to get cleaned up. He watches us with pale, almost translucent blue eyes, like a cloudless sky that's had most of the color sucked from it. The other men and I—the foundlings, he keeps calling us—seem to always be on our knees, and I'm smart enough to realize it's so we can learn our place. Based on that alone, I'm starting to think we'll be slaves, and this *ceremony* is really an auction of some kind.

After we've gotten cleaned up, Zachariah looks us over again before nodding his approval. "You will follow me."

When he heads for the door, motioning for us to stand, I'm the first one on my feet. I'm no one's doormat, but I saw what happened to Deacon yesterday, and to John, the man who got knocked on his ass by the giant woman, and I don't have a problem playing along for now. These people, especially the women, aren't weak. They're nothing like the women we're used to dealing with, meek and tired to the bone. The women in this village are as broad as trees, and their muscled arms could easily be mistaken for a man's, and their glares alone are enough to put me in line, while the homemade weapons are an added incentive. Until I know what the hell is going on, I plan to take these people seriously.

When I step out onto the porch, Zachariah motions toward the rope in front of him. Copying what I saw him do yesterday, I grab hold and swing out, realizing once I'm on my way down it has some kind of pulley system attached. I go down with little effort, hitting the ground sooner than I expected and stumbling back a couple steps, but somehow managing to catch myself before I fall on my ass.

A guy in his early twenties stands in front of me, leaning against one of the hut's stilts. He laughs and pushes himself off, and eyes the color of fall leaves narrow on my arms as he walks my way. When he stops, he shoves his wavy blond hair back. It comes to just above his shoulders and doesn't seem to want to obey him, though, because seconds later it's back in his eyes.

"What are these pictures?" He waves to the tattoos on my arm. "How do they not wash off?"

"They're tattoos. They're drawn on with needles so they don't go away."

He studies them more closely. "You let someone cut pictures into you?"

"I paid them to do it."

Someone drops to the ground behind me with a huff, but I'm too focused on the guy in front of me to look back. A few other men stand not too far from us, watching our exchange, and past them a handful of young boys pull weeds in the garden. There are others around, too, all different ages, but like yesterday, they're all men or boys. No women.

"Where are the women?" I ask as more people drop to the ground at my back.

"In their village," he says. "You are a foundling, but you will see. This is the men's village. We do not go to them unless invited. We do not touch them unless invited. We farm and we tend the animals. That is our job."

Invited?

I start to ask what the hell that's supposed to mean, but the question gets cut off when Zachariah calls out, "Let us go."

"You should leave," the guy in front of me says.

"What's your name?" I ask as I back away.

"I am called Hawk," he says then motions to the forest behind me. "You must go."

Zachariah is watching me when I turn, and I lower my head as I join him and the other men, hoping the gesture comes off as submissive. Based on the gleam in the older man's eyes, I don't think he's fooled, but it does seem to amuse him, because he smiles. It's also possible he's insane, because that grin seems as permanent as the tattoos on my body.

He leads us into the forest, looking back every few seconds to make sure everyone's still in line. Every step feels like knives are jabbing into my soles. The shoes they gave us are little more than a strip of leather tied to our feet and do nothing to protect me from the sharp rocks and sticks littering the ground, and I can tell by the pained expressions on the other men's faces they're having the same problem. I was wondering why the beefy women didn't come back to escort us to wherever we're meant to go, but now I know why. We'd be idiots to make a run for it with nothing on our feet but these pathetic excuses for shoes.

Zachariah is wearing the same thing on his feet, but he doesn't seem bothered by the rough terrain. He must be used to it.

"Stop here," he says when we reach what looks like a clearing. "We do not go in uninvited."

He sticks two fingers in his mouth, and I jerk away when he lets out a loud whistle. The same war cry the warrior let out yesterday follows only a second later, and Zachariah starts walking again.

He waves for us to move. "Follow me. Do as I say."

He steps into the clearing, and we follow one after the other in a straight line like obedient dogs. I go fourth, pushing past branches that scratch at my bare chest, and make it out of the forest to find tree houses with thatched roofs hanging high above my head, numbering in the dozens, with rope and wood plank bridges floating between them, going from platform to platform. But the sight of those houses isn't what makes me freeze, or why I feel like I've been thrust into a different world for the second time in twenty-four hours.

Standing in the clearing are dozens and dozens of women. Every age is represented in the group, from toddlers to an ancient woman who's propped up on a chair carved from a tree trunk, and they're all dressed in fur, with leather strips swirling around their bodies to hold their clothes in place. Some are tall like the woman who grabbed me, while others are petite. There are redheads and blondes, and women with mahogany skin standing next to others whose complexions are snowy white in contrast. The diversity of the group is overwhelming, but they all share one trait, and it stands out above everything else. They are strong. They stand tall and meet our gazes head on. Their backs are straight and their shoulders squared, and even the oldest of the women, the one sitting front and center, seems unyielding.

The uneasiness from yesterday returns as Zachariah leads us forward. The broad women who dragged us here stand at the front of the group, distinguished from the others by the black paint on their faces. I look from them to the women at their backs, and then to the old lady at the front, but none of their expressions are very welcoming. It's like they see us as intruders, which makes no sense, considering they're the ones who brought us here.

There's a lot to take in, but the fact that the rest of the women aren't as muscular as the ones who collected us from the camp doesn't escape my notice. Everyone is thin and fit, with arms that seem capable of carrying any load thrown their way, but the women with the black paint on their faces are twice as big. Anything feminine about them has been swallowed up by muscle, and they have no breasts or curves to soften them. Their thighs are as thick as logs and their shoulders broad like a man's, and they stand as straight as a board and stare at us with eyes made of steel, making them the most imposing things I've ever seen.

"Do not come closer," the old woman says when we're still several feet away from the group. "Kneel."

She has to be at least ninety, possibly pushing a hundred, and her brown eyes are milky with age yet somehow exude intelligence when she looks us over. Wiry hair the color of snow flows down to her waist, contrasting with her brown skin, which is the color of old chocolate and excessively wrinkled, making it seem like she's been soaking in a bathtub for decades.

Zachariah takes a small step back, his head bowed, and motions for us to do as we're told. I drop to my knees on the soft ground, afraid of what might happen if I resist, repeating a mantra in my head like I'm trying to reassure myself I'm actually the one in control here, not them.

Just do as they say. Bide your time. You'll get out of this soon.

On both sides of me, the other men do the same, one after the other falling to their knees until only the blond guy who was kneeling next to me when we first got here is left standing. His name is Eric, which I learned last night after we went into the hut, but other than that, I don't know a thing about him.

I'd put him in his mid-twenties, close to my age. His wavy, blond hair softens his features even though I know he's hard on the inside, and in contrast with his light brown skin, which is tan from hours of physical labor under the sun, his features are almost delicate. He's a pretty kind of guy, except for the sneer on his face, that is.

"I don't kneel for anybody," he growls as he gives the old woman a cold look.

Zachariah starts to move, but the warrior woman with the dark skin beats him to it, bringing the staff of her spear around and slamming it into the back of Eric's legs, sending him to the ground.

Once he's down, she grabs his chin and lifts his face so he's looking her in the eye. "You will do as you are told, foundling, or we will end you."

I shudder, remembering how Deacon's throat was slit right in front of us. Once he'd stopped breathing, two of the women dragged his body into the forest, but what they did with it from there, I don't know. Based on their brutality so far, I'd guess they left him for the animals.

Eric jerks his face out of the woman's hand. He doesn't argue, but he's still glaring at her, and I can practically see the images in his head as he pictures shoving her down and slitting her throat. I'm sure I'm not the only one who knows what he's thinking, either.

The warrior's upper lip curls and her hands coil into fists, making the muscles in her biceps flex. She's a tall woman, but still shorter than Eric, only I don't think it would matter. If these two had to go head to head, no weapons and no help from anyone else, this woman would be able to take Eric down without breaking a sweat.

After a moment, the warrior steps back. She spits on the ground in front of Eric, and the other Amazonian women whoop. She smiles, revealing teeth that are shockingly white next to her dark skin and much healthier than they should be, considering *this* is where she's spent her life, but her grin looks dangerous.

When she's once again taken her place in the crowd, the old lady pulls herself to her feet. It seems to take a great deal of effort, but no one helps her, and when she's standing, her head is high.

Her milky eyes stare straight ahead, but they don't seem to focus on anyone when she bellows, "Welcome to the Gleaning."

A murmur moves through the crowd of women, and like a knife slashing through a loaf of bread, they part and a procession comes into view. Despite my unease, I crane my neck in hopes of getting a better look, but I can't see much from my position on the ground. Then a woman with ashen hair and a crown of feathers on her head materializes from the crowd. She gives off the air of royalty, standing tall and regal and possessing an age-defying beauty, and although the furs wrapped around her body conceal her thin frame, they can't hide the power exuding from her. Every move she makes is precise and planned, meant to let everyone—the men kneeling on the ground, especially—know she is in control.

When the newcomer takes her place at the front of the crowd, the old woman collapses onto her chair like standing is too much work, and I find myself holding my breath, waiting for the woman with the crown of feathers to say something, but she doesn't utter a sound. Seconds pass when the only noise is the rustling of the trees above our heads, then five other women step from the crowd.

They're young, early to mid-twenties, all of them wearing a crown as well, only theirs are made of wildflowers, each one a different shade. Yellow, purple, white, orange, and pink. The girl with the yellow flowers looks like she is the youngest, probably only eighteen, but the others can't be much older. They stand in a line next to the other two women, and I study them, trying to figure out what's happening and what these women, who are young and fresh and vibrant with life, have to do with it.

Despite their youth, the women stand as tall as the warriors and don't give off even a hint of discomfort or weakness as they each meet my gaze head on. I study them one by one, trying to size them up and make sense of it all, but I get the feeling they're trying to size me up as well. Except there's something much more calculating in their eyes. Something that has my scalp prickling under their scrutiny.

"You know our history," the woman with the feather crown begins, raising her arms over her head as she turns to face the crowd of women at her back. "We came here to start fresh after the Great Plague wiped out most of the world. Before that, there was a time when women were beholden to men. When we were women and mothers only. When we were the weaker sex. We came here to escape those things, and thanks to the Great Mother, we have thrived." She turns, her arms still up, and drags her sharp gaze across those of us kneeling on the ground. "You do not take. You have no power here. We invite you in. We give you permission. At the Gleaning, we choose our husbands, giving us the control."

Husbands.

The realization of what's about to happen hits me like a sledgehammer to the gut, and the sudden urge to run is stronger than ever. I'm not sure if I'd be this scared if I thought they were going to eat us, because at least then I'd understand what the hell was going on. But this? Husband? Gleaning? None of *this* makes sense.

"Wilderness," the woman says, not taking her eyes off the men in front of her.

The girl wearing the crown of purple flowers steps forward, but it still takes a few seconds for me to realize that *Wilderness* is her name. Her small stature made me think she was hardly out of her teens, but now that I've had a chance to get a better look at her, I gauge her to be closer to her mid-twenties. Her golden hair hangs to the middle of her back, twisted into an intricate braid, and the red fur dress she wears is short and revealing, dipping between her breasts and barely covering her ass. It contrasts with her sun-kissed skin, making her look bright and youthful. She's muscular, not broad like the women who brought us here, but fit and healthy, with a splash of freckles on her nose and sharp, brown eyes that seem to take in every detail.

Her gaze moves over the men lined up in front of her, studying each of us. It lingers on me for a little too long, and my back stiffens, but before I have a chance to get too worried about being chosen, her eyes snap to Eric. She stares at him so long my muscles begin to uncoil. A part of me is relieved she's going to pick him, but another part wants to warn her. She wasn't here when he tried to defy the old woman, so she has no idea what she's getting into.

Then, as quick as a bolt of lightning, her gaze snaps back to me. "Him," she says before I've had a chance to register what's happening. "I choose the man with the pictures on his arms."

My stomach drops to the ground, and the warriors yank me to my feet so fast I don't have time to pick it up before I'm dragged off.

CHAPTER SIX

Wilderness

WHEN I TAKE MY PLACE AT THE FRONT OF THE crowd, the man I chose—now my husband—is dragged forward and forced to kneel in front of me, giving me the chance to study the drawing on his shoulder. Now that I am closer, it looks nothing like a hawk, but I can put no other name to the bird. Perhaps the species does not live around here. Perhaps it is common wherever this man came from.

The Gleaning continues with the other women, each of them choosing their husbands, but I am too focused on mine to take much of it in. In the light of day, his shoulders are much broader than I thought they were, his muscles more defined, and I notice a few scars on his arms, small but dark against his pale skin. His hair is dark brown like a bear's fur and much shorter than most of the men in our village, only a little more than fingertip length, and his face is angular, his jaw wide. He is not as pleasing to look at as the blond man, but he will make strong daughters and yieldlings, which is why I chose him.

Blossom, the last woman to get a husband today, chooses the man with the blond hair, and when he goes to join her, he does not look happy. His sour expression gives me confidence in my own choice. The medicine will make even the most defiant foundlings comply inside the hut, but we cannot administer it all the time, and I have a feeling the blond man will not give up without a fight.

I thought of that man all night, even while I slept, but I still felt certain that his looks would not be as pleasing when I saw him again today. Only they were, and had it not been for the exchange in my hut right before the ceremony, I might have picked him simply because his appearance pleased me. But my mother and the other Elders reminded me of my duty to the village, of my responsibility to bear healthy daughters, and so I chose the strong man instead. The one with the pictures on his arms and muscles that tell me he will produce sturdy offspring.

The Gleaning comes to an end, and the women begin to disperse, but I stay where I am and wait for my mother. She will want to congratulate me, and Zachariah will no doubt want to as well, assuming she gives him permission. She always does, but he is still a good husband who stays were he is and waits for her signal.

My gaze goes to the foundling who was not chosen today, still on his knees in the clearing. He is rounder than the others, softer, which is why no one picked him. The man wears a relieved expression, and something about it tugs at my heart. His fate is in my mother's hands, but it is doubtful she will allow him to remain in the men's village if he is not to be a husband, meaning he will very soon meet his end. Although I would not say it out loud, something about it feels wrong. Almost like we have stolen something from him, which I know makes no sense. Still, I cannot help feeling that way.

My husband looks back at me, tearing my focus from the leftover foundling to the man I chose. He is still on his knees, an expression of confusion on his face, but instead of speaking to him, I continue my wait in silence. I want to see how he will react. If he will remain on his knees, or if he will move without waiting for a signal from me.

"What do we do now?" he asks when I say nothing.

"We will wait for my mother." I nod toward Raven, who is helping Mother Elder to the pulley cart.

My husband, whose name I still do not know, lifts his eyebrows in surprise. "That's your mom?"

"Raven, yes. She is High Elder."

My mother motions to Zachariah, who is still standing beside the extra foundling, and he says something to the man before hurrying to Raven's side. Zachariah holds out his hand when he reaches her, and she slips hers into it, allowing him a brief moment to press his lips against her fingers. Then they head our way, walking side by side. Not touching.

"Stand, husband," I say when my mother and Zachariah have stopped in front of us.

He does as he is told, and the unquestioning obedience causes a smile to tug at my lips. Perhaps I made the right choice in this man. Perhaps he will be like Zachariah and find a special place in this village.

My mother gives me a rare smile when she says, "Congratulations on your husband, Wilderness."

"Thank you, Raven."

"Congratulations, Wilderness." The smile Zachariah gives me is as open and welcoming as the forest on a spring morning.

"Thank you," I repeat.

My mother turns to my husband and dips her head once, a gesture meant to give him permission to speak. "I am Raven, High Elder of this village. You already know my husband, Zachariah."

My husband's eyebrows jump up in surprise, but all he says is, "I'm Jameson."

Jam-e-son.

I roll the name around in my mouth, but do not say it out loud. It is an odd name, which is normal for a foundling. I was almost five years old before I could pronounce Zachariah's name, and even then it felt like I was trying to spit something out every time I said it.

My husband turns his gaze on me. "Your name is Wilderness?"

Working to keep my body straight and my head high the way my mother does when she addresses her own husband, I give a small nod. "That is what I am called."

Jameson's lips move as if he intends to say something, but my mother speaks before he can. "You have the day off from hunting, Wilderness. Now is the time to invite your husband to your hut."

My husband's gaze flits to my mother and then back to me, and the knowing expression in his eyes causes flames to move up my neck to my face.

Once again, he acts like he is on the verge of saying something, but Zachariah gives a slight shake of his head, and Jameson remains quiet, pressing his lips together.

I choose to focus on my mother instead of my husband's deep, brown eyes. "Thank you, Raven."

She gives me a small smile before turning to face her own husband. "I know you are responsible for the foundlings, but perhaps you can get Hawk to help out this evening? I would like to invite you to my hut tonight."

The smile on Zachariah's face does not change, but the way his eyes light up tells me the invitation pleases him. "I will ask him."

"Good." Raven nods to me, then to my husband, before turning away.

"Good morrow, Wilderness," Zachariah says before also taking his leave.

Jameson and I stand in silence, watching them walk away. His reserve has more to do with confusion than wanting to know where my mother and her husband are going, but mine is so I can gather my strength. The hardest part is yet to come.

My husband's eyes are full of questions when he finally turns to face me, but there is a certain amount of understanding in his expression as well, and it makes my cheeks flush. My mother is right. I must invite Jameson to my hut today. He is a foundling and needs to get used to how things work here, something that will never happen unless I fulfill my duty.

"I would like to invite you to my hut," I say, trying to sound as sure as my mother did when she invited Zachariah to hers.

Jameson gives a slight shake of his head, and even more heat spreads across my cheeks. "I don't—I mean—"

"You are my husband," I say, no longer needing to fake confidence. I refuse to let any man tell me no, especially a foundling. "You *will* come to my hut."

My husband swallows. "Okay."

"Follow me."

I head for the ladder without looking back. If he chooses not to follow me, or if he tries to run, the warriors will detain him. Their position in the village is always vital, but even more so following the Gleaning. I only pray Jameson is not foolish enough to test them.

I begin my climb and have to swallow a sigh of relief when the ladder sways beneath me only a few beats later, telling me Jameson is also on his way up. He moves slowly, but steadily. His obedience is a good omen. Unlike Blossom's husband, the man with the blond hair, who will need a large dose of medicine and possibly even a warrior to guard him, Jameson will do as he is told.

When I reach the top, I barely pause to wait for my husband before heading across the walkway to the next platform. He follows, holding onto the rope railing like he is afraid the bridge might break, and it almost makes me smile. But I hold back, knowing I must maintain control. I cannot show any weakness in front of the foundling. It is too dangerous, especially when I am still establishing my dominance over him.

I reach my hut and stop, turning to face my husband. He is still standing on the walkway, staring down in awe, but when he lifts his head and meets my gaze, I motion for him to keep moving. He seems more certain of his safety than he was when he first climbed up, but he still moves carefully, still stares at the ground with a mixture of wonder and trepidation.

"This is incredible," he says when he reaches the platform outside my hut. "Did the men build these tree houses?"

Anger boils up inside me. Jameson is a foundling, so it is natural for him to assume the men would build the huts, but he will soon learn how things work in our world.

"When we came here, there were no men." I lift my chin, trying to give off the impression of looking down on him though he is much taller than I am. "We did this. Women."

His eyebrows lift in surprise, and I can see the questions in his eyes, but he still does not voice them. He will, though. He has a lot to learn, and it will take both Zachariah and myself to teach him.

His first lesson will happen in my hut.

"Come," I say, turning to open the door.

The hut is dark with the shutters closed, but I make quick work of lighting a lantern, and in no time the soft glow of firelight floods the room. My husband takes in his surroundings, his gaze lingering on my bed of furs. When he studies the bearskin on my floor, the knowledge that I took this animal down fills me with pride. Why, I cannot comprehend, but I find myself wanting my husband to know what a good hunter I am, wanting him to know that someone of great importance has taken him as a husband.

Jameson swallows like the sight of the animal skin frightens him then turns to face me. "Now what? Are we married already, or is there a ceremony later?"

"You are my husband," I tell him. "The ceremony is me choosing you."

His head bobs twice, but he still seems uncertain. "I have no say in it? Because I'm a *foundling*?"

"Because you are a man," I say firmly. "We do things differently in our village, something you will soon learn." I gesture to the bed. "Sit. I will get you a drink."

He lowers himself onto the bed, and once again I almost sigh with relief. I had imagined this night going many different ways, had envisioned a struggle or disobedience, and the fact that he has so far been compliant is a relief. I have no wish to bully my husband, but he must understand that I have people to answer to as well. My mother and the other elders especially, but not them alone. All the women. We depend on one another to keep the village strong, and that means we must teach the men their place. Even if it is not always easy.

I turn to face the table. The medicine is ready, dropped off earlier by our Healer, but I hesitate before moving to pick it up. Giving it to the foundlings on their first night is customary, and most need it for many nights after, but my mother never had to use the medicine on Zachariah. Not even on the first night of their union. It is rare, and I know it, but my hands still tremble when I pick the bowl up and bring it to the bed where my husband sits waiting.

"Drink this," I say, holding the bowl out to him.

He opens his mouth as if to protest, but closes it again when I give him a firm look. Instead of arguing, he takes the bowl, and as he brings it to his lips, his gaze holds mine. He takes a tiny sip, tasting the liquid, and winces, but drinks the rest without complaint. The medicine is bitter, or so I have heard, but it will go a long way toward helping with his transition. Hopefully, it will ease my worries as well.

When the bowl is empty, I take it from Jameson and set it back on the table. Then I go to him, settling onto the bed at his side where I study the pictures etched into his skin. He watches me from the corner of his eye but does not turn his head. Not even when I trace the lines with my fingertip. Like I thought when I first saw them, the lines wrap around his bicep as if tying his muscles together, and every time he flexes his arm, they seem to move and shift.

"Why do you have these pictures?" I ask after a moment.

"They're tattoos. Decorations."

"Decorations." I repeat the word as I get to my knees, moving behind him, but it has little meaning to me. When I run my finger over the bird, Jameson shivers in response, and I almost smile. "What is this? A hawk?" I know it is not a hawk, but it is the closest I can guess. "I have never seen a bird like this."

"It's an eagle," he says, looking back over his shoulder at me. "An American eagle."

He blinks, but the gesture is slow and his eyes are less focused, telling me the medicine is taking effect. Soon we will have our union, and if the Great Mother chooses to bless me, my husband will give me a daughter.

"What did you give me?" he asks after a few seconds.

"The medicine. It will help."

I climb to my feet so I am standing in front of my husband. When I pull on the leather cord wrapped around my waist, it comes free, unwinding from the dress until there is nothing left to hold the pelt against my skin, and the fur slides down my body and drops to the ground at my feet, leaving me naked.

My husband blinks again, and his brown eyes take me in, focused despite the medicine. I take his hand and pull him to his feet so I can repeat the process of untangling the leather cord, freeing him from his clothes, and like my dress, his pants drop to the ground, giving me the opportunity to look him over. It is the first time I have seen a man naked, but he is much like my mother described. Although larger than I imagined.

I look up to find him staring at me, his expression a mixture of confusion and desire. It is the medicine, I know, and I cannot help wondering how he would have reacted had I not given it to him. If he would still look at me with the same need in his eyes. If he would still want me.

It is inconsequential, though, because no matter what Jameson does or how I feel, I have a duty to the village, and I cannot let my people down. So, with a tremble in my voice, I say, "I invite you to touch me."

MY HUSBAND DOZES AT MY SIDE, HIS LARGE BODY TAKING UP MORE than half the bed. I consider sending him on his way now that our union is complete, but he is worn out from the medicine, and I know he needs the rest. Instead, I cover him with a fur, pulling it up to his chest to keep him warm, while I lie at his side naked and uncovered. Watching as his chest rises and falls, memorizing the way his eyes twitch. In the soft light of my hut, his looks are more pleasing than I previously thought. His jaw is strong and defined, his nose straight. The firm line of his lips made it surprising how soft they were when he kissed me. His skin, too, was smooth against mine.

He knew what he was doing during our union, which is no surprise for a foundling, and much to my astonishment, I enjoyed the intimacy we shared. The pain was brief and was followed by a pleasurable ache I had never felt before.

Still, staring at him now, I find myself once again wondering what would have happened if I had not made him drink the medicine. Would he have tried to resist? Would he have wanted me on his own, unaided by the medicine? Even more importantly, would I have wanted him to want me?

I watch him sleep, heat licking at my cheeks as the memories of our union flicker through my mind. He will not remember it in as much detail as I will, and it suddenly strikes me how unfair that is. Almost like I have stolen something from him.

Next time he comes to my hut, I will not give him the medicine. Next time my husband and I become one, he will be present, he will remember it, and I will make sure he enjoys the act.

CHAPTER SEVEN

Jameson

I WAKE TO BLACKNESS AND A BRAIN THAT FEELS LIKE IT'S floating in soda pop, and at first, I have no idea where I am. Not in the work camp, that much I know for sure. Whatever I'm lying on is hard and unyielding, but it isn't cold like the ground. Plus, the blanket covering my body is softer than any blanket I've ever had, both in the work camp and before. I run my hand over it as I shift, and when the fibers tickle my fingers, it all comes screaming back. The warrior women, the village, my time in the hut with the woman who calls herself Wilderness. My wife. I don't remember much of what happened, and the memories I do have are fuzzy, like they, too, have been soaking in soda, but there are some images impossible to erase from my mind. Her body under mine, her smooth skin, how she gasped. Those things replay themselves over and over again like an echo.

She gave me something, something she called medicine, only it wasn't medicine. It was a drug, and it made me feel like I wasn't in my body, made it impossible to think straight, especially with a naked woman standing in front of me. The effects of whatever it was have dwindled but haven't worn off completely, causing disorientation and fuzziness in my brain and making my body ache.

It's blacker than the pits of hell, but I don't need to see to know I'm not in Wilderness's hut anymore. The room is too big, too open, and the snores echoing through the space are too masculine. I'm in the men's village, but I don't have a single memory of coming back, not even a fuzzy one.

The floor creaks to my right, and I twist to find a figure moving through the darkness on the other side of the room. I push myself up, suddenly afraid one of the warrior women has come to slit my throat now that Wilderness has gotten what she wanted out of me, and every inch of my body throbs. It takes a hell of a lot more effort than it should to sit up.

"Who is there?" a voice says, and right away I recognize it.

"Zachariah," I whisper as I climb to my feet.

I move forward, stumbling over furs and bodies as I try to reach him. It's the middle of the night, but I want answers. About how I got back here, about what happened today, about what will happen tomorrow. I want to know everything.

"Jam-e-son." He says my name the way Wilderness and her mother do, like it's a foreign object they're trying to spit out or like they can't decide if it tastes good or bad.

I've almost made it through the mass of furs scattered across the floor when my toe catches on something and I stumble, but Zachariah catches me before I can fall. His hands are like ice against my skin, and I realize he's just come from outside, then remember that he's the husband of Raven, and she invited him to her hut tonight.

"Why are you back already?" I ask, keeping my voice low so I don't wake anyone, although, if the other men got the same medicine I did, they may be out for a while.

"This is where I sleep," Zachariah says.

"You don't stay with your wife?" I ask, still trying to make sense of the whole thing. I definitely got the impression Raven was looking forward to Zachariah's company, so why didn't he stay?

"There is no wife. There is only husband."

I shake my head, though he can't see it, and when I do, it feels like my brain is swirling around, bouncing around inside my skull.

I grip my head between my hands and squeeze as I murmur, "What?"

"Come." He turns toward the door and motions for me to follow, something I can barely make out in the darkness of the room.

I hesitate, but not for long, because I have too many questions, and the things I've seen over the last day and a half have too many terrifying possibilities to put off this conversation.

Zachariah leads me out onto the porch and uses the rope to swing to the ground like it's nothing. My muscles are tight and sore, but I do the same, and when I hit the ground, I nearly fall on my ass. He's already moving away from the huts, and when I right myself, I have to jog to catch up, the ground digging into the bottoms of my feet. The air is cool against my bare chest, and steam rises in front of me when I exhale, making me wish I had one of the many furs in Wilderness's hut.

Zachariah only leads me to the edge of the forest, right next to the fire that's now little more than embers, before motioning for me to sit. "Here."

I do as I'm told, dropping to the cold ground even though I know it'll be as hard and unforgiving as the plank floor I've been made to sleep on. My legs are too unsteady to remain standing, though, and now more than ever, my head feels like it's spinning in circles.

Zachariah sits in front of me with his legs crossed and his back straight, resting his hands on his knees as he studies me with serious, blue eyes. What's left of the fire makes it possible for me to see him, even if his face is cloaked in shadows, and his expression makes me shift uncomfortably, but I meet his gaze head on. I'm not afraid of this man, even if I do think he smiles too much, but I'm terrified of what he might tell me about this place.

When he doesn't say anything, I take a deep breath and start asking my questions. "I'm married to Wilderness?"

"You are her husband," Zachariah says, then he repeats the confusing phrase he already said in the hut. "There is no wife. Only husband."

"I don't understand."

"There is no father, there is no brother, there is no son."

The words are confusing by themselves, but combined with everything I've seen, they almost make sense. Here, men have no titles, no privileges, and the women call all the shots, make all the decisions. Men exist only to satisfy the needs of the women.

But it doesn't even come close to explaining everything, so I ask, "Then you aren't Wilderness's father?"

Zachariah's body jerks ever so slightly, and something that almost looks like pain flashes in his eyes, but his back is still straight when he shakes his head. "No. I am her mother's husband."

I try to wrap my brain around the information, but no matter how hard I try, it doesn't work, because there are too many holes and I'm too tired from the medicine. The more I try to focus on it, the more my head throbs, and I rub my temples, hoping to ease the tension, but the ache is deep inside my head and the effort futile.

"Explain," I finally say, the word coming out as a sigh. "Please."

"The women stay in their village, and we stay in ours," Zachariah begins. "You are not to enter the women's village unless invited. They can come here if they desire, but most do not. We are here to serve the women, to give them daughters and strong yieldlings. That is our purpose."

"What's a yieldling?" I ask before he can go on, still rubbing my temples. It isn't working. The more Zachariah talks, the more my head pounds.

"A man born of this village."

I swallow, remembering the little boys I saw in the men's village. There were a few in the women's village, too, but they were all very young, babies and toddlers, under the age of three. The older boys are here, living with the men.

"You're telling me the mothers don't raise their own sons?" I ask, my fingers frozen on my temples, my headache forgotten at this revelation.

"There. Are. No. Sons." Zachariah emphasizes the words like if he pronounces them right I'll be able to understand. "There are only yieldlings. They come to us, to the men's village, after they are weaned from their mothers."

The callousness of the whole thing hits me in the gut, and for a moment I can't say a word. I inhale then blow the breath out, trying to understand, but it's impossible, because I can't comprehend women handing their children over simply because they're boys.

"What else?" I ask when I've gathered myself. "You call me a foundling. What does that mean?"

"Foundlings come from outside the village. When a woman comes of age, the Elders match her with a yieldling so she can produce daughters. But we do not always have enough husbands to go around, so every five years, the warriors go out and get foundlings for the women." He pauses and looks me over. "It is a hard transition, and only the strong make it."

He continues looking me over, and the expression in his eyes is one of a father sizing up his son-in-law. Despite his claim that Wilderness isn't his daughter, he acts like he cares about her, and I can't help wondering how he fits into this village.

Zachariah wasn't born here; that much I know. He has too much understanding of me and the other men who came in with me, but he fits in so well I almost can't believe he was brought here like us. Maybe there's another way to come. Maybe he volunteered somehow.

"Are you a foundling?" I ask.

"I am." Zachariah's shoulders relax a little, and the smile he gives me is even more unsettling than all the earlier ones, because it's accompanied by the knowledge that he was once like me. Yet, somehow, he's happy to be here. "I was brought to the village thirty years ago, taken from Salt Lake City. I was only twenty-two, but I had a…fee-on-say." He pronounces *fiancée* like he isn't sure it's the right word. "We were to get married. I thought I loved her. I thought I wanted to return to her, so when I was brought here, I did as I was told. I cooperated so I would be able to escape when no one was looking. Just like you are doing." He gives me a knowing look, and I shift, hating that he can see through me so easily. "Raven chose me. She was seven years older, but beautiful, just like Wilderness is. Just like she still is. When Raven invited me to her hut, I went willingly. When she invited me to touch her, I did so willingly. I did it again the next night and the next, every time telling myself I would run soon. I did not run, though, and before long, I realized I did not want to.

"She got pregnant, but back then I did not understand the ways of the village, which is why I am telling you all this now. That way, you will know what to expect." His smile doesn't disappear, but it does change into something that almost looks sad. "The child was born, but it was a boy. I saw him on nights when I went to her hut, but I did not yet realize that to her he was just a yieldling. She took care of him, but she was distant, and when he turned two, she brought him to the men's village to live. By then, she was once again expecting, and I realized she would not be happy unless she had a daughter. That she would not think her life was complete unless she had a girl. When Raven gave birth the second time, there were two babies. A yieldling and a girl."

The news makes my back straighten. "Was the girl Wilderness?"

Zachariah nods. "It was."

"She has a twin brother?"

This time, his expression is definitely tinged with sadness. "There are no brothers."

Except there are, and somewhere in the men's village Wilderness has both an older brother and a twin. Does she even know? Does she even realize the significance of those things? It doesn't seem like it, not if she sees the world the way her mother does.

And what about the brother? Does he remember Raven at all or know who she is? If she sent him to live in the men's village when he was only two years old, he probably doesn't. The knowledge that she gave up her sons like they were nothing blows my mind. Even worse, she isn't alone. I think of all the young boys in this village, and all the women who have handed them over to be raised by someone else. It seems cold. Heartless.

Then there are the girls. If a woman has more than one daughter, do they acknowledge the relationship? Based on what I've seen of the village, I'd guess they do, which means Wilderness could have a sister she knows about, even if she isn't aware of her brothers.

"Did Raven have other children?" I ask. "Do sisters exist, and does Wilderness have one?"

"Sisters exist in our world, but it is less significant here. All the women are sisters. They are all family." There's an expression of almost pride in Zachariah's eyes when he says this, and it makes my stomach turn. "After Wilderness was born, Raven had two other children, both yieldlings," Zachariah continues. "Wilderness is Raven's only daughter. She is special. You must take care of her."

The end of the speech feels like the classic *be good to my daughter* warning, and the irony isn't lost on me. But I'm still curious how this village came to be in the first place. The little announcement Raven gave at the beginning of the Gleaning didn't tell me much except that something bad must have happened to the women who settled here, which isn't a surprise.

In school, we learned all about the history of the plague and how it wiped out most of the population, as well as the many horrible things people did to survive those early days. The atrocities people committed against one another were horrifying, and I have no doubt that the women who settled here were victims of something awful. But what?

"What happened to send these women here in the first place?" I ask him. "They've been here since the beginning, but why?"

"That, you will find out at the Festival of the New Moon," Zachariah says. "Now you just need to know *your* job. You are a foundling, and you must work to learn what is expected of you. You stay in the men's village. You do not leave the perimeter unless you earn my trust. You tend the animals and go to Wilderness when you are invited. You do not talk to other women. You do not touch any woman, not even Wilderness, unless you are invited. Do you understand?"

I don't understand, but I nod. I don't get why these men allow themselves to be treated like cattle, and I don't understand why the women feel the need to live separate from the men, why they keep them at arm's length even when they care about them. The look in Raven's eyes when she talked to Zachariah made it seem like she at the very least enjoys his company, but I think it goes deeper than that. She loves him, but she holds back, not even allowing him to spend the night in her hut, and it makes no sense.

"Good." Zachariah stands like his little speech has explained everything, but I have a million more questions than I did before. "Now you must sleep. Tomorrow we have work to do."

He heads toward the hut, not even waiting for me to stand, and I drag myself to my feet. Climbing the ladder is more difficult than it should be, and every move has me feeling like I put in hours of hard labor the day before. Hopefully, whatever Wilderness gave me wears off by morning, because I can't imagine trying to do anything with my body feeling this stiff.

THE CREAK OF ZACHARIAH'S FOOTSTEPS DRAGS ME FROM A dream in which I'm tied down and surrounded by the warrior women. I knew men in Baltimore who would savor the idea, but to me it feels like a nightmare, and even though it can't be much past dawn, I'm thankful for the escape.

On the other side of the room, the man in charge of keeping us in line slips out the door. He couldn't have gotten much sleep, but already he's up and ready for the day. I don't know how he does it. How does he live here and follow these rules with a smile on his face? It seems insane.

I roll onto my back and stare at the ceiling. The hut's roof, like all the others in the village, is made of bundles of sticks woven together and secured with vines. Thick layers of mud are pressed into the crevasses, and between that and the tight weave of the sticks, not a single ray of sunshine has been able to break through. I doubt rain water would be able to penetrate it either. It's actually amazing how well made this place is. As a child, my family was poor and moved often, going from one shitty apartment to the next, where most of the time plumbing didn't work and electricity was scarce. I didn't live in a single building that wasn't crumbling and decayed from decades of neglect, and in comparison, this hut almost feels like a palace. The floor is hard, but the furs and animal pelts piled around the room keep the cold out and add a certain amount of comfort most people wouldn't expect in a village like this. I know I didn't.

Around me, the other men from my group—the foundlings—stir, and I turn toward them. Eric is the only one already sitting up, and the puzzled expression on his face tells me that he, too, was drugged. Since the effects seem to have faded for me, I can only guess he either got it later, or received a much bigger dose than I did.

He catches me looking at him and shakes his head. "They drugged me."

"Me, too," I say, pushing myself to a sitting position.

The three other men nod, and it hits me that the sixth man isn't here. Sully was his name. He was the oldest in our group, and while I haven't taken the time to get to know anyone very well, Sully's good nature made it impossible to ignore him. He was also fond of a drink—or ten—at the end of the night, and his round gut told me it wasn't a new thing.

"Where's Sully?" I ask.

"You know as much as I do, man." The guy next to me sits up and looks around.

I don't know his name, and a part of me doesn't care to learn it. When I do make a run for it, I don't know if I'll have time to think of anyone but myself, and keeping my distance from these men will be the only way to not feel guilty about leaving them behind. Regardless, I find myself asking the man's name, as well as the name of the other guy I haven't met. The first guy is Michael, and then there's David. Eric and the other guy, John, I already knew—he's the one who got kicked down by the large warrior woman, something I doubt he'll try again.

"We have to get the fuck out of here," Eric hisses.

The other men look down, and I know they're thinking the same thing I am. Running isn't going to be easy, and we can't rush into it. Eric, though, strikes me as the type of guy who would take off into the woods with no plan, and I know exactly how that will end. The warriors know these woods, have lived on this mountain their whole lives. They'll go after him if he runs, and they'll find him.

I push myself up, glad the stiffness in my limbs is minimal, and head for the door. "Later."

Behind me, Eric grumbles and at least one man joins him, but only a second passes before the wood creaks, signaling they, too, have gotten up. They don't know all the stuff I learned last night, so they don't yet understand that no real harm will come to us as long as we learn our place, or at least pretend to. I have to bide my time and wait for the right moment.

Like Zachariah did…

Doubt nags at me, but I push it away and step outside.

The sun is low, and the distant horizon is painted orange and pink by its rays, but despite the early hour, the men's village is already alive with activity. Boys tend to the garden while three teenagers head toward the huts, loaded down with buckets of water in each hand. Their muscles strain, but they don't seem to be struggling under the heavy weight, and it suddenly hits me that *this* is why Wilderness chose me. I'm the biggest guy in our group, and the most muscular. It comes from years of hard work, of scavenging old buildings for scrap metal to sell, hoping to earn enough money to feed my family, then later, working at the docks, hauling crates of fish. I've only had a handful of days to rest in my entire life, yesterday being one of them. Ironic that one of my few days of leisure was my first as a prisoner.

Zachariah stands by the fire, stirring the contents of a big cast iron pot, and when he lifts his head, his gaze stops on me. He waves his arm, the spoon still in his hand as he motions for us to come over, and little drops of whatever's in the pot drop onto his head.

"Come," he calls, his voice seeming to boom through the village the way thunder booms through the city right before a storm.

In the early morning light, his scalp is even more visible through his thinning hair, but somehow he also looks younger. Despite the crinkling at the corners of his eyes when he smiles, the healthy glow of his skin takes years off him. He looks less rundown than men his age in the city, which probably has something to do with being out in nature and away from the pollution clogging the urban areas, not to mention the life of ease here compared to what the average man has these days.

In the city, it isn't uncommon to work twelve hours a day, seven days a week. A few people—those who have more education—get weekends off, but most of us are lucky to grab one day a month. Before getting pulled from my tent, I hadn't had a day to myself in over six months. I'd go back to my dingy apartment after a twelve-hour shift and scarf down a meal so I could grab some shuteye. Occasionally, I'd forego a few hours of sleep so I could check out a fight, but most of the time I couldn't even scrounge up enough cash for that. Even a buck is tough to come by when you don't make shit. I kept telling myself I was going to save my money and get the hell out of the city, but between rent and food and paying for utilities—which didn't always work—I never seemed to have enough. Plus, I wasn't even sure where I'd go. Rumor had it things were better in other parts of the country, but they were just stories people latched onto in a desperate attempt to keep hope alive. I'd never seen an ounce of proof that every other city in the world wasn't as shitty and beaten down as Baltimore, not that it stopped me from clinging to those stories as frantically as every other sucker I knew.

When the damn plague came, people flocked to the coasts and crowded into cities where the previous government had set up refugee camps before what was left of civilization disappeared. Back then, close to ninety percent of the population died—at least that's the best guess—and those left didn't know what the hell to do. Not even when things began to return to something resembling normal did they venture out, which is something I never could wrap my brain around, especially growing up the way I did.

Standing on the platform outside the hut, I pause and take a deep breath, expecting to be assaulted by the typical smells of the city. Garbage and urine, the stink of burning fuel. Instead, I'm greeted by the sweet scent of spring. Greenery and flowers and fresh air. Excrement and dirt, too, but different than the city. It isn't the stink of unwashed bodies and soiled clothes, but instead smells of nature, of animals and freshly laid soil, ready to bear food for the village. It's almost enough to make me forget I'm a prisoner here.

Too bad all it takes is one look at Zachariah for the truth to slam into me.

I grab the rope and swing to the ground, this time prepared for the impact when my feet hit. Behind me, the rope goes back up, and a whoosh follows only a second later, telling me another man is swinging down as well, but I don't look back to see who before heading across the village to the fire.

Zachariah still stands next to the fire, but his attention is now focused on the guy I met yesterday, Hawk, he said his name was. The younger man is nodding, listening intently, but most of what Zachariah is saying goes over my head. I'm too focused on Hawk's face. On brown eyes the color of fall leaves and the blond waves he seems to be constantly pushing out his face.

This is Wilderness's twin brother. It has to be. I only met the woman who calls me husband yesterday, but the expression on her face when she chose me is tattooed on my mind. The way her mouth scrunched up when she was thinking looks the same as Hawk's does right now. They hold themselves the same way, too, with their shoulders back and self-assurance radiating from them, and I can see both Zachariah and Raven represented in the man in front of me, the two of them mixed together perfectly. Hawk has his mother's eyes and his father's chin, and the freckles across his nose make me think of his sister. There isn't a doubt in my mind.

I draw closer, and Zachariah turns my way, frowning when he notices the way I'm studying Hawk. Whatever's going through his head, he keeps to himself, though.

"Hawk will teach you to tend to the goats," Zachariah says. "He butchers the game, but before that he was the goat man. You will be the goat man now."

I've never been around goats in my life, but I nod like an obedient dog because that's the part I've decided to play, and Zachariah's grin says he can see right through me. That he knows I'm playing the game while I wait for a chance to get away. Eric isn't the only one who needs to be careful, I realize. Not only will Zachariah be watching me, but if he suspects I'm considering taking off, he might have some of the warriors keeping an eye on me as well.

"First," he says, turning back to the fire, "we eat."

He lifts the cast iron pot off a hook and motions to the ground. I sit, knowing chairs are a luxury these people don't have, and when the other men from my group come up, they join me on the dirt. The air is cool, as is the hard ground, but the heat from the fire helps chase away the chill I should be feeling thanks to my lack of a shirt.

A couple dogs drift over, either drawn by the scent of food or the presence of new people, and they sniff me, then the other men. One of the mutts wanders off, but the other comes back after having checked everyone else out. He's thin but healthy, with eyes that barely peek through his shaggy, black fur. He nudges my arm as his tail works behind him, swishing back and forth, and when I scratch him behind the ears, his tail moves faster, making me smile despite the uncertainty of everything.

"Zip likes you," Hawk says, nodding to the dog.

I look at the scruffy thing in front of me. "Zip?"

"He is fast," Zachariah replies as he carries the cast iron pot to a rickety table that's seen better days. "Much faster than the other dogs."

He doesn't look very fast, but I don't mention it.

Jars and wood bowls, as well as a few ceramic ones, are stacked up on the little table, and I remember how the warrior women took the jars from our supplies, but threw away the prepackaged food. These people probably have no idea what to do with the processed food of the outside world, and I have a strong suspicion if they did eat it, they'd throw it back up. I doubt their bodies would respond well to the chemicals and preservatives found in our food. The jars are useful, though, either to drink from or even to fill with soup, which is what Zachariah is doing now.

The liquid he pours into the glass jar is a murky brown color and thin, with lumps of something off-white floating in it. He hands me the first serving, grinning like he can't wait to see me dig in. The warm glass threatens to scorch my skin, but I doubt it's hot enough to do any real damage, and it feels good in the chilly morning air.

Since there don't seem to be any spoons, I lift the jar to my lips and take a small sip of the broth, which is earthy, like the wild onions I found growing in the city park when I was around seven years old. I'd eaten them right there, shoving them in my mouth despite the dirt covering them. They'd tasted horrible, but my stomach had been so empty I would have eaten a hundred if I'd found more. There were only three, though, not even enough to stop my stomach from growling, and I'd gone to bed hungry, which wasn't anything too unusual.

Now, just like then, the stew is welcome, even if it isn't great. Wilderness didn't feed me anything last night other than the medicine she made me drink, and all it takes is one small sip for my stomach to growl greedily. Just like it did that day in the park. I take a bigger drink, this time getting a chunk of something that crunches when I bite into it. The texture reminds me of uncooked potatoes, but the flavor is pleasant. I'd guess it's some kind of root.

As I chew the vegetables, I look up to find Zachariah's eyes trained on me, making my scalp prickle. I fight not to shift under his gaze, not wanting him to see me squirm.

When I look away, he lets out a low chuckle.

The other men eat in silence, some of them drinking out of jars while others sip from wooden bowls. As a whole, we resemble a pack of beaten dogs, our heads down like we're afraid of what we might witness if we dare look up. Eric alone studies our surroundings, scanning the area like he's trying to memorize every inch of it, his intent so obvious it seems like he has the words *I'm going to run* written across his forehead. I want to tell him to knock it off—if he doesn't cool it, he's going to make it more difficult for the rest of us to get out of here—but that would give me away, and right now all I want is to fly under the radar.

"Where's Sully?" he asks after a few minutes of silence.

Zachariah tears his penetrating blue eyes off me and focuses on the other man, chewing his stew slowly, a bowl in one hand while the other rests on a homemade knife strapped to his hip. "Sully?"

"The other guy who was with us," Eric says, meeting the older man's gaze without blinking. "The one who didn't get a wife."

"No wife." Zachariah shakes his head. "Only husband." He takes a second to finish chewing, and when he's swallowed, says, "Your friend met his end yesterday. He was not needed, and he was not healthy enough to live in our village. We need strong men, not men who let their bodies get round and soft. It is better this way."

The men around me shift uncomfortably, each of them no doubt thinking about how Deacon had his throat slit on our first night here. I know I am. Hopefully, Sully's end came fast. He was a good man, even if he was a drunk.

"Finish." Zachariah sweeps his arm out, motioning to each of us. "We have work to do."

I swallow the rest of my stew and climb to my feet. "What do I do with my jar?"

"There." Zachariah nods to a bucket on the ground. "The yieldlings will take care of it."

I do as I'm told, once again the obedient dog, and the behavior continues when I turn to find Hawk waiting for me. He takes off toward the goat pen, and I trail after him with Zip on my heels. We're pretty much on the same level right now, both of us trailing after their masters, only, if I had to guess, I'd say the dog probably ranks higher in this village.

Doesn't matter, I tell myself. *Do as you're told and bide your time.*

The sound of Zachariah's chuckles chases me, and I glance over my shoulder to find him watching me. It feels like he's reading my mind, and it makes the hairs on the back of my neck stand up. I hate that he can see through me so easily.

When we reach the goat pen, Zip drops to the ground. The goats wail and shift away from the dog as Hawk lifts the latch holding the door closed, then he motions for me to enter.

I have to duck when I step through, but once I'm inside, there's plenty of room to stand up straight. The ceiling is high—ten feet, at least—and the fence keeping the goats inside is made of vines and sticks woven together. It's intricate, like the roof of the huts, and seems as secure.

Inside the pen, the stench of animal shit is overpowering. You can smell the stuff the second you set foot in the men's village, and even up in the hut, but here it makes my eyes water, and I have to resist the urge to cover my nose because I have a feeling it would make me look weak. After Zachariah's comment about needing strong men, the last thing I want is to seem like I'm anything but resilient and capable.

"You must clean the pens," Hawk says.

He waves to the piles of shit and then to a bucket, and my recently filled stomach lurches. Just what I didn't want to do this morning. I look around for a shovel or scoop of some kind, but there's nothing other than a bucket already caked with animal feces.

"What do I use?" I ask, turning to face Hawk again.

He looks pointedly at my hands with an expression in his eyes that says he thinks I'm a moron.

No way. He's insane.

"I'm not picking up piles of shit with my hands."

"Shit?" He pronounces it slowly, the way Zachariah did when he said *fiancée* the night before.

"Poop," I clarify.

Understanding crosses Hawk's face. "Fertilizer."

Of course.

"Whatever," I mutter.

I spot a small bundle of sticks outside the pen and step out so I can grab one. When I return, Hawk watches me curiously as I lay the bucket on its side in front of a pile of shit, then use the stick to flick it inside. I succeed in getting only a few specks on my hands when the stuff plops in, which I call a win, considering I'm literally standing in shit.

Hawk nods approvingly before turning to leave, not even glancing back at me as he says over his shoulder, "Good. After you clean, you will take the bucket to the field." He waves to the other side of the men's village. "The yieldlings will take care of it. Then you will wash yourself. Then milk the goats."

"Milk the goats?" I step toward him, the bucket of poop in one hand and the shit-covered stick in the other. "I've never milked a goat in my life."

Hawk glances back at me, and his grin makes him look exactly like his father. "You milk yourself, do you not?"

I turn away, so irritated I don't want to dignify the comment with a response but unable to stop myself from pointing out the insanity of the statement. "I don't think it's the same thing."

IT'S EARLY AFTERNOON, AND I'M IN THE MIDDLE OF LEARNING how to tan an animal's hide when Wilderness steps into the men's village, and the sight of her materializing from the trees makes me freeze in the middle of scraping fat from the skin. Not for the first time, Zachariah, who's standing at my side, grins like he can read my mind. Maybe he can. It's possible he knows what I'm thinking better than I do, because I have no clue why my stomach contorts when I look at her.

It's only the second time I've laid eyes on Wilderness, and unlike yesterday, she isn't wearing a skimpy fox fur dress. But it doesn't make her any less attractive. The fur from a wolf's leg is tied around her waist like a belt, keeping her leather skirt in place, but the pelt covering her upper body is secured with the typical leather cords. The fur is gray and matches the belt, and I can only assume it came from the same animal. Her golden hair hangs loose around her shoulders and down her back, and is wavy like Hawk's. She also has the same pointed chin and golden-brown eyes.

"Good morrow, Wilderness," Zachariah calls.

She returns his smile, but it's reserved, almost hesitant. Raven had the same cold demeanor about her yesterday when addressing her husband, but the women I saw talking to one another at the Gleaning were much more open. It's almost like they've erected an imaginary wall between themselves and the men, and they're terrified of what might happen if it comes crumbling down.

"Good morrow, Zachariah," Wilderness says when she stops in front of us. "Good morrow, husband."

She doesn't glance my way, which makes me feel cheap and used like a prostitute, and the thought is both uncomfortable and insane. Uncomfortable because the comparison isn't much of a leap, and insane because it isn't how most men would feel in this situation. Even the other men in my group. They're pissed to be here against their will, but I doubt they mind being used for sex all that much. Maybe that makes me an oddball, I don't know, but I do know the feeling only grows more intense as Wilderness and Zachariah talk and she still doesn't glance my way.

In the light of day, I notice that Wilderness's freckles aren't confined to her nose and cheeks alone, but are also sprinkled across her shoulders and chest, growing heavier as they dip between her breasts. Last night in the privacy of her hut, it was too dark or I was too drugged to notice them, but now it's all I can look at, and the sight of her flesh sparks memories of our time together. The feel of her naked body under mine, how soft her skin was, and how eager she seemed to please me and have me please her.

I only remember bits and pieces of what happened, but what I do remember is enough to send blood rushing to my groin. The woman in front of me was obviously a virgin, but she had no qualms about exploring every aspect of sex, and she asked for things I never would have thought to do with someone so inexperienced. I've been with other women—quite a few, actually—but I've never had one respond the way she did, and it occurs to me that this is how they keep the foundlings in line. To these women, sex is a weapon, a way to trap men and trick them into doing their bidding. It could work, I know, because even now, with part of my brain focused on how I'm going to get away, the other part is wondering when Wilderness will invite me to her hut again.

"You are hunting?" Zachariah nods to the bow in her hand.

"I am. I missed yesterday because of the Gleaning, and spring will be drawing the animals out." Wilderness lifts her head to the sky and smiles at the sun. "It is a good day to hunt."

"Good luck to you, Wilderness," Zachariah says.

When she turns her gaze back to him, her smile is more open than it was before, and it changes something about Zachariah. Makes his eyes light up and his smile widen. He loves this girl, even if he claims there are no fathers in their world, just like he loves her brother, Hawk, and I can't help wondering once again if Wilderness even realizes the significance Zachariah has in her life.

"Thank you," she says.

Wilderness doesn't glance my way before leaving, and I hate how much it disappoints me, hate that she heads across the men's village and doesn't bother looking back. Hate even more that I want her to.

"Do not worry." Zachariah has already retuned his attention to the deer hide, and the scrape of his knife against the skin seems loud in the quiet village. "She will invite you again."

"I'm not worried about that."

He lets out a low chuckle. "You cannot lie to me, Jam-e-son."

"Why do you say my name like that?"

Zachariah shrugs, but his gaze doesn't stray from the hide as he runs his homemade knife across the skin, sending bits of flesh and fat into the air. "Words and names from the old world are hard to remember sometimes. I have been here so long. I forget a lot of what I knew before."

"Things out there have changed a lot in thirty years," I tell him. "Maybe you'd want to go back if you saw it now."

He shakes his head but still doesn't look up from his work. "No. Here, I am happy. Here, life makes sense. Before, I had a fee-on-say—" He pronounces the word slowly again, as if still unsure he's saying it right. "—but life was very hard. My family was poor, and so was hers. She worked in a factory, and I delivered coal. We made very little money, and the home we had was not nice."

"It sounds like how I grew up."

It's an understatement, and like earlier, I find myself comparing the hovels I lived in as a kid to the huts here in the men's village. Even without a bed, there isn't much of a comparison. Most of Baltimore should have been torn down twenty years ago, and the few nice places left are reserved for the wealthy. Just like fuel and decent food and education and clothes. Just like houses with indoor plumbing that works and electricity that doesn't cut out on the coldest nights of the year.

In school, we learned that there used to be a middle class, but it disappeared a long time ago, and these days there are a handful of rich people who control everything while the rest of us live in squalor. We scrape by, existing only to make the lives of the upper class easier, or at least that's how it's always seemed to me.

"Then you understand." Zachariah finally stops working so he can focus on me, giving me a look that makes it seem like he knows something I don't. "You see how it can be better here. Easier."

Suddenly, I get why he stares at me so much. I remind him of himself, of what it was like when he first arrived here, and it probably even amuses him to remember how out of place he felt when he was a new foundling like me.

The comparison may be entertaining for Zachariah, but I don't find it amusing at all. The opposite, actually. It gets under my skin, makes me feel even more out of control than I already do and makes me want to take off running even if I know I wouldn't get far.

"I'm not going to give in like you," I say against my better judgment, mainly because I don't like getting lumped in with the man at my side. "This is wrong. They captured me and brought me here as their prisoner. I'm being held against my will."

He tilts his head, his knife less than an inch from the deer hide, frozen in mid-air. "Are you a prisoner?" His grin widens. "I see no chains. I see none of the things that held you captive before you came here. I know, because they held me captive, too. I went to work every day feeling like I had no control over my life, but here I have control. You will see. You have not been trapped the way you think. You have been set free."

I don't respond because I know he wouldn't agree even if I did. He's only as free as Raven allows him to be, and that isn't even the biggest problem with this place.

CHAPTER EIGHT

Wilderness

MEMORIES OF LAST NIGHT FOLLOW ME THROUGH the forest like a second shadow, making my blood sizzle and long for a repeat, but also making me feel like I am not the one in control.

I had hoped a few hours of hunting would clear my head, but even the singing birds and clicking branches have not been able to calm my mind or body. Evening is closing in, and already I have three squirrels and a raccoon that foolishly came out during the day, drawn by the promise of spring, but I cannot make myself head home.

Before leaving my village this morning, I saw only one of the other women matched at the Gleaning. Blossom chose the man with the blond hair, the one who is pleasing to the eye but has fire raging inside him, and although she said her union was successful, I could see the concern in her eyes. Like me, she worries this foundling will not work out. Hopefully, the Great Mother will bless her with a daughter before this man forces us to end him.

I finally head back toward the village when the sun begins its slow crawl toward the horizon, but take my time, enjoying the warmth still clinging to the air and the scent of spring flowers. Above me, the trees are dotted with buds, and it will not be long before they have opened, once again bringing life to the forest.

When I reach the men's village, I pause at the edge and look around. Two gray-haired husbands sit by the fire whittling as a handful of yieldlings run by, letting out delighted whoops while the dogs charge after them. They disappear into the woods, the animals right behind them, and a second later a few birds burst from the trees, squawking at the disturbance.

Most of the men are nowhere in sight, my husband included, but I spot Hawk sitting by himself in the shade of one of the huts, weaving a basket, and head his way to drop off my game. The memory of running into the forest with him the way the yieldlings just did adds an excited skip to my step and makes me want to grab his hand and pull him into the woods after them. It is an old urge that clings to me like a leech even though I have tried to push it aside. Hawk is not my husband, and we are no longer children, but the stolen moments spent with my childhood friend are always comforting, especially in moments like this, when I suddenly feel like I am lost in my own life.

"Good eve, Hawk," I say when I stop at his side. "I have some game for you."

"Good eve, Wilderness."

He barely looks up when I drop the dead animals at his side, and a pang spreads through me.

"The village is quiet." I look around again and spot Oak by the fire, rocking in his usual way. "Where have all the men gone?"

"Zachariah is showing the foundlings where the river is." Hawk finally looks up, his soft, brown eyes meeting mine for the first time. They sparkle, taking me back to our years of climbing trees and throwing rocks, to the twinkling laughter that followed us through the forest. It was so long ago, but at times it seems like only a season has passed. I have never missed being a child, but I do miss the freedom I had back then. How I could choose who I wanted to spend my time with. In my own village, the women gather and eat together, talk and laugh, but I have never felt a bond with anyone like the one I shared with the man in front of me. Even Dove, who has been a good friend over the years.

"We used to swim in the river," I say, wondering if Hawk thinks about that time as much as I do.

He smiles and lowers his basket, his weaving forgotten. "I remember. You dragged me in when I said the water was too cold."

"It was not too cold," I say with a laugh.

"It was barely spring." Hawk's smile widens, making him look younger and more like the boy I knew so many seasons ago. "It was too cold to swim."

We smile at each other, and the part of my heart that clings to those memories aches. He is the husband of Dawn, and walking away would be the right thing to do, but I do not, because I know this feeling has nothing to do with husbands or yieldlings. It is only about Hawk.

"Are you looking for your husband?" he asks when I say nothing else.

He is still smiling, but there is sadness in it as if, like me, he seems to realize our time together has come to an end.

"No." Heat flames at my cheeks, and I look away, focusing on the crackling fire in the center of the village.

Once again, I am thinking of last night, but the man in front of me and the one I have welcomed into my bed feel like they should exist in two different worlds. It is something impossible to explain; I just know they are very different to me.

"He will be a good foundling." Hawk turns back to his basket, weaving the grass together with nimble fingers, and a few strands of blond hair fall into his face, blocking his eyes from view, but he seems not to notice. "Zachariah is teaching your husband, and he listens well. Some of the other foundlings may not work, but yours will be okay."

"That is good to hear," I say, but I am uncertain whether I actually mean it. I have no desire for Jameson to cause trouble, but I am unsure how this man, this stranger, will fit into my life.

Movement catches my eye, and I turn to find Dawn standing at the edge of the forest, her blue eyes narrowed on me. The sun has dipped even lower, painting the sky the same color as her hair, orange and brilliant.

Guilt twists my insides into knots, and I take a step away from Hawk. "Dawn has come to see you."

When he lifts his head, the small smile he had for me is replaced by another, bigger one, and in a blink I am forgotten, and Hawk only has eyes for Dawn. It is right, it is how it should be, but it still feels like a part of my childhood is being stomped out.

"Good eve, Wilderness," he says, not looking at me.

"Good eve, Hawk," I reply as I back away.

Dawn moves toward her husband as I head for the forest, and we meet in the middle of the village where she pauses at my side, looking me over, but not smiling. We have never been close. Dawn is older than I am and was made a warrior very young, and spent most of her childhood training. The role was natural for her because of her thick build and tall frame, but her cold nature makes it even more fitting.

"Where is *your* husband, Wilderness?"

"He is at the river with Zachariah and the other foundlings."

She says nothing, but her eyes snap like the fire burning at her back.

Dawn has always hated it when I speak to Hawk, but I have tried to ignore it, knowing my actions are innocent. Now, though, she acts like she caught me inviting her husband into my bed.

"Good eve, Dawn," I say, anxious to take leave of her.

She sniffs before continuing her trek across the men's village while I head for home, and it feels like the trees are sucking me in when I cross the threshold into the forest. I welcome it, hoping the branches will conceal not just me, but the uncertainty swirling through me as well.

I think about Hawk and Dawn and Jameson as I walk, and how my position in the village has changed, wondering when everything will feel normal again. It is possible it never will, and the thought is unsettling.

The women's village, like the men's, is quiet when I step out of the trees. High over my head the huts are lit up, and the flicker of firelight shines through the open doors and windows as if the eyes of everyone are on me. That is how it feels. I am the daughter of Raven, the High Elder of the village and the first woman to successfully tame a foundling, and the weight of what I need to do makes it difficult to breathe. My mother's success is twice as impressive, considering most of the men we bring into the village do not last longer than five years.

It pains me to admit it even to myself, but I have never felt like I would be able to live up to my mother, and I am even less certain of it now. After only one night with my husband, I already find it difficult to control my body. No, impossible. Just being near him made me feel like I was on fire, but it should not be that way. I am the woman, and I should be more in control. I should not allow him to affect me like this.

The desire to talk to someone smarter and stronger sends me to Raven's hut, and I arrive to find the door open and my mother sitting in the middle of the floor, weaving a few pelts together. When I stop in the doorway, she smiles and pushes her gray hair behind her shoulders so it is out of her face.

"Wilderness."

"Raven," I say, nodding once.

She waves toward a pile of furs, and I go to it, lowering myself to the floor across from her.

"I have not seen you today, so I did not get a chance to ask how your union was. Did your husband please you?"

"He pleased me very much," I reply, trying not to let the heat licking at my cheeks show. "I gave him the medicine. I know you did not give it to Zachariah after your Gleaning, but I worried Jameson would resist."

I look down, afraid to meet my mother's gaze, afraid she will see the fear and weakness I have been fighting to keep inside. The medicine is standard, but it still feels like I have failed by giving it to my husband.

"Wilderness." She touches my knee, and I lift my head to find her smiling. "Zachariah is very special. There are few foundlings like him. You did right to give your husband the medicine."

I nod even though her reassurance does nothing to ease my worry, and she must sense my uncertainty, because she presses her hand more firmly against my knee. It is a comforting gesture, made more so because she rarely does it. My mother is a strong woman, and she has strived to cultivate strength in me, which means I am often forced to work things out for myself.

"What else is bothering you?" she asks when I say nothing.

"I was in the men's village talking to Hawk," I tell her. "Dawn saw us together and was unhappy. I know she dislikes it when I talk to her husband, but I do it anyway. Am I wrong? Should I keep my distance from him?"

My mother withdraws her hand, and already I miss the comfort of her touch. "No. You are not. I will speak to Dawn, but you did nothing wrong. She cares for Hawk very much, just as I care for

Zachariah, and seeing another woman speaking to her husband makes her uneasy. But that is not how we should act. The women in our village must always be sure of themselves. Especially the warriors. We must be strong, and we must not look at one another with suspicion. She does not understand the bond you and Hawk have. That is all."

"Why do we have this bond?" I ask Raven. "It is not normal in our village, and I know that, but no matter what I do, I cannot make it go away."

My mother's smile tightens, and something in her expression changes, almost as if a wall has gone up. "You are the same age. You were young together. That is all."

She does not blink as she holds my gaze, but I find that I cannot believe her. Is she lying or simply keeping the whole truth from me? Either way, I cannot accuse an Elder of being deceitful, not even my mother. Raven is above reproach, and if she is withholding something from me, there must be a reason. She has the best interest of the village at heart. Always.

After a moment, her expression relaxes. "Will you invite the foundling to your hut again tonight?"

"No." I try to keep my head up, but fail and find myself staring at the fur beneath me. "I had not planned to."

"This is an important time for him, Wilderness." She is frowning when I venture a look up, her expression having morphed from an interested mother to Raven, High Elder of the village. "He is a foundling, and everything is new to him. It is your job as much as it is Zachariah's to show him the way. *You* must lead your husband. *You* must show him what is expected of him without the medicine."

I swallow, knowing she is right but terrified of having him in my hut without the medicine. Terrified of the way my body reacts to him. He is a foundling and a man, which makes him doubly untrustworthy, and whatever happens, I have to keep my guard up. I cannot let him have the upper hand in anything.

"Do you understand?" my mother says when I say nothing.

"Yes," I reply, bowing my head so she cannot see the uncertainty in my eyes. "I understand."

I REFUSE TO TAKE THE INVITATION TO THE MEN'S VILLAGE myself, instead sending one of the young girls to deliver it, but I do wait for my husband's arrival just outside the forest that separates our two villages. Above me, the sky is black and clear, and the stars twinkle as if winking down at me. My insides feel like they have been filled with grasshoppers, and though I know I should not use the medicine for a second night in a row, I consider giving it to my husband anyway. It would not be wrong, not really, because Blossom will be forced to use the medicine on her husband for several days to come—possibly even weeks. Still, I think it would disappoint my mother, and keeping it from her would be impossible since I would have to go to the healer to get it.

Before my husband has even made an appearance, I decide against using the medicine, but seeing him step through the trees makes my resolve waver. He fits into our village nicely; the leather pants suit him, and being bare chested shows off his broad form as well as the pictures on his body. He said they were for decoration, and looking at him now, I can almost understand it. They make him stand out.

"Wilderness," he says when he sees me.

He stops at the edge of the forest like he knows he should to wait for an invitation, and I marvel at Zachariah's strong leadership. Behind my husband, something stirs, and a dog with shaggy black fur comes into view, wagging his tail. He stops as well, but he seems to be waiting on Jameson.

"Good eve, husband." I push off the tree and nod at the dog. "You have made a friend."

My husband looks down and smiles even as he shakes his head in disbelief. "Zip's been following me around all day."

Zip. I was unaware of the animal's name, but it fits him. I have seen him in the men's village, playing with the yieldlings and other dogs, running with the warriors, and know he is fast.

"Did you learn much today?" I ask, my attention back on my husband.

"I learned how to tend to the goats, and how to milk them. Then Zachariah taught me how to tan a deer hide."

"Yes," I say, "I saw you. I killed that deer the day before your arrival. It was a good size doe. The hide will come in handy."

"You killed it?"

His gaze moves down, taking me in, and I find myself shifting, wondering what he sees and what he thinks, curious how I compare to the women from his world, and how I compare to the women from mine. It is something I have never given much thought, not even when I feel like I am standing between Hawk and Dawn, but now I cannot help it, cannot stop myself from wondering if my husband finds me desirable, if he thinks about last night and longs for a repeat.

"I am a hunter." I straighten my shoulders so I come across as strong instead of uncertain, which is how I feel right now. "It is my job to bring in game so we have food and clothing. I am the best hunter in the village."

My husband smiles like something I said impressed him, only I do not know what it could be. Yes, I am a good hunter, but any of the women in our village could bring in game if they needed to. Other women have different jobs, different gifts, but we all know how to provide.

"Why do you look at me like that? Do the women you know not provide food?"

"They cook, yes. I don't know anyone who hunts, though. Man or woman."

I try to picture a world where no one hunts, but all I can imagine is starvation and misery. "How do you get food if you do not hunt? Do you not eat meat?"

He tilts his head to the side and presses his lips together like he is trying not to laugh, and it makes me feel like a silly child. My back straightens and my blood heats up, and I glare up at him, wishing I were as tall as Grove so *he* would have to look up at *me* instead of the other way around.

"Do not laugh at me, husband."

"I'm sorry." His smile disappears, and he shifts from foot to foot. "I think it's cute."

"I do not know *cute*," I snap, unable to let go of my annoyance despite his apology.

"Never mind." Jameson lets out a sigh of frustration. "We buy our food from a store."

"Buy?" Another word I do not understand.

"Yes..." He lets the word fade like it has been caught by the wind and carried away. "I guess you don't buy things. We work, have jobs, and we get paid money. With the money we can buy things like food and clothes. That way we don't have to hunt or make our own things."

"Who makes them?" I remember the strange clothes my husband and the other foundlings were wearing when I first saw them. They did not come from any animal I recognize, so someone must have made them, although I cannot imagine how or from what material. "You do not make them, but someone must. Who does it?"

"Whoever has that job." He shrugs like he is as uncertain as I am. "They're made in buildings bigger than all your huts combined. Factories are what we call them. There, people work every day to make clothes. The same way you hunt every day to provide food."

I try to picture what he is describing, big huts that tower over my head, people crowding into them all day so they can make clothes. The needs of the outside world are very different from ours, which is something I understand very well, but this sounds like a miserable way to live. Stuck inside all day and hidden from the sun. I go to my hut at night to sleep, but during the day I am outside. Even in the winter when the air is frigid, I try to be out as much as possible. I remember many years ago when a heavy storm swept through the village, how the snowdrifts came up to my shoulders, forcing me to cower in my hut for almost a week. It was maddening.

"I do not like that," I say, turning my back to my husband. "We are meant to be outside."

I head for the nearest rope ladder, and he follows without me telling him to.

"It's different in the city," he says from behind me. "We don't have clear skies like you do. There's pollution, and the trash litters the streets."

I pause at the base of the ladder, once again trying to picture the world he came from. Pollution and trash are things I do not understand, except from stories passed down. Stories about the motor vehicles people had before the plague and how there were so many that in places skies were murky and brown instead of blue, and how the air was not fresh and clean the way it is here. You could not smell the trees when you breathed, could not taste the rain in the air before a storm. Back then there was waste, and people always wanted more. More clothes to wear, more useless items of technology they thought they needed to survive, more of everything even if they had no need for it. Perhaps that has not changed. It sounds like it, based on my husband's description.

"Then it is a good thing you are here," I tell him before turning back to the ladder.

I begin to climb, but he does not follow, and halfway up I pause and look down, only to find him standing at the bottom of the ladder, staring at me in confusion. Zip sits next to him, his head tilted to one side like he is as unsure of what to do as my husband is.

"You must come," I say when Jameson still does not move.

My husband begins to climb without comment, and as if told to stay, the dog drops to the ground at the base of the tree.

When I am sure Jameson is on his way, I continue my climb. I can feel his presence behind me, his breath brushing my heels and his heat warming me even though we have not yet touched. Just being in Jameson's presence feels like someone has thrown a log on the fire inside me, like it never died down, but has instead simmered in my blood all day.

We say nothing when we reach the top. My husband walks behind me, his feet pounding on the wood with every step he takes, and I keep my eyes straight ahead. The walkways sway when we cross them, and like the day before, Jameson holds onto the rope like he is afraid he will fall. It makes no sense to me, this large man being scared of walking across a bridge.

"Are you afraid?" I ask when we reach a platform.

He looks at the rail, then at the ground, and although he shakes his head, I can tell he is lying. "A lot of people are scared of heights."

Scared of heights? I look over the railing as well, but his apprehension still makes no sense.

"The earth will not come up to get us, and the distance can do nothing. We will not fall if we are careful. Being in the air keeps us safe from predators. Up here, we do not have to fear the animals in the forest. If a bear wanders into our village, it cannot harm us because we are high above its head."

"I guess that makes sense."

"It does," I say, turning my back to him once again.

We remain silent as we cross the walkways to my hut, and once there I open the door and motion for Jameson to enter, and he steps inside, sitting on the edge of the bed while I go about lighting the lantern. My back is to him, but his overwhelming presence makes me feel like he is standing at my side, his body flush with mine, and my hands tremble as I strike the flint together. Sparks burst through the darkness, and when the wick catches, the scent of burning animal fat fills the space. The odor is pleasant because it is familiar in the midst of so many different and new sensations.

Even after the lantern is burning, I stay where I am for a moment, taking deep breaths while I think about how much has changed. Everything in my life has turned upside down, and it makes me feel like I am someone else. I do not recognize this person, the one who brings a stranger to her hut and is expected to take control, but still I know it is what I have to do. I must be the one to dictate what happens here, because it is my job to lead my husband and teach him, to make sure he fills his role in the village so he does not meet his end. If I am a strong enough leader, like my mother, I will succeed.

"Are you going to drug me again?" Jameson's voice breaks through the quiet, and I almost jump.

My heart is already pounding when I turn to face him, and seeing him on my bed only makes it thump harder. He stares at me, his brown eyes uncomfortable, and some of my confidence wavers. He looks like he dreads what we are about to do, and the expression makes it impossible to keep my head held high as something like guilt twists inside me, but I cannot say why. I am not hurting Jameson—the opposite, really. He enjoyed being with me last night, I know because his body responded to mine just as mine responded to his, which means there is no reason for me to feel guilty. This is our way. It has always been our way.

"I will not give you the medicine as long as you do as you are supposed to," I say after a moment.

Jameson frowns, and the guilt I had just managed to push down resurfaces. "You mean have sex with you?"

"Yes." Heat spreads across my cheeks, but I do my best not to let it show. "That is what I mean."

Jameson lets out a resigned sigh, but still he does not get to his feet. "And if I refuse?"

Anger and embarrassment, and even a little bit of guilt, war with one another inside me. As a foundling, Jameson has no right to deny me, but something about his expression gives me pause.

Why does he act like I am forcing him to do this? I know he wants me, and I know all I have to do is slip off my clothes and his body will respond the way it should, and yet he still acts like he wants to be somewhere else. Anywhere but here.

"I can drug you," I say, trying to mimic the firm tone my mother uses with Zachariah.

"You can't force me to drink it, though. I'd still have to be a willing participant in that."

"You do not think Grove could force you?" I lift my eyebrows, challenging him to deny the truth. "How do you think Blossom's husband will take the medicine? He will be held down. That is how."

Jameson jerks like my words have slapped him. "Then I guess I have no choice."

Again, the expression on his face gives me pause, and I find I can say nothing. I had thought mimicking Raven's brusque tone would make me feel stronger, but it has done the opposite. Jameson has shrunk away and now sits further back on the bed, almost like he wants to put more distance between us, and the look in his eyes fills me with shame. It is distrust and disgust, and it is directed at me.

"I have no wish to do that," I say, softening my voice, hoping the soothing tone will help. I wave to the table and give my husband a gentle smile. "See, I have no medicine."

Jameson eyes the table for a moment in silence before looking back at me. "All I have to do is have sex with you?"

"That is all. I have a duty to my village," I tell him, stepping closer so I am standing right in front of him. "As my husband, you have a duty to me."

Resignation flashes in his eyes, and he scoots forward so he is back on the edge of the bed, and once again guilt shoots through me.

The feeling fades when he reaches out.

I take a step back, narrowly avoiding his touch. "You must not touch me unless invited."

"I have to touch you if we're going to have sex," he says, his frown becoming more prominent.

"You must have permission," I say firmly, yet gently, mimicking the tone I have heard mothers use when speaking to their children. "You must never touch me unless you have permission."

The instruction helps me feel more in control, and when Jameson nods, the last little twinge of guilt in my stomach disappears. It is my job to look out for my husband, and this is the most important lesson he must learn, because a mistake like this could lead to punishment, and although the blame would be on my shoulders as much as it would be on his, it would hurt him much more than it would hurt me.

I pause for a moment to let my words sink in and then step closer. "I invite you to touch me."

His eyes roll in their sockets like a child who hates the rules. I have the urge to scold him, but it disappears when he pulls at the fur wrapped around my waist and it comes loose, the leather covering my lower half falling to the floor. A couple beats later the fur wrapped around my chest has also made its descent, leaving me bare.

My husband looks me over, staring at me like a starving man faced with his first meal. He does not touch me as he drags his gaze down my body, over my breasts to my stomach, and then to my female parts, and heat flares inside me. It is a magical thing, this man's ability to warm me with just a look, but like earlier, it makes me feel out of control. I should not want him the way I do, but I cannot help it.

When he finally reaches out, his touch is more hesitant than it was the night before. Last night during our union he was passionate without reserve, but it was the medicine that made him behave that way. It takes away the foundlings' inhibitions and opens them to the sexual experience. It connects the man to the woman who has taken him as a husband.

The medicine explains why he responded to me the way he did, but it does nothing to explain why I responded so much to his touch, or why I want him right now. It cannot account for the tremor in my legs as I reach for the leather strap holding his pants up, or the ache between my thighs when I think about being with him again. I just know it is there, and the only thing I can do to stop it is be with Jameson.

Despite his initial hesitation, Jameson performs exactly as he should, pleasing me with his hands and his mouth before filling me with his seed, and when we have finished, I find I am glad I chose not to use the medicine. The timidity he showed when he first touched me was short lived, and once his restraint faded, he was eager to please me.

But he was more aware of what he was doing this time. He would pause in the middle of kissing me or exploring my body and stare at me, his gaze searching mine, and it made the act more intimate than it had been the night before. Made me feel like a bond was forming between us that I had not seen coming.

It is late when we finish, but I do not ask him to leave my hut. The flicker from the lantern is bright enough to highlight the contours of his face, and I find myself tracing them with my gaze, taking him in the way he took me in during our union. He is very pleasing to look at, I decide. I know it is wrong to think, but I cannot help it. Just like I cannot help wondering if other women feel this way about their husbands, and if they crave not just the pleasure the union brings, but the closeness as well. The intimacy of the act is something I have never experienced, and one thing my mother did not prepare me for.

Jameson turns to face me, half covered by the fur of a black bear. His calf is visible, the muscle round and firm, and unlike the blonde hair on my own legs, which is soft and fine, the hair on his is coarse and almost as dark as the pelt wrapped around us. It makes him seem very masculine, very capable of giving me strong offspring.

He reaches out to touch me but stops himself. "Am I still allowed to touch you?"

"The invitation is good until you leave my hut," I tell him. "Then you will have to wait for another one before you can touch me again."

Jameson smiles when he cups my breast, which is round and heavy and ideal for motherhood, although I know that is not what he is thinking about when he touches me. My breasts are made for sustenance, but it came as no surprise last night when my husband touched them for the first time. My mother was diligent and thorough in her teachings, making sure I was prepared for everything in life, including how to please my husband.

"You were a virgin before yesterday, weren't you?" my husband asks, his hand still on my breast.

"Virgin?" I repeat the word, shaking my head to let him know I do not understand.

There is so much about the man in front of me that is foreign, so much he has seen and done that I cannot understand, and it makes me wonder how he will ever fit into this world. How can anyone who comes from the outside make a home here?

My husband frowns like he is unsure how else to word the question and then says, "You've never been with a man before."

"No." I run my hand over his arm as I talk, tracing the black lines on his bicep with my fingertip and marveling when bumps rise up on his skin. "The women and yieldlings do not mix except at festivals, and even then there is very little interaction. Here, men come of age when they turn twenty-four, and then they are husbands. It is not right to spend time with another woman's husband."

My mind wanders to Hawk, and a tinge of regret, as well as shame, goes through me. Even now, with Jameson at my side and my desire for him so strong, I cannot let go of my childhood playmate.

"If last night was your first time, how were you so eager? How did you know exactly what to do?"

"Raven has spent a lot of time preparing me for what to expect. As soon as I passed the threshold into womanhood, my mother began instructing me in my duties to my husband. Not just outside the hut, but in it as well." She had told me, in detail, the things she and Zachariah did in private. What he did to please her, and what she did to please him. "In our village, it is important for everyone to be happy, the men as well as the women. Sex is part of that."

Jameson shakes his head like something I said makes no sense. "But you don't want to live with your husbands?"

"Men have their place," I say firmly, my finger frozen in the middle of tracing his tattoo. "In their village."

He presses his lips together like he wants to ask more but says nothing. Instead, he leans closer and runs his lips across my chest, causing tendrils of heat to move through my belly and settle between my thighs. My husband's hand is still on my breast when he urges me onto my back, and I oblige, lying down so he can climb on top of me. His lips are warm and soft when they cover mine, and his manhood is already stiffening in anticipation.

I return his kiss, running my hands over his shoulders and arms, feeling his muscles flex under my palms as his hard body moves against mine. With him on top of me, I am at his mercy, and it makes me feel weak and vulnerable, and all the things I have been made to fear, so I twist our bodies and urge him onto his back, taking the dominant position on top, my legs straddling him.

The soft glow from the lantern flickers over us as I stare at the man beneath me. His gaze looks hungry in the darkness of the hut, his eyes roving my naked body like he cannot get enough of me, and the expression makes me feel powerful in a way I never have before.

This man is a stranger, and yet he is mine. It is an odd reality to be faced with, but one I must get used to if he is to be as successful as Zachariah has been. I need Jameson to know this is how it should be. Me on top. Always.

CHAPTER NINE

Jameson

BARKING JOLTS ME FROM SLEEP WHAT FEELS LIKE seconds after lying down, and I bolt upright, expecting to see the outline of Zip in the dark hut. He was waiting for me in the women's village, still lying on the ground exactly where I left him, but he isn't here, and I know it. The dog couldn't have made it into the hut.

The realization comes to me only a second before shouts echo through men's village, followed closely by the high-pitched war cry I've heard a few times since being taken by these women, and my foggy brain can only muster up one explanation—we're being attacked by an enemy village. Of course, that would mean another village exists in this area, and I don't think that's true since no one has mentioned it, and it doesn't make sense with how secluded they are. Not that I can come up with another explanation for shouts waking me up in the middle of the night.

Feet scuffle against the floor on the other side of the hut, followed by sparks breaking through the darkness. Seconds later, light floods the room, illuminating Zachariah's icy, blue eyes as he looks us over.

"Missing two." The flickering light casts shadows across his face, exaggerating his frown and making it look freakish. "Knew he would make trouble, but I did not think it would be this early."

It takes one look at the space next to me to figure out what he's talking about. We're short two people. Eric and John have made a run for it. Like Zachariah, I knew it would happen, but I'd hoped they'd be smarter about it. Now, thanks to their impulsiveness, my chances of escaping just went down to almost zero.

"Not far," Zachariah mutters as he heads for the door. "They did not get far."

I jump to my feet and hurry after him, unable to talk myself into staying still when the world seems to be exploding with activity.

Outside, the men's village is lit up. The bonfire is still going, and a few women are loading more logs onto it while a group of warriors gathers in the village, holding torches. The fires blaze through the night, while around them five dogs bark in anticipation. The Elder Warrior stands in the middle of the animals with something in her hand, presenting it to the dogs, and I spot Zip just as he presses his muzzle into the bundle of fabric. Clothes, I realize. If I had to guess, I'd say they're what Eric and John were wearing when they got here.

The warriors are going to send the dogs into the forest.

The sudden realization makes Zip's wagging tail seem less cheery and more sinister.

"You stay," Zachariah barks.

He hands me the lantern, which I barely have a chance to take before he jumps out, grabbing hold of the rope with expert ease. He flies to the ground and takes off the second his feet touch down, charging across the men's village toward the warriors.

I do as I'm told and stay put, watching from the platform as Zachariah talks to the women. From where I'm standing, I can't hear a single word, but it looks like the warriors aren't interested in listening to whatever he has to say. Most of them ignore him, and even when he does manage to grab the attention of the tall woman—the one who dragged me from my tent only a few nights ago—she looks irritated by his presence.

The dogs take off, and all the warriors except the one Zachariah is talking to hurry after them. When she tries to move past him, Zachariah grabs her arm, and the look she gives him could kill a man in his tracks. I know what's going to happen before it does, but I still cringe when the tall warrior slams her knee into his groin. Zachariah drops to the ground like dead weight and curls into a ball, and she walks away without looking back.

"Shit."

He told me to stay, but I can't leave him curled up in the middle of the village, so I set the lantern down and jump for the rope, once again going down much faster than I anticipated. My feet hit, landing on a pointed rock, and the sharp pain forces a hiss out of me. I ignore it and jog forward.

"Are you okay?" I ask when I drop to my knees at Zachariah's side.

He rolls to face me, his hands cradling his injured balls. "My fault. I know better. My fault."

"All you did was touch her."

"Not okay." He hisses and closes his eyes. "There will be punishment."

I don't know what that means, but as far as I'm concerned, a knee to the balls is punishment enough. Since these women don't have the first clue how much pain Zachariah is in, I doubt they'd agree with me.

I wait until the pain has subsided a little to help Zachariah to his feet and back toward the hut. Getting up isn't as fast or easy as getting down is—especially when he's still hurting—but he manages to pull himself up the rope ladder with little issue. Once he's reached the platform safely, I climb up after him.

Back inside the hut, Zachariah collapses on his bed of furs, letting out a painful groan. Michael and David are awake now, too, but unlike me, they're still sitting on their furs like they're too afraid to move a muscle. They stare at Zachariah like he's a monster, and deep down I know I should feel the same way, but for some reason, I can't. He may be a little crazy, and he's definitely been brainwashed by these women, but I'm finding that I like this man. A lot. Who knows? Maybe I'm a little crazy, too.

"What will they do to the men if they find them?" I ask.

"They will find them." Zachariah lets out a deep breath. "Been a long time since foundlings ran. Usually the problem ones meet their end very early."

I want to tell him that no matter how they phrase it, what they do is murder, plain and simple, but it won't do any good, and I don't feel like having a debate right now.

"Is that what will happen to them?" I ask. "Will they meet their end?"

"They will be punished. It will be up to Raven." He winces and looks away. "She will not be happy."

I kneel in front of him. "Will you be punished?"

"Yes."

Zachariah keeps his head down, and I let out a deep breath. After my evening with Wilderness, I was feeling better about this place, but this changes things. They have dogs and punishments, and who knows what the hell else, and it isn't right. No matter what Zachariah said earlier, I'm a prisoner here, and I have to get away.

WE DON'T GET ANY MORE SLEEP AFTER THAT, AND ZACHARIAH IS out of the hut at the first sign of light, and even though he doesn't tell me to follow, I do. So do the other two men. Like me, they've each been assigned an animal pen to care for, and the three of us go about the business of cleaning them without being told, but the work is quiet and feels more tedious than before, and after last night, I can't help feeling like weights have been shackled to my legs.

When I've finished, I take the goat shit to the field and clean up, using the bucket of water the teens collected from the river. I splash some on my face and over my head, ignoring the goose bumps that pop up on my skin. The cast iron pot sits close to the fire, but the water hasn't had enough time to warm up. Not that I care. Anything is better than smelling like shit, and I haven't bathed since arriving. I'd love to have the chance, but I'm not even sure it's something these people do or where they would do it. The river, possibly, and although it has to be barely above freezing this time of year, I'd welcome even that at this point.

Michael comes up beside me so he, too, can wash, and out of the corner of his mouth says, "Did you know they were going to run?"

"No." I look around.

No one is paying attention to us, but I still keep my eyes straight ahead. You never know what can happen. They could have dozens of surprises up their sleeves.

The man at my side splashes water over his face. His skin is dark compared to mine, partly from heritage, but it's been made darker by the sun. His arms are muscled, too, and the scars on them tell me he's use to working hard.

"Where are you from?" I ask.

"Chicago, but it's been a long time. I did a stint in the coalmines and since then have been working on the railroad." He shakes his head as he scrubs the dirt from his hands. "We've come across groups of backward people out in the middle of nowhere before, but I've never seen anything like this. That's for damn sure."

"Cannibals?" I ask out of curiosity.

"No. As far as I know, they're gone, but I've seen a lot of inbreeders. People who are afraid of outsiders, so they keep to themselves. A lot of idiots in those groups."

He jerks his head to the right, and I turn to see a boy sitting next to the fire. I noticed him the day before, sitting in the same place while Zachariah and I tanned the deer hide, but I hadn't paid much attention to him. Now, though, I recognize the vacant look in his eyes and how he rocks back and forth. I've seen kids like him in the city, usually orphans who live on the streets and only get by thanks to the scraps other people throw them. They're slow, born with something wrong in their brains. In the city, I attribute it to drug or alcohol use by the mother, maybe even a lack of medical care while pregnant or being exposed to something dangerous at a factory job. Here, though, I think Michael's right. These people may bring in new blood every five years, but there's no way the gene pool hasn't gotten thin. Not living the way they do. I'm actually surprised there aren't more children like this.

"I don't know how groups like that make it. Of course, they aren't much better here," mutters Michael.

A dog barks, and I turn just as Zip dashes out of the woods. Seconds later, another dog follows, and then the entire hunting party steps out of the trees. The hounds and the warriors—including the one who kneed Zachariah in the balls—and John. But no Eric.

"Looks like the asshole got away," Michael grumbles.

"Yeah," I say with a sigh, unsure if I'm happy for him or pissed that he jumped the gun.

John is carried forward, supported by two of the warriors, the Elder and the one with the bright orange hair, and Michael and I watch as they drag him forward. He's bleeding from a big gash on his head and barely on his feet. When the women reach the center of the village, they release him, and he drops to the ground. John's eyes flutter but don't stay open, but I can't tell if he's injured or exhausted from running all night. Either way, whatever punishment they have in store for him is bound to be worse than what he's already been through.

"Son of a bitch has no idea what's coming," I say. "He might have been better off if he'd thrown himself off the mountain."

"Maybe we all would," Michael mutters.

"Zachariah," the Elder Warrior calls.

The older man steps forward, his head bowed.

"We could only locate one of the foundlings, but we can look no further. The men reached the outskirts of our territory before we could get to them, and we only located this one because he was injured. The other is gone." Elder Warrior pauses long enough to look toward the man at her feet, giving him a cold stare that makes me hate her. "Feed and clean him, then prepare for the punishment."

Zachariah keeps his head bowed, and I can't help comparing him to a dog I once saw on the streets. The poor wretch had been so beaten down he couldn't even hold his head up to beg for food. And this man thinks he's free?

The warriors leave, each of them shooting John a look of disgust on their way by. Only the tall warrior looks toward Zachariah, and when she does, the vengeance in her eyes makes even me sweat.

"What do you think they'll do to him?" Michael asks me.

"I don't think I want to know."

WE'RE CALLED TO THE WOMEN'S VILLAGE ONLY A COUPLE hours later, and by then John is up and moving around, his wound cleaned and bandaged. Zachariah walks at the front, leading us with his head held high despite what he's about to face, while the other foundlings and I walk directly behind him. The rest of the village comes last. All of them, from the old—which there aren't many of—to the very young and even the simple-minded boy. It's like the women want every man present to witness whatever punishment John has earned, and it makes me both sick to my stomach and uneasy.

The damn dog, Zip, trots at my side like we're best friends. I'm not sure why the thing has decided to adopt me, but at the moment I can't look at him without thinking about the warriors and how they charged into the forest in search of the men. I know it's irrational, but I can't help feeling like the dog is part of it.

Like the day of the Gleaning, the women stand waiting for us, only this time Raven is already in place. The crown of feathers is on her head once again, and at her side sits the old woman. Her hands are knobby and gnarled from arthritis, and her eyes milky and unfocused, but she holds her head high when we cross into the village like she can see everything we do even though I'm starting to suspect she's blind. Or at least very close to it.

Once we've come to a stop, Raven steps forward. "Bring the foundling."

Zachariah complies, pulling John forward by the elbow.

At my side, the dog sits, swishing his tail. It hits my heels and makes me want to push him away, but I hold back, knowing my anger isn't directed at the right place. He's a victim like me. Like John is about to be.

"Kneel," Raven roars once John is standing in front of her.

He does, and when Zachariah joins him, I shift, not liking what's about to happen but knowing I can't do a damn thing about it. Behind Raven, someone steps forward, and I don't have to strain to see who it is because she towers over everyone else. The tall warrior stops at the High Elder's side, and my gaze is drawn to the item in her hand. The sight of it makes me want to take a step back. Several pieces of leather have been braided together to create a whip. It's long, at least six feet in length, and as thick as one of my fingers. This can't be real. Men being whipped by women, punished like they're children. What kind of life is this?

Another woman steps forward, and I recognize her from the night of the Gleaning as the one who chose John as her husband. In this light, standing next to Raven and with the warriors so close, she looks impossibly small and young. She can't be more than nineteen—still a child, when you think about it—and I can't imagine her taking part in this. It's sick. This whole thing is sick.

"Foundling," Raven says, drawing John's gaze to her, "you were chosen by Brooke, but instead of pleasing her as you should, you ran. Where is the man you left with, the husband of Blossom?"

John swallows, his eyes wide as they shift between Raven and the whip. "I got hurt and couldn't go on, but he kept going. He's gone."

Raven frowns like John personally dragged Eric from the camp. "We have not had a transgression like this in a long, long time, and I want to be sure the other foundlings do not follow your example." She takes the whip from the warrior's hand and passes it to the girl at her side. "Brooke, your husband will receive twenty lashes for his disobedience."

I balk when the girl steps forward and want to shrink away, but I know better than to move an inch. Two of the warrior women do move, though, each of them grabbing one of John's arms and dragging him to the ground until he's sprawled out on his stomach, his cheek pressed into the dirt. He begs them to stop, his words coming out as hiccups, but he barely fights. Maybe he knows it will only make things worse.

Brooke steps forward, her eyes focused on the man in front of her. She doesn't even blink before raising her arm, lifting the whip into the air, and I hold my breath, bracing myself. When she brings the whip down, my whole body jerks. The echo of the leather cracking against John's back rises above the crowd and bounces off the trees, ringing through the forest and mixing with the sound of his screams. The noise gets cut off when the whip comes down again, followed quickly by a third time. Red welts rise on his back, thick and angry, and before Brooke has even reached thirteen lashes, his skin has been ripped open by the leather strips.

Blood pools on his back, dark red against his tan skin, but it isn't over yet, and I can't stomach the thought of seeing more, so I close my eyes and turn my head away. It's impossible to block out the snap of the whip or the high pitch of John's screams, though. They ring in my ears, pound against my temples, and make me want to scream right along with him.

I keep my eyes squeezed shut, counting each crack until number twenty breaks through the air. It fades away, and my body relaxes, and I finally open my eyes. But my relief is premature. John is up, dragged off to the side by the two warriors, but Zachariah is still kneeling in front of Raven, and she's looking down at him with sad eyes. Eyes that say she has no desire to punish him. For a brief moment, I think she might let his transgression go unpunished, but then she holds out her hand, and Brooke sets the whip in her palm.

"Zachariah," Raven's voice is thick with remorse, "you were not invited to touch Grove, were you?"

"No," he says, raising his voice so everyone can hear him. "I was not. I was wrong, and I will accept my punishment."

Raven looks at him like a mother who knows her child has learned an important lesson the hard way. "How many lashes do you think you deserve?"

He doesn't even hesitate. "Ten."

Raven glances toward Grove, who is glaring down at Zachariah. "Do you think the number is sufficient?"

The tall warrior nods once.

"Do you wish to give the lashing?" Raven asks.

Grove's stony expression falters, uncertainty flashing in her eyes. "No," she says after a few seconds. "He is your husband."

"Very well," Raven replies.

Zachariah turns without being told. He doesn't lie on the ground the way John did, but instead stays on his knees, his hands clenched into fists at his sides. He takes a couple deep breaths and grits his teeth, and without thinking, I find myself doing the same.

Raven raises the whip above her head, and sunshine glints off the drops of blood already clinging to the leather. She brings it down, and Zachariah grunts, but he doesn't move, and the same thing happens when she does it a second time. I want to look away, but I can't, because I'm too mesmerized by the expression of raw determination on Zachariah's face as Raven brings the leather down again, over and over. Sweat beads on his forehead, but he holds his ground. Not once does he make a sound louder than a grunt. The crack of the whip against his skin is as loud as it was during John's punishment, but witnessing it is a hell of a lot less traumatic without the accompanying screams.

The ten lashes are over quickly, and when they're finished, a murmur of approval moves through both crowds.

Facing me the way he is, I can't tell if the whip has broken the skin. But when Zachariah gets to his feet and turns to Raven, I see that his back is lined in red, but most of the blood seems to be left over from John's punishment. The welts are big, though, the skin swollen to a bright shade of pink, and just looking at it makes my own back throb.

"You did well, husband," Raven says.

He turns to face Grove. "I apologize for touching you."

The venom has melted from the warrior's eyes, and when she looks at Zachariah now, there is only admiration. "You are a good foundling, Zachariah. I know we can always count on you to do what is right."

Raven lifts her hands and turns in a circle, studying everyone gathered around. "The punishment is over, but let this be a reminder to all the men here. In this village, women are not the weaker sex."

The women hoot, lifting their arms above their heads in a strange kind of salute, and I search the crowd for Wilderness. It only takes a moment to find her, standing not too far behind her mother, and like all the other women, she has her arm raised. There's a look of triumph on her face, too, and the sight of it makes me sick.

CHAPTER TEN

Wilderness

I WATCHED MY HUSBAND DURING THE PUNISHMENT, AND his expression told me everything he was feeling. He was appalled. Disgusted. Outraged. But I cannot understand why. The stories I have heard about the outside world are filled with horrors much greater than this. During the Great Plague, people did unspeakable things to one another. Horrible things. It is why we are here. Surely, those atrocities have not been abolished. Surely, my husband has seen those things with his own eyes and must know a society cannot survive without rules and punishment.

All around me the women begin to disperse, heading to the trees or to jobs. The men, however, stay where they are. Although Zachariah does not bear the title of Elder since the men do not have such things, he has slipped naturally into a leadership role over the years, and it is normal for the men to wait for him the way they are now.

Zachariah has not moved because he is waiting for my mother.

Raven helps Mother Elder to the pulley cart so she can be lifted into the trees before finally going to her husband. The expression on her face tells me that Zachariah will once again go to her hut tonight, only this time the visit will not be for intimacy. She will take care of him, just as she did two winters ago when he got the sickness and could not keep any food down. It was the only time I have known my mother to let him stay in her hut both day and night, but she had, nursing him back to health just as she did with me when I was a small child.

"Zachariah," she says when she stops in front of him, "you please me more and more every day."

"I am sorry, Raven. I did not mean to grab Grove."

"I know, husband. I know you. I know the evilness is weak in you."

My mother urges him to turn so she can look at his back, and the pain in her eyes is as deep as the wounds left by the whip. She did not like having to punish Zachariah, just as I know I will struggle to do the same to my own husband if the time ever comes. But duty is not always pleasant, and as women, we are called to lead men on the right path.

"I will take care of it later," my mother says, keeping her voice low and soothing. "I invite you to my hut tonight."

Zachariah turns to face her, but I am too focused on my own husband to follow their exchange. Jameson is staring at my mother, and the scowl on his face reminds me of a petulant child who has just discovered that there are consequences to his actions.

At my husband's side, Zip sits wagging his tail, which doubles in speed as I make my way toward them. The dog may be excited by my approach, but my husband watches me with eyes full of hesitation and anger. He pulls away when I stop in front of him as if missing the distance, but we have been together two nights already, and I know how easily his body responds to mine. He wants me as I want him.

"I invite you to my hut tonight," I say, looking up at him through lowered lashes.

"What if I don't want to come to your hut?" he asks, but he keeps his voice low like he knows he should not say such things.

"You do not have a choice," I tell him. "You are my husband, and your job is to please me."

He blows air out of his nostrils like an angry sow. "This is insane."

"You use so many words I do not understand." Zachariah passes us, and the rest of the men turn to leave. I take a step back but say, "You will come to my hut tonight, husband."

Jameson's head dips once before he follows the other men, but his expression is still defiant. Angry. Hurt.

I watch him go, the dog trotting at his side. Like me, the animal seems to sense there is something very special about this man, and it warms me despite the knowledge that Jameson is angry. He will come to understand our ways in time, just as Zachariah did. I can feel it already. Can feel him slipping into our village the way my mother's husband did when he arrived.

When I turn, Raven captures my gaze with hers. "How is your husband?"

The runaway foundlings have her worried, and the concern is not just about my husband, but about all the foundlings. About our future and what will happen if things continue like this. We depend on the new blood the outsiders bring in to keep us strong, to prevent us from having children whose minds are slow and whose bodies are weak.

"He is fine," I tell her. "Obedient. I chose not to use the medicine last night, and he performed as he should have."

Fear flashes in her eyes. "Maybe it is okay to use it more. Maybe we have let Zachariah blind us to what the foundlings are capable of."

I look toward the trees my husband and the rest of the men disappeared through, thinking about the man I chose and how different he is from this place. Despite those differences, he has done well and pleased me, he has asked the right questions, and he seems eager to learn. When we are alone, he explores every inch of my body as if I am the woman he chose for himself, and not the other way around.

"I am not concerned about Jameson. I will lead him where he must go," I say with confidence, and for once I feel certain I have the strength inside me to do what needs to be done. Being on top of him last night helped put things into perspective and helped me understand the power I have over him. "Zachariah has taught him well."

"Good." My mother lets out a deep sigh as she turns away. "I must go see the healer. Zachariah will need herbs for his wounds."

THAT NIGHT, I ALLOW MY HUSBAND TO FIND HIS OWN WAY TO my hut, and when he opens the door, I am already naked and waiting. He steps inside and takes me in, his gaze moving over my flesh like I am a succulent berry he is considering taking a bite of even though he suspects it is poisonous. He remains just inside the door, though, and I know his hesitation has nothing to do with waiting for an invitation. It is because of the punishment. He is having trouble getting the image out of his mind, and he is scared of what the future will bring.

"Come," I say, holding my arms out and motioning for him to step closer. "I invite you to touch me."

He crosses the hut, his eyes taking me in as he walks. When he reaches the bed, he sits on the edge, but once again only studies me. I am eager for his touch, but allow him the time to take me in, knowing he will not be able to resist. To my surprise and pleasure, the expression in his eyes when he looks at me is almost as pleasing as having his mouth on my body.

"You're beautiful," he says after a moment, but I have a difficult time understanding the bite in his words. It is as if my beauty makes him angry, not just at me, but at himself as well. "You know that, right?"

"My mother tells me I am beautiful, but she should not have." I run my finger down his arm, over the lines curling around his bicep, and he cringes but does not pull away. "Here, we do not place importance on physical appearance the way you do in the outside world."

Jameson lifts his eyebrows the way he does when something confuses him, but his expression remains hard and detached. "Physical appearance doesn't matter? Why?"

"It's part of our history," I tell him. "Part of why we are so strong. There was a time when women who were more attractive were held in higher esteem, even if they had less to contribute. Here, we value gifts. What we can do to help the village. I can hunt, so I am valued for that, not because I am pleasant to look at. My mother is a good leader, but she would be so even if she were not attractive. These things are much more important than beauty. They are what will keep us strong."

When my husband frowns, it seems as if he does not believe me. "I don't think it's very realistic. We all judge other people by their appearance. Like the Gleaning, for instance. Sully was the only man who wasn't chosen, and he was also the only one who was overweight. Are you telling me that didn't matter?"

I think back to that night, to the men lined up and the choice in front of me. I weighed them all in my mind even though I was more drawn to the blond one, Blossom's husband who is now gone. At the time, I thought very little of my husband's looks. His features seemed too hard, too severe. There was no softness to him.

"I remember the man you call Sully. He was round, not healthy or as young as the others. To me he was poor choice because I want my offspring to be strong. If I had chosen a husband based on looks, you would not have been my choice, Jameson. The blond man, the one who ran, was very pleasing to me. But you are stronger, tall and broad, and I knew you would give me strong yieldlings and healthy daughters."

His eyebrows jump like a startled rabbit, and his expression softens for the first time since stepping into my hut. Suddenly, he lets out a laugh. It is a deep sound, but free, like the croak of a bullfrog on a summer morning. It also lights up his eyes in a way I have never seen before and creates a dimple in his cheek.

I reach up to touch it, sticking my finger in the little crater, and he catches my hand in his. His eyes hold mine for a second before he presses his lips to my fingertips. The touch is soft and gentle, but there are as many meanings behind the gesture as there are stars in the sky.

"I like when you laugh," I tell him.

"Even if I'm not pleasing to look at?" he asks.

I laugh this time, letting the sound float out of me and fill the room. "You please me very much, Jameson. Both in how you look, and in how you touch my body."

He drops my hand and crawls onto the bed with me. "Let me please you, then."

WHEN I WAKE, MY HUSBAND'S BODY IS WRAPPED AROUND ME like ivy, and light is streaming in through the cracks in the shutters.

He stayed all night.

My first thought is one of terror. Have I given away too much of my power by allowing him to stay?

Then Jameson moves, and his hand brushes my thigh, and the warmth of his touch pushes the feeling away. Even my mother allows her husband to spend the night at times, and there are many women in the village who do as well. Dawn, for one. I have seen Hawk climbing down from the trees early in the morning on many occasions.

"Jameson," I say, shaking my husband's shoulder. "You must wake."

He rolls onto his side and looks up at me. "Is it morning?"

"It is, but you must go."

He stretches, not making a move to leave. "I like your bed better than the hard floor in the hut."

"It is just the naked woman," I tell him.

Jameson chuckles, and my lips curl up at the sound. It is only the second laugh I have been able to pry from him, but I want more. The more he laughs, the more certain of his comfort I will be, and I find that I am desperate to know he is learning his place. To be assured that he won't follow Eric down the mountain. And away from me.

"The naked woman does help," he says as he climbs to his feet.

I watch from the bed as he works to wind the leather straps around his pants. His struggles make my smile stretch wider, and though I know I should allow him to figure it out on his own, I sit up so I can help.

"Like this." I weave the leather straps around his waist and tie them tight.

"I don't know how you do that," he says, his eyes holding mine.

I smile up at him, my hands still on his hips. "You will figure it out."

For a second, he does not move. Then he turns to leave, and a pang shoots through me, and I find myself getting up, swiping a fur off the bed and wrapping it around my body so I can walk with him. Jameson stops without opening the door, staring at me, and the expression in his eyes makes my heart beat as fast as the wings of a dragonfly.

"That looks good on you." He fingers the fur wrapped around me.

"I told you. We do not—"

"I know. Looks don't matter. Except they do, and you're gorgeous." He plants a kiss on my forehead before turning to the door. "Good morrow, Wilderness."

"Good morrow, Jameson."

After he leaves, I crawl back into bed and burrow under the furs. They are soft against my skin, and under me the bed is firm but supple, and it suddenly occurs to me how uncomfortable sleeping on the hard floor would be, even with a pile of furs. How has Zachariah put up with it for all these years?

I have a cot made of deer hide, but many of the other women in the village use hammocks. Not only would those be easy to make, but they would also give the men a comfortable place to sleep at night. I would have to kill a lot of deer, though. I could do it, I know I could, but I also know it is something I would have to talk over with my mother first. She is High Elder, and even a decision as small as this cannot be made without her permission.

CHAPTER ELEVEN

Jameson

THE SUN HASN'T YET BROKEN OVER THE HORIZON, BUT already the sky is lit up with the promise of dawn. Throughout the village, other men make their way across walkways to ladders, heading back to their rightful places. Just like I am. There aren't a lot of them, six or seven, but I do spot Ash as he descends a ladder, as well as another man I recognize but haven't yet been introduced to. Canyon, I think his name is. Do all the women kick their husbands out at the first sign of dawn?

I'm crossing one of the many walkways, holding on for dear life, when Zachariah comes out of Raven's hut. He sees me, and a look of surprise crosses his face, but it's quickly replaced by a smile.

"Good morrow, Jameson."

His grin feels out of place after what happened yesterday. I witnessed his apology, but a part of me thought he was feeding them a line so he didn't have to face a more brutal punishment. Now, though, it seems like I was wrong.

"Good morrow, Zachariah."

The man waits on the platform and pats me on the shoulder when I reach him. "Did you have a nice sleep?"

"Better than the floor in our hut."

Zachariah laughs and starts walking, motioning for me to follow. "Yes, the cots are much softer."

"Don't you think it's weird that you aren't allowed to have a bed?"

He shoots me a look that feels a little too much like a warning. "No, I do not."

I follow him, studying the red welts on his back. They're less inflamed this morning, and the couple areas where the skin was broken have already scabbed over. Under them, though, are older marks, scars from punishments he must have received in the past, and a shudder shakes my body at the sight.

How common are whippings?

The longer I stare at the other man's back, the more the euphoria from the night wears off, and the more I have to accept that Wilderness did this on purpose. She knew I was pissed after the punishment, but she also knew if she was naked when I got to her hut it would distract me, and it did. Like a weak-minded fool, I let her body draw me in. No wonder Zachariah walks around oblivious to the shit going on around him. Raven has probably done the same thing since the beginning. It's like these women have the ability to cast a spell over us, and it pisses me off even more than the damn whippings.

Zachariah and I don't talk again as we climb down, and like the day before, I find Zip waiting for me at the bottom. I don't quite get why the dog has adopted me, but whatever the reason, he jumps excitedly when I reach the ground. I scratch him behind the ears, and his tail goes nuts, and Zachariah grins like the dog's acceptance is somehow proof I belong here. I'm still petting the dog when I shake my head in disgust.

The three of us head across the clearing together. A handful of women have gathered around the fire, eating a stew similar to the one we have every morning, and like we don't exist, none of them glances our way when we pass.

When we step through the trees, it seems safe enough to ask the question nagging at me, so I say, "How are you feeling this morning?"

Zachariah narrows his eyes, and this time the look is definitely a warning. "I am fine."

"You were whipped yesterday, and you're telling me you're fine?" I let out a deep breath, trying to control my anger, but it doesn't help, and I feel on the brink of exploding. "Aren't you mad?"

He stops, and I do, too. Zip, who's gotten ahead of us, turns around and trots back. He sits at my side, but my eyes are focused on Zachariah. The expression on the man's face seems like more than a warning, but I don't quite understand where it's coming from or what it means.

"I am fine, Jameson," he begins. "You need to let it be. I was wrong. I know the rules, and I chose to grab Grove. To you it may seem like a heavy price, but to me it is securing the peace of mind of this village. I like what we have here, and although you do not yet understand, you will."

"When will I understand?" I snap. "When will I think it's okay to whip a man?"

"The Feast of the New Moon is tomorrow, and you will hear the story then." Zachariah pats me on the arm before he starts walking again. "I know you will see reason."

I head after him, fuming, and Zip jumps to his feet.

I don't believe Zachariah's claims that I'll understand. I can't think of a single thing that would make me understand the way these people choose to live. The men are treated like dirt, and the women live like royalty. Raven obviously cares about Zachariah, but still refuses to let him get close to her, plus she's given up four sons like they were nothing. It blows my mind.

Back in our hut, I find John sprawled out on his stomach, snoring. His wounds seem to have been treated, but unlike Zachariah's, they're raw and painful looking.

"He will sleep today," Zachariah tells me. "He needs time to heal."

"Is that allowed?" I spit at the older man.

Zachariah shakes his head like I'm a foolish child. "It is required."

I go about my day, seething. Last night when I went to see Wilderness, I was determined not to let her suck me into this world with sex, but when I'd walked into her hut and found her already naked, my resolve fizzled until I couldn't remember why I'd been angry in the first place. But I'm not going to let them trick me today. I watched two men be whipped only a day ago, and it was meant to serve as a warning to me and the other men in my group. To make me do as I'm told unless I want the same thing to happen to me. It was wrong. All of this is wrong, and one way or another, I'm getting out.

I'm still angry when Wilderness shows up. Like yesterday, she's carrying a bow, but this time when she sees me, she smiles. The way it lights up her face has me freezing in my tracks and cursing my body, but I can't stop it from reacting to her presence the way it does. One look at her sends blood shooting to my groin, and the closer she gets, the more I find my anger fizzling away.

"Husband," she says, her tone a hell of a lot less formal than it has been every other day. "I am going to hunt. I thought about what you said, and I have decided you should have a hammock. I do not want you to be uncomfortable."

I have to bite back a retort about how she shouldn't force me to watch my friends get whipped, and instead say, "Your mother is okay with this?"

"I spoke with Raven, and she has agreed, as long as I can bring in enough deer. It will take some time, and you will have to tan the hides, but soon you will have a bed."

She smiles like she's proud of herself, and I'd be lying if I said the gesture didn't touch me, because it does, which is part of the problem with this place. It's harmonious and relaxing, making it easy to forget they dragged me here against my will. I work hard, but I don't toil all day for nothing the way I did back home. Here, even if I get sick and can't clean out the goat pen, I'll still have food and a roof over my head. It's easy to get confused, especially when the woman in front of me wraps her naked body around mine, but I won't let her confuse me again. Even if I'm dragged down to the center of the village and whipped, I refuse to give in.

Her smile wavers when I don't reply. "Are you not happy?"

"No, Wilderness, I'm not happy, but I'm grateful you're thinking of me."

Her smile fades even more, and the pain flashing in her eyes feels like a knife in my chest. I hate that she looks hurt, but even more, I hate that I hate it.

THAT NIGHT, WILDERNESS DOESN'T INVITE ME TO HER BED. I'M still stewing in my own anger, though, and even lying on the hard floor in the men's hut, surrounded by darkness and the stench of animal shit, I can't bring myself to wish I was with the woman who calls me husband. Zachariah, who once again goes to Raven, has promised over and over again that I'll feel differently after the Festival of the New Moon, but I don't believe him. No explanation can justify what's happening here.

John's groans welcome me to a new day. He's in pain, and I know it, but I can't stop irritation from surging through me. It's like a wave rolling over my body the way it covers me from head to toe. John did this to himself. No, he didn't deserve the whipping, but he ran without thinking it through and left a trail so long the warriors probably didn't even need the dogs to find him. If he'd taken his time, he might have gotten away, but because he rushed into things, he brought punishment on himself and extended the sentence the rest of us are going to have to serve. It makes sympathy difficult, if not damn near impossible.

After breakfast, I clean the goat pens, doing my best to stay as far away from Zachariah as I can. I blame him almost as much as I blame the women. He was punished, too, but he pretty much asked for it. He's like a warden in a prison full of men he knows are innocent, going about the day, doing his job, and refusing to help the people who are being held unfairly. Telling them they're better off as prisoners. What a load of bullshit.

Zip is a constant shadow in my life. Even when the yieldlings and other dogs run into the forest whooping in delight, he stays at my side. I watch how his gaze follows them, and how he wags his tail, but for some reason, he sticks with me.

After everything that's happened, I enjoy the company. I talk to him as I work. About the world I came from where cars drive up and down streets and lights flick on with the flip of a switch—assuming the electricity is working that day. I tell him about the ocean and how beautiful it can be if you get the chance to make it far enough away from the pollution of the bay. I only had the opportunity to do it twice—both times filling an empty position on a fishing boat—but it was the most amazing thing I'd ever seen. The waves, the sun sparkling off the water, the way it seemed to go on forever. Like paradise.

The dog listens to everything I say, or at least he seems to, and he happily scarfs down the scraps of fat I toss him while tanning another hide. I don't understand why he's decided to latch onto me, but I'm grateful for the distraction it brings.

It's late afternoon by the time Wilderness steps into the men's village, and the very sight of her sucks away the good mood I've managed to conjure up by talking to Zip. There isn't a single part of me that wants to see her, but I'm not allowed to tell her no unless I want to be the next person forced to kneel in the women's village. So, I do the only thing I can do, continue with my work, forcing her to come to *me*, which is the most defiance I can afford in my current situation. It isn't the least bit gratifying.

"You will come with me," she says when she stops at my side.

I take my time turning, and when I'm facing her, it hits me for the first time how small she is compared to me. She can't be more than two inches over five feet and only a little over a hundred pounds, and yet the power she wields blinds me to her size. No one this tiny should be able to control me with a single look, but she does.

"Where are we going?" I ask instead of giving in right away.

When she frowns, I brace myself for a lecture about how it isn't my place to ask questions, but instead she holds up a small bundle and says, "A bath. We will get clean for the festival."

I was beginning to think these people didn't take baths, and I'm glad to learn they do. She seems to know it, too, because her frown eases, and in seconds a smile that feels like a peace offering has replaced it. I take it, if for no other reason than because I've been shoveling goat shit every morning, and no matter how well I try to clean myself, there's only so much you can do with a bucket of cold water. But I tell myself I'm not happy about it.

She leads the way toward the forest with the bundle tucked under her arm, and I follow at a safe distance while Zip skips along at my side. The woods are thick, and the branches scratch at my bare skin, making me wish I had a shirt. In the summer, I'm sure this no shirt bullshit will be nice, but right now it's still spring, and it sucks. I'm covered in goose bumps half the time, and the other half I feel like I'm naked, and a little bit on display, especially with these idiotic pants that aren't actually pants.

"Why don't the men wear shirts?" I ask, realizing I've never questioned the practice. I have to stop that. I have to force myself to question everything or I'll end up a puppet like Zachariah.

Wilderness glances over her shoulder at me, frowning like she doesn't understand the question. "They do not need them."

I almost laugh. "What about staying warm?"

"In the winter, you will wear fur, but why wear a shirt if it is not cold? You have no breasts. Your pants cover your male areas."

It's hard to argue with that logic.

"I'm not used to it," I say anyway, because I refuse to give in to her today, refuse to make it easy on her like I did last night. I won't fight and leave myself open to punishment, but I won't be the obedient dog who rolls over every time she tells me to. Not anymore.

I glance toward Zip and give him a sympathetic look like I think he can read my mind and knows I insulted him, and he wags his tail in response.

"If you would like to wear a shirt, Jameson," Wilderness says, "you may wear a shirt. You do not have to ask permission for such a thing."

I don't know how to respond, so I don't. I expected her to tell me it was to keep the men in their place, but this makes it seems more like custom, like something they've always done and continue to do more out of habit than any form of punishment or control. Like it never occurred to the men to put a shirt on when it isn't necessary to keep warm.

Wilderness leads me deeper into the woods, and the ground beneath my feet grows rocky. The ridiculous shoes—if you can even call them that—do little to protect my feet, so I take my time, doing my best to step on smooth areas and avoid the places where the stones jut up in sharp points. Before long, we come to a wall of rock that towers over us by more than twenty feet. I look up at the tree and bushes hanging over the edge and growing into the natural stone crevices. Here and there, plants have sprung up on a ledge or from cracks and seem suspended in the air, their green leaves a burst of life against the otherwise gray rock.

Wilderness follows the wall, running her hand across the surface as she walks. I do the same, marveling at the smooth texture the rock has taken on, thanks to centuries of water running over the edge of the cliff and down the wall. This is what happened to Zachariah. He came here with hard edges and enough defiance to want to leave, but Raven was able to wear him down one night at a time until there was nothing of that person left.

When the rock wall comes to an end, Wilderness turns the corner, and I follow, only a couple steps behind her, and stop dead in my tracks. Zip does, too, wagging his tail in excitement, but I don't look at him because I'm too focused on the small pool of water in front of us. It isn't huge, no more than six feet across, but it's surrounded by pine trees and secluded from the rest world, and the water is clear and blue, with steam rising from it and getting caught on the wind.

"Is this a hot spring?"

Wilderness turns to face me, already untangling the leather cords from her clothes. "We come here to bathe, but we take turns. I asked that today be our day."

The leather she's wearing slides to the ground and collects at her feet, leaving her naked, and desire builds in me, pushing down the anger I've been clinging to. Damn her. It's impossible to remain unaffected when she's standing in front of me like this, and she knows exactly what she's doing and, even worse, how I'll react.

She turns her back to me, and my gaze moves over the curve of her ass. Wilderness may be a small woman, but she's fit and healthy, and every inch of her is perfect. Soft, yet firm and inviting. She steps into the water without looking back, and I watch it engulf her silky curves. The pool isn't deep. The water only goes up a little past her waist, and when she turns to face me, her breasts are on full display, once again distracting me from my anger.

"Come into the water, husband."

As I pull on the leather strap, freeing myself from the pants, I tell myself I have no choice, because not only is it impossible to deny her unless I want to be punished, but I'm also dying to be clean. The leather falls to the ground beside the clothes Wilderness has already removed, and as if sensing we'll be here for a while, Zip drops next the discarded fur.

The water is warm when I step in, and next to Wilderness, it's the best thing I've felt in years. Even back home in Baltimore I didn't get warm baths, which isn't uncommon these days, and the luxury of this moment isn't lost on me. I sink down, allowing the water to engulf my body, my gaze on Wilderness as she moves to the side of the pool. She's so confident, so certain of her place in the village and her supposed responsibilities to her people that she seems decades older than her mid-twenties. It's something I'm not used to. The outside world is too uncertain to produce people like her. Every day you wake up wondering if your hard work is going to be rewarded or if it will once again be futile, and every night you go to sleep feeling like it was all a waste. When I think of my situation in that light, it's almost understandable how Zachariah got sucked into this world.

Wilderness turns back to face me after digging through the bundle she carried through the forest. She has a small bar in her hand, which she dips in the water and rubs between her palms, creating a lather. The ache that started in my groin increases when she runs her hands down her chest and over breasts, and even though I hate myself a little, the urge to reach out and touch her is overwhelming.

I don't because she hasn't invited me to touch her, which makes me hate myself a little bit more than I already do.

"Stand up," she says as she moves behind me.

I do as I'm told, standing so the water is barely covering my waist. After the warmth, the air feels colder than ever, but heat flares through me a second later when Wilderness runs the bar over my shoulders and back. The scent of pine is heavy and pleasant, and for the first time in days, I'm positive the stink of goat shit won't follow me wherever I go.

"Do not move," she whispers, this time reaching around my waist. Her fingers wrap around me, and I groan but do as I'm told and hold still, and Wilderness presses closer, her nipples hard points against my back. "I want you to be happy, husband."

She tightens her fingers on me in a deliciously torturous way as she moves her hand faster, making it impossible to utter a word. I want to tell her this won't make me happy, but there's no blood left in my brain to form the words, so I close my eyes and once again give in.

WE'RE CLEAN AND BOTH VERY SATISFIED WHEN WILDERNESS and I leave the hot spring. The sun has begun to set, painting the sky in bright colors made even more vibrant by the surrounding beauty of the forest. Zip trots along at my side, having gotten a good nap in while he waited for us, and on my other side, Wilderness's steps seem just as light.

I try not to look at her, but it's impossible. Wildflowers are tangled in her long, blonde hair, and when the remaining sunlight shines down on it, the tendrils gleam like gold. She's a sight to behold, more beautiful than the sunset and more tempting than the damn apple the serpent gave Eve, and that's exactly how she feels to me. Like a temptation that would be impossible to resist even if I could tell her no. When she comes to me like she did in the hot spring, I try to convince myself I'm only giving in because I have no other choice, but it isn't true. Even if she gave me a choice, I would go to her. Every single night.

Everyone is already gathered in the women's village when we arrive, the men and women intermingled for the first time since I got here, and for once they don't look like two separate groups, but rather one happy village. There's a large fire in the center with a boar on a spit, its skin charred and black from the flames, and the scent of roasting meat makes my mouth water. But the boisterous atmosphere doesn't seem to fit with the image I have of this village. The women don't look like tyrants. They're with their husbands, many of them with arms around each other, and they're smiling. Happy. In the afterglow of the hot spring, it's almost possible for me to convince myself this place is normal.

Wilderness smiles up at me when we reach the edge of the crowd, her amber eyes sparkling in the soft light of the setting sun. "You have permission to touch me tonight."

My own smile wavers, but it's impossible to keep it at bay. I've only known this woman for a few days, but when she looks at me like this, I can feel it all the way in my soul. There's something about her, something good and strong and right that defies every one of my qualms about this place, and I can't escape it.

She holds her hand out, and I take it without hesitating, entwining my fingers with hers, and together we move toward the festival already underway.

Zip disappears, drawn away by the smell of food, and I search for him in the crowd, but spotting him is impossible. All around us, people laugh and talk, and children run in circles squealing. The women, like Wilderness, have adorned their hair with fresh flowers, and like me, most of the husbands look enthralled by the presence of the women at their sides. Almost like these women really do have the ability to cast spells on the men.

In the center of the crowd sit Raven and Zachariah. He's on a stump with her perched on his lap, her arm draped around his shoulders and her long, gray hair hanging down her back, shining in the light of the fire. He catches me staring and lifts what looks like a hollowed out gourd in a silent salute, grinning from ear to ear, then he takes a drink.

"What's he's drinking?" I ask Wilderness, leaning down so she can hear me over the noise of the crowd.

"Dandelion wine." She smiles up at me, and her brown eyes shimmer with a feeling I can't name that causes a pang in my stomach. "The children gather the flowers in the spring so we can make it. It is very sweet."

I chuckle, and her grin grows wider.

"What?" I ask. "Why are you smiling?"

Her hand tightens around mine. "I told you. I like it when you laugh."

I focus on the way her lips curl when she smiles, remembering how soft and warm they are. The urge to kiss her is strong, but I hold back because I feel like it would be giving away a part of myself, and I'm still trying to hold on to who I am. I don't belong here. I'm not one of these people. It's gets harder and harder to remember every day, I realize, and it makes me understand Zachariah a little better.

But I can't let the woman at my side cast a spell on me the way Zachariah has with Raven. I have to remember who I am.

The party goes late into the night. There's food and drinks—Wilderness was right about the dandelion wine being sweet—and plenty of laughter. Some dancing, too, accompanied by homemade drums made from wood frames with animal hides stretched tight over them. I even catch John laughing with Brooke, although I don't know how he manages it after the whipping. Maybe the wine has something to do with it, though. Alcohol can ease the pain of most wounds if you try hard enough.

It has to be nearing midnight before I spot the old woman moving through the crowd, which parts for her like Moses and the Red Sea. The men and women kneel as she passes, settling on the ground, and a hush falls over the group that seems heavy after the noise of the party.

My head is spinning from the wine, but not enough that I don't remember what Zachariah told me, and when I find him in the crowd, his expression is for once somber. Wilderness kneels, pulling me with her, as the old woman hobbles by. When she reaches the front, she takes a seat in the same wooden chair I've seen her in every time we've gathered here, and in the silence that has fallen over the village, even the crickets seem loud.

Raven alone is standing. She takes her place at the woman's side, the crown of feathers on her head and her expression as subdued as her husband's. Her gaze moves across the crowd, and when it rests on me longer than anyone else, I shift. I'm about to have all my questions regarding this place answered, but I'm not sure if I want them to be, because the last thing I want is to learn something that will justify the way these women act, which is what Zachariah assures me will happen.

"We have gathered not just to celebrate, but to remember our past and what brought us here," Raven begins, her voice rising over the crowd and seeming to bounce off the village hanging high above our heads. "Mother Elder has been here since the beginning and is the last of us who was alive back then. She survived The Great Plague and what followed. Our ancestors came here not to hide, but to start a new life and to protect themselves, and because of that, none of us will ever again be forced to endure the atrocities they suffered. Now we listen, so we do not forget."

Raven turns to face the old woman, who closes her eyes and takes a deep breath like she's preparing for a long story. At my side, Wilderness's body seems as stiff and unyielding as the mountain beneath us, and all around me, the other women shift as well. Shoulders straighten and they sit taller, holding their heads higher, while the men do the opposite. They look down like they're ashamed of something they've done.

"Each of us came to that place in a different way," the old woman begins, her scratchy voice rising louder than I thought possible, considering her age. "I was taken from a camp in the middle of the night, away from people who had survived the plague and wanted to start over. They were good people, but the men who took me were not. They brought me to a large building called a hotel. It had hundreds of rooms, but the women they stole were crowded together, dozens of us to a room. The men fed us little, gave us almost nothing to wear. They used us however they liked. Treated us like animals. They did not hear our cries or care when we begged for mercy." When the old woman opens her milky eyes, they seem to stare through the crowd, almost like she's able to look into the past and watch it all play out again. "After a time, someone set us free. Who it was, I do not know. Those of us who made it out were weak and scared. Beaten down. Tired. Hungry. The external scars we wore were nothing compared to the scars we carried inside. I was just a child then, only fifteen years old, but the things I endured at the hands of those men had changed me into a woman overnight."

I look around and find tears on the cheeks of most of the women, their eyes shimmering in the glow of the fire and mirroring the pain in the old woman's voice. She sits tall, her head held high, but she, too, has tears on her cheeks. My own eyes are dry, but the tightening of my throat is impossible to ignore. No matter what these women have done to me, I can't remain unaffected by this story.

"Not everyone was strong enough to go on, but those of us who were fled the desert, hoping to leave the men and the hotel and the memories behind. We traveled for weeks, hiding during the day in empty stores and houses, moving at night when the darkness concealed us better. We lost more along the way, women who could not forget, who could not escape the pain, and by the time we reached the mountains, only twenty of us remained. We settled in as best as we could, built shelters and gathered food. The determination to survive was the only thing that could have pushed aside the horrors of those weeks in Vegas.

"Shortly after we arrived at our new home, one of the women discovered she was with child. In those days, The Great Plague took most of the babies born, and we were not even sure the child would survive. Only it did." For the first time, the old woman looks down, almost like she's reached the most painful part of the story. "The child was a boy, and despite how he had come about, he was loved."

Raven places a firm hand on Mother Elder's shoulder, and the old woman takes a deep breath before continuing her story. "The memories of what we endured at the hands of men had not faded, though, and we began to worry what would happen once the boy came of age. We knew a great evil lived inside him, and we worried it would come out and destroy everything we had built. By then we had made our home in the trees, keeping us safe from predators, and so we decided to build the boy a separate home on the ground. We built it on stilts so he would be safe like us, but we kept him away. He was an outcast, living on his own from the age of twelve. He tended the animals, kept watch over them to make sure no predators stole them in the dark of night. It was all he knew, and he accepted his role in our village without complaint.

"He grew older, became a man, and it was not long before the women began to visit his bed at night. He was a husband to all, and it was his seed that helped bring about the first generation of children born in this village."

The old woman nods like she's trying to convince herself everything they did was okay, but I can't help thinking about the boy who grew up and became the only man in this village. If I felt cheap and used the morning after my first time with Wilderness, I can't imagine how he felt. His only purpose was to please the women. It's sick. Even worse, it isn't that much different than what happened to the women in that hotel.

"The first generation of children born in the forest gave us three boys," the old woman says, continuing her story, " and like the man before them, when they were old enough, they left the trees and lived on the ground, tending the animals and taking their place in the village. And like before, the daughters of that generation visited the beds of these boys. The next generation was offspring of those half siblings, but we knew continuing down that road would make us weak. We knew that if we wanted to remain strong, we would have to bring new blood to our village."

At my side, Wilderness sniffs, and I watch as she wipes the tears from her cheeks. As the old woman begins the next part of the story, though, Wilderness's expression changes from sorrow to pride. Her shoulders relax, and she smiles like she's anticipating a happy ending. But I have a strong suspicion I won't be able to agree with her about that.

"And so the Gleaning began. Warriors from our village left, the strongest and bravest among us, and went down the mountain in search of men. On that first trip they found two, but they went back only a few weeks later and brought more. In the beginning, the need for husbands was strong, but as time went on and more yieldlings were born, we began to spread out our trips. Now we go down the mountain only once every five years. For more than forty years we have lived this way, and it has served us well. Babies are born, and our village has grown stronger." All around me, the women nod. "The men take their place in the huts and tend the animals, while the women hunt and gather and lead." The old woman pushes herself up, standing so she can look out over the crowd, and despite their milky hue, her eyes blaze with fire and pride and hope for the future. "We will never return to the way things used to be, back when men took and used and hurt. We will never be weak and helpless again. We are strong. We are one. We will not fall."

A cry rises up when she stops talking, the women and even the men whooping out a shout of triumph. I don't join in. I've heard part of this story, back in school while studying the events leading up to and following the plague. There was a group of men who captured women and trapped them in a Las Vegas hotel, using them as currency. They were raped, tortured, and starved. People, not just men, will do sick things when there are no consequences, and I can't even begin to imagine what those women went through. Eventually, the group was broken up and the women set free, but it was believed that only a handful of them survived to tell their story. Now I know that isn't true. Twenty more made it out of that hotel, and this is what they built out of the ruins of their lives.

Zachariah told me once I heard this story I'd understand everything, and I do. I understand what drove these women here, why they hid and why they fear men, but I understand something else, too. I understand what they're doing is no different than what those men did all those years ago. They took women against their will and used them, and now these women are doing the same thing to men. It doesn't matter if Zachariah is happy about where he ended up, how he got here is still wrong. All of this is wrong.

Once she's finished telling her story, the old woman returns to the trees, and it isn't long before Wilderness leads me up as well. I climb the ladder behind her, my mind still spinning from what I heard and what I know. I'm not unaffected by what these women are feeling, and I'd like to say I'm angry, but the emotions inside me are more complicated than that. I'm disgusted, sickened by the way Wilderness has been misled. Because of her mother and the other women in this village, she's missed out on so much. She doesn't know who her father is or that she has brothers. She doesn't understand what a real relationship between a man and a woman can be like. It makes me ache for her, and by the time she's led me into her hut, I find all I want to do is hold her close. To comfort her.

When I wrap my arms around her, she smiles up at me. "What is that for?"

"I just—" I swallow. "I was thinking about the story the old woman told."

"Mother Elder," she corrects me.

"Yeah."

She sits on the bed, pulling me with her, and I don't let go of her hand even when I've taken my place at her side.

"That is why we keep the men in a separate village," she says, her eyes boring into mine like she wants to make sure I understand. "To protect us from the evil nature living inside them."

I don't know what to say at first, too dumbfounded by her logic, and I'm not sure if she'll even understand me when I do manage to get it out. This is all she knows, after all. To her, this is normal. Her only frame of reference for the outside world is the story of those sick and twisted men who captured her ancestors.

"But not all men are bad, Wilderness," I tell her. "There are good men, too. Like Zachariah. Don't you think he's a good man? He is your father."

When her nose wrinkles, it confirms all my suspicions, but it still feels like a slap when she says, "What is this word, *father*?"

I clench my free hand into a fist when the urge to punch someone comes over me, fighting to get out. Part of me wants to tell her, to lay it all out for her, but I have a feeling doing that would only get me in trouble. With the punishment Zachariah and John endured still fresh in my mind, I have no desire to do anything to bring that down on myself.

Still, I don't get how Zachariah can put up with this. Especially with his own children.

"Never mind." I brush her question off with a shake of my head. "It's something I can't explain right now."

"I do believe there are good men," she says when I go silent. "Some have less evil than others. Like you and Zachariah. I can see it in his eyes when he talks to me. I can hear it in his laughter. That is why I enjoy your laugh so much."

"What about the other men in the village?" I ask her. "Don't you see good in them? What about the little boys?"

She presses her lips together for a moment before saying, "Hawk and I were small together, and I remember playing with him. He and I have a bond I do not understand, but whenever I am near him, I want to talk to him. He is Dawn's husband, though, and she does not like it when we spend time together."

I shift when an uncomfortable thought pops into my head. "Do you have sexual feelings for him?" If she has no idea Hawk is her brother, she might not understand why she's drawn to him. Another reason not to keep people in the dark about who they're related to.

"No." Wilderness peers up at me through lowered lashes, a small smile on her lips. "Are you jealous, husband?"

I snort, wishing I could explain why Hawk means so much to her but knowing I can't. "Not at all."

"You have nothing to be jealous of. I enjoy your company much more than I thought I would."

Wilderness snuggles closer to me, and the pang in my chest is so real and violent I almost can't believe it. I just met this woman, and I don't understand her or her culture, but I can't deny I'm falling for her. Hard. At this point, I'm not sure there's anything I can do to stop it either. Other than leave, that is.

CHAPTER TWELVE

Wilderness

WITHOUT FOUNDLINGS, OUR VILLAGE WOULD NOT have thrived the way it has, but the transition is not an easy one, and most of the matches do not turn out like the one my mother and Zachariah share. Too often, women find themselves indifferent to their husbands, inviting them to their huts only when they are ready for a child, but it is a feeling I cannot understand. Having Jameson in my bed, at my side, fills me with more joy than I could have anticipated, and already I can picture a future for us like the one my mother shares with her own husband. Like Zachariah, Jameson will lead the men while I lead our village as High Elder, and like my mother, I will still call him to my bed thirty years from now. Still long for his touch, his closeness.

It is more than the pleasure he brings to my body, though. I enjoy every moment with Jameson, every look and touch and caress, and every smile I manage to coax out of him. I long for him to be happy here, which is why the sting of his words when he told me he was not happy felt as sharp as the bite of a snake. Jameson is here to please me, but it is my duty to make sure he wants to, and I am failing him.

That is why, for the second time since he came to the village, I allow my husband to remain in my hut all night.

Jameson's hard body is pressed against mine when I wake the next morning, his heat warming me better than any fur could. I know I should wake him and send him on his way, but instead I take a moment to watch him sleep. I was not lying when I told him that his looks please me more than they did when we first met, and staring at him now, I find myself wondering how I was ever able to look at him and see anything but beauty. Jameson is all man, all hard muscle, but every inch of him is beautiful.

When I nudge him awake, he groans but rolls out of bed without complaint. His eyes are half closed as he dresses, and the early morning light streaming in through the cracks in the shutters highlight his movements as I watch from my position on the bed, marveling at him once again. An ache spreads through me, turning into a sudden and overwhelming desire to do more for him. To not just allow him to sleep in my hut, but to do something that shows him how much I am starting to care.

"Good morrow, Wilderness," he says once he has dressed.

He turns to the door, still groggy from sleep, and on impulse, I get to my feet.

"Jameson." I sweep a wolf pelt up off the floor and hold it out to him. "A gift. For you."

Jameson's eyes widen, suddenly more alert, and he stares at the fur for so long without moving that I begin to worry he does not like it. Finally, he reaches a timid hand out and runs his fingers over the fur like he is afraid he will hurt it.

"Did you kill this?"

"I did," I say, and I find myself squaring my shoulders.

It has been ingrained in me since I was a small child to make sure I always appear strong in front of men, but something about doing it now seems to wash away some of the intimacy of the moment. Once it is gone, I find I miss it, only I have no idea how to get it back without making myself vulnerable, and doing that would go against everything I have been taught.

"It was a very noble wolf," I continue. "He came into our village quite often, but he never bothered us. It was as if he wanted to check on how we were doing. But two winters ago, a bear cornered him, and by the time I came upon them, the wolf had already been injured. I took the bear out, hoping to save the wolf," I nod to the rug under our feet, "but his injuries were too severe, and I knew even our healer would not be able to save him, so I put him down. His pelt has been a prized possession ever since, and I would like you to have it."

Jameson takes it from me, holding it in his hands like it is a delicate flower. "It's beautiful. Thank you."

"You are welcome, husband."

He glances from the wolf's pelt to the bear under our feet, and the awe in his eyes is clear as day. This is how he should look at me. It is right. It is what our village is all about. Still, I miss the softness from before.

"Go to the men's village and work," I say after a moment. "I will see you tonight."

My husband shoots me one final look before stepping out of my hut and heading down the walkway, and I lean against the frame with my arms crossed to keep the morning chill away, watching his progress. Jameson is more confident than he used to be, and he no longer holds onto the rope quite as hard as he walks, no longer stares at the ground like he is afraid it will jump up and bite him.

The bird on his back is dark against his pale skin, but soon summer will come and the sun will grow warmer, and my husband will tan to a nice brown. When that happens, he will no longer look like he has spent his life in a far away land where they cover themselves with strange clothes and hide inside large huts. He will look like he belongs here. With me.

Is it normal to stare at the man lying at my side as if I cannot get enough of him? To watch him walk away and think about the next time we will be together? Am I alone in this desire, or is it something all women feel about their husbands?

I have no clue how to answer those questions, but I know who will.

After I have dressed, I head to Raven's hut. The day is still so new that the sun has not yet made it above the trees, and all around me the village is on the verge of waking. Women move across walkways in the distance, waving when they see me, and I return the gesture. Two platforms away, Ash descends a ladder, and for some reason, seeing him reminds me about my discussion with Jameson the night before. *Father*. This is a new word for me, something from the outside world, but to my husband, it seems very important. In most instances I have no qualms about talking to my mother, but I instinctively know this is not something I should bring up. I cannot risk getting my husband in trouble.

Perhaps Zachariah can tell me what it means. Like Jameson, he is from the outside and will no doubt know why *father* is so important to my husband.

It is still early when I reach my mother's hut, and I pause to knock on the door in case Zachariah is inside. He is rarely allowed to stay the night, but it does happen from time to time, and I want to be sure I do not interrupt their time together.

The door opens only a couple blinks later to reveal my mother, wrapped in the fur of a brown bear, her gray hair a tangled mess around her shoulders.

When she sees me, she smiles. "Good morrow, Wilderness."

Behind her, barely discernable in the darkness of the hut, something moves, and a moment later Zachariah appears, dressed but flushed.

He kisses my mother on the forehead. "Thank you."

"You are always welcome, Zachariah," Raven replies, beaming up at him to show she means it.

"Good morrow, Wilderness," he says, throwing me a smile as he moves past me.

"Good morrow," I say in response.

Zachariah jogs off, down the walkway to the platform beyond, looking much more confident than my own husband. From the open doorway, my mother watches him with sparkling eyes. Once he has disappeared, she turns to me, still smiling, and the expression in her eyes seems like a reflection of my own developing feelings for Jameson. I have always known my mother cares for her husband, but until I had one of my own, I had never given it much thought.

"It is nice to see you so early in the morning." Raven steps back so I can enter her hut. "Let us have breakfast."

The air is thick with the scent of warm bodies and sweat, and together Raven and I work to open the shutters so the wind can carry it away. Once that is done, we sit and eat bits of dried meat and fruit, my mother still wrapped in her fur and her gray hair still a tangled mess, making it impossible to forget why I came to her in the first place.

"Do you find Zachariah pleasing?" I ask after a silence that feels heavy and serious.

My mother presses her lips together like she is not sure what I am asking, but nods as well. "In what way do you mean?"

I pick at the fur beneath me, trying to figure out how to explain my feelings. Raven has always been honest with me, revealing the intimacies she and Zachariah share, how they make her feel, how he makes her feel. It should make this conversation easier, but instead my insides are as tangled as her hair.

"In every way, I guess, but mostly his looks."

This time, Raven smiles like thinking about him brightens her day. "He did not seem like much to look at when he first came to the village. He was too skinny and seemed very small compared to the yieldlings, but I was old and needed a husband, so I took him anyway. He pleased me from the beginning, though, and before long I discovered that I liked his looks very much. Now he seems like a different man, and I can barely picture who I thought he was on that first day."

I pop a berry into my mouth and chew it, thinking her words through. I understand what she means because already Jameson does not resemble the man I saw kneeling in front of Zachariah only a few days ago. He seemed so dark and hard at first, but since then I have seen a softer side to him. A side that cares about others, that takes his time with me. A side eager to please me even though he was not brought here of his own free will.

"Why do you ask, Wilderness?" Raven urges when I remain silent.

"Jameson was not my first choice," I admit. "I know physical appearance should not matter, but at the Gleaning I thought the blond man, Eric, was very nice looking. I chose Jameson because I knew the feeling was wrong, but now I find my husband's looks very appealing. Is this normal? Is it wrong for me to think of him like that?"

My mother pats my leg the way she does when she is trying to reassure me, but it has the opposite affect. It turns me back into a small child. Will there ever be a time when Raven does not make me feel small and weak?

"It is very normal, Wilderness," she says. "It is also why we avoid putting emphasis on physical appearance. If your match is good, an unattractive person can become attractive after you get to know them. This is what you are experiencing. Nothing else."

Her words ring true. Despite my husband's hesitation to immerse himself in our ways, I know that deep down we are a good match. Still, I cannot help thinking of how Jameson called me beautiful. I chastised him for it at the time, but I enjoy knowing he finds me desirable, and I like when he stares at me as if I am the most beautiful thing on this mountain and never want him to stop.

Worried what she will think of me, I say in a low voice, "He tells me I am beautiful."

My mother's smile widens, chasing away my fears of rebuke. "And he should. Zachariah tells me I am beautiful every day. It is okay for your husband to think this. When you care about a person, it is much harder to see their flaws."

Her face lights up when she talks about Zachariah, making her look younger. Raven loves her husband, I am sure of it, but not once have I heard her say the words out loud. While saying *I love you* is not customary in our society, it is also not unheard of. Only I cannot imagine my mother saying it. Not even in the privacy of her hut.

"Do you tell Zachariah you love him?"

Raven's smile fades until it is nothing more than a memory, and she straightens her shoulders, reminding me that she is not just my mother, but also the High Elder of our village.

"That is something I choose not to say. Every woman must make up her own mind, but I fear saying those words will make me weak in my husband's eyes. That if he knows how I feel about him, he will use it against me."

No matter how hard I try, I cannot imagine a scenario in which Zachariah would use my mother's feelings against her. He has never done anything but adore her, has obeyed every command she has ever given. Even some of the yieldlings have not been as dedicated of a husband as Zachariah has been to Raven, and yet she does not trust him completely. It makes me wonder if all my instincts are wrong. My mother's husband is a foundling, an outsider, and nothing will ever change that, just as nothing will ever change that my own husband came from the outside world.

Raven must see the doubt written on my face, because she sighs and reaches out to take my hand. "All men have evil in them, Wilderness, and you must choose how best to guard yourself against it. Never let your walls down completely, even if the man at your side is your husband."

Her words make me feel like I am standing on uneven ground. She has never spoken to me like this before, and until now I had no idea she felt this way. When she and Zachariah are together, Raven seems so free and open, but even after all these years, she still holds a part of herself back. Does he even know it?

When I take leave of my mother, I head into the forest, anxious to spend some time alone. My thoughts are never far from my husband, though, making me feel like a fly caught in a spider web. I struggle to think about something else, but no matter which way my mind twists, it seems to become more and more tangled in thoughts of Jameson. How he looks at me, how much I enjoy looking at him, his touch, his kiss, his words and what they mean. Even the things my mother said about Zachariah and what it means for my husband and myself.

By the time a buck steps through the trees in front of me, I feel like I have been spinning in a circle. The animal catches me off guard, and I almost raise my bow too fast, which would most certainly scare him off. I blow out a breath and lift my weapon, working to calm my thoughts and focus. It is a difficult task when Jameson has so thoroughly wrapped himself around my life.

When I release my arrow, it hits the mark, piercing the heart right where I wanted it to, and the buck jumps once before taking off running. I climb down from the tree so I can track him, knowing he will not make it far.

I follow the trail of blood through the forest, tracking the animal to a ravine. He stares up at me with glassy eyes, and against the green of the forest floor, his ten-point rack appears starkly white. The antlers will come in handy for making many different weapons, but more important than that is the pelt, which I can use to make my husband a bed.

After I have prepared the animal, I drag it back to the men's village, only to find it quiet. Most of the men are nowhere in sight, my husband included, but Zachariah is by the fire, the simple-minded child, Oak, at his side. He never seems to stray too far from the inferno—even in the heat of summer—and right now he's in the middle of helping my mother's husband prepare a stew.

"Good eve, Wilderness," Zachariah calls when he sees me.

His smile is wide and welcoming, seeming to contradict everything my mother said this morning. This man would never do anything to hurt her, or anyone else, for that matter. Of that, I am certain.

We cross the village to one another, meeting outside the rabbit pen, and the animals scurry around, their noses twitching in protest of the unexpected visitors.

"Another deer?" Zachariah asks, looking past me to where I left the animal.

The wind blows, and the stench of rabbit waste fills my nostrils. "A buck."

He nods his approval as he sticks two fingers in his mouth and lets out a loud whistle. A blink later, two teens appear on the platform of one of the huts and drop to the ground, and I watch as they take off toward the animal carcass. One has dark skin, but the other is blond like Hawk. Talon is his name, and he walks with a limp leftover from a break that did not set right. This boy and I have only spoken a few times, but his presence always tickles a memory at the back of my mind, and today is no different. I remember him from my childhood even though he is several years younger and was not a playmate like Hawk, but something else. Something I can't quite name.

"Your husband went to the river," Zachariah says, drawing my attention from the teens.

"I will see him later in my hut."

"It is a fine gift you gave him," he says with a grin. "I remember the day you brought that wolf in very well."

I return his smile and for the first time all day begin to feel at ease. "Only because you and Hawk had to help me drag the bear in."

Zachariah belts out a laugh, and like with Jameson, the sound warms me more than the rays of the summer sun. "That is very true. That would be a hard thing to forget."

"How is my husband doing?" I ask, curious what Jameson does when I am not with him. If he is adjusting as well as he seems to be, or if he is more defiant when I am not around. "Is he fitting into the men's village?"

"He is well, for a foundling."

There is so much about my husband I do not understand, but there was a time when Zachariah was also a new foundling, and there is a chance my mother's husband can help me understand the man who now shares my bed.

"You are a foundling, Zachariah," I remind him.

He grins, and the way his blue eyes flash makes him look several seasons younger. I study his features, trying to see what my mother sees. His looks are not unpleasant, but he is not a man most would find attractive. His forehead is too high and his hair thin, and even the icy blue of his eyes looks wrong on him. But there is something I never noticed before. Something agreeable that brings Hawk and Ash to mind.

"What is father?" I ask after studying Zachariah until my mind once again becomes tangled with thoughts, like an animal caught in a snare.

As fast as a startled cricket, his eyebrows jump. "Who told you this word?"

"My husband. He has many questions about husbands and yieldlings, and why we choose to live apart. He asked about my father." I do not tell Zachariah that Jameson mentioned his name because I have no desire to get my husband in trouble. Even if I do not understand everything, this is not the way we choose to live, and I know there is a reason.

"It is a word from the old world." Zachariah waves his hand like he is trying to swat the word away. "It is nothing."

But his eyes tell a different story. With his mouth he makes it seem as if *father* is nothing, but the expression in his eyes reminds me of the longing I get when I am around Hawk. As if, like me, Zachariah wants more.

"Do not worry yourself about it," he says when I do not respond. "I will talk to your husband, and he will learn that such things belong in the old world. Here we live in harmony, and changing things will only bring about friction."

"Thank you," I say, though I want to ask more, want to know more and understand why this word brings a look of longing to Zachariah's eyes. "Please tell Jameson to come to me tonight." I take a step back, toward the forest.

"I will do that." Zachariah nods once as if to reassure me, and I turn away.

When I reach the forest, I pause and glance over my shoulder. He is standing in the same place, watching me with a sad and distant expression in his blue eyes.

CHAPTER THIRTEEN

Jameson

ZIP IS ONCE AGAIN AT MY SIDE WHEN THE OTHER foundlings and I follow Hawk and Ash to the river. No. Not foundlings, men. I hate thinking of the people who were dragged here with me as *foundlings*, but since I haven't taken much time to get to know them, it's become a habit. One I need to break.

I slow, wincing when a rock pokes my foot through my shoes. It's gotten easier walking around in the things, or my feet have gotten harder, but there are still times when I step on something sharp and it hurts like hell.

John walks at the rear of our group, faster today but still slower than the rest of us. His back is healing, but gradually, and every breath he lets out makes it obvious he's still in pain. Since he and I haven't spoken about the punishment and I don't plan to anytime soon, I move to walk at David's side instead.

"We haven't talked much," I say when he looks my way.

At the age of nineteen, he's little more than a boy, and the hair on his face still grows in sparse patches—although it hasn't stopped him from trying to grow a beard. Young or not, the glower on his face was a permanent fixture even before we came here, telling me David's had a hard life.

"Probably 'cause you're too busy getting brainwashed." He curls his upper lip like the sight of me disgusts him.

"I'm not brainwashed," I protest, but even as I say it, I have to stop and think.

When was the last time I thought about leaving? After the punishment, I did, but then Wilderness took me to the hot spring, and it was like she washed the thoughts away. The story the old woman told appalled me, but once again, Wilderness was able to ease my thoughts of escape away. It's like she has some kind of magical powers that make it impossible to hold onto my free will, and I have to wonder if David isn't far off.

"Right." He spits at our feet. "You can't even see it."

I lower my voice and say, "I'm biding my time. You can't rush things or you get caught." I jerk my head back, indicating John.

David spits again and starts walking faster.

I wasn't planning to be his best friend or anything, but the fact that he thinks I'm getting sucked in has crawled under my skin. David can't be right. Zachariah told me the story at the Festival of the New Moon would help me understand, but he was wrong, and it only succeeded in making me think he might be the one who's brainwashed. No matter how Wilderness makes me feel when we're in her bed, I won't end up like him. I still want to get out of here.

I avoid David when we reach the river, but it doesn't escape his—or my—notice when I find myself standing with Ash and Hawk instead. It turns out Ash, who is a couple years older than Hawk and the husband of the tall warrior, Grove, is as interested in my tattoos as the younger man.

"Did it hurt when they drew these pictures on you?" he asks, leaning closer. He stares at them like they hold some mystery, and if he looks hard enough, it will all unravel for him.

"Like hell." The two men frown, and I have to work not to roll my eyes. "Yes, it hurt."

They nod in unison, and it hits me how much they resemble one another. Ash has dark brown hair, but like Hawk, he has his mother's brown eyes and father's pointed chin. The resemblance is so striking I don't know how I didn't notice it before. Probably because I wasn't looking for it, but with them standing in front of me now, it's all I can see.

The two men show us where the stream dips deeper and how to catch crawfish. It takes a lot of holding still and being patient while they wait for the little creatures to slink out of their hiding spots, and when they strike, it's with an animalistic speed. They're good at it, though, and when they catch the things, they toss them into a waiting bucket to take back.

"The women let you do this?" David spits at Ash and Hawk. "Don't they do all the hunting?"

Ash, unaware that the younger man is trying to emasculate him, shakes his head. "We eat these. The women do not enjoy them."

David only snorts.

I watch the men—the brothers—catch a few of the clawed creatures before turning my attention to the stony river floor. The sun's rays reflect off the surface of the water, but also catch a few of the rocks, making them sparkle. A deep blue stone catches my eye, and I bend down to get a closer look. The color stands out against the other rocks, making it impossible not to pick it up. It's a good size, only a little smaller than the tip of my thumb, and when I wipe the dirt off, the blue is even more vibrant.

"Sapphire," Hawk says from behind me.

When I glance his way, he nods to the rock in my hand.

"This is a sapphire?" I ask, studying it again. "How do you know?"

The other men, even David, make their way toward me so they can get a better look. If it is a sapphire, it's a big one, and I can't even imagine how much it would be worth if I took it back to Baltimore.

Ash joins his brother, and he, too, nods. "It is a sapphire."

"But how do you know?" Michael asks, repeating my earlier question.

"We just know," Hawk says.

David snorts and turns away, but I stare at the little rock in my hand. The light catches it, making it sparkle even in its uncut state. If it were polished, it would be magnificent, but even the way it is right now, the sapphire is pretty.

And it's a perfect gift for Wilderness.

I slip it into the palm of my hand, tightening my fist around it. I don't know why I have the urge to give her a gift, but I chalk it up to the wolf pelt and how touching it was that she gave me something that means so much to her. It's insane and makes me wonder if David wasn't onto something when he called me brainwashed, but I can't push the feeling away, and I find myself suddenly excited to see Wilderness again so I can give her the gift.

BEFORE I'VE EVEN HAD A CHANCE TO WALK TWO FEET INTO THE men's village, Zachariah is charging toward me. "You, boy."

I freeze, suddenly uneasy. His scowl says he's unhappy about something, and with his fury aimed at me, it's clear I'm the culprit, but I don't have a clue what the hell I did.

When he reaches me, he grabs my arm and pulls me back into the forest with Zip trailing after us. Hawk and Ash watch with accusations in their eyes, while the men from my group look like they think I'm headed off to face a firing squad. I sure as hell hope not.

Zachariah doesn't stop until we're a good distance from the village, and when he finally starts talking, he keeps his voice low. "You tell her about *father*, did you?" He narrows his eyes while lifting his brows, a feat I doubt I would be able to accomplish. "You think you can come here and tell her things and change what we have, but you cannot. That is *not* how we live."

I can't believe he's mad about *this*. Of all the people in this village, he should be the one fighting to tell her, not fighting to hide it.

"She doesn't have a clue you're her father or that Hawk is her twin brother, or that such things even exist. It's insane." I look down, too frustrated to meet his gaze, and find Zip staring up me with his head titled, making him look as confused as I feel.

"So you figured out who Hawk is. Very smart." Zachariah waves his hand in front of my face, and I jerk away. "You think you know everything because you came from out there, but you do not."

"You're going to tell me you aren't Wilderness's father and Hawk isn't her twin brother? And what about Ash? I guess you're going to tell me he isn't your son, too?"

"Not what I said." Zachariah sucks in a deep breath like he's trying to control his anger, but his eyes still flash. "That is not how we live. We are happy here. We like things as they are. I know you do not understand, but that is because you do not try. Did you have a father?"

I pause when a pang thunders through my chest. "No. My dad died when I was five, and after that, my mother was a single parent. But I did have two younger brothers." The years come back to me in a monsoon of memories, working in a factory at seven, coming home to find my little brother crying because he didn't have anything to eat, seeing my mother passed out drunk. I swallow the emotions threatening to burst out and look down, not wanting to meet Zachariah's gaze. "It was hard."

"Always hard out there." He points to the forest at my back like he can point to Baltimore or Salt Lake City. "Here, we make it easy. We do our jobs. We are *all* family, and we look out for each other. Wilderness would not choose to give Hawk more meat, because to her the men are *all* her family. We are equal."

I still can't wrap my brain around it completely, but I can kind of see what he's getting at, because the harmony here makes sense for them. There's no fighting and only mild jealousy, like with Dawn and Wilderness, and the people work together and are happy when their hard work benefits the entire village.

But Zachariah still has five kids, and *he* knows who they are. That has to affect him, has to hurt at times.

"Wilderness wouldn't choose to favor her brothers, but what about you? What if she and Grove both needed something, and you had it? You would choose Wilderness, wouldn't you? She's your daughter, and you love her. I can see it when you look at her. Just like you love Raven. And your sons?"

Zachariah flinches and looks past me, focusing on the forest like it will somehow hide the emotion in his eyes. "It is not the same."

"It is," I say, but in a softer tone, hoping to take some of the sting from the words, "I won't tell her anything else about fathers and sons and brothers, but I still don't agree with you."

I push past him so I can head back to the village.

I've only taken two steps when he calls, "Do you still want to run?"

I stop walking but don't turn around. The sapphire is still in my hand, and it feels suddenly hot against my palm. Right before I found it, I was thinking about leaving, about not letting Wilderness win again, but finding the stupid little rock pushed the thoughts from my mind. It seems to always happen here, and every day I get sucked in a little bit more. Like Zachariah did thirty years ago.

"I don't know," I say honestly, still not facing him.

"You love her?"

"I just met her." I let out a deep sigh, but I'm powerless to stop the sensations surging through me when I think of Wilderness. "There's a lot about her to like."

"That, there is," he says, sounding almost sad.

I walk on, leaving Zachariah—my father-in-law—behind.

LATER, AFTER THE SUN HAS SET, I GO TO WILDERNESS LIKE I'M told. Despite the hour and the fact that the women's village has usually settled down by now, I'm greeted by a flurry of activity when Zip and I step from the forest. As usual, he drops to the ground at the base of the tree while I climb, only to find the walkways clogged with women, making it difficult to pass without getting close to the edge. I've gotten a lot more comfortable with how high off the ground the huts are, but being on the edge of the walkway still makes me nervous.

Wilderness is waiting for me outside her hut, and she smiles when she sees me, but the gesture doesn't quite reach her eyes. Like all the other women in the village, she seems to be waiting for something bad to happen.

"What's wrong?" I ask, looking behind me at the women milling around. "What's going on?"

"One of the women, Spring, is in labor. It is taking a very long time, and the midwife thinks she will not survive."

"I'm sorry," I say and reach out to comfort her.

It's an automatic response, wanting to ease some of her hurt away, but she steps back, avoiding my touch, and a sting moves through me. I suck in a deep breath, but unlike other times, she doesn't remind me that I need an invitation to touch her, and I'm not even sure if she knows I'm standing in front of her. She's too focused on what's happening in the village.

"Do you want me to leave, Wilderness?"

She drags her troubled gaze up to meet mine and blinks. "No. Please stay," she says and holds her hand out. "I invite you to touch me, Jameson."

I take her hand, the sapphire I found resting between our palms. When she lifts her eyebrows, the expression reminds me so much of Zachariah that it feels like a slap, especially after our earlier conversation. Wilderness looks from me to our hands, and when I pull mine away and flip it over to reveal the stone, she smiles.

"A sapphire."

"Yeah. I found it today at the river. It's for you. A gift."

Her smile stretches wider as she takes it from my outstretched hand and studies it. "It is a big one."

Once again, she lifts her gaze to meet mine, and something inside me pulls tight, almost like there's a string attached to my heart, and she's holding the other end. The feeling isn't unpleasant, but I hate myself for it just the same.

"I love it," she says. "Thank you."

The words are whispered, her tongue moving over them like a caress, and it sends an ache shooting through my body and straight to my groin. For what has to be the tenth time, I wonder if this woman might have some kind of magical powers, because my body has never responded to anyone like this before.

"Come into my hut, Jameson," she says, walking backward. "There is nothing we can do for Spring."

IT TURNS OUT THERE IS NOTHING ANYONE CAN DO FOR SPRING, because she and the baby die sometime during the night. The mood in both villages the following day is somber, even the men feeling the loss. Spring's husband, Canyon, spends the morning sitting in front of the fire, staring at the flames like he's considering throwing himself into them, not moving until late afternoon when the women appear almost out of nowhere, carrying Spring's body. The baby was never born.

The following processional appears to be the entire village, but Canyon is the only man who falls in with them as they head into the forest. He walks behind the warriors, who are carrying Spring's body, and for the first time since I got here, it seems like the husband's status is actually going to be honored. It's a relief, because watching him stare into the fire all day made *me* want to throw myself into the flames.

Once all the women have passed through the village and headed into the forest, the rest of the men follow, only the very old and very young staying behind.

For once, Zip doesn't follow me, and I wonder if it's because he can sense the mood. Instead, I walk beside Zachariah, with Hawk and Ash on his other side. The three of them seem to always be this way, and I can't help wondering if the younger men have any idea who Zachariah is. There's no way he's told them outright, but that doesn't mean they can't sense the connection.

We don't talk, not even when we come to a stop in a circular, well-maintained, and obviously manmade clearing I've never been to before. There are no fallen branches littering the grass, which is thick and lush thanks to the sun shining down on the clearing, and purple wildflowers dot the green field, only broken up by the dozens of stones lined up in perfect rows. A hole for Spring has already been prepared at the end of the last row, only a few feet from the edge of the forest.

The men stay back while the women and Canyon gather around the grave. He keeps his head down, even when they lower Spring into the hole, and the crowd gathered in the clearing is so silent that the thud of her body hitting the earth is audible from ten feet away.

Raven, who is once again wearing her crown of feathers, stands at the head of the grave. "We have come to say our final goodbye to Spring, a daughter of the Great Mother. Though we are sad, we are called to rejoice, for Spring's end in this village may have come, but her time with the Great Mother is only beginning. Even now, Spring and her child are in Paradise."

The women around her nod and murmur in agreement, and I search the sea of faces for Wilderness to find tears glistening on her cheeks as she stares down at the grave. Zachariah's words ring in my ears. They are all family here, so for Wilderness and the other women, they have lost a sister, but to Canyon, she wasn't even his wife. What was she to the other men, then? A slave master, as far as I can tell, even if they don't realize it. That's all the men here are. Slaves.

Raven continues to talk as the women around her move forward and scoop up handfuls of dirt, tossing them into the grave one at a time. It seems to take forever for the hole to get filled, and the entire time, Canyon doesn't move an inch. He stands at Raven's side with his head down, staring at the hole as the woman who called him husband slowly disappears.

When the hole is finally filled, Raven turns to face him. "Spring's husband." Canyon lifts his head. "Now that Spring has met her end, it is time for you to find yours. We pray your journey is swift and that soon Spring will once again have her husband at her side. Go, Canyon, and find your end."

The crowd of women parts, and a path opens behind Canyon. He turns his back to the grave and moves toward the forest, making his way between the women with his head once again down.

"Where's Canyon going?" I ask Zachariah.

"He has gone to find his own end."

I turn to face him, my head spinning, and find Hawk and Ash watching me, Hawk's brown eyes so like his sister's it's almost unnerving.

"What?"

"If he is no longer a husband, he has no purpose in this village," Zachariah says, his blue eyes intent and focused, warning me not to make a scene.

Only I'm not sure I can keep quiet about this.

"He will wander the forest until he finds his own end," Hawk adds, "and then the Great Mother will allow him to enter Paradise and be with Spring once again."

I was wrong, because the explanation has rendered me speechless. The idea that Canyon is worthless without Spring makes me sick, like ancient civilizations where widowed wives used to throw themselves on their husbands' burning bodies. Only backward. Everything in this village is backward.

"So he's not allowed to stay?" I manage to get out.

At his father's side, Ash blinks like he's trying to figure out what I'm getting at. "Why would he want to? His purpose is to be a husband, which he is no more."

"What if Canyon was the one who had died?" I ask. "Would Spring have gone off into the forest?"

"No." The warning in Zachariah's voice rings loud and clear despite his hushed tone.

"She is a woman," Hawk says. "The village is as much her responsibility as her husband is."

"So men are only worth as much as the women allow them to be," I snap. "Why not bury him alive with Spring, then?"

Ash jerks away from my words. "That would not be a noble end."

"There's nothing noble about any of this," I mutter.

Ash and Hawk don't say anything else, but Zachariah presses his lips together like he's holding something in that's desperate to get out.

When the women leave the clearing, the men follow like dogs trailing after their masters. I'm still fuming. Every time I think I have a handle on things, something new comes my way and knocks me on my ass all over again.

We make it back to the men's village, but Zachariah grabs my elbow, keeping me at the edge of the forest as the rest of the men pass. I try to jerk away, but his grip is too tight, and I know better than to fight.

Once we're alone, he releases me, and I take a step back, wanting to put distance between us, wanting to put distance between myself and everything here.

"You will cause trouble for yourself if you continue down this path," he says. "These men are happy with how things are. Canyon was happy to go find his end, because he wants to be with Spring."

"It's sick," I say.

"To you, but there are many things in this world you do not understand. That does not make them wrong."

"This is wrong, Zachariah." I shake my head, too angry to do anything else. "Why can't you see that? The story about the hotel, about Vegas, it didn't make me feel okay about any of this. What these women do is no different than what those men did."

Zachariah jerks back and says, "It is not the same."

But the expression in his eyes says he's had the same thoughts, and I know he's lying. He's seen the similarities, but something has a hold on him, and he can't break away. Raven, or the peaceful atmosphere. In that instance, he's right. On the surface, life here is easier and more enjoyable, but the illusion is broken when a man gets whipped or sent into the forest to die because he's no longer a husband.

"You know the truth," I say, turning away from him.

My anger still hasn't subsided by nightfall, but since refusing Wilderness's invitation is out of the question, I have no choice but to go to her hut. My conversation with Zachariah swims in my mind as I trudge through the bit of forest separating the two villages. If I stay here, if I can't get away and I somehow manage to find a place with these people, I will be bound to Wilderness for the rest of my life.

If she asks me to come to her hut, I'll have no choice. If she thinks I've done something deserving of punishment, I'll have to submit. If she dies, I'll die, too.

Is this the kind of life I want for myself?

It's been easy to get pulled into this world, to confuse the ease of life in this village with happiness, but after today, I can't imagine I would ever be able to find peace or fulfillment in a world where I have no value. I need to do more to resist Wilderness, to hold onto who I am, because if I don't, I'll lose myself forever.

She's waiting for me when I arrive, on the bed but not naked. Even the way she is, covered but with her long legs stretched out, the rush of blood to my groin makes my head spin. She's not magic, though, I know that, and I also know I can resist her.

Wilderness rolls onto her side and pats the bed. "Come here, husband."

I do, but only because I have no idea how to exert myself in this situation. Impulsiveness will only get me whipped, but if I take my time, if I try to appeal to the tenderness I know this woman feels for me, she may listen. Maybe.

She moves over when I take a seat, and the fur around her shoulders falls away. The sapphire is around her neck, wrapped in twine so it's secure and hanging from a thin strip of leather. It rests against her chest, the blue stone dark against her creamy skin.

"You made a necklace," I say, nodding to the sapphire.

She fingers it, a smile curling up her lips. "I want to keep it with me, always."

This time the pang isn't in my groin, but in my chest.

Wilderness pushes herself up until she's on her knees, but when she leans forward to kiss me, I pull away. Hurt flashes in her eyes, and seeing her in pain threatens to kill me, especially knowing I caused it, but I refuse to back down. Refuse to end up a puppet like Zachariah, no matter how much I'm starting to care for this woman.

"What is it?" she asks.

I look away and swallow, trying to figure out how to voice my feelings so she'll understand. Here, everything is complicated, but in a different way than it was in the outside world, and I'm not sure how to maneuver the set of obstacles in front of me without getting hurt.

"It's been a rough day for me," I finally say.

"Jameson, look at me." When I don't look up, Wilderness grabs my shoulders and turns me to face her. "Are you hurt? Did something happen to you?"

"Nothing happened to me." I pull out of her grasp and get to my feet, avoiding her gaze as I say, "It's Canyon."

"What about him?"

"I don't understand why he had to leave." I venture a look her way and find her studying me, confusion in her brown eyes, and I once again focus on the floor. "The way things are set up here makes me feel worthless, and I don't understand any of it. So I want you to explain it to me. Make me understand."

Out of the corner of my eye, I watch as Wilderness tilts her head to the side, and her blonde hair falls over her shoulder. "Canyon left to find his end. So he could join Spring in Paradise."

"Don't you get it? That makes no sense to me," I say in exasperation. "Why did he have to go *now*? He could have still joined Spring in Paradise later, after his end came naturally. Why is a man only valuable as a husband? Why can't there be more for him?"

"Spring was responsible for Canyon, but now she is gone, and there is no one left to guide him," she says, her tone making it seem like she's talking to a small child. "His purpose was to be a husband, but that ended with Spring."

Half afraid of what I'll see, I tear my gaze from the floor and focus on her, searching her face for a sign she understands where I'm coming from. There's nothing, though. She looks as confused by my questions as I am by this ridiculous tradition.

"You don't think there's anything wrong with that?" I ask after a heavy silence. "Sending a man out to die because he isn't a husband? You don't think it's wrong to treat men like they're meaningless?"

Her brown eyes are penetrating as she turns my words over in her mind, and even when she finally shakes her head, she acts like she's still considering them.

"I do not see it that way," Wilderness finally says. "The men are not meaningless. They are husbands, and they must join their wives in Paradise to fulfill their duty."

Maybe I'm crazy, or even brainwashed, but despite her words, I have a strange feeling she's listening to me. That what I'm saying is sinking in, maybe only a little at a time, but I can't help hoping I'll eventually be able to get her to understand where I'm coming from.

Then what? It's a question I can't even answer for myself. The idea of changing everything about how these people live is too far-fetched to even consider, but what other goal do I have, and does this mean I've given up trying to leave? There's nothing for me outside this village, not really, and the thought of leaving feels like someone has driven a knife into my heart.

I let out a deep breath, trying to figure out a way to explain it all to her, to make her see things through my eyes, and say, "You know the story Mother Elder told about the hotel?" Wilderness nods to let me know we're on the same page. "The women came here so men wouldn't be able to treat them like they were nothing, but what you're doing is no different. It's just reversed. Men took your ancestors to that hotel against their will, and now you bring men here against theirs. You say you don't want men to have all the power, but instead *you* have all the power over your husbands. It doesn't have to be that way. There can be balance."

Wilderness's forehead scrunches up. "But we do not force men to do these things."

"You drugged me, Wilderness."

She blinks, and then stares at me without talking for so long I start to believe she understands, and I hold my breath, hoping and praying.

"No," she says finally, and I let out an exasperated sigh. "The medicine does not make you do anything you do not want to do. Your body responded to mine. You did not cry. You did not tell me no. We want our husbands to be happy. We do not keep them locked away."

"Just because I'm not locked up doesn't mean I'm not a prisoner." The words are hard to get out, but I know I have to press forward. If I don't, if I let her get away with everything she's doing and say nothing, I'll be a prisoner forever. "I'm not free, Wilderness. I have no choices. You call me to your bed, and I'm expected to perform. What would happen to me if I refused? I would get punished. You can't tell me that's freedom."

Wilderness frowns up at me, hurt and concern in her eyes. "Do you not want me?"

I exhale but force myself not to look away. "After today, after what happened with Canyon, I can't. I know you don't understand, but what your people did to him hurts me. It makes me feel like I'm nothing."

"You are not nothing, Jameson. You are my husband." She gets up, but I take a step back, making her freeze when she's still two feet away. "Are you not happy with me? Do you not enjoy the time we spend together? I thought you did, but maybe I am wrong."

I swallow, afraid to say the next words because it might validate what these people are doing, but also unable to lie because I'm afraid it will hurt her. "I enjoy the time we spend together, enjoy being with you in every way," I say quietly, "but I want to have a choice in it."

Pain flashes in her eyes, and she looks down. She clasps the sapphire I gave her and stares at it, twisting it between two fingers while I hold my breath and wait for her to say something, and the silence between us seems to stretch out forever. She could choose to punish me just for saying these things, meaning I could be kneeling in the center of the village tomorrow, waiting for a whip to slash across my back. Only, I don't think she will.

The more time that stretches out, though, the harder my heart pounds. Was I a fool for thinking she could understand where I'm coming from?

When she finally speaks, it's little more than a whisper. "If you do not wish to lay with me, Jameson, you are free to go."

I blink and then shake my head, not sure if I heard her right. "I am?"

"I want you to want me." Wilderness finally looks up. "I thought you did."

"I do," I murmur, and hate how much the pain in her eyes hurts me, hate that I have the urge to wrap her in my arms and take her to bed despite the little bit of freedom I've won. "Just not tonight."

Wilderness turns away. "Then go back to your hut, husband. I will see you tomorrow."

For a moment, I stay where I am and watch her, the ache in me growing when she slips the fur from her body and climbs onto the bed. If I said turning my back on her was easy, it would be a damn lie because it's one of the hardest things I've ever had to do.

I do it anyway, and as I head back down the walkway and through the women's village, my steps are lighter than they were before. Even if she doesn't know it, she's starting to understand me a little more, and it gives me hope. What I expect to come of it, I'm still not sure, but I know one thing for certain. The outside world holds nothing for me, but there's a very good possibility this secluded, backward village will give me a future.

CHAPTER FOURTEEN

I DO NOT WATCH MY HUSBAND LEAVE MY HUT, BUT THE sound of the door shutting vibrates through my body. His rejection is like a knife slicing me, but it has nothing to do with weakness or me relinquishing power to him. It is because I want Jameson.

It is wrong, letting him make his own decision, but the pain in his eyes was too much to bear. There is something else as well, something I cannot understand and would never admit, not even to Jameson. Back in the clearing when I watched Canyon head into the forest to find his end, my thoughts had gone to my own husband. I had imagined him making that same trip, and it had saddened me. Why? I have seen dozens of husbands make the journey, and not once did I give it a second thought. Not until Canyon passed me, leaving Spring's grave behind, and the image of Jameson flitted through my mind had an ache spread through me.

It is the right thing to do; it will allow Canyon to be with Spring once again. Plus, his time as a husband is over, and he must join her in Paradise. It is how things are done, how they have always been done, and I know this. Still, the knowledge does not stop the pain inside me from spreading.

These are our traditions, though. It is how we have lived for the past seventy years, and it has worked for us. We have harmony here. Peace and happiness. Who is Jameson to question these things? He is a foundling, nothing else. He is just a man.

Except I allowed him to question it. Even worse, I allowed him to turn his back on me, to leave even as I longed for him to be in my bed. Does this mean I will let him choose from now on? If he decides he does not want to come to my hut tomorrow, will I allow it to happen?

I know the answer almost as soon as the question enters my head. Yes. I will let Jameson choose, because I want him to be happy even more than I want him in my bed. If he is unhappy here, he will never find his place in the village the way Zachariah has, and despite our short time together, I cannot bear the thought of my husband going away.

Raven would never approve. Even worse, my mother would be disappointed in me if she found out. She would say I am giving Jameson all the power, and it is possible she would choose to punish my husband even though the decision is mine, but I cannot take it back. Not when his pain is still present in my hut. This is my husband, and I must do what is best for us.

Raven does not need to know.

THE MEN'S VILLAGE IS NEARLY DESERTED WHEN I STEP OUT OF the trees. A few yieldlings tend the crops, which have grown taller, thanks to the sun's warm rays, and Oak is sitting by the fire, but otherwise no one is in sight, and my disappointment at not finding Jameson in the clearing is impossible to ignore. After last night, I need to see him. To know he has not pulled away from me completely. To know we still have a chance of building a life together.

I thought of him all night, barely able to get any rest as the worry gnawed at my insides like a woodchuck sinking his teeth into a tree. The feeling had not disappeared when I woke this morning, and I found myself leaving my hut much earlier than usual, telling myself I was going to hunt when all I wanted was to see Jameson.

Except he is not here.

I strain my ears, searching for sounds that might tell me where the men have gone. To the river, or possibly into the woods to collect mushrooms. Beyond the village, though, the forest is still and silent except the rustling of the trees and the singing of a few birds. No laughter or barking, nothing to indicate where they have gone.

So I head into the forest, knowing my duty to the village does not change just because things with my husband are uncertain.

Spring is in full force, and the buds have now opened, painting the trees above me green and shading me from the sun's harsh rays as I leave the men's village behind. The further I go, the more alive the forest becomes. Animals scurry away at my approach, their tiny feet crunching against the brittle leaves left over from fall. I keep my ears open, listening for the footsteps of bigger game, like a deer or even a forest cat. Something that will provide meat for the village.

When I reach my usual hunting ground, I stop and kneel at the base of a tree. The hot spring I took Jameson to is nearby, the rock wall visible in the distance, and once again I find myself distracted by thoughts of my husband. Thinking about where he is right now and wondering if he will decide to come to my hut tonight when given the choice.

The snap of a stick drags me from thoughts of Jameson. My bow is already out and an arrow nocked when I spin toward the sound, raising my weapon. I hold my breath and remain still, and only a beat passes before another snap breaks through the silence, this time closer.

I pull the string on my bow back.

The cat steps through the trees only a stone's throw away, and before it can catch wind of me, I release the string, and my arrow flies through the air, hitting the mark. The animal jumps and lets out a roar, and I reach for a second arrow, but the cat takes off before I have a chance to wrap my fingers around it.

I am on my feet in a blink, charging through the trees after him. I dodge branches and jump over fallen logs, pumping my legs as I chase the cat. He breaks through some foliage in front of me, and I lose sight of him, but only for a moment because I'm right on his trail.

I push my way through the brush and skitter to a stop, losing the cat but unable to care. My heart is pounding, and my legs ache from the run, and I gasp as I try to fill my lungs. My chase led me to the rock wall, but it is not what made me stop.

Canyon is in front of me, leaning against the rocks with his eyes closed.

Is he sleeping?

I take a step closer but freeze again when I notice the strange way his head hangs to the side and the pale hue of his skin. The sun's rays are bright, shining down over the cliff, and I shield my eyes, hoping once I block out the light the image will change, but it does not. Canyon's body is only a shell. He is gone, off to Paradise where he will once again be Spring's husband.

What was it? An animal, or a poisonous snake? I look him over but find no injuries. No cuts and no blood. Nothing to indicate how he died. His hand rests in his lap, his fingers curled as if holding something, and I take a step closer, catching sight of something brown in his palm. Instantly, I know what it is. Mushrooms. Canyon chose to bring about his own end rather than continue to wander the forest without Spring.

I drop to my knees, my gaze trained on his face, and despite his peaceful expression, my eyes fill with tears. He was so young, only a couple seasons older than Hawk, and healthy. Fit and strong. I remember seeing him in the men's village when I passed through, how he laughed as he spoke with Zachariah, or how kind he was to Oak. I remember running with him as a child, back before I realized he was just a yieldling.

Now Canyon is gone, though, and despite how serene he looks or that he chose this end for himself, I cannot help thinking Jameson was right. This should not have been Canyon's end. If I were gone, off to Paradise and the Great Mother, I would not want *this* to be my husband's fate. Picturing

Jameson's lifeless body like this, alone and cold, makes me want to weep.

Tears fill my eyes and spill over before I can stop them, sliding down my cheeks like a stream, and though I rarely cry and hate doing it now, I cannot control them. Before long, I am sobbing, clutching Canyon's cold hand while my body shakes. My mind spins, and my heart aches for what our village has lost. For how little we valued this man and how we have cheated him.

It takes a while for me to collect myself, and by the time I climb to my feet, the sun is directly above me. Leaving Canyon's body does not feel right, but I have no way to dig a hole, and even if I did, the terrain here is much too rocky. Carrying him back on my own is impossible. He is too big. I would need help.

Zachariah.

I think back to the day I found my wolf friend cornered by the bear. My arrows had taken the large animal down without a problem, but he had been too big to bring back on my own, so I had gone to the men's village for help. Working together, Zachariah, Hawk, and I managed to drag the bear back.

That is what I will do now. I will go to the men's village and talk to Zachariah. He will make sure Canyon is brought back. He will make sure this man is not left to rot in the forest.

The cat I shot is nothing more than a shadow of a memory when I turn away from Canyon's body, wiping the tears from my cheeks as I head home. It seems to take no time at all, and unlike earlier, the village is buzzing with activity when I step into the clearing. The men have returned from wherever they were, and I find Zachariah standing by the fire, once again talking to Oak while he stirs a pot of stew.

On the other side of the village, I spot my husband with Hawk, the two men standing side by side as they tan a deer hide. The pang in my chest when I see Jameson makes me want to run to him, to drag him back to my hut right now and tell him everything I am thinking and feeling. But Canyon is alone in the woods, cold and waiting for his final resting place, and before I can talk to my husband, I must make sure he is taken care of.

Zachariah looks up as I draw near, his usual grin lighting up his face, but the expression is short-lived. He studies me, his blue eyes clouding over as his smile fades until it is nothing more than a memory.

"Wilderness—" He sets his spoon down, the stew forgotten. "What is it?"

"I must speak with you," I say, keeping my voice low. Why, I cannot even say. Maybe my own husband's heartbreak over Canyon has affected me more than I thought, because I find I do not want to upset the yieldlings by telling them I found Canyon's body. "In the forest."

I move back to the trees I just fled, Zachariah only a few steps behind me and my husband's gaze burning into me with each step I take.

Once we are away from the men's village, I turn to face Zachariah. "I have found Canyon's body."

He bows his head, letting out a deep sigh, and a moment of silence passes. When he looks up, his eyes are more somber than I've ever seen them, and they're rimmed in red and shimmering with unshed tears. "It is done, then. He has found his end."

"He chose his end," I say. "Mushrooms."

Zachariah sighs again, but the news does not seem to surprise him. "It is not uncommon. Many men choose a quick end. Those are usually the bodies we find."

"You have found others?" We hold funerals for women, and for the husbands who die first, but I have never attended the burial of a man who went off to meet his end. Until Jameson brought it up, I had never given it much thought. "What do you do with them?"

"I bury them," Zachariah says simply.

"In the clearing?"

He gives me a sad smile. "No, Wilderness."

Pain throbs through me, and once again I think about how wrong this is. Why is Canyon undeserving of a grave? It almost feels like he has been punished for outliving Spring, which was not his fault, not his choice, and it makes no sense. He was a yielding, a man, but he was still part of our village, and we should honor him the way we would honor anyone else.

Zachariah lifts his arm as if to reach out and touch me, but it does not get far before he curls his fingers into a fist. "I will take care of him. You do not need to worry."

"Where will you bury him?" I ask, not even caring that my words are laced with sadness.

"In the forest," Zachariah says. "I have a place."

"Thank you," I murmur.

His blue eyes are intense as they hold mine, searching, and he almost acts like he has more he wants to say, but he remains silent.

After a moment, he lets out a deep sigh and lifts his gaze from mine, looking past me toward the expansive forest. "Tell me where he is."

"By the stone wall."

I explain where I found him, as well as what he looked like even though Zachariah will very soon see Canyon for himself. The memory is enough to once again fill my eyes with tears, and I wipe them away almost violently, angry at my own weakness.

My mother's husband gives me another sad smile, acting yet again like he has something else to say, but he does not utter a word before heading into the forest, leaving me with my tears and bitterness.

I watch him go, but only for a moment. The pain has grown until it is twice as intense, and for a reason I cannot comprehend, I feel like seeing Jameson is the only thing that will make it better.

So I head back to the men's village and to my husband.

Jameson is watching for me, and I have only taken one step from the forest when he is moving toward me, leaving Hawk and the deer hide behind. We move toward one another, each of us focused on the other. My heart pounds with the anticipation of his nearness, and I cannot bring myself to look away, not even when he is standing right in front of me and the thump in my chest intensifies. To my relief, he does not look away either.

"What's wrong?" Jameson asks, his voice thick with concern as his brown eyes search mine.

"Nothing." I swallow when the lie almost sticks in my throat. It is wrong, I know it is, but I worry telling him the truth will damage things between us even more, and I cannot risk it. Not now. Not when I am about to give him a choice no other man in this village has. "I want you to come to me tonight."

Jameson's eyebrows lift, and I know why. Usually when I invite him to my bed, I am not as forthcoming with my feelings. It is because of Raven, because she has always told me to hold a part of myself back, but I can no longer do it. Not after last night, not when I need Jameson to know how much I want him.

"Is it up to me?" he asks.

"It is. I want you to want to be with me, Jameson, so from now on, I will leave the decision up to you." I pause for a beat. "But I also need you to know that I want you with me tonight."

The corner of his mouth twitches like he is holding a smile in, and his head bobs twice before he says, "Then I'll be there."

CHAPTER FIFTEEN

SPRINGTIME MOVES INTO SUMMER, BRINGING WARM weather and flowers with it, and every morning I'm greeted by the chirp of birds, making me feel like I'm living in a cartoon. I saw a few at the nickel theater years ago. We'd scrimped and saved, and my mom had stopped drinking long enough to get us a nicer apartment. She was doing better then, going to work and staying away from the men who fed her liquor and talked her into taking her clothes off, and I had one year when I was able to be a kid. That's when I saw the westerns about cowboys and Indians, and the cartoons where animals sang. Both felt unreal to a boy living in a crowded, polluted city who had only seen a handful of trees in his life, but both now felt amazingly tangible.

I follow through with my promise to Zachariah and don't mention fathers to Wilderness again. She doesn't ask about it, or about anything else from my past, and I still have to ask permission to touch her, but she always gives me a choice in whether I sleep with her. With the decision left in my hands, I find I want her more than I did before.

Several times a week I'm invited to her hut, which is a hell of a lot more often than any of the other foundlings. We've been in the village for months now, and like me, they seem to be trying to make the best of the situation, but I can tell when they start to grow restless, and I know it won't be long before one of them tries to make a run for it. My money is on David.

The idea of leaving still exists in the back of my mind, but it's often overshadowed by the intimacy I share with Wilderness. Her eagerness to please me never fades, and neither does her desire for me to fit into the village. She never asks about my past, almost like she wants it to disappear completely, and the simplicity of life makes it easy to forget a world outside this forest ever existed in the first place.

The way these people live may not make sense to me, but I've come to understand they're happy with it—both the women and the men. There are festivals several times a year where both villages come together to celebrate, and it's these events that help me see the people for what they really are. It's also at one of these that I spot Blossom for the first time since Eric ran. She's a good distance away, but I can still make out roundness of her stomach. She's thin, so the difference is subtle, but it's there.

"Is that Blossom?" I ask Wilderness. "Is she pregnant?"

The way she smiles up at me, her brown eyes glowing, is enough to drive me to distraction. As is the sapphire necklace she always wears and the way it dips between the curves of her breasts.

"She is with child. Hopefully, the Great Mother will bless her with a girl, and her union will not be wasted."

The image of the two of us tangled together flips through my mind but is pushed away by Wilderness's words. It's always been obvious that the women here put more stock in girls, but hearing her say the words out loud is more effective than having a bucket of cold water dumped on my head.

"If she has a boy, it will be a waste?"

Wilderness tilts her head and studies me the way Zip does when I talk to him. "A yieldling is good because he will help continue our bloodline, but it would be a disappointment. Blossom will not get matched again, so this will be her only offspring."

Boys are a disappointment. No wonder Raven was able to send four children away without a second thought.

I ignore the first comment and instead focus on the second one, because it's something I'd never thought about before. "Blossom can't get a new husband?"

"One husband. Is that not how it is in the outside world?"

"Not at all. A woman can have several husbands in her lifetime. If she decides she doesn't want the one she has, she can divorce him and choose another. Sometimes the husband is the one who chooses to leave."

"Yes." Wilderness shakes her head like the whole thing saddens her. "Women in the outside world have no power, which makes them unhappy. Here we choose our husbands and we know our roles, so we are content in our matches."

I want to point out that Blossom's situation proves the opposite, but I don't. Timing is everything when it comes to Wilderness, and the middle of a festival, surrounded by the other women, isn't the best place to try to make her see the contradiction in her words. Plus, despite how improved things between us have been, I still need to be careful what I say.

Blossom, as it turns out, isn't the only one who's pregnant. Early summer brings news for both John and Michael as well, although neither of the men acts like the announcement is welcome. Not that it's a surprise.

That night, as I lie in Wilderness's bed, I find myself wondering how I'll feel when she finally tells me I'm going to be a father. I can't imagine living the way Zachariah does, having children but not being able to claim them. I don't remember my own father, and my mother was a poor excuse for a parent, but I'd always promised myself that if I did have children one day, I'd do a better job. Here, though, I'm not sure I'll be able to, because in this village the role of father doesn't even exist.

"Thank you for coming to me tonight," Wilderness says, staring at me through lowered lashes.

"Thank you for giving me a choice."

"I told you it was my job to make you happy." She pauses, smiling up at me as she does, and brushes her lips against my chest. "If this is what you need, I will do it."

"What about Raven? What would she think of this arrangement?"

Wilderness's smile wavers but doesn't fade completely. "My mother must choose what is right for her husband, and I will choose what is right for mine." She twists away from me, pulling the fur up to cover her breasts. "Tonight, you will return to your own hut."

I try to ignore the way her words sting, but it isn't easy. While the choice of whether I sleep with Wilderness is now up to me, she still doesn't allow me to stay in her bed every night. There's no pattern or reason to it either, making it impossible to predict when she'll let me stay and when she'll send me packing. Plus, it's obvious she's keeping me at arm's length even though a part of her wants to pull me close, almost like she feels it's her duty to keep a wall between us. I can't help thinking it has something to do with Raven and Zachariah, because it hasn't escaped my notice that the High Elder does the same thing with her own husband.

It's dark when I step out of the hut, and though there's still a slight chill in the air, the warmth from the sunny day has held on longer than usual. Behind me, Wilderness stands with a fur draped around her body, and next to the brown pelt, her skin looks ghostly pale. Her blonde hair is a wild and tangled mess, the waves cascading down her back and covering half her face. Since the fur only goes to mid-thigh, her legs are on full display, and their shapely firmness calls out to me, begging me to come back to bed and let her wrap them around me once again. I want to, more than I've ever wanted anything, but despite the small amount of freedom she's granted me, it's something I can't do. In this world, I'm not even allowed to touch her without an invitation, and the second she asks me to leave, our time together is over. When that happens, I can't help feeling like a mosquito, like I'm a pest she won't hesitate to stomp out if I hover too close.

"Good eve, Wilderness," I say, pausing outside her door.

"Sleep well in your new hammock, husband."

I swallow when a lump I don't understand rises in my throat. It's gotten more and more difficult to leave her hut, but I can't bring myself to address the emotions welling up inside me when she looks at me like this. She's a beautiful woman, exotic and intoxicating, and I choose to attribute my feelings to that as well as how she makes me feel when I'm in her bed. The idea of looking for deeper meaning is more terrifying than the thought that I might be punished if I fall out of line.

"I will," I say and turn away from her.

I can feel her gaze on my back as I move down the walkway. It sways with each step, but it doesn't scare me the way it used to, and I no longer think it will snap at any second or that the creaking of the wood beneath my feet is a sign of weakness. These women are strong and smart, and they created a world that's both achingly beautiful and as resilient as they are. They keep up with it, too, just like this bridge, and a day doesn't pass that the women don't tighten a loose rung or fix a cracked plank. Nothing gets by them.

I use the rope pulley system to lower myself to the ground, something I rarely did in the beginning because it goes down so fast and the platforms are higher than the ones in the men's village. It doesn't scare me to take the plunge anymore, and I'm prepared for the impact when my feet hit the ground. The thud seems loud in the quietness of the night.

Zip jumps to his feet, wagging his tail in excitement, and I motion for him to follow me to the forest as I head toward the men's village, thinking back on the last few months. Time moves differently here. The week isn't marked by work or worship, even though these women do have their own religion, and there's no day of rest. Instead, the days move forward in perfect harmony, blending together to create a peacefulness I've never known before.

The serenity of my time here has made it difficult to mark the passing of days, though. How much time has gone by since the warriors dragged me up this mountain? Two months? Three? It was late April when they took me from the work camp, and I can tell by the growing warmth of each passing day that it must be early July by now. It feels like I've only been here for a matter of days until I focus on how much my view of this village has changed. In the beginning, I was biding my time until I could get away, and I saw the women around me as savages and enemies. Some of those negative feelings have hung on, but most have changed into something that resembles pity more than anger. I feel bad for them. Bad that the women who started this group went through something so horrific they felt the only way to stay safe was to completely shelter themselves from men. Because of that, these women are missing out on one of the greatest parts of life. Having a family.

I'm halfway through the patch of forest separating the two villages when a shadow emerges from the darkness, moving toward me. At my side, Zip lets out a growl, and despite the fact that I haven't encountered a single dangerous thing since coming here, my pulse quickens the way it used to when the landlord came knocking on my door.

"Jameson." A voice I recognize as Michael's cuts through the darkness.

"Shit," I say, and at my side, Zip relaxes and once again starts wagging his tail. "You scared me."

Michael steps closer, and I notice two more shadows behind him. It doesn't take a genius to figure out who they are. John and David.

"We're leaving," Michael says. "Taking our chance in the woods."

I knew this moment would eventually come, but it still almost knocks me on my ass.

"No." I reach out but stop myself, a habit now ingrained in me from living in a world where touching another person is a privilege. "You know what happened last time."

"We have to try," John says. "We think they may not try as hard to find us since the women are pregnant. That's all they want, anyway. Babies so they can keep this shit show going."

"Come with us," Michael hisses.

I shake my head automatically. "No."

I'm pretty sure something is wrong with me, because all I can think is that these men are abandoning Brooke and Rose, and how their lives will be a waste if they don't have girls. Even worse, Ivy, the woman who took David as her husband, isn't pregnant, and if he leaves, she'll never have a child.

Maybe David was right. Maybe they have brainwashed me. I don't feel like it, but the thoughts going through my head aren't normal, and I know I should *want* to leave. I should be willing to try anything to get away from the people who captured me and dragged me into the middle of nowhere. No matter the risks. But I don't.

"I told you," David says. "That woman put a spell on him. They're witches. That's why Zachariah is still here, why he thinks all this is okay."

"Screw them," John growls. "I'm not staying here."

David and John start to back away, but Michael grabs my arm and squeezes it, pulling me close. "You have to cover for us. I don't care how you do it, but you can't let anyone realize we're gone until morning. That will give us enough of a head start."

I shake my head even as I say, "Okay."

The trees above us are thick, blocking out most of the moon's light, but even in the darkness I can see the hesitation in Michael's eyes.

"Let's go," John hisses.

Michael releases my arm and takes a couple steps back, not turning until he's a good five feet from me. Then he takes off, running through woods after David and John, not once looking back.

Zip sits when I don't move. I can't, not with my mind reeling. What should I do now? Zachariah must not be in the hut, which is why the men chose now to make their escape, but the second he gets back from Raven's, he's going to know something isn't right. The women haven't invited Michael and John to their beds a single night since they found out they were pregnant.

When the sounds of the other men's footsteps have faded to nothing, I force myself to move. Zip and I continue our trek through the woods, and when we step into the men's village, it's dark and silent like it should be. Still, the thick dread inside me makes it seem like there are figures hidden in every shadow. Watching me, judging me.

I leave Zip to join the dogs and climb the ladder to the hut I share with Zachariah and the other men, finding it empty. His absence isn't a surprise, but Hawk should be here. They usually take turns watching the foundlings.

In the corner of the room, the hammock Wilderness gave me swings back and forth like it's taunting me, a reminder that more is expected of me here. That as Wilderness's husband, I have a duty not just to her, but to the entire village as well. The thought makes me sick, both because I'm going to disappoint her, and because it won't go away.

I sink onto the floor and wait, my insides feeling like I'm at the center of an epic battle of tug of war. I'm not sure what's right and wrong anymore. The lines have become blurred until they're nothing but a shadow of what they once were, and I'm pretty sure no matter what I do right now, I'll feel like it was the wrong decision.

I don't have to wait long before the telltale sound of feet hitting the platform echoes through the hut, and I get to my feet as the door opens. Zachariah steps inside, an expression of surprise on his face that's quickly replaced with worry, and then suspicion.

"Jameson." He looks past me to the empty beds, then around the room. "Where are the foundlings? Where is Hawk?"

"Gone," I say, hoping he won't ask any more questions, but feeling with almost certainty that I won't be able to escape them completely. Not for long.

Zachariah steps closer, and when he narrows his icy blue eyes, it feels like he can see right through me. "Where?"

"They were gone when I got back from Wilderness's hut."

He spins on his heel without another word and rushes outside.

The night is a whirlwind after that. Like the first time John ran, a group of warriors comes to get the dogs—Zip among them—torches already in hand. In the center of the village, the fire crackles, the flames rising higher when more logs are thrown on. Sparks fly into the air, getting lost in the darkness as they fizzle out, while the warriors prepare to head into the forest and search for the foundlings.

I watch it all unfold from the platform, knowing it won't be long before I'll have to answer for my part in all this. Zachariah will have more questions, and a part of me doesn't know if I can lie. Only I'm not sure why. Is it because I have some strange loyalty to these people, or because I don't want to disappoint Wilderness?

Before the warriors have even made it into the forest, Wilderness steps out of the woods on the other side of the village, her mother at her side. The women stop in front of Zachariah, and Raven holds out her hand. He takes it and they talk, and even though I'm too far away to hear anything, I know he's filling her in on what happened. When all three of them turn to face me, the hair on my scalp prickles.

A few seconds later, Wilderness heads back into the woods, and the warriors leave as well, following the dogs as they charge into the forest. I stay where I am, unable to make myself go down to join the others but knowing I can't go back into the hut right now.

Before long, three figures emerge from the woods. Wilderness, with Hawk and Dawn only a step behind her. When the trio approaches Raven and Zachariah, I'm no longer able to keep my distance. I want—no, need—to find out what they're talking about.

I jump from the platform, grabbing the rope and swinging to the ground, then take off across the village. The group is already talking, and I walk up in time to catch Hawk's confession.

"I knew I was supposed to stay with the foundlings, but I went to Dawn's hut instead. They were asleep, and I thought it would be okay. I did not think anyone would know."

Zachariah shakes his head while Raven turns her gaze on Dawn. It's hard to tell for sure, but it seems like she's purposefully avoiding looking at Zachariah. Almost like she's afraid to learn he's played any part in what happened. Like the thought of having to punish him again hurts her.

"Did you know your husband had other duties?" Raven asks.

"No." Dawn straightens her shoulders, and at her side, Hawk stiffens. "I would have told him to return to the foundlings."

Hawk doesn't lift his head, but his eyes do dart Dawn's way, and I can't help thinking that she's lying. Only it *can't* be true. She has to know he'll be punished, and I've seen them together. Dawn cares about Hawk. She wouldn't want him to get in trouble for something he didn't do. Would she?

Raven turns her hard gaze on me. "What about you? What did you see when you returned from my daughter's bed?"

Everyone is looking at me now, but I keep my gaze focused on the High Elder. "I got back to find our hut empty."

Raven lifts one eyebrow, and even though she's shorter than I am, it feels like she's looking down on me. "That is not an answer."

I'd hoped she would accept my explanation at face value, but a part of me knew she wouldn't. She isn't a woman who allows gaps. Just like the huts' thatched roofs, she wants every hole filled so nothing can leak through.

"I saw the men in the woods on my way back to the hut."

Wilderness takes one step toward me, but Raven lifts her hand, motioning for her daughter to stay where she is.

"And you spoke to them?" the High Elder asks in an even voice, giving away no emotion.

"I did."

"They told you they were leaving?"

"They did."

At her side, Zachariah stares at me, but it's hard to read his expression. Is he disappointed in me? Concerned?

"This is not welcome news. We will find the men, but the punishment for this…" Raven lets out a deep sigh and lowers her gaze to the ground. "Maybe we give the foundlings too much freedom. Maybe Zachariah's success has blinded us."

"Raven—" Zachariah reaches out, but he doesn't touch her.

She turns to face him, her expression sad. "This is a troubling moment for me. I will have to consult the other Elders, but we cannot let things continue like this. We have already lost one foundling, and even if Blossom's union was successful, we must think about how this could affect the village. What if these men return to the outside and tell others about us? We cannot risk our way of life like this." She turns her back on her husband. "Come, Wilderness. We will meet with the Elders."

Wilderness doesn't look at me before following her mother, and the throb of disappointment inside me is even more painful than I imagine my punishment will be.

CHAPTER SIXTEEN

Wilderness

THE LOOK ON MY HUSBAND'S FACE STAYS WITH ME AS I follow my mother back to our village. He knows, just as I do, that he will face punishment, but I cannot help thinking Jameson did what he thought was right, both with the foundlings and now. He let the men go because he knew they were not happy, and he confessed to my mother even though he knew it would get him in trouble because he knew it was expected of him.

His actions are as confusing to me as they probably are to him.

Raven does not speak the whole way back to our village. She is troubled, both by the foundlings who have run and by what she will have to do. I, too, am troubled. My husband chose not to leave, but he has involved himself by not alerting us. He should have come to me.

Once we are back in our own village, Raven and I return to the trees, winding our way across the walkways until we reach Willow's hut. There is a flurry of activity already. The shutters and doors are open, and several lanterns have been lit, and the soft glow of firelight seems to accentuate the worry on the faces of the other Elders.

"Have all the foundlings run?" Willow asks when my mother stops in front of her.

"Wilderness's husband remains, but he did help the others."

A murmur of shock and disapproval moves through the crowd, and I have to fight to keep my head up.

"We must discuss what will happen next." Raven turns to me. "I have brought Wilderness to the meeting so she can learn what we do. I hope it will also help her learn how to successfully guide her husband."

This time, I find it impossible not to lower my gaze to the floor.

The women file into the hut and sit in a circle on bundles of fur. Only Mother Elder sits in a chair, and it seems like she is looking down on me from high above. It has been many years since she was able to see well, but it is hard to remember because she has always been such a big presence in my life. I cannot think of her as old the way Jameson does. She survived The Great Plague and the hotel, and she was among the women who came here and started over. They created this world for us, made something good and strong out of the ruins of so many horrible things, and that makes her almost omnipotent in my eyes.

"We have not had foundlings run in many years," Mother Elder begins, "and this is the second time since bringing this group in."

"Perhaps there are too many of them," Summer says. "It has been a long time since we had five at once."

"They have too much freedom," my mother replies. "I believe we have let Zachariah's successful integration blind us to what the foundlings are. They are not like us, and before Zachariah's time, it was not normal to allow the foundlings so much freedom. They were not allowed to roam the way they do now. We guarded them both day and night. After this, we may need to go back to the old ways."

I sit up straighter when the meaning of my mother's words threatens to knock me down. "You mean using the medicine more? Locking them up?"

My mother does not look at me when she says, "I do."

I hate what this could mean for Jameson. He has just reached the point where he seems to be finding his place, and this would make him feel more like a prisoner. High Elder or not, I cannot stand by and allow my mother to lock my husband up like he is a criminal. Jameson has done nothing wrong, and even if it means fighting Raven, I refuse to remain quiet in this face of this injustice. Somehow, I must stand up to her.

I say nothing while the Elders discuss the foundlings, giving myself a moment to collect my thoughts. They do not say it, but I know what will happen to the husbands of Brooke and Ivy if the warriors find them. The women are already with child, meaning the foundlings have fulfilled their duty and there is no reason to keep them around. Especially after they have caused so much trouble.

But what of the third man, and what of Hawk? What of my husband? Jameson's actions were not right by the standards of our village, but he told my mother the truth, and in my mind that means he deserves mercy. I doubt Raven will agree with me, though. Jameson is a foundling, and to the other women that means he has more evil in him than the yieldlings. They do not trust outsiders, no matter how much they have come to love Zachariah.

There seems to be very little decided during the meeting, but it is still almost morning by the time we leave the hut. The horizon is aglow from the rising sun, and soon the orange will change to yellow and blend into the blackness above, chasing away yet another night while bringing my husband one step closer to punishment.

My mother stands tall as she heads down the walkway, and though she does not say it, I can tell she wants to have words with me. I follow, a sinking feeling in my stomach as if a small forest creature has burrowed its way inside me and created a home, weighing me down.

When we are alone, she stops in the middle of the walkway and turns to face me. Above our heads, the trees sway with the morning breeze, and the chirping of birds joins the rustling of leaves, but the cheery sounds are at odds with the dread inside me.

"Your husband will be punished," my mother says, her unblinking eyes looking hard and cold.

"But he did not run," I argue as the heaviness in my stomach grows more intense. "He had the chance, but chose not to go with the foundlings."

"He also chose not tell anyone what was happening even though he knew he should. You saw it in his eyes, daughter, do not tell me you did not. Your husband has guilt over what he did. If this goes unpunished, he will learn nothing. Maybe this way he will do the right thing next time."

My mother is right; I know she is. Still, I do not savor the idea of watching my husband be punished, let alone being the one to wield the whip, which I know is what she expects me to do.

"You must take responsibility for him," she says, mimicking my thoughts.

I turn my eyes down, focusing on the bridge beneath me so I do not have to look her in the eye. "You cannot ask me to do this."

"I must." When my mother sighs, the sound is more annoyance than weariness. "You have seen me punish Zachariah. You must know I did not enjoy it, but I did it anyway. It is my job. To teach my husband what is right and what we expect of him. You saw him after his most recent punishment, and you know he thanked me for it."

"Jameson is not Zachariah. He will not thank me. He will be angry. He will pull away, and I fear I will lose him. He is making good progress. He is finding his place." I take a deep breath, realizing I have said all this without pause, and finally lift my eyes to meet my mother's. "Please."

"You know this must be done. He will not be alone. Hawk will be at his side, and Dawn will do her duty."

"Mother—"

"I am High Elder, not your mother." Her voice booms through the village, and above our heads, a bird bursts from the trees and flies off, squawking. "This is what is going to happen, and there will be no more discussion about it, Wilderness."

She turns her back on me, and as I watch her walk away, my body goes cold. Not once in all my life have I felt alone the way I do right now.

I have watched Zachariah be punished more than once, and every time it has hurt me. It is something I have never told anyone, and even now I cannot fully understand it, but seeing my mother's husband hurt has been painful. Watching him get punished feels like I am the one being whipped, like the lashes are hitting my skin and like I am the one bleeding. Seeing Jameson go through it will be so much more difficult, and I cannot even begin to imagine how agonizing it will be if I am the one inflicting the pain.

I turn, intending to go to my hut so I can compose myself, but freeze as if a sudden snowstorm has come in and turned me to ice. Dawn stands on the platform in front of me, watching. Smiling.

"What?" The predatory expression in her eyes makes my voice tremble.

She turns away without answering me, still smiling.

I stay where I am, my gaze following the other woman as she moves through the village, crossing walkways to her own hut. The sun shines down, highlighting the orange in her hair, and for a reason I cannot name, a shiver runs through me.

Instead of going back to my hut, I return to the men's village. The sun is high when I step out of the forest, and the village brightly lit, and all around the clearing men have started their daily duties. Young yieldlings tend the rabbits and the fields while older ones, like Hawk, tend the larger animals. My husband is in the goat pen, and despite the dread inside me, I head his way.

The closer I get, the stronger the stink of animal dung becomes. I am in the center of the village when Jameson sees me, and he stops what he is doing, waiting, watching as I cross the village to him.

I think of him being here against his will, taken from a different life and a different world, forced to be the husband to a woman he does not know and to obey customs he cannot understand. I have no knowledge of what his life was like before he came here, but it was no doubt very different, and for the first time I understand how unfair this must seem to him. To be ripped away from everything he knew and forced to scoop up goat dung, then sleep with a woman he did not choose for himself. To us, to the women in my village and the yieldlings, nothing about this is strange, but to him it must be very difficult.

Yet he stayed. He could have run with the other men or any time before and he would have been justified, but he stayed. Why? Was it for me?

He is watching me through the fence when I stop outside the pen. The sun's rays shine through the crisscrossed sticks, creating a honeycomb pattern on his chest and arms. He is a very beautiful man, I have come to decide, and I am grateful for the chance to know him, but I do not want to be unfair.

"Why did you stay?" I ask.

He tilts his head, and I notice for the first time how much his dark hair has grown. It was short when he arrived, barely longer than one fingertip length, but it has grown to four finger widths, and now curls around his ears as well as at the back of his neck.

My husband takes a deep breath as if trying to figure out how to answer. "I don't know."

"Until today, I never thought about what you gave up. I did not ask what your life out there was like or if you had loved ones. This is normal for me, having men brought to the village to be husbands, but I now realize it is very unfair." I take a deep breath and ask the question I am almost certain I do not want to know the answer to. "Do you have a woman out there?"

Jameson blinks before saying, "No."

I sense, though, that there is more to the story. "Do you have other people out there?"

"I have a mother," he says, "but I haven't seen her in a long time. I have two brothers—" When I shake my head, he sighs. "Never mind. I don't know where they are, anyway."

Jameson looks past me, over my shoulder, and when I turn, I find Zachariah watching us, his expression intent. Almost nervous.

When I look back at my husband, he says, "That's why I didn't run. My life before I came here wasn't anything special. It was hard. I had to work hard. Most of the time, though, I felt like I couldn't get ahead. Like I never had a moment of rest. It's been that way most of my life, but it's been different since I came here. Stealing men and forcing them to do this is unfair, and I don't agree with everything you do, but I'm starting to think this is where I was meant to be. Here, I sleep well at night, and when I work, I'm doing it for a reason, so the whole village can survive and not just so someone else can get rich. I know you don't understand what that means, but it's the only way I can explain how I feel."

I turn his words over in my head as he watches me, waiting for a response or for me to ask another question, and my insides tingle under his gaze. Something about his expression tells me that the question he is waiting for is already on the tip of my tongue.

"Did you stay for me?"

Jameson swallows as if finding the answer difficult. "I did."

I let out a deep breath, and even though the answer is what I wanted to hear and it fills me with joy, the happiness is chased away by the dread of what will happen next. As well as the fear that what we have built will not be able to survive it.

"My mother says you must be punished."

He flinches but nods. "I knew it was coming."

"I do not want it to happen, but I am powerless to stop it."

He reaches out, curling his fingers through the holes in the fence, and without knowing how it got there, I find my hand on his. "I'll be okay."

A dog barks, and I turn away from Jameson, facing the forest as Zip bursts through the trees. The other dogs follow, and a blink later the warriors step out. The men are with them. All three of them.

CHAPTER SEVENTEEN

Jameson

WILDERNESS LEAVES ME WHEN THE WARRIORS appear, but I can't move. Instead, I stand surrounded by goat shit while the bleating animals nudge my hands, vying for attention as the warriors drag the men forward. Last time they retrieved John, it was up to Zachariah to take care of him and clean him up, but that isn't what happens now. This time, the women tie all three men up and leave them in the center of the village, bloodied and bruised.

I don't believe for a second their injuries are a result of anyone falling.

Even after the women return to their own village, I can't make myself move. This is my fault. These men asked me to cover for them, but I couldn't, and now they're here, and nothing good will come of it. Whatever happens, their blood will be on my hands as much as it is on the hands of the women, because I let them down.

Eventually, I finish scooping up the goat shit and need to get cleaned up. The bucket of water is next to the fire, which is next to the men who now hate me for double-crossing them, and even Zip trotting along at my side can't distract me from the furious looks they throw my way.

"Prick," David hisses.

"You gave us up," Michael says. "You promised to cover for us, but you gave us up."

John glares at me for so long without talking that I'm sure he's going to stay silent, but he finally says, "I hope you burn in hell," hurling the words at me like daggers. They hurt more than blades slicing into my skin possibly could.

I lower my head, unable to look them in the eye when I say, "Zachariah knew what happened the second he set foot in the hut. There was nothing I could do about it."

No one answers.

I turn my back on them and spot Hawk on the other side of the village, in the middle of cleaning the animal pens left neglected by the foundlings who ran. That's something I hadn't even thought of.

I go to him, intending to help, but freeze when he lifts his head. "What's wrong?"

"We will be punished," he says, but I can tell there's more to it, so I wait. Hawk presses his lips together like he's trying to decide what to say and then sighs. "Dawn did not speak the truth."

"She knew you were supposed to watch the foundlings?"

Hawk's eyes stay focused on the pig shit in his hand. "She knew, but she invited me to her hut, so I had to go. I had no choice."

The unfairness of it all hits me like a train. He's about to be punished—whipped—and yet he had no choice in the matter. None of the men do—

except me. If the women call them, the men have to run to their beds like slaves. If the women *invite* their husband's to touch them, it's their duty. It's so twisted and sick it makes the world around me tilt and go out of focus.

"You have to tell Raven," I say.

Hawk goes back to scooping the pig shit up off the ground. "I cannot."

I wait for him to say something else, to change his mind and take his future into his hands, but all he does is pick up handfuls of shit and drop them into the bucket, one after another after another.

I turn my back on him, too disturbed to talk right now, and my gaze lands on Zachariah. He's in the middle of cooking a large pot of stew, the simple boy once again at his side, his head bobbing as he listens to the older man talk.

The boy seems to always be there, by the fire and alone. Who the hell does he belong to?

The truth hits me like a punch. He belongs to no one. Like all the other boys in the village, this boy's mother gave him up, and he has no father. He's alone in this world, and the realization makes my legs wobble and threaten to give out. Knowing all the boys are cast off is bad enough, but this kid, this boy who sits by the fire hour after hour, seems so lost I can't help thinking it must be twice as difficult for him. Not only does he not understand the world around him the way the rest of us do, but he has no one to guide him. I'm sure Zachariah has taken on a lot of the responsibility, but he can't be everywhere, and he can't be everyone. He, like the rest of us, has limitations, and this kid will probably suffer because of it.

The heaviness of this, combined with the knowledge that Dawn lied to Raven, weighs on me as I cross the village. Zip walks by my side, but he seems to understand my mood, because he doesn't wag his tail the way he usually does.

The three men are tied up less than ten feet from the fire, and I do my best to avoid looking their way when I pass. It doesn't stop them from hurling insults at me, though, and one of them—I'm not sure which one since I don't look—even spits at me. It lands in the dirt a good three feet away.

Zachariah doesn't smile when I reach him, a sign of how grave this day has become. "You should have told Wilderness."

"Maybe," I say but then shake my head. "But I don't think so. I had to do what I thought was right. Those men don't belong here."

The older man holds my gaze for a few seconds before saying, "Not like us, you mean?"

I shrug because contradicting him is useless. "Maybe."

Zachariah nods solemnly, and I let out a deep breath. It's a subject I can't understand and have no desire to talk about, especially not right now.

Instead I say, "Dawn lied."

Zachariah's brows lift, but I can tell he doesn't believe me. "What are you saying?"

"Hawk told me. Dawn knew he was supposed to be with the foundlings."

Zachariah looks past me to where his son is busy scooping up pig shit, and then back to me. "This cannot be."

"It is," I say firmly.

The man in front of me looks down, and at his side the simple boy continues to bob his head. He's listening, but I haven't had the opportunity to talk to him yet, and I'm not sure how much of what's going on he actually understands.

When Zachariah finally lifts his head, he wears a torn expression, and I don't get it, can't understand his hesitation. Hawk is his son, and he's going to be whipped for something he couldn't control. If it were me, I'd be charging off to the women's village. I'd break Raven's door down if I had to. But Zachariah hasn't moved, and he acts like he isn't sure what to do with the information.

"Tell Raven."

"It is not that simple," he says. "We have rules. I cannot go to her unless invited. I cannot speak against a woman as if I am an Elder. I am just a man here. Have you learned nothing?"

I stumble back like he's hit me, my mouth hanging open. "Have *you* learned nothing? Can't you see how wrong this is? How can you still justify what happens here?"

Zachariah stares at me, his gaze expressionless, and says nothing.

"I'll tell Wilderness," I say. "*I* won't stand by and do nothing."

"You will not."

It isn't an order, and when he turns away, I'm forced to step back as the urge to punch him slams into me. Everything is starting to spiral out of control, and despite what I said to Wilderness earlier, I'm not sure why I'm still here. I should have run, too. I should have thrown myself off the mountain months ago, not stuck around like a fool who can't think straight in the presence of a nice pair of tits.

Just as this thought goes through my head, a group of warriors and Elders steps from the forest, and my stomach drops until it feels like I'm standing on it. They head our way, but they aren't looking at Zachariah or me. They're looking at the three men they brought back only a short time ago. The foundlings.

"The men will now learn their fate," Zachariah says, but I already knew it.

He moves past me, heading toward the women. I want to go back to the hut and close the door so I don't have to be a witness to this, but I find myself following Zachariah. The women don't even glance our way when we approach, not that it's a surprise. We're only men, after all. Only a little more useful than the pigs.

They warriors untie the foundlings and force them to kneel in a line. David first, and then John and Michael.

"We have decided on the punishment," Raven says, her voice floating through the village.

Behind me, the other men have moved forward, and I can't help looking around. They're yieldlings, but they have to know this is wrong, have to understand that these men deserve more. That all of us do. The faces of the men around me are somber, though. There's no anger. No disgust. No one seems care.

"Bring the husbands of Rose and Ivy," Raven calls out.

Rain and Grove pull Michael and John forward and once again force them to kneel, this time in front of Raven. The warriors stay at the men's sides. They're both shaking, John more so than Michael, and when I realize I am as well, I clench my hands into fists and take deep breaths, hoping to calm myself. I know what's coming, but I have to stay in control.

"You have fulfilled your duty to our village and will now meet your end," Raven says without preamble.

She steps back, nodding once, and before either man has a chance to react to the news, the warriors have made their move. Grove slides the blade of her knife across Michael's throat at almost the exact moment Rain does the same with John, and blood sprays across the dirt, followed by a sickening gurgle. John grabs his throat while Michael drops to his hands and knees, blood pouring from his neck like a faucet has been turned on.

Only a few moments pass before both men are on the ground, motionless, while beneath them a pool of red is slowly sucked up by the dusty ground.

David, who is only a kid, is hysterical. "No! No. You can't do this. No!" He won't stop screaming, not even when Dawn kicks him in the side and he goes down.

Raven frowns at the warrior, but she doesn't correct her. "Bring him here," she says instead.

Dawn drags David forward, and I take a step back. He won't get his throat slit because Ivy isn't pregnant, but the sick feeling in my stomach tells me something bad is about to happen. Something that will make him wish he was on the ground with the other two men.

"You ran, but we cannot have it happen again." Raven pauses like she's unsure but then says, "You will receive forty lashes."

"Raven," Zachariah whispers, so quiet only I can hear him.

Dawn releases David when the other warriors head for the forest, and he crumples into a ball. I doubt he'll ever consider running again after watching the other two men get their throats cut. Forty lashes? I think about how bloodied John's back was after twenty, and my stomach lurches. This kid will never be the same.

Raven hasn't moved, and the way her gaze focuses on Zachariah makes it obvious she wants him to come to her, but he turns away. Irritation and worry flash in her eyes, but she doesn't call after him. Instead, she turns and follows the warriors into the forest.

CHAPTER EIGHTEEN

Wilderness

DAWN STANDS WITH HER BACK AS STRAIGHT AS AN arrow like she is not the least bit uncomfortable carrying out her husband's punishment, but I cannot do the same. Instead, I keep my eyes focused on the ground while my mother speaks to the crowd, not even venturing a look up when Ivy steps forward to deliver the forty blows to her husband. This is the most severe sentence I have ever heard of, and for the first time in my life, I find it impossible to understand what my mother is thinking. How can she believe this is okay? How can any of us believe this is okay?

My insides twist when Ivy takes the whip from my mother. The uncomfortable feeling intensifies when I think about what happened earlier in the men's village. We brought the two foundlings here against their will, and all they wanted was to be free, and we killed them for it. Until Jameson came, I never thought we were bad people, but what he said to me after Canyon was sent into the forest now rings true. What we are doing is no different than what the men in that hotel did seventy years ago. How can we say we are better after what has happened here today? We cannot. It is impossible.

The whip cracks against David's skin, and the sound of his screams solidifies everything I am feeling. I want to look at Jameson, to make sure he is okay, but I find it impossible to lift my head. Is it shame? Jameson said he does not blame me, but I cannot understand how I could remain faultless in his eyes, because not only am I a part of this village, but it will be my hand holding the whip.

By the time Ivy has finished delivering the forty lashes, the warriors have to drag David away. The sight of the blood streaked across the dirt makes my stomach twist harder. Getting out of this is impossible, but I cannot deliver my husband's punishment with that much brutality. He does not deserve it. No one does.

"Kneel, Hawk."

My mother's voice booms through the village, and my head jerks up. Like Zachariah, Hawk keeps his head held high when he steps forward. The strength he displays is impressive, and when my legs begin to shake, I feel like a weak mouse in comparison. Until now, I could only think of Jameson, but watching Hawk prepare to take his lashes makes me want to run and hide. In all his years, he has never done anything that required punishment, and the very thought of witnessing his pain hurts me.

"Dawn will deliver ten lashes for your part in the foundlings' escape," my mother tells him.

Escape.

The word hits me like a fist. These men wanted to escape our village just like the women wanted to escape the hotel. How can the other women not see the similarity? How could I not see it until Jameson pointed it out?

Hawk turns to receive his punishment, kneeling in the dirt, his knees coming to rest on top of David's blood. For a few blinks, the red beneath him is all I can look at. Even when I do manage to lift my eyes, I cannot make out Hawk's face because his back is to me. That does not mean I am unaffected. The blond curls I remember from my childhood are so familiar that I can picture his smile, and the urge to run to him, to throw my body over his so Dawn cannot hurt him slams into me. I want to scream to the others that we must stop this, but I do nothing, and the powerlessness settling over me feels like leather binding my wrists.

My mother holds the whip out, and Dawn takes it. A drop of blood falls to the ground, red against the dark earth, and bile rises in my throat, but Dawn does not even blink when she takes a step forward. Her blue eyes flit from her husband's back to me, and her expression hardens. Suddenly, I remember the way she smiled at me earlier, and the sick feeling in my stomach increases.

Dawn's gaze moves back to Hawk, and she raises her arm. She brings the whip down, cracking the leather against his skin, and my entire body jerks. Hawk grunts but does not cry out. He keeps his body straight as she delivers another blow, leaving a second red welt on his skin. The lines cross, making an X on his back, but they are quickly joined by a third one, and then a fourth.

The fifth blow draws blood, as well as a cry of agony from Hawk. Zachariah steps forward like he is going to stop Dawn, but he does not take more than one step. Six. Seven. Eight strikes. Hawk cries out with each crack. On the ninth, he falls forward onto his hands and knees, but it does not stop Dawn from delivering the tenth blow. It strikes him on the left shoulder, so high up that the tip of the whip curls around and makes contact with his cheek. When blood pools on his face, I find it impossible not to react, crying out and stepping forward, reaching for my childhood friend. Dawn spins to face me, her eyes narrowed the way a bird of prey looks at a mouse.

"Raven," Zachariah says.

His voice is breathy, like a gasp of pain, and agony distorts his features. He balls his hands into fists like he wants to hit someone or is trying to stay in control, but he does not move. He just looks back and forth between my mother and Hawk.

My mother inhales, stretching it out, and when she releases the breath, words come out as well. "Dawn, help your husband."

Dawn drops the whip, and when the leather hits the ground, it sounds like a crack of thunder in the quiet forest. I cannot take my eyes off it. Cannot think. Cannot focus on Hawk or his bloody body, do not register the sounds he makes when Dawn hauls him up off the ground.

"Foundling."

My mother's voice draws my gaze up, and I watch in frozen horror as my husband steps forward. His eyes are on me, and like Hawk, he does not hesitate. He holds his head high like he is a yieldling, not a man we dragged here against his will.

"Did you take part in the escape of the other foundlings?" my mother asks.

Jameson nods once. "I did."

"You did not run, though. Why?"

His gaze moves to me, his brown eyes holding mine as he whispers, "Wilderness."

My mother flinches, but it is so slight I doubt anyone else notices. "Because you did not run, we will show you mercy, but you must still be punished for your part in the deception. Ten lashes, like Hawk."

Jameson turns his back to my mother, his head held high, and drops to his knees. He balls his hands into fists, and the muscles in his back ripple and pulse like he finds staying still difficult, but he does not move. The eagle tattoo is dark against otherwise flawless skin, and I find myself trying to imagine what his back will look like after this. I cannot, though.

"Wilderness."

I turn when my mother calls my name, but still I cannot move.

"This is your husband. It is your duty to show him the way. Pick up the whip."

My gaze moves down almost on its own, but I do not move. The whip is on the ground, covered in dirt and blood. It looks like a poisonous snake, and I fight the urge to shrink away from it. How can I do this to someone I care about? How can anyone?

"Wilderness." I look up again and find my mother watching me. "Pick it up."

Something moves in the corner of my vision, and when I turn toward it, Zachariah's gaze captures mine, his icy eyes soft and gentle. I inhale slowly through my nose then blow it out through my mouth, trying to regain control. Trying to decide what to do. This is my village. These are my people. I have a duty to them, and I must follow through. These are our traditions.

But my mother is right; I have a duty to Jameson, too, and I cannot do this. I cannot inflict pain on someone I care so much about.

Zachariah's head bobs ever so slightly, and I begin to relax. He understands the thoughts going through my head, and he agrees. Why his approval means so much, I cannot say, but it does, and knowing Zachariah is on my side gives me the strength I need.

I tear my gaze from his and turn back to my mother. "I will not."

A murmur moves through the crowd, and Raven's expression hardens. "I am High Elder, Wilderness. You must do this."

"I cannot," I say, louder this time.

She sucks in a deep breath, but before she can say anything, Dawn steps forward and grabs the whip, cracking it against the air and making me shrink away.

"I will deliver the punishment if Wilderness cannot." Dawn's eyes feel like spears of hatred when she looks at me.

At first I think my mother will not allow it, but then I see the anger in her eyes and realize I have pushed her too far, disobeyed and challenged her, and now my husband will pay.

"Ten lashes," Raven says, nodding to Dawn.

The orange-haired warrior grins, and I reach out to stop her, but before I can do anything, she brings the whip down. The leather snaps against Jameson's back, right below his eagle tattoo, and all the air leaves my lungs. He flinches but stays upright, not making a sound.

Dawn's expression hardens even more, and she raises the whip again. This time she brings it down harder, faster, and my husband screams. I step forward, but my mother grabs my arm and pulls me back. Her fingers dig into my skin, but I barely notice the pain. My gaze is trained on my husband, on the blood trailing from the red welts left behind by Dawn's blows.

The third lash sends him to the ground, but he catches himself with his hands. He is still on his hands and knees when the fourth blow rains down on him, this one breaking the skin in a way I have never seen from a whipping.

"Raven," I say, just loud enough for her to hear me, my voice coming out as a plea.

My mother remains immobile, but her twisted expression says she realizes her mistake. Dawn's jealousy drives her to hit my husband harder, and by the eighth blow, he is no longer conscious. I drop to my knees on number nine, my mother's nails scraping along my arm as I fall, but I do not feel an ounce of pain. At least not physical pain. Inside, though, I am a ball of ripped flesh, matching my husband's back.

When the crack of the last lash has faded away, I crawl forward until I am at my Jameson's side. The crowd is hushed, but I am too focused on him to know what they are thinking. Too focused on his damaged back, on his face, so slack it seems as if all the life has bled out of him. I cannot look away, not even when Zachariah kneels beside me and takes my hand.

I HAVE NO MEMORY OF GETTING MY HUSBAND TO MY HUT, BUT I know Zachariah helped. Jameson is awake but in so much pain he has yet to utter a single word. Sweat beads on his forehead and upper lip, and I do my best to keep him hydrated. His back is a tangle of bloody flesh, his once beautiful tattoo now unrecognizable, and I can see my name in every line. This is my fault. I should have done more. I should have tried harder.

A knock echoes through the hut, and I stand, barely able to tear my gaze from Jameson long enough to cross the room. I pull the door open, and when I come face to face with my mother, I am torn between the desire to slam it in her face and the urge to scream. She wears a pained expression, but it is nothing compared to what Jameson feels right now.

"Wilderness," she says.

I raise my hand, signaling for her to stop, and step outside. Before I shut the door, I look at my husband. He has his eyes closed, but I can tell by his scrunched expression he is not asleep. There is too much pain for him to rest.

I ease the door shut and turn back to face my mother. "Why are you here, Raven?"

Too ashamed to look me in the eye, she focuses on the platform beneath us. "I have come to apologize. I should not have let Dawn deliver the punishment. I did not realize—" She swallows but says nothing else.

"I told you Dawn had jealousy with me."

"I spoke with her, back when I said I would. I explained that there was nothing between you and Hawk. I thought she understood."

"She did not." My mother is too close, and I want to pull away from her, but she is High Elder and I cannot, so I cross my arms instead. "She did this to hurt me."

"I know." For the first time in my life, Raven looks uncertain. "I knew after the first blow, but I did not know what to do. I was unprepared. I thought stopping her would be a sign of weakness."

"Something must be done," I say.

My mother lifts her head so she can look me in the eye. "What can I do? We have never punished a woman."

"Perhaps we should."

"It is something I cannot decide on my own. I will need to talk to the other Elders." My mother lets out a deep breath and holds a jar out to me. "I brought you this. This salve will help with the pain and healing. Once upon a time, when Zachariah first came here, he was punished. Thirty lashes." My mother hangs her head again. "He says this helped."

I take it but do not thank her.

I turn toward the door, but only halfway, pausing when I realize I am standing between the hut—Jameson—and my mother—the village—one of them on each side. It is how I have felt lately, like I am stuck between two worlds, and I have no idea how to break free.

I do not look at Raven when I ask, "Who is tending Hawk?"

"Zachariah. He did not want to go with Dawn."

I study her out of the corner of my eye, uncertain what to say but knowing I cannot keep quiet after what happened. "You allowed him to make his own decision?"

This time when she looks down, the expression in her eyes is not shame, but something else I cannot name. "In this, I did."

I leave her standing on the platform.

I am hurt and angry, but there is more to it. Jameson's words refuse to quiet themselves in my head, and all I can think about is the look on Dawn's face as she whipped first her husband, and then mine. I have heard the tale of what happened in the hotel hundreds of times, but I have never truly seen the face of evil until today. Only it was not a man who showed it to me, but a woman.

THE SALVE DOES HELP, BUT THE FOLLOWING WEEK IS STILL difficult for Jameson, and for me as well. He is restless, never comfortable, and I can do nothing to help him. Every groan he lets out is like a fresh strike against my own back, and I begin to wish I had thrown myself over him after that first blow. That is what I would have done had I been able to think, had I been able to react faster when Dawn picked up the whip. But I was frozen, too shocked to do a thing. When my brain finally began working again, my mother was there to stop me.

A week after his punishment, I wake to the sound of my husband calling out to me. I push myself up off the floor and move to the bed where he sleeps, only to find his hand grasping for me in the darkness. He has not left the hut since his whipping, has barely moved from the bed where he now lies. Day and night, Jameson has been here while I do everything I can to make sure he is comfortable, ignoring every other duty.

"I am here," I say, wrapping my hand around his. "I am here for you."

He scoots over, letting out a small groan in the process. "Sleep with me. I miss having you at my side."

Although I worry he will be uncomfortable, it is impossible to deny him after what he has endured. Plus, I have missed his warmth as much as he has missed mine.

Jameson is on his stomach, forcing me to lie on my side, perched on the edge of the bed, and he drapes his arm across my hip so I cannot fall. His breath brushes over me with every exhale, and it is the most intimate moment we have ever shared. The knowledge that he still wants me fills me with relief, but also guilt because I know I do not deserve it.

"I am sorry," I murmur into the darkness. "I should have done more. I should have stopped Dawn. I should have stood up to my mother."

"Shhh," he says, his lips brushing my face. "It's not your fault. You did everything you could."

I do not think I tried hard enough.

THE NEXT DAY HE GETS UP AND MOVES AROUND FOR LONGER than he has in the last week. His wounds have scabbed over, but we both know the healing has only begun and that there will no doubt be scars left behind. He wants to get out of the hut, and though I worry about his wounds opening back up, I let him because he is both restless and anxious to check on Hawk.

I do not allow him to climb down the ladder, though, but instead insist on using the pulley cart we use for Mother Elder. Zip, who has spent the last week sitting at the bottom of the tree waiting for Jameson to appear, pushes himself up when he spots us. He wags his tail, but it is more reserved than usual.

I have never given the dogs much thought before now. They live in the men's village, play with the yieldlings, and the warriors train them to track, but Zip's attachment to my husband has forced me to pay attention.

"Hey, boy," Jameson says when he reaches the ground.

I help him out of the pulley cart while the dog waits patiently, his tail moving faster and his body language telling me how worried he has been. My husband scratches him behind the ear for a moment, and then the dog circles him, sniffing.

He whines, and Jameson pats his head. "It's okay. I'll be okay."

It feels like someone is gripping my throat in their fist as, together, the three of us head for the forest.

The sky above us is flawless, completely unencumbered by clouds, and stepping out of the shade is like moving closer to a fire. The sun's heat is almost blistering in intensity, but it has not stopped people from going about their business. The village is alive with activity, and women throw curious glances our way when we pass.

They were all there when my husband was whipped, yet not a single woman asks how he is or even mentions the punishment. Their callousness leaves me feeling cold even under the heat of the sun and reminds me of the expression in my mother's eyes before Jameson's whipping.

Thankfully, we make it into the forest without running into Raven. I have seen nothing of her since the day she brought the salve to my hut, and though I know I cannot avoid her forever, I have no desire to see her today. I need more time to heal, assuming it is even possible after what happened.

The men's village is as busy as the women's, but when we step out of the trees, men and boys stop what they are doing and hurry to Jameson. He moves slowly, and I can tell every step causes him pain, but when the yieldlings scurry over to say hello, his smile is genuine.

I spot Hawk and wave, and for once he comes to me. His wounds were not as bad as Jameson's, but he, too, seems to walk with great effort. The cut on his cheek has scabbed over, but will no doubt leave a scar, just as the cuts on his back will, and knowing this punishment has marked him for life hurts almost as much as the memory of watching it happen.

"How're you doing?" Jameson asks him before I am able to find my voice.

Hawk blows out a long breath as if to illustrate how difficult things have been. "I am healing, but it has been slow."

"For me, too," my husband replies.

A whoop rings out, and I turn as Zachariah swings to the ground. He waves as he jogs over, smiling like he is greeting long lost friends, and his grin, as always, is infectious, so that by the time the older man stops in front of us, even I am smiling.

"You are up, foundling." Zachariah reaches out as if to smack Jameson on the shoulder, but seems to remember the whipping and drops his hand to his side. "I am glad to see you."

"He is not healed yet," I say, so no one will expect him to return to his duties yet. "But he is better."

Hawk lowers his head like he is personally responsible for Jameson's state. He carries none of the blame, but I understand how he feels. Dawn is the one who wielded the whip, but Hawk knows where her anger came from. He is her husband, but he is also only a man, and even if he had not just endured his own whipping, he could have done nothing to stop it.

But I could have.

"It will get better," Zachariah is telling my husband. "I promise."

His grave tone reminds of what my mother said when she brought me the salve, about how Zachariah had endured his own harsh punishment many years ago. Thirty lashes. Ten is standard, and other than the foundlings who continue to fight our ways, I have never seen a punishment more severe. Even in the past when my mother's husband has had to be reprimanded, usually for touching a woman without permission, it is only five or ten lashes. But thirty? What could Zachariah, who is the most successfully integrated foundling we have ever had, done to require such a harsh punishment?

"How are the goats doing?" Jameson asks, and I know it has more to do with changing the subject than because he cares about the goats.

"Nan is pregnant." Zachariah shakes his head like the goat has disappointed him. "Again."

The men talk for a moment about the animals while I stare at Hawk. Something about him has changed, but I cannot say what. He seems more closed off. Sad, even. Does it have to do with Dawn?

When Zachariah looks toward Hawk, an expression of pain scrunches up his face, and he lets out a deep breath, almost like he is trying to push the hurt away, then he says, "Hawk, take Jameson to the goat pen. He has been away for a week, and he must miss the animals."

Hawk turns, and Jameson goes without protest, Zip trotting along after him. My husband must realize Zachariah wishes to have a private word with me, because I know he does not miss the animals or their shit—as he calls it.

When they are gone, Zachariah says, "Hawk is healing, but his relationship with Dawn may not."

I have no idea how to respond to this. It is unheard of, at least with a yieldling. If Dawn finds herself displeased with her husband, she can stop inviting him to her bed, but she can also choose to end the relationship. Which will result in an end for the man. I cannot comprehend something so extreme happening, but I also cannot forget the gleeful way she picked up the whip when Jameson was kneeling in front of her, or the evil expression on her face when she looked at me. Dawn is a cold person, dark on the inside like a cave.

"What does my mother say?" I ask Zachariah.

"I do not know." He looks down, but he cannot hide the sadness in his eyes, and for the first time I realize how much this punishment has shifted things in our village. "She has asked me to come to her, but I have not. I know I risk punishment," Zachariah winces at the thought, "but I cannot make myself go. Hawk's screams stay with me at night, and I cannot forget how Raven stood by and let Dawn whip Jameson. It was wrong. What happened that day was more wrong than anything I have seen since coming here."

I reach out, placing my hand on his arm in a way I never have before, and as suddenly as a bolt of lightning, a memory comes to me. I remember Zachariah kneeling at my side after Jameson's punishment, and how he slipped his hand over mine, giving me the warmth and comfort I needed during such a horrible moment. I had forgotten all about it, too wrapped up in my husband's pain to remember how Zachariah risked punishment so he could comfort me.

"I am sorry, Zachariah."

I want to say more, to thank him not just for that moment, but for all the times he has been there for me over the years. My mother and I have always had a close relationship, which is normal in our village, but she is not a warm person. When I was young and got hurt, Raven rarely comforted me, and even though I know she was only trying to teach me to be strong, it was a difficult thing to live with as a child. I craved her hugs, her comfort, but I rarely got them.

Zachariah, however, did fill that role for me at times, and when he lifts his head and meets my gaze now, those moments come back like a waterfall of memories.

"You have grown to be a very good woman, Wilderness." Like so many times before, the expression in his eyes is confusing, reminding me of the way my mother looked at me when I was young and made my first bullseye, only the emotion in Zachariah's eyes goes much deeper than pride.

I let my hand drop, feeling like I should say or do something, but unsure what that something is.

This man means a lot to my mother, but he means something to me as well. It is difficult to put into words, and even more difficult to understand. All I know is that in this village, a man who is not my husband should mean nothing to me, and yet Zachariah does.

"I will make sure nothing happens to Hawk," I say instead of addressing my feelings. "Dawn will not go unpunished for her jealousy and hatred."

"I fear you are overestimating Raven. She is strong in almost every way, but her fear makes her weak, and she is very afraid of what will become of this place if she embraces her feelings. She does not understand that love can make you stronger."

Zachariah's words are the opposite of what my mother told me not too long ago. She believes love is a disadvantage, that it will cloud your judgment or make you weak, which is why she has never told Zachariah she loves him. Back then, I was not sure how I felt, but a lot has changed, and I now know I do not agree with her. I cannot. Not after everything I have seen.

"I believe she will see things differently after what happened with Dawn," I say.

Zachariah exhales, but there is very little hope in his voice when he says, "I pray you are right, Wilderness."

CHAPTER NINETEEN

Jameson

THREE WEEKS GO BY BEFORE WILDERNESS LETS ME GO back to work in the men's village. Her concern touches me in a way I didn't even know possible, but being cooped up in her hut all day and night makes me feel like a prisoner for the first time since she took me as her husband. Even if I thought the women would be okay with me wandering around their village, I wouldn't want to, but I can't bring myself to admit to anyone other than myself why.

Dawn. The expression on the warrior's face when she picked up the whip still haunts me. I pictured it every time the leather slashed across my skin, and felt her evilness seeping into my wounds as my blood seeped out. Why she has so much hate inside her when there seems to be nothing in this village but harmony is a damn mystery, but the last thing I want to do is risk bumping into her on one of the walkways. She's liable to push me over.

On my first day back in the men's village, Zachariah refuses to let me do anything strenuous, so I end up pulling weeds with the younger yieldlings. I'm on the edge of the field, hunched over and trying to ignore the throbbing in my back, when a teenage boy with blond hair and freckles stops at my side.

"Water." He sets a bucket on the ground and nods to it.

"Thanks." My scalp prickles when his brown eyes focus on my back.

I scoop out a handful of water and suck the cool liquid down, repeating the process two more times before offering a handful to Zip. The dog laps it up while the boy watches in silence. The longer he stares, the more the tingles spread across my scalp until it feels like my hair is sticking straight up. He has to be close to seventeen, which makes him a good eight years younger than Wilderness, but the striking similarity is impossible to deny. This is one of her brothers.

"What's your name?" I ask.

There's a slight unsteadiness in his movements when he shifts from foot to foot, and I notice the way the lower half of his left leg bows out. Like it was broken years ago and didn't set right.

"Talon," he finally says.

"I'm Jameson." I stick my hand out but drop my arm when he frowns, reminding myself they don't shake hands here. "Thanks for the water."

The boy scoops the bucket up. "You are welcome, Jameson," he says before turning away.

I smile at the way he rolls my name around in his mouth, exactly the way his father, sister, and brother do. Hawk, I already figured out, and Ash, and now Talon, but according to Zachariah, there should be one more brother somewhere in the men's village. One more boy Raven gave up without a second thought.

I spend the rest of the day studying the yieldlings in their late teens and early twenties, searching for one who resembles the rest of the family, only there are none. I'm sure of it, and when we meet around the fire for dinner, I become even more certain. Most of the men in this village have dark hair and bronzed skin, meaning Zachariah's fair hair and easily sun-scorched complexion stand out. Hawk and Talon take after him, as does Wilderness, and Ash has darker hair, but the same pale skin, while Raven, too, is fair, making me think her father was a foundling as well. Possibly even her grandfather, considering how predominant the fair skin and blond hair seem to be.

So, where's the fourth boy?

After we've eaten, the boys and young men run toward the forest, whooping in excitement, and oddly enough, Zip takes off after them instead of waiting for me. He isn't alone, and when the other dogs run into the forest as well, as excited as the yieldlings, I turn to Zachariah with my eyebrows raised.

"The pond," he says, answering my silent question. "You have missed the swims because you were healing, but we take turns with the women during the hot summer months."

Swimming. It sounds like a fairy tale.

Growing up, I remember a couple times when the hydrants in our neighborhood broke and kids would run through them, reveling in the cool water. I never got to go to a pool or a pond or the ocean, though, at least not for fun. I worked at the docks and came home every night stinking of fish and pollution from the bay, and even the two times I went out on the sea, it was nothing but work—although the view helped ease the ache of dragging nets full of fish from the ocean. But I've never once jumped into a pond so I could cool off.

"What is it?" Zachariah asks as we head to the forest side by side.

"It's strange to feel at home after everything that's happened. I didn't choose to come here, and I was beaten to within an inch of my life—" His expression hardens, but I wave my hand to let him know that's not why I brought it up. "But this world is better than anything I could've imagined, and I do feel oddly at home." *Almost.*

I don't add the last word because I don't want to dampen the good mood, but of everyone here, Zachariah would be the one to understand. He's happy here, but he could be happier, because if it were up to him, he'd choose a house with his wife and five children.

"I am the same," he says after a few seconds. "Before coming here, I did not understand that life could be easy or happy. It seemed everyone I knew accepted that things were hard. Here, though, things move like the seasons. Even the bad things have brought me joy. I cannot explain it, I just know this is where I was meant to be."

His mention of bad things makes me think of Talon's bowed leg, and then the missing son. I wonder how Zachariah's son broke his leg. In the city, a doctor would have been able to set it right and put it in a cast, meaning Talon wouldn't have a limp. Maybe something similar happened to Zachariah's fifth child. Maybe the boy got sick, and they didn't have the right medicine to make him better. Maybe he fell from a tree or got attacked by a bear. Maybe he would have survived whatever killed him if he were in the city instead of out here in the middle of nowhere.

It takes a few minutes of Zachariah and me walking in silence before I work up the nerve to ask. "What happened to your fourth son? I already figured out who the others are, Ash, Hawk, and Talon. But there was another."

Zachariah looks my way out of the corner of his eye, but he doesn't act like I've overstepped by asking, and something about his expression warms me. It's welcoming and familiar. Like he and I share a bond. That's something I've never had before—a man to look up to. A father figure.

"There was," he says quietly, nodding. "Come."

He veers off to the left, in the opposite direction the other men and boys ran, and motions for me to follow. I walk behind him, trying to avoid my back getting too scraped up by branches, and find my gaze drawn to his scars. The new ones, mostly healed now but still bright against his skin, and the older ones. There are more of those, and though they've faded over time, it's criminal that they exist at all. Not only because the punishments are so wrong, but because this man can't possibly have done anything to deserve a beating that would have left so many scars behind. He's the picture of compliance.

Zachariah doesn't stop until we've stepped through the trees and into the same clearing we came to when Spring died, and when he does, I freeze. It's been months since we were here and Canyon went off to find his end, but since then the grass has grown thicker, and the purple flowers have given way to other wild blossoms. It's still clear of debris, though, and something about it feels so clean and pure that it's hard to imagine this is where the villagers lay their dead.

"This is where he is." Zachariah sweeps his arm across the clearing, and my gaze is drawn to the stones poking up through the grass. "Reed came to me after Hawk but before Talon. He was only two, but joyful. He smiled a lot and laughed even more, and everywhere he went, he left happiness behind.

"When he was four, he was playing in the forest with some of the other yieldlings. I heard his scream from across the village, but there was nothing I could do. Not for a rattlesnake bite. He met his end a day later in my arms." Zachariah lets out a deep sigh, and when a tear rolls down his cheek, he doesn't look at me, but he also doesn't try to wipe it away. "It was the only other time I felt like a mountain stood between Raven and me. I could not understand why she stayed away when our son was hurting so much, and I had a hard time forgiving her. I had just made up my mind to leave, to go into the woods and find my own end so I could be with my son, but when I went to her hut to tell her, I heard her crying. She did not want me to see her pain, but I went in anyway. That is when I understood. She does what she must to keep the village strong, and even if I do not always agree with her decisions, she does not make them because she does not care. She cares very, very much."

I listen to Zachariah in silence, hurting because he hurts. I've grown to despise Raven, but I don't disagree with him. She does care about this village and the people here, but she doesn't understand what she's doing. Not to her husband, not to her daughter, and not to her people.

I say nothing, and after a moment he turns to face me. In the bright light of the sun, his pale, blue eyes look translucent, and it feels almost like I can see every thought and emotion swirling through him.

"I have thought about the things you said," he begins, "about this place and how these women are not unlike the men in Vegas. You are wrong, but you are also right. The difference is that they are not doing these things to hurt the way those men did. They are not right, but they do not mean to be evil, and they believe what they are doing is the only way to stay safe.

"For a long time, I thought Raven would be the one to change things. Even after she gave up our first two sons, I believed she could be better. I no longer believe she has it in her, but I can see something in Wilderness that gives me hope. You cannot push these things, though. You cannot force change to come about if the women are not ready. I know you have bitterness toward Raven over what happened to you, but trust me when I tell you she is not evil. Things are much better now than they were when her mother was High Elder, and when Wilderness is in charge, they will be better still. Patience is rewarded."

"Is that what happened to you?" I ask, nodding so he'll understand I'm referring to the scars on his back. "Did Raven's mother do that?"

Zachariah looks down. "It was a long time ago."

"Not long enough for the scars to fade."

He exhales but doesn't lift his head. "There is much truth in your words, but I have no desire to talk about it. Not right now.

"Let us join the other men at the pond." Zachariah heads toward the forest. "It is hot, and I could use a swim."

IT'S DARK WHEN WE RETURN FROM THE POND, AND I STEP INTO the men's village to find Wilderness waiting. She crosses to me, worry written in every line of her face. When she stops in front of me, she makes me turn, her touch gentle, and rests her hand against my wounds, her soft touch reminding me of the salve she spread across my injuries when they were fresh.

"I was worried about you," she says.

I turn to face her, not even hesitating to take her hand, but she doesn't blink, doesn't tell me I don't have permission to touch her. She only stares up at me with eyes swimming with worry.

"I'm okay," I tell her. "I told you I would be."

Wilderness walks backward, toward the forest, our fingers intertwined as she pulls me with her. "Come. This is not your home."

We pass Zachariah, who for once isn't smiling, but instead watches us with a hopeful expression on his face as if, through us, he's able to glimpse a different future.

Wilderness leads me from the men's village and through the forest, her hand in mine as we walk side by side. For the first time since arriving here, I don't feel like a second-class citizen. We're equals, Wilderness and I. Partners. Husband and Wife.

Once we're back in her hut, I reach for the leather ties holding her clothes in place. It's been weeks since we were together, and all I want right now is to be one with this woman.

"Your back is not healed enough," she says, trying to push my hand away.

"It is," I whisper.

I hold her gaze and pull on the string, and she smiles up at me as the fur covering her flesh falls away, sliding to the floor and leaving her exposed. I take her in, every inch. From the first moment I laid eyes on her, I thought Wilderness was a beautiful woman, but something about the way I see her has changed over the last few weeks. The small scar on her chin from when she fell out of a tree at the age of ten doesn't look like a flaw anymore, but is instead a tiny piece of the puzzle that when fit together makes her who she is. The scar represents tenacity, because she didn't let the tree win, but climbed it again the very next day, making it all the way to the top.

I hold her face in my palm, rubbing my thumb against the scar, then move my hand down to touch the one on her arm that she got when scaling the mountain, and another on her side, the result of an altercation with a wild cat. Then I kneel in front of her so I can see the one on the inside of her knee, which is the product of yet another tree climbing incident, only this time she was running from a bear and cut her leg on the way up. Every mark, every scar is beautiful.

"What is it?" she asks when I don't say anything.

I look up at her from where I kneel on the ground, but the way she towers over me no longer feels like she's the master and I'm the slave. Something in her eyes tells me she doesn't want it to feel that way either, and when she kneels in front of me, it cements the thought in my head. We're eye level now, Wilderness and me. Equals.

"I love you," I whisper, saying the words that have been churning through me since my punishment. At first they felt wrong, like letting them out would be another lock on my prison door, but not anymore, because now I know this woman isn't a prison guard, and she doesn't want to be my master. No matter how I got here, things are different now. "Even if I have to face a thousand more punishments, it will be worth it because I'm with you."

Her eyes shimmer, and when she leans forward and presses her lips against mine, she says, "I love you, and I am not afraid of these feelings. I do not think they will destroy me or make me weak. As long as I am standing, you will never again have to face a punishment."

PART II: Husband and Wife

CHAPTER TWENTY

Wilderness

JAMESON DOES NOT RETURN TO THE MEN'S VILLAGE TO sleep, but instead stays with me. We are one almost every night, and in the darkness of my hut, when he tells me he loves me, I repeat the words without shame. Despite my mother's fears, I know my love does not give my husband an advantage over me. It does not make me weak.

The guilt does not come until after the sun has risen and I rejoin the women. My feelings for Jameson are not what bring it, but the sense that my place in the village has changed, and with it comes uncertainty for the future. My mother's words about keeping a wall between her husband and herself have not faded, only I now know she is wrong. All this is wrong. The rest of the women do not share my feelings, my mother especially, and the rift between us has grown until it feels like we are standing on opposites sides of a great canyon.

Three cycles after we ended the two foundlings, David, the third one, is still little more than a shadow of his former self. Jameson tells me how the foundling walks like a ghost through the men's village, doing his work but never talking to anyone. He looks at the people who pass him like they will slit his throat at any moment, and even when he goes into Ivy's hut, he acts like the wind is out to end him. She is not yet with child, but I fear it will not be long before she chooses to end her husband simply because he is too much work for the village.

Hawk has returned to Dawn, but like David, the punishment has changed my childhood friend. We see one another in passing, but he refuses to look me in the eye, and I do not know if he blames me for what happened or if he is afraid it will happen again if we talk. His distance stings even more than the chasm separating Raven and me, but I have to believe my childhood friend can come back from this. He is a yieldling, and much stronger than the cut of a whip.

Dawn is who I worry about the most. Something in her snapped that day, and it seems as if she is always watching Hawk. I find her standing in the forest at the edge of the men's village throughout the day, watching her husband like she believes he will be the next man to run. In the evening when he comes to her, she waits for him on the walkway and watches as he ascends the ladder. Her gaze is more predator than human now, and I worry that if Hawk looks the wrong way, she will swoop in and cut his throat.

Long after Zachariah has returned to Raven's bed, the distance between my mother and me remains. He and I do not speak of her, but the longing in his eyes tells me he aches for things to go back to the way they were, but I fear that the part she played in Jameson's punishment has made reconciliation impossible. Dawn wielded the whip, but my mother's hand was on it as well, and the memory of my husband's screams have not faded. Perhaps they never will.

The leaves above us change from green to brown and orange and gold, then drop to the ground, covering the village. The days grow shorter, the air cooler, and I find myself out in the woods more and more, hunting to prepare for the winter ahead. The bite to the wind tells me it is coming much sooner than usual, and I want to be sure no one goes hungry.

"It's weird having a shirt on after months of not wearing one," my husband says as we dress for the day, while at his feet, Zip wags his tail like we are discussing throwing him scraps instead of our clothes.

I wrap myself in fur as Jameson adjusts the pelt covering his own chest, acting like the feel of it is unwelcome.

It makes me smile, and I say, "I remember a time when you thought not wearing one was strange."

A flicker of light plays with his features when he looks my way, making them sharpen and change. "That's true. It seems like a long time ago, but it was only a little more than six months. That's it."

We do not mark the passing of time the way the outside world does, but I have gotten used to hearing him speak this way, so I nod. "Yes, there have been many cycles since then."

And my own cycles as well, which I do not mention.

Despite the time my husband and I have spent together, my cycles have continued, each one signaling that Jameson's seed is not yet growing inside me. With each passing day, my worry that I will never know the joy of having a daughter grows, but it is something I keep to myself. These things take time; it is normal and nothing to worry about, or at least that is what I try to tell myself. Hawk and Dawn have been together for much longer, and she is not yet with child. It will happen for me.

I pull a thick fur off the bed and wrap it around my husband's shoulders. "It will be cold today. I can smell the snow in the air."

He lifts his eyebrows like he suspects I am lying. "Can you?"

I grin, marveling at the man in front of me, of how much we have come to care about one another and how much my life has changed. "Wait. You will see."

We leave the hut together, Zip trailing behind us like a shadow. Jameson rests his hand on my lower back as we walk, and the women we pass shoot me looks of disappointment or confusion, but I no longer care if they approve. Jameson is my husband, and he can touch me whenever he wants because it is what I want. All my life, I have been taught that an uninvited touch is bad, but no one ever told me how good it can feel to have someone you love rest their hand on your back. It is like he cannot bear to have me away from him. Like he wants us to never be apart.

When we reach the pulley cart, Zip climbs in just as he does every morning. Bringing the dog up to my hut every night was awkward at first it, but it felt wrong to leave him on the ground when he refused to go back to the men's village without Jameson. Now, Zip is used to the ride and knows to lie down and wait while we pull him up and down.

He hops out when the cart reaches the ground and sits at the bottom of the ladder, waiting for us to descend. The bite in the wind tells me I was right about the snow, and I lift my face to the sky when I reach the ground, half expecting to find flakes already falling. They are not, but it will not be long.

Jameson, Zip, and I cross through the forest and into the men's village. There is already a flurry of activity as the yieldlings work to secure pens, covering the sides to block out the wind and snow they, too, know is on the way. When they finish, they will bring piles of leaves in from the forest so the animals can keep warm during the long winter. Soon the snow will fall, and like the animals, we will burrow into our huts, spending more and more time curled up under furs to stay warm. For the first time, I will have someone to keep me company, and the thought of Jameson's naked body curling around mine makes me long for a blizzard.

"It looks like Zachariah needs help with the goats," I say, nodding to my mother's husband, who is in the middle of securing a wall of wood to the side of the pen.

Jameson plants a kiss on the side of my head. "Shoot straight."

"I do not know how to shoot any other way."

He smiles before running over to help with the goats, and Zip charges ahead of him like they are in a race.

I head through the village, nodding to the men I pass. Like Zachariah, Hawk is preparing an animal pen for the snow when a gust of wind whips through the village and grabs the wall, pulling it from his grasp. He kneels to lift it once again, gritting his teeth under the weight, and instinctively, I go over to help. Together, we manage to get it in place, but the wind fights us every step of the way.

"I will hold it if you secure it," I say, putting my weight into the wall.

Hawk nods but says nothing, and the way he avoids my gaze makes my heart ache for the little boy I played with. I hate the distance between us. Hate that he refuses to look me in the eye.

The wind beats against the wood at my back, and I have to dig my heels into the ground to keep it in place, but it takes no time at all for Hawk to get it nailed to the side of the pen, and then I am able to relax.

Once it is up, he turns and looks at me for the first time in many cycles. "Thank you, Wilderness."

"You are welcome." He starts to walk away, but I stop him by saying, "Do you blame me?"

Hawk turns halfway back to me, but keeps his eyes on the wall we just put up. "I do not."

"Then why do you refuse to look at me?"

"I am not your husband, Wilderness, and Dawn does not like it when I talk to you."

I knew it, but it still fills me with sadness. "I am glad you are okay, Hawk."

He still refuses look at me, and when I turn away and head through the men's village, there are tears in my eyes. Dawn is right, Hawk is not my husband, but I do not care about him in that way. There was a time when my feelings for him confused me, but they no longer do because I know what it is to love a man. Hawk was the first friend I had, and the years have not been long enough to push those feelings away completely.

Once the sounds from the village have faded, I force all thoughts of Hawk from my mind and focus instead on keeping my steps light. My feet crunch against the forest floor, but my steps are quiet enough that they should not alert any nearby animals to my presence.

The sharp scent of earth fills my nostrils with every breath I take in, but it cannot chase away the moisture clinging to the air, and when the first flake drifts to the ground, I am not surprised. More follow, and in only a few blinks the snow picks up, growing thick and making it difficult to see more than a stone's throw in front of me.

That is when the sound of footsteps reaches me. They crunch against the forest floor, and I stop walking, lifting my bow as I scan the surrounding trees, but see nothing other than a wall of fluttering, white flakes. More footsteps cut through the silence, headed my way, and I turn toward the sound. Still, the snow and trees are thick, and the animal is not yet visible, so I hold my breath and wait.

When it finally rips out of the forest, it takes me completely by surprise. I release my arrow, but the shot is wide, and I only have a moment to be glad I missed before the streak of orange slams into me and pushes the thought from my mind.

Dawn and I hit the ground in a painful ball of arms and legs. She lands on top, and before I have even had a chance to fill my lungs, she is sitting, her legs straddling my stomach and her body forcing the little bit of air left inside my lungs out in one painful whoosh.

The hate and anger in her eyes snaps my brain to attention, and I realize she is attacking me. My bow is still in my hand, and I bring it up on instinct, slamming it against her head. Dawn cries out but stays where she is, her weight pressing into me, and a beat later she rips the weapon from my hand and tosses it aside.

"Dawn," I grunt, trying to push her off. "Stop."

She is a warrior, though, and much stronger than I am, making it impossible to gain any ground. I do not stop struggling, not even when she brings her fist down and her knuckles make contact with my eye and upper cheek. The sharp sting of bone hitting bone is enough to knock the wind out of me a second time, and when her hands slide around my throat, my lungs are already empty.

She squeezes, her fingers tightening on my neck until it feels like it will break, and I claw at her hands and kick my legs but cannot get free. Above me, Dawn's eyes snap and crackle like fire, her face a picture of calm as she tries to squeeze the life out of me.

Pain spreads through my neck and down my body, settling in my lungs until it feels like they are burning. Darkness claws its way across my vision, and my mouth opens and closes as I try to fill my lungs, but all I get is a mouthful of snow. I barely have time to register the icy chill before the flakes have melted, but it seems to seep into my bones and turn my blood to ice. Even as blackness overtakes my vision, I begin to shiver.

She is ripped off me so fast that her nails leave a trail of pain behind on my neck, and air rushes into my lungs, thick and wet with snow, and I cough. I roll onto my side and gasp like none of the oxygen made it into me, and each time I inhale, it feels as if the air is scorching my insides.

"Get off!" Dawn screams from behind me.

My vision is still fuzzy when I turn, and it takes a moment to register what I am seeing. Hawk is holding Dawn, his arms around her waist, and she struggles against his grasp while his face reddens like holding onto her is difficult. Her face is a mask of anger, her eyes crackling more than ever.

"I did not invite you to touch me!" she growls, twisting in her husband's grasp. "You will pay for this. You do not have the right to put your hands on me."

That snaps Hawk out of it, and he releases her.

Dawn drops to the ground and scrambles back, but she does not get to her feet. I am still on the ground, shivering as snow falls on my body, and her fiery gaze snaps back and forth between her husband and me. Every breath I take in feels like fingernails scratching the inside of my throat, and my head sways like it is not attached to my body.

"What did you do?" Hawk asks after a moment, staring down at Dawn.

"You will be punished," she spits at him. "You do not touch me. Not unless I invite you."

The image of the whip cracking against Hawk's back makes my stomach twist, and I find the strength to push myself up on my knees. "No, Dawn. Do not—"

Her cold eyes focus on me, cutting my sentence in half. "You. I have been watching you. I knew you would not be able to stay away from him. You have a husband, but you have always wanted mine. I know. I know the spell you have cast on him, and the one you have cast on me. We have been together for over a year, and I am still not with child. This is your doing!"

"It is not like that," I say. "Hawk and I were children together. We were friends. That is all."

"I will not hear it." She pushes herself up, climbing to her feet with great effort even though she is not injured the way I am. "Raven will hear of this, and Hawk will be punished."

She dashes into the forest, leaving us behind.

I am still on the ground, snow falling on my head and fur and covering me like it wants to bury me alive while Hawk stands over me. He does not move, and the way he stares at the ground makes it look like he is wishing for his end, or even expecting it.

"My mother will not let this happen," I tell him.

"She did before."

He is right, and I want to tell him I do not believe it will happen again, but it is impossible because I cannot speak for anything my mother does or will do. If she allows this to happen, though, it will change everything about the village. It could set something in motion that will destroy us, rip us apart the way nothing has been able to over the last seventy years.

"How did you find us?" I ask instead.

"I saw her standing at the edge of the forest after you left the men's village, and I did not like the expression in her eyes." Hawk lifts his gaze so he can look at me, but his head is still down when he says, "Dawn has changed. In the beginning, she treated me like I was a prize, but now she acts like I am a possession. Her jealousy controls her, not only with you, but with the other women as well. Even with Zachariah. She does not want me to talk to anyone else."

"I am sorry, Hawk."

I pull myself to my feet, coughing when the breath I suck in scratches my throat. I can imagine the purple bruises Dawn's hands have left behind. There are no punishments for women, my mother said, only men, but this cannot stand. Dawn tried to end me, and she cannot be allowed to go on like everything is normal.

"We must return to the village, Hawk. Dawn must answer for what she has done."

I sweep my bow up off the ground before heading into the forest, Hawk following me, keeping a distance and saying nothing.

The men's village is empty when we reach it, and Hawk still has not uttered a word. He acts like he can barely lift his head, and the fear and sadness in his expression beg for me to protect him. I cannot let anything happen to Hawk, not again. Dawn cannot be allowed to win.

We cross through the empty village to the forest and have only made it a few steps when the sound of voices reach us, rising and falling, bouncing off the trees and swirling around us with the snow. The closer we get to the women's village, the louder the commotion becomes, and we step out of the trees only to be met with anger. The crowd gathered around Dawn turns on us like a pack of wild animals, the accusations in their eyes making me want to shrink away even though I know I have to keep going or they will never know the truth.

"Bring the whip!" Dawn calls when she spots us. Her hair is a tangle of orange around her face, and her pale skin as white as the snow currently falling from the sky.

"Dawn." I turn at the sound of my mother's voice. "If a punishment is to be dealt, it is not up to you to decide."

She and Zachariah are the only voices of reason, but I am not sure if it will be enough to save Hawk. Unless I do something, unless I find the strength I lacked when Jameson faced his punishment, not even Raven will be able to change the course Dawn has set us on.

The orange-haired warrior's eyes flash when she looks from Hawk and me to my mother, and I see it again, the same evil that glinted in her eyes when she struck my husband. I want to run forward, to knock her to the ground, but if I do that, no one will bother to listen to what I have to say. No one will be able to hear me if I attack Dawn now.

"They have betrayed me." She points a shaky finger at me. "Wilderness has cursed my womb and treated my husband like her own. Hawk will answer for what he has done, and then we must deal with Wilderness."

A murmur moves through the crowd, louder among the other warriors than anyone else. These are the women Dawn is closest with, and like her, they have blood and vengeance on their minds. Hawk must sense this, too, because he shrinks back.

Rain moves like she is going for the whip, and I step forward, no longer able to remain silent. "Stop. The things Dawn said are not true."

Her face contorts, twisting her features until she looks like a rabid animal, but doubt flickers across the faces of the other women, and it gives me courage.

"Hawk is innocent of what she says, as am I. We were children together, and I remember that, so I talk to him, but nothing else. I have a husband." I look toward Jameson, who is standing on the other side of Zachariah, half expecting to see the same accusations on his face, but there is only worry. Only fear. "I love Jameson, as you can all attest to. He is in my hut every night. When would I have time to be with Hawk? We work during the day.

You all see the game I bring in." I turn my gaze on Dawn. "I have done nothing wrong, but she attacked me in the forest. Tried to end me. She would have succeeded, too, but Hawk came to my aid. If he had not pulled Dawn off me, I would have met my end today."

I pull my furs aside to reveal my throat, and the gasps that move through the crowd tell me the bruising is as bad as I thought it would be.

Jameson is at my side in the blink of an eye, and when he strokes my injured neck, another murmur moves through the crowd. I look at no one but him.

"Are you okay?" he murmurs.

"I will heal."

He leans down and kisses my throat, and at the touch of his lips, I let out a deep breath.

"Enough!" Raven's voice rises above the murmurs, and the crowd goes silent.

Snow falls from the sky in steady flakes that are big and fat. They land on the leaves at our feet but do not melt. Already around the base of the trees there is a coating of white, and I know that soon the forest will be covered in a thick blanket. Winter has arrived.

My mother turns on Dawn. "Is this true?"

The other woman looks around with wide eyes that radiate madness. "She was trying to steal my husband. That is why I attacked her. I had to stop them."

My mother lets out a deep breath, and steam rises up in front of her, carried away by the wind. "We have never had something like this happen in our village, but it cannot go unpunished." She turns to Rain. "You will take Dawn to her hut and stand guard so she cannot hurt anyone else. The

Elders and I will meet to discuss what happens next."

Rain hesitates, her dark eyes moving to her friend, but Dawn's eyes are still wide and angry, not afraid but full of vengeance. Rain must be able to see the madness as well, because she finally moves to her friend's side.

Dawn only fights a little when Rain pulls her through the crowd. They part for her, creating a wide gap like they fear the madness is catching, and once she has disappeared, the men and women begin to disperse. They are silent, though, the shock of what happened still thick, but the snow is coming down harder now, and there is much work to be done.

When the crowd has thinned, my mother crosses to me, as does Zachariah. She reaches out to touch my neck just like Jameson did only a moment ago, and though we have not spoken in many cycles, I do not shrink away. The pain and worry on her face make it impossible to stay angry with her, at least for the moment.

"I am sorry," she says, her fingers brushing my injured neck. "This is my doing. You told me something needed to be done about Dawn, but I did not listen. I was afraid to alter our customs, and my fear almost cost your life."

"Hawk was there to save me," I say.

My mother's expression does not change when she looks at Hawk, almost like his pain hurts her as much as mine does. "Thank you."

He lifts his eyes to meet hers, nodding twice, but still says nothing.

"You do not need to be afraid," she tells him. "There will be no punishment. There should not have been last time, either. I have learned from my mistakes, and I will not repeat them."

"Thank you, Raven." His voice is cold, icier than even the winter air.

She smiles, but it is sad, and when she turns to Jameson, my entire body stiffens. Is she going to mention how he touched me in front of everyone?

"Take my daughter to her hut and look after her," is the only thing my mother says.

When my husband reaches for me, I take his hand, and together we head for the trees.

CHAPTER TWENTY-ONE

Jameson

WILDERNESS AND I ARE LAID OUT ON HER BED, naked and wrapped in one another's arms, but no matter how many times I kiss the bruised skin on her neck and face, it doesn't feel like enough. Inside me, anger twists into a ball until it threatens to explode, and I have to stop myself from running out the door to hunt Dawn down so I can kill her.

"I want to strangle her," I say against Wilderness's skin.

She threads her fingers through my hair and pulls me closer. Her bare skin is like home these days, and at the moment I feel like I can't possibly get close enough.

"She will be punished."

I pull back so I can look Wilderness in the eye. "How? Will they whip her?"

"It is hard to say, but I doubt it. After the last time, I do not think my mother will be so quick to hand out whippings. But Dawn is dangerous, and she cannot be allowed to stay here."

"Exile?" I ask, wondering if it's something these people even understand.

"Perhaps, but most likely she will meet her end."

I look away because I'm afraid to let Wilderness see the vengeance in my eyes. The thought of watching Dawn die feels right. Every time I think of what she almost took from me, I imagine my own hands wrapped around her neck or that I'm the one holding the knife as it slices her throat open. It's a feeling I don't like, but I can't push it away. She almost killed Wilderness.

"The bigger question is, what will become of Hawk?" When Wilderness frowns, it accentuates the bruise at the corner of her eye. "If Dawn is no longer here, then he is no longer a husband."

The anger I felt the day Canyon left bubbles up inside me, momentarily overshadowing my fury at Dawn. He was never seen again, at least not that I know of, but since that day I've found myself thinking about him hundreds of times, imagining what might have happened to him. Every image I conjure up is different, but each one is as senseless as the last. Sometimes a bear attacks him, while other times he falls off a cliff and dies a slow and horrible death, and at times I imagine it was nothing but a simple case of starvation or dehydration.

"Would your mother send Hawk away?"

Wilderness shakes her head, but there's fear and uncertainty in her brown eyes when she says, "I do not know."

The whole thing with Dawn was a shock, but at the same time, it wasn't. The women built this world around the idea that men are evil and need to be kept away, and yet Dawn—a woman who was sworn to protect the village—was the one who tried to murder someone.

"Wilderness," I say, keeping my voice low and gentle.

"Yes?" She puts her hand on my cheek, and I lean into it. "What is it?"

"I need to say something about Dawn."

She shifts so she's facing me, her body pressed up against me as her gaze holds mine. "Tell me what is going through your head."

I take a deep breath, gathering strength before going on, not because I'm afraid to tell Wilderness what I'm thinking, but because I'm afraid of what it might do to her. Afraid it will change how she sees everything. This world is a lie, and it's something she needs to know, but I don't like the idea of hurting her, and the truth could hurt her very much.

"What happened to your ancestors in the hotel was wrong and horrible, and it was evil," I begin, "but this whole thing with Dawn should prove it isn't men alone who have the capacity to be evil. Women, too, can do horrible things. Just like there are good women and evil women, there are evil men and good men."

She says nothing, and when her silence stretches out, I start to wonder if she heard me at all even though we're only inches apart. Then, out of nowhere, she kisses me.

"You are good," she says against my lips. "I do believe you, but I am powerless to change the way things are. At least right now. One day, maybe we will be something different, but the women are not yet ready to face such a big change. All we can do is wait for the right moment and hope it comes in our lifetime." She looks into my eyes, her lips so close they tickle my mouth when she says, "Can you wait?"

I wrap her in my arms, rolling her onto her back so my body is over hers. She moves, spreading her thighs until I'm nestled between them, her warmth begging for me to be closer.

"As long as I'm with you," I say, "I can wait for anything."

THE NEXT DAY IS SO WHITE IT FEELS LIKE A DIFFERENT WORLD. The Elders call a meeting early in the morning, and everyone gathers in the women's village. Dawn is on her knees in the snow this time instead of a man, and even the frightened expression in her eyes can't make me regret what's about to happen. She showed too much pleasure in fulfilling my punishment, and she came too close to taking Wilderness from me. Maybe the thing I'm feeling is the evilness these women believe exists in all men, or maybe it's human nature. Maybe it's both.

Raven is as somber as I've ever seen her when she steps in front of Dawn. Snowflakes cling to the feather crown sitting atop her head, but she doesn't seem to notice the cold even though all around her the other women shiver in the early winter snow. Raven, however, doesn't even blink.

I stand with the men, at Zachariah's side as usual, and the distance between Wilderness and myself feels like miles rather than ten feet. She shivers, and I have to stop myself from crossing to her so I can wrap her in my arms. The bruise under her eye seems dark in the snowy day, and I feel like I should be there to hold her hand.

"This is a dark day in our history," Raven says, raising her voice so everyone can hear it over the groaning of the wind. "For decades, we have lived in peace, our unity giving our village strength. This act has gone against everything we stand for, and it has made us rethink how we do certain things. We have always punished the men as if they are the only ones who do wrong, but Dawn has proven that is not so. From this day on, punishments will be different. We cannot look the other way when someone has done wrong." She pauses and takes a deep breath, and when she looks down at Dawn, it seems to take a great deal of effort. "The Elders discussed showing mercy, but we fear we can no longer trust you. Not only did you try to end Wilderness, but you also told us a falsehood. Today, Dawn, you will meet your end."

A scattered murmur moves through the crowd, but it doesn't sound like shock or even anger, and it seems like most of the women knew this was coming. Based on Dawn's expression, she did as well.

"What of my husband?" she calls out, much louder than necessary. "If he is to leave after I am gone, then he should meet his end with me. Let him kneel at my side so we can be together in Paradise."

This time, the sound moving through the crowd is closer to a roar, as if Dawn's suggestion has horrified the other women. Wilderness shifts like she's about to move toward her mother, and Zachariah does take a small step forward. Raven doesn't look away from Dawn, but she must see it, because she lifts her hand in her husband's direction, motioning for him to stay where he is. Hawk, who stands on Zachariah's other side, is the only one who seems unaffected by the warrior's suggestion.

"Your request shows how twisted your mind has become. Hawk will not meet his end with you today, and the council has decided that he will not leave the village either. He has fulfilled his duty as your husband. He has stood by you, has stopped you from committing the ultimate transgression, and for that, he will be rewarded."

Dawn's face contorts and her eyes flash, but she doesn't speak. She keeps her gaze locked on Raven, and when the High Elder steps forward and pulls a knife from its place on her hip, Dawn raises her chin like she's offering herself.

"I hope you are able to find peace in Paradise," Raven says then draws the blade across the other woman's throat.

Blood flows from the cut, dark red against Dawn's pale skin, and her eyes grow wide as she falls forward, catching herself on her hands and knees. From where I'm standing, I can just make out the way her lips move, almost like she's trying to speak, but she doesn't utter a sound.

Blood pools under her, painting the snow, and it only takes a few seconds for her to collapse. All around her, the ground turns bright red as the life flows from her body, and when she finally goes still, the color drains from her skin, leaving her as white as the snowflakes dropping one by one onto her lifeless form.

CHAPTER TWENTY-TWO

Wilderness

AFTER THE OTHER WARRIORS HAVE DRAGGED DAWN'S body away, my husband and I return to my hut. We have not yet retired to bed when someone knocks on the door, and before I have even opened it, I know who will be standing there. Outside, a blanket of white covers the forest, and the snow sparkles like twinkling stars. It is still coming down, just as I predicted it would, and tomorrow it will no doubt go past my ankles in places.

My mother stands outside my door, her fur pulled around her and her gray hair looking suddenly dark against the fresh, white forest at her back. "Good eve, Wilderness."

"Good eve, Raven."

She looks past me, into the hut, and when she spots Jameson curled up on my bed, my mother shakes her head. "Your husband is here every night."

"He is." I straighten my shoulders to show her I will not back down. "I said as much yesterday when Dawn tried to accuse me of relations with Hawk. I will not apologize or ask Jameson to leave. He is my husband, and I want him here."

My mother exhales, and her breath comes out in a puff of steam. "I would never ask you to send him away, Wilderness, but I do worry you have given him too much of yourself. You must remain strong. You must be the leader. He should not touch you the way he does, not without an invitation."

I look my mother in the eye when I say, "I have invited him to touch me whenever he likes."

She shakes her head in disappointment yet again, but it does not surprise me. Raven and I do not view love the same way, and it makes me sad for her. Zachariah is a good man, as good as Jameson, and my mother has missed out on so much by not giving in to the feelings I know she has for him.

"I do not want you to be angry with me anymore," she says instead of continuing the conversation. "I know what happened at your husband's punishment hurt you, and I understand. I have told you I am sorry. I have told you I was wrong. Today, I hope you feel as if I have stood up for you."

"I do, and I am glad you chose not to send Hawk away."

The certainty in my mother's gaze wavers, and her eyes flick down like she does not want me to see the emotion swimming in them. "I could never do that."

I wait for her to say more, to explain why she stood up for Hawk, but she says nothing. Still, something is bothering her, I can tell. Something that has to do with Hawk…

"I remember playing with him." The words tumble out, but as soon as I have uttered them, I know it is what I wanted to say. I feel like there are gaps in my life, and I know Raven is one of the few people who can fill them in for me. She could answer some of the questions I have about the connection I share not only with Hawk, but with Zachariah as well, and if she would just do it, everything will start to make sense.

Though my words should not come as a surprise, my mother's head jerks up like they have shocked her. "Hawk?"

"Yes. I remember spending time with him before he went to live in the men's village. I remember us playing together in the trees."

"You spent much time together," is her only response.

Those memories are the strongest, but they are not alone. The tickle of memories has gotten more persistent since Jameson's arrival, and lately I have found it impossible not to think about my childhood and the yieldlings who played at my side.

"I remember others, too."

My mother swallows as if trying to hold her emotions back, but she remains silent, a pleading expression in her eyes. But what she is begging for, I do not know.

"Other yieldlings," I say, pressing her now, giving her the same look of pleading she is giving me.

"There are always yieldlings around," she whispers.

I wait for her to tell me more, to tell me she bore the yieldlings I remember, but she does nothing but stare at me like she cannot talk.

Disappointment surges through me when I realize she will not give in, and I let out a deep breath. "It was a long time ago."

"It was." She swallows again. "One day you will bear children, and you will understand it all more. It is not always an easy thing to talk about, and though it is how we choose to do things here, that does not mean there is no pain involved."

"I do not know if I will bear children."

I look over my shoulder at Jameson, who is still lying on the bed waiting for me, but see no indication that he is listening. He is undressed and covered in fur, and the sight of him causes a now familiar pang of desire to shoot through me. There's something else, too. Sadness. Fear.

I swallow the feelings down and turn back to my mother. "Jameson and I have been together for many cycles now, but I am still not with child. I fear it will never happen for me."

My mother places her hand on my arm, something she does so rarely that it makes the gesture twice as comforting. "You will be fine, Wilderness. It takes longer for some women than for others. Just be together as you have been. The winter is a good time to focus on it. Many children are born in late summer and early fall for this reason."

"I hope you are right," I say.

"I am."

My mother smiles, but the gesture seems hollow and empty now. There was a time when she could comfort me more than anyone else, but that is no longer so, and though it makes me sad for the past and how much has changed, I cannot bring myself to wish for things to go back the way they were. Not if it means Jameson disappearing from my life.

Raven steps back, and when the wind blows, she pulls the fur tighter around her body. Already the bloom from summer is fading from her complexion, and compared to the dark pelt, her skin seems pale and almost ghostly.

"I must return to my hut," she says. "Zachariah is waiting for me."

"Good eve, Raven." I step back into my own hut.

"Good eve, Wilderness," she replies.

I do not shut the door even after she has turned, but instead watch as she moves down the walkway. She is strong but thin, and although she does not tower over others the way Grove does, it sometimes feels like she is bigger than everyone else in the village. Raven is a born leader and can do many things to change the way we live, making it better for everyone, but she does not seem to understand that. Like the other Elders, she is stuck in the old ways and cannot see the damage they have inflicted on us.

What happened with Dawn is a product of that. I now know Hawk came from my mother just as I did, and that this is where our bond comes from, but because we did not grow up in the same hut, Dawn saw me as a threat. If my mother had taken the time to tell Dawn the truth, things might have turned out differently. Only she did not, and now Dawn has met her end. It was a costly mistake to make.

WINTER BRINGS SNOW AND ICE, AND DAYS THAT SEEM TO stretch out forever, and Jameson and I gladly take shelter in my hut, wrapping our bodies in fur and each other to keep warm. His presence is a constant I never thought I would have. He is at my side when I go to sleep and when I wake up, and I take him with me when I hunt despite the knowledge that my mother and the other Elders would never approve. I teach him to shoot a bow, how to take down a deer, and how to cut it open, and even show him secret places I went to as a child. A small cave on the side of the mountain only accessible by climbing along a rock ledge, and the tree I used to climb so I could see far into the world beyond our territory.

We go to the hot spring as well, undressing each other in the snow so we can slip into the warm depths of the pool. The steam wraps around us while we kiss, and I find myself believing that even if the water was as cold as the air, Jameson would be enough to keep me from freezing to death.

But we are not the only ones who brave the cold and wander the forest, and one afternoon during late winter, we come across Blossom and Hawk together in the woods. Thanks to the long winter days, I have seen very little of Hawk since Dawn met her end, and finding him with Blossom is not only a surprise, it also sends fear shooting through me. Her round belly serves as a reminder that the end of her pregnancy is approaching, but also that she had a husband who is no longer here. He has been gone for many cycles, but it has never been our custom for a woman to take a new husband, and in our village, Hawk has no right to spend time with a woman like this.

The guilt in their eyes answers all my questions before I have even had a chance to voice them, but I ask anyway, "What brings you to the forest on such a cold day?"

Blossom stares at the snow-covered ground, but Hawk has no trouble meeting my gaze. "We ran into one another. Blossom was walking in hopes of hurrying her baby along, and I was gathering sticks."

The falsehood comes out so smoothly I want to believe my friend, but I cannot. Not when the truth is staring right at me.

"Be careful, Hawk. My mother has shown you mercy, but it is not bound to happen again. Give her time, and she may see things in a different light, but if you challenge her now, it will be like poking a bear when it is already angry."

Fear swims in Blossom's eyes, but I cannot regret the warning. My mother is afraid of allowing our traditions to slip away, and letting Hawk stay was a turn of events she could come to regret. Especially if he tries to force her hand.

When they have gone, I turn to my husband. "Raven will not change, and I worry Hawk is moving in a direction that will lead to his end."

"She wouldn't do that to him," Jameson says, but his frown tells me the same fears live inside him.

Hawk may have come from her womb, but there are many things my mother is willing to sacrifice to maintain our way of life, and to her, he is still nothing more than a yieldling.

EVERY PASSING CYCLE HAS ME WISHING FOR NEWS, BUT disappointment follows me like a shadow through the cold winter months. The days grow longer and the ice begins to melt, and soon flowers poke their heads through the snow, decorating the ghostly forest in spots of color. Then the sun gets hotter, and the news I have been waiting for finally comes.

I mark the passing days by carving lines into a wooden post in my hut, wanting to be certain before I tell Jameson. When there are fifteen marks lined up in a row, and my cycle still has not come, I know it has finally happened. I expected the relief that surges through me, but not the swell of happiness. All my life, I have been told motherhood is my duty, but I did not anticipate the joy. I also could not have predicted the excitement I would feel at the thought of telling Jameson, or the devastation his indifference brings.

He sits on my bed, balanced on the edge as if wanting to leave but unable to make himself get up, and he does not look at me when he says, "You're sure?"

I do not understand his reaction. We have been happy together these last few months, and he has stayed with me day and night since his punishment. It never occurred to me that he would be anything other than happy, but he acts like he cannot even bring himself to look at me.

"I am sure," I tell him. "My cycle should have come fifteen days ago. I am with child."

My husband says nothing, and Zip gets to his feet so he can nudge Jameson's hand like he senses his master is sad. I watch in silence as my husband scratches the dog's head, waiting for him to say something, but still he remains quiet. Subdued.

Pain twists my heart like a vine of thorns is wrapped around it. "Are you not happy?"

Jameson lets out a deep sigh, and when he finally lifts his head, I find myself wishing he had kept his gaze on the floor. "I don't know what you expect from me, Wilderness. I love you, but this isn't how I ever planned to have a family. I never thought I'd be a husband but have no wife. I never thought we would live together, but I would have a different home, too. I never thought that if the baby was a girl she would stay with her mother while I was sent away, and I never thought I wouldn't get to be a dad, or that if it was a boy, his mother would kick him out the second he was old enough to eat solid food. It's no secret I don't understand why things are the way they are here, and I don't think it should surprise you that I'm not thrilled about it."

Tears pool in my eyes against my will, and I want to push them away, but it is impossible because Jameson is right. Even if some of the things he said are foreign to me, I know this is not how he wants to live. I thought having him stay with me every night would make it better, but it cannot change some things. If I have a girl, she will be mine, but not his, and if I have a boy, he will be a yieldling and will go live with the men. Again, he will not be Jameson's, but will instead belong to the village. There is nothing in this for my husband. It is all for me and the other women in the village.

"I am sorry." I sink down next to him and take his hand. "You are right. I never thought about what this would be like for you."

"It's twisted," he mumbles.

Perhaps it is. I am starting to think everything we do here is just a little twisted.

WHEN JAMESON HEADS OFF TO THE MEN'S VILLAGE TO TEND the goats, I go to my mother. We have not talked about what is happening in my life much lately—

not since before our rift over my husband's punishment—but I am suddenly desperate for the kind of guidance only she has been able to give me. I need to understand where my husband fits into this world, and what I can do to make everything okay in his eyes.

She is in her hut, the door open to let in the spring air, and the way she stands when I approach is more formal than it used to be, as if, like me, she is unsure how to fix things between us.

"Good morrow, Wilderness."

"Raven," I say, forgoing the customary greeting. "I need to speak with you."

My mother blinks, and the hesitation in her eyes is as clear as the sky above our heads, but she steps aside anyway and motions for me to enter. "Come in."

Her focused gaze when I pass makes me feel like she can tell I am with child just by looking at me, and fire spreads across my cheeks that I cannot explain. Maybe it has to do with the questions I am about to ask and the fact that I am certain she will not approve of the things I have been thinking and feeling.

We sit, and I do not give her a chance to say a word before sharing my news. "I am with child."

My mother's smile changes, becoming more genuine and lighting up her brown eyes, and she pats my knee twice before saying, "I am so pleased, my daughter."

Tears well up in my throat, making me feel like I have swallowed a boulder, and I remain silent, too afraid my emotions will take over if I open my mouth. I hate showing weakness, especially in front of Raven, but it is impossible to control my tears.

When I say nothing, her smile fades. "What is it?"

"Jameson." His name comes out shaky, and I pause to swallow. "He was not happy."

My mother blinks, and like that she has disappeared, replaced by the High Elder who seems to approve of nothing I do these days. "This has nothing to do with your husband."

How can I respond to a statement like that? To me, this has everything to do with him, because we created this baby together, Jameson and I, and to say it has nothing to do with him seems… Twisted. Wrong.

"Wilderness," Raven says with a sigh, "you are the woman. If the baby is a yieldling, you will give it nourishment and protect it, help it grow strong. Then, when it is weaned, it will go to the men. If it is a girl, you will be a mother, and then all this will make sense to you."

It. She talks about the yieldlings like they are not even people, and I cannot understand her coldness. Raven had yieldlings—how many, I do not even know—but she must have had feelings for them. Did she not love them the way she loves me?

"How many yieldlings did you have?" I ask.

My mother sits back as if trying to put distance between herself and the past. "We do not talk about things like that."

"Hawk."

She jerks like I have slapped her, and something like a mixture of pain and anger flashes in her eyes. "Wilderness, I am warning you. This is not what we do."

"There were others. I told you I remember them."

My mother gets to her feet so suddenly it is as if she has jumped even though the movement is as controlled as she is. "You are hysterical. You should go see the healer. Get some herbs so you can sleep, and then we will talk about this again."

I get up as well but do not leave. "Jameson wants to stay with me all the time. He wants the baby to be his, too."

"That is not how it works. You know this."

My mother takes a step closer, her eyes flashing more than ever. I could be pushing her close to the edge, but I refuse to back down.

"I want him to be with me."

"Do not do this, Wilderness," she says, the words hissing their way through clenched teeth. "He is a foundling. He is not from here. You cannot let him come in and change how we live. You are letting your feelings affect how you see things. I warned you, did I not? I told you it would make you weak."

"Loving Jameson does not make me weak. Refusing to let love into your life has made you blind."

She slaps me, and the force of her hand slamming across my cheek makes my head whip back. The sting from the blow pulses through my cheek and eye, and the crack rings in my ears, but still I refuse to back down.

I turn to face her, ignoring her shocked expression. "You cannot beat the love out of me, just as you could not have the loyalty whipped out of Jameson. He let those men go because he knew it was wrong for us to hold them prisoner, and he was right. What we do, bringing men here against their will and forcing them to be husbands, is no different than what those men did to our ancestors in the hotel. *We* are no better."

She stumbles back as if my words have punched her, and though she does not reply, the raw shock on her face tells me they have hit home, and I turn away. I want to give her time to think about what we have done. How we have captured and killed and tortured men because they are evil, all the while ignoring the evilness in our own hearts.

CHAPTER TWENTY-THREE

WHEN I FINISH TENDING THE GOATS, ZIP AND I HEAD over to where Zachariah is tanning a deer hide, and I fall in beside him while the dog drops to the ground at my feet.

After my earlier conversation with Wilderness, I'm a bundle of emotions, my insides so twisted I find it impossible to talk. Instead, I focus on the task in front of me, scraping fat and muscle from the animal's pelt, moving the small homemade tool faster and faster until my biceps ache from the repetition.

Zachariah watches me from the corner of his eye, his usual smile a ghost of itself and coming across as sad and labored instead of happy. It's like he only wears it for my benefit, which seems like a shame, because at this moment I can't imagine anything in the world worth smiling about.

"Wilderness brought this one in yesterday," Zachariah says after a lengthy silence, still watching me from the corner of his eye.

"I know. I was with her." He stares at me, waiting, and I say what he already knows. "I killed it."

His smile doesn't change. "I thought as much. You have done well, fit in and found a place, but this..." He stops scraping and turns so he's facing me. "Dangerous ground, Jameson. Men are not hunters."

"I know." I scrape at the hide harder, gritting my teeth as bits of fat fly into the air. "We're nothing."

Zachariah doesn't turn back to his work, and his blue eyes stay focused on me, making my scalp prickle. "What is it?"

I stop scraping the hide, but don't look at him when I say, "She's pregnant."

I sigh and so does he, but saying the words out loud isn't a relief, and it doesn't feel like I'm putting the burden on someone else's shoulders. Especially when Zachariah nods, because the gesture is sad.

"I understand," he says.

I believe he does, and for the first time it occurs to me that the news might hurt him as much, if not more, than it hurts me. Wilderness is his daughter, a daughter he has no claim over and one who doesn't even understand the significance, which means this will be a grandchild who will never get to know him.

"How do you do it?" I ask, finally turning to face him. "How do you watch your children grow up knowing they have no clue who you are?"

"They know me," he says.

"No, they don't, not really."

Zachariah exhales and sits on the ground, his back to the hide, and when he motions for me to do the same, I give in without a fight, sinking onto the dirt at his side like the useless lump I am. Zip gets up long enough to come to my side, resting his muzzle on my knee like he knows I need the comfort, and I find myself scratching his head without even thinking about it.

"I had four boys with Raven, and I raised them all, buried one," Zachariah begins. "Ash, Hawk, and Talon know me. They come to me when they need something. They ask me for advice. They love me, respect me, and talk to me. I know more about them than you will ever know. So what if they do not call me father?"

"What about Wilderness? To her, you're just her mother's husband."

"Wilderness loves me, too, even if she does not know it."

"But it could be so different—"

"It could also be worse," he says, cutting me off. "I did not have a father, and my mother was never home. She worked three jobs. I raised myself. Alone in a stinking apartment, barely enough food and no love. Here, there is love and food and family. It is hard at times, but as a whole, it is easier than what is out there. Do you not agree?"

He gives me a challenging look, and I find it impossible to argue, because this *is* better than anything I had before; the fact that I joined that damn railroad detail is proof. If I went back to Baltimore, I doubt I would ever see my mom again. She's probably dead. She was halfway there the last time I saw her eight years ago, and it wouldn't surprise me if my brothers had followed in her footsteps down the steep and dangerous staircase leading to the world of drugs and alcohol. It's an all too common story these days, and the end is always the same. Heartbreak.

Zachariah pats my leg when I say nothing. "It will be okay."

All I can do is stare at my hands. "If I hadn't come here, I don't know if I would've ever gotten married, but if I had, I know I wouldn't have had a better father-in-law than you."

Zachariah tilts his head like the thought hadn't occurred to him before now. "Guess I am." He laughs and pats my knee again, harder this time. "I would not have chosen a different husband for Wilderness. I knew you were the right one for her the second I saw you. Knew she would pick you, too, because she is smart, and like her mother, she has the ability to lead. I thought Raven would be the one to change the old ways, but she is too scared. She is strong, but her fear keeps her trapped. Wilderness, though, she does not have her mother's fear."

"No," I say. "She doesn't have an ounce of fear inside her."

Zachariah lets out a deep sigh. "Raven's mother was High Elder when I came here. She was a hard woman. Cold as ice. In those days, the foundlings were given very little freedom. We were locked in the hut at night unless we had been invited to the women's village, and the warriors guarded us during the day.

"My group was small, just me and one other man, but there were others who had been here for years. They were given the medicine every night so they would perform their duties, but Raven never gave it to me." He gives me a small smile. "I know you have not forgiven her for her part in your punishment, but back then she was as much a rebel as Wilderness is now. Raven's mother was not happy when we grew close so fast. She did not trust any men, not even the yieldlings."

He pauses, giving me a moment compare the man at my side to myself and the other men I was brought in with. The other foundlings. The warriors go out every five years to bring in new blood, and Zachariah has been here for thirty years, yet I've met no other men from the outside world. It's something that's been nagging at me for a while, but something I haven't wanted to face. Until now. Now, sitting with Zachariah and feeling like we've finally reached a point where we understand one another, I find I can't keep the words in any longer.

"There's something I've been wanting to ask you," I say before Zachariah can go on, and when his eyes meet mine, for once there's no warning in his expression. "I've been around long enough to realize we're the only foundlings left in the village—and David. Were all the others killed? What happened to the man you were brought in with? What happened to the others who were already here?"

Zachariah lets out a long breath. "They all met their ends in different ways. Some because they could not adjust, others because they outlived their usefulness." He shakes his head, his gaze on the ground again. "There was an uprising, too."

"An uprising?" My pulse quickens when I think about what that most likely meant for the men.

"It was before I came here, but Raven told me about it. A few of the foundlings worked together and tried to escape. They injured one of the warriors and killed the yielding who was guarding them." He frowns, and the expression seems to darken his eyes. "It is the reason there were so few foundlings left when I came here, and why there are so few now. After that, the women worried about keeping us around, and when Raven's mother was still in charge, she had little tolerance for the men brought into the village. Including me."

"What happened?" I ask, my mind switching gears as I remember the scars on his back and realize they're why he brought Raven's mom up to begin with.

"My punishment was thirty lashes, but my only crime was loving Raven," Zachariah says. "I did as I was told, performed my duties at night, and worked during the day, but her mother knew Raven cared about me a great deal, and it scared her. She claimed she was beating the evilness out of me, but she really wanted to put me in my place."

I shift, my back aching from the memory of my own punishment. Zachariah's must have been a hundred times worse.

"How could you stand staying here after that?"

"Love." He shrugs like it should be obvious. "Raven did not wield the whip, and that night in her hut she cried for my pain. You do not know the woman I do. She is different in private. She may not tell me she loves me, but she shows me. The scars on my back do not hurt, and Raven's mother is gone. She died, and things have been better. Change takes time, Jameson, and if you love someone enough, you can get through anything."

Zachariah's words stick with me long after our conversation, and I spend the rest of the day thinking about what I'm willing to endure for love. Anything. That's the conclusion I come to. For Wilderness, I'm willing to put up with anything.

I still don't love or understand why things are the way they are here, but I do know I'm stuck, both because I love the woman who chose me as her husband and because we're going to have a baby. Girl or yieldling, it doesn't matter, because I trust that Wilderness won't let who I am go unacknowledged the way her mother has with Zachariah. Things for us will be different, even if it takes years to get there.

Later, when Zip and I return to her hut, I wrap my arms around her and whisper in ear, "I'm happy."

She pulls back, still trapped in my arms, so she can smile up at me. "I have decided I will fight for you, Jameson. You want a family like the one you know, and I want you to be as happy as I am. My mother may not like it, but she will not be High Elder forever. We have been trapped by the fear of our ancestors for too long, and I will not allow it to continue."

"As long as I'm with you, I'll be happy. We'll figure the rest out as we go."

Wilderness's smile widens, and she lifts herself up on her toes so she can press her lips to mine. I hold her closer, feeling the beat of her heart against my chest and thinking about the baby inside her, the life we created together. If it's a boy, I'll do everything in my power to raise him to be strong and good, and if it's a girl, Wilderness will do the same.

CHAPTER TWENTY-FOUR

Wilderness

THE CHILL FROM WINTER IS STILL HANGING ON WHEN Blossom gives birth to Eric's baby. It is a girl, which makes the village rejoice for her good fortune. I rejoice as well, but only because I know it would make a difference to Blossom. When my own time comes, I will be happy either way.

Brooke and Rose are not as fortunate. Springtime blooms, bringing new life to the forest in shades of green and white and yellow, and the women give birth only a few days apart. Both babies are yieldlings, and since their husbands are gone, neither woman will have another chance to be a mother. I mourn for the babies more than the women, though, because they are innocent and do not yet realize that the world they have been born into does not know their worth. They do not yet understand that their time on this earth will be marked by how long they are husbands.

Ivy's husband, David, no longer goes to her hut, and I worry more and more that the village Elders will decide it is time for him to meet his end. After what happened with Dawn, they are hesitant to end the foundling, but it cannot last. He is not fulfilling his duty. He has not helped Ivy produce offspring, and he no longer does his work in the men's village. Day after day he sits in the hut by himself, staring at the wall like it is a cell. I know it must feel that way to him, and the unfairness of it sickens me. We have done this man a grave injustice.

Above me, the sky is clear and blue, and buds dot the trees, a sign that spring will soon be in full bloom. The men's village is alive with activity, and it is the first day warm enough for my husband to go outside without a shirt. His broad shoulders are a welcome sight, but the tattoos on his arms and the now distorted eagle on his back are reminders that he is not from here. Just like David.

"Have you tried to talk to the other foundling?" I ask Jameson.

"No. He isn't a fan of mine." When I shake my head to let him know I do not understand, he sighs. "He doesn't like me."

"But you are like him. That must give him some peace."

"I'm the enemy, like Zachariah. I'm not trying to leave. I don't want to."

It makes sense, even though it does not.

"What do you think they'll do to him?" my husband asks after a moment of silent reflection.

"I am not sure. He may meet his end, or the Elders may let him live as he is."

"They won't let him go?"

"There is too much at risk," I say gently.

My husband gives a sad nod as we walk toward the forest hand in hand, headed for the hot spring to bathe.

Only days later, David makes the decision to bring about his own end by breaking a glass when no one is looking and using the sharp edges to slice his wrists. By the time Zachariah discovers the foundling, he has already passed over to Paradise, and I find I cannot be anything but happy for him. He is at peace now. Hopefully, a happier existence waits for him in the afterlife.

Springtime sweeps in, but the passing time does nothing to heal my relationship with my mother. After our last conversation, she looks at me with suspicion, and she does not speak to my husband at all. It seems like she watches his every move, like she is waiting for him to slip up so she can end him, and every day feels like I am tiptoeing through the forest so a wild animal does not find me. Never before have I felt unsafe in my village, not even when Dawn was alive, because it never occurred to me that she would try to bring about my end, but the way my mother watches my husband makes me feel like I am walking toward the edge of a cliff with my eyes closed.

I go to Zachariah, which is the only thing I can think to do. He has always been one of the people I am most comfortable with, and the only one who might be able to help me understand my mother's mood.

"I fear for my husband," I tell him.

Zachariah reaches out to me, and for the first time ever, does not hesitate to grab my arm. His grip is gentle but firm when he pulls me away from the center of the men's village and into the forest. We do not wander far, stopping just inside the trees, but it is far enough away that no one will be able to hear our conversation.

He releases my arm and stares at his hand like he just realized what he has done, but then shakes his head and says, "Talk."

"My mother and I spoke after I found out I was with child, and since then she has been different. Distant." I tell Zachariah everything I said, about the baby and Jameson wanting to live with me, as well as the questions I had about the yieldlings and Raven's refusal to talk about it. "I told her we are no better than the men in the hotel. We bring men here against their will and force them to be husbands. We steal their lives. We kill."

Something flickers in Zachariah's eyes, and an expression of pride crosses his face. "You said these things to Raven?"

"I did."

"But she did not take it well."

It is not a question, but I shake my head anyway. "She did not."

He sighs but his expression remains unchanged. "No, she would not." He places a hesitant hand on my shoulder and says, "You are braver than she is, Wilderness, and I am proud of you."

I blame the baby growing inside me when tears well up in my eyes, and my heart swells at Zachariah's words like it wants to rip its way out of me.

"Thank you."

He opens his mouth like he wants to say more, but shuts it for a blink before trying again. "Things will be okay. Your mother has said nothing to me about the situation. She worries about you, and she has a lot of distrust in her heart, which makes it hard for her to see things the way you do, but that does not mean you should fear her. She will do what is right eventually. Just wait."

I try to take his words to heart as the days move forward, but find it difficult, because my mother does not warm to me or to Jameson. Not even after the snow has melted completely and the trees are once again thick with leaves.

The day that marks one full year of Jameson being with me arrives, and we spend it wrapped in one another's embrace. There is a subtle roundness to my stomach now, but it is small enough that no one but my husband and I would notice.

"I can't believe it's been a year already," Jameson says to me in the darkness of my hut.

"You did not come here of your own free will, and I am sorry, but you have made my life full."

"I stayed of my own free will, though."

"I am glad you stayed."

When he kisses me, it feels like the world is shifting, as if the future in front of us has changed. Like a caterpillar emerging from its chrysalis. That is how I feel, like a butterfly spreading its wings for the first time and seeing that there is beauty in the world, and the promise of change almost takes my breath away with its brightness.

Only it does not happen the way I expect it to. It does not come in a burst of colors, but instead shows itself on a warm spring day when I am out hunting.

I am perched in a tree, waiting for game to cross my path, when I spot them. The men are still a good distance away. There are two of them, their faces masked in wiry hair and their bodies covered in clothes as strange as the ones my husband wore the day he was brought into our village. Pants made of material I do not recognize, and shirts as colorful as the flowers in spring. They carry objects I have never seen before but instinctively know are weapons. The items are black and small, with blunt ends that are hollow instead of sharp.

The men move closer, and I press my back against the trunk, holding my breath and praying they do not spot me. In the seventy years since our village was established, no one has ever wandered this far up the mountain, and I find myself unsure how I should react. Should I let them pass and hope they do not make it to the villages? I could end one of them before they realized I am up here, but I do not know how their weapons work or if the second man would be able to end me before I ended him as well. The villages are a good distance off, but if these men keep heading in the same direction, they will run right into them.

I am still trying to decide what to do when one of them pauses, and I have hunted enough animals to know he senses my presence, so it does not surprise me when he starts scanning the area. It takes only a few blinks for him to find me in the trees, and when his eyes meet mine, he jerks back but does not raise his weapon.

Not wanting him to see me as a threat, I remain still and silent.

"Look," he says to his friend, nodding toward me.

The second man turns, and he, too, jumps in surprise. "Holy— Whatcha' doin' up there, girlie?"

The sound of his voice scratches the inside of my ears, and I have the urge to cover them. All the foundlings who have come into our village sound different, but I have never heard anyone whose voice sounded like this. It is like his words are being raked over hot coals.

"We're not going to hurt you. We just heard there was a village up this way and wanted to say hello." The other man's voice is not as unpleasant. It is more like the way Jameson talks, combining his words like he is too lazy to pronounce them all.

"Maybe she don't speak English," the man with the voice of flames says.

"Don't know for sure," his friend responds, narrowing his eyes on me. "You don't have to come down if you're scared, but say something at least. Let us know if you understand."

I press my lips together as I try to decide what to do. I will lose control of the situation if I do not respond, and they may decide to continue up the mountain, and then I will be forced to use my bow. With the uncertainty of how their weapons work, I cannot risk it.

"I understand," I finally say.

The man with the less offensive voice nods. "Good. We're settlers, and we've moved to the town at the base of the mountain. The railroad company has fixed the tracks, and there's going to be a stop down there. We heard there was a village up this way and thought we might be able to help one another out."

Like when Jameson talks about the old world, I do not understand most of what this man says, but one part rings loud and clear. These men knew we were up here, and they came looking for us. How? Who has seen us, and when? Other than the warriors who go out every five years, we never leave our mountain.

"How did you hear about us?"

"Rumors," the man says.

"I do not know *rumors*."

He scrunches his mouth up then says, "People talking to each other. That's all."

"Is your village nearby?" asks the man whose voice makes me cringe.

"You cannot go there." I swallow, trying to decide what to do. I could run and try to lose these men in the woods, but they might find the village anyway. On the other hand, they might be willing to wait if I give them the option. "If you stay here, I will bring the Elders to you."

The two men discuss this, their voices too low for me to hear, and after a beat they nod in unison.

"Okay," the first man calls. "We can do that."

I sling my bow over my shoulder and scoot forward so I can climb down. Having my back to them makes me feel like the animal instead of the hunter I am, but it is the only way to get out of the tree, so I have no choice. I scurry down as fast as I can, moving from branch to branch the way a squirrel does when it hears a predator. Except I am going toward the danger, not away from it.

When my feet touch the forest floor, I spin and press my back against the trunk. "You must stay here. Do you understand?"

The men nod, and the one whose voice does not make me want to pull my ears off lowers himself to the ground. "We'll stay."

I turn and take off through the forest.

It is unclear whether I can trust these men, but I do know if I run fast enough they may not have a chance to catch me. So that is what I do, dodging trees as I go and jumping over logs with my heart pounding in my chest while I strain my ears, listening for the sound of footsteps moving after me. My own footfalls and heavy breathing make it impossible to know for sure if the men are behind me, though.

I do not slow until I reach the village, and even then it is only so I can scramble up the ladder, headed for my mother's hut. We have barely spoken lately, but she is High Elder, and even if we do not see eye to eye on most things, I still trust that she will know what to do.

I am out of breath when I stop outside Raven's door, and despite my panic, I find it impossible to step inside. When my mother sees me, she gets to her feet, and the stiffness of her movements tells me she feels the same way. Her back is too straight and her eyes too guarded. We are like strangers now.

"Wilderness." The cold indifference of her tone is almost as shocking as finding the men in the forest, but in a blink her expression changes, and I know she has finally registered my panic. She steps forward, her hand out, but she does not touch me. "What has happened?"

"Men," I say through gasps. "In the forest. There are two. They were looking for the village and saw me hunting. They want to talk, but I told them they could not come here. We must go to them before they try to find the village themselves."

My mother blinks like my words have no meaning. "Men? Looking for us?"

"Yes."

Reality hits her like a boulder, and I see a crack in her strength, but it is like a fissure in the side of the mountain, small and insignificant compared to the overwhelming magnitude of the structure.

It is gone before I can really take it in, and then Raven is back to her normal self, moving past me and down the walkway. "I will get the Elders, you gather the warriors. We need weapons. We must not look weak."

I do as I am told, flying up and down the walkways in search of the warriors, but find only Elder Warrior, Rain, and Grove. The three women spread out to find the others while I hurry for the men's village. I am the only woman who would consider letting them know what is going on, but I cannot leave without telling Zachariah and Jameson what is happening. I will not leave them in the dark like they do not matter. If something happens and these intruders make it here, the men are even more vulnerable than the women. They need to prepare.

They are eating their afternoon meal when I break through the trees. Zachariah sees me and sets his bowl down, getting to his feet, instantly aware something is not right, and before I have reached them, Jameson is up as well and has already started moving toward me.

"What is it?" Zachariah asks, and behind him the other men and yieldlings freeze. "What has happened?"

"Men in the forest. Raven is gathering the Elders and warriors. We are going to meet them."

My husband takes a step in my direction, concern clouding his vision. The worry is for me, but it is also for the baby, and I know I would be feeling the same way if he were the one who ran into outsiders. I care about my village and about the people living here, but my first thoughts would be of him and his safety.

"You aren't going," Jameson says.

"I am the only one who knows where they are."

"No, Wilderness. It's too dangerous."

The violent way my husband shakes his head shocks me. How he was before he came here is a mystery, but since he arrived, he has never tried to tell me what to do, not like this, anyway. It should make me angry, but it does not, because I understand. I would feel the same way if he were the one going. Frightened of what could happen, scared he could get injured or his life will come to an end.

But I have no choice.

I step back. "I must go."

Before he can argue, I take off, knowing the group will be preparing to leave and that I must get back to the women's village.

They are already assembled and waiting when I arrive. The warriors are loaded down with weapons, wearing fur and leather, and the Elders are armed as well. The women in front of me are as fierce as a pack of wolves, and pride fills me despite the confusion that has clouded my life lately. This is my village and my family, and even if I do not agree with everything that happens, I am proud of what the women here have achieved.

My mother stands at the front of the pack, and when she sees me says, "We must go."

I have only taken one step when Zachariah calls out from behind me, "Raven."

The women turn, as do I.

Zachariah is not alone. My husband is with him, as well as Hawk and Ash and some of the other men, all of them armed with spears.

"What are you doing here?" my mother asks, her voice colder than a burst of winter wind.

"We are going with you," Zachariah says.

She lets out a sound of disbelief, and all around her the warriors and Elders shake their heads.

Elder Warrior curls her upper lip and spits out, "We do not need men."

"You can't go there without us," Jameson says. "Those men don't know how strong you are. If you go and all they see are women, they'll think you're weak and susceptible. They'll come here. I know you can beat them, I know you don't need men to keep you safe, but if you want to prevent them from even thinking about coming here, you need to bring as many people with you as you can. And you need men at your side."

"Do not tell me what we need, *foundling*." My mother's voice booms through the village, making her seem ten times bigger than she is. "You are not one of us!"

Jameson jerks away from the venom in Raven's words.

"You must listen to the boy," Zachariah says, his voice low as he tries to reason with her. "Jameson knows about the world. We do not. He is right about the men, but he will also be able to give us insight no one else can. He will know how to talk to these people. He will know if they are spouting lies."

"You are overstepping, Zachariah," my mother says. "It is not your place."

"No, I am not!" he bellows, sending gasps through the group of women. "I love you, Raven. I have never said it, but you know I do. You know that is why I stayed all those years ago, but I have come to love this place and what we have here as much as I love you, and I will not see it destroyed because you are too afraid to ask for help. What happened to your ancestors was wrong, but the men here are not like that. We are a family, and that means being here for each other."

I look back and forth between them, but even before she speaks, I know my mother will not back down. She lifts her head, and the rage flashing in her eyes reminds me of how Dawn looked in the woods after she tried to end me.

"You are not coming. Do not try to follow us or you will all be punished. *Fifty lashes.*" The last two words hiss through her teeth the way the leather hissed through the air when Dawn brought it down on my husband's back. "Let us go."

Raven turns away from the men and heads into the forest.

I do not move, too shaken by what she has done. The past year has made me see my mother in a different light, but until today I never thought she was weak. Now, watching her walk away with her head held high, I can see the fissure I first spotted in her hut growing, can see the cracks spreading from her to the women around her, and I am afraid there is no stopping it at this point. Even worse, I am worried it will be our undoing.

"Wilderness!" my mother shouts.

Jameson's gaze captures mine, and he silently begs me to stay, but I cannot. No matter how much I disagree with my mother, I must go. For the village. For my husband. For the baby growing inside me.

I take one step backward, then spin on my heel and run after her.

The trek through the forest is a silent one, but I am not sure what the other women are thinking. Are they on my mother's side? Elder Warrior is, but some of the younger women do not seem as sure. Even Rain, who I have come to know as a cold woman, has uncertainty swimming in her dark eyes. This is something we have never faced, men in their environment, not in our own. We have no real control here and no knowledge of what to expect. Zachariah was right when he said Jameson would be helpful, but my mother is too blind to see the truth in his words.

"Tell me about your conversation," Raven says as we walk.

I repeat everything I remember, describing the men and their clothes, as well as the weapons they carried. My mother blinks like picturing them is difficult, but I can think of no other way to describe them, and I have no clue what they do.

"Jameson would know what these weapons are," Rain says.

My mother keeps her eyes straight ahead. "We will be fine. They want to talk, so we will, and we will let them know we do not want to trade with them. They are not welcome on our mountain or in our territory."

Dread pools in my stomach at her harsh tone. She will be difficult to deal with like this, and it will not bode well for our village if she does something to anger the outsiders.

We find the men sitting right where I left them, and at our approach, they climb to their feet, studying us. We are a strong group, ten warriors and all five of the Elders, plus me. Still, right away I can tell by the men's expressions that Jameson and Zachariah were right. They do not see warriors and Elders standing in front of them. They see women. These men come from a world where we are the weaker sex, and because of that, they may not take us seriously.

"Good eve," my mother says when she stops in front of the men. "I am Raven, High Elder of our village. My daughter, Wilderness, tells me you wish to speak."

The first man scratches his beard as he looks my mother over a second time then studies me. "Wilderness and Raven?" He shakes his head and sticks his hand out. "I'm Tim, and this here is Abraham."

My mother stares at the man's outstretched hand without blinking until it finally drops to his side.

I study the man who calls himself Abraham, the one with the voice that beats against my eardrums. His name is as strange to me as my husband's once was and feels rough on my tongue, impossible to spit out. Abraham studies me in return, and something about the gleam in his eyes makes me want to pull out my knife. I do not trust this man. I do not like the glint in his eye or the way he smiles.

The man who seems to be in charge, Tim, keeps his focus on my mother. "Like I told your daughter, we're fixing to settle into the town at the base of the mountain. The railroad track is finally fixed, and this will be one of the stops. The company is paying us a stipend to move here with our families and start a town. We heard you were up here and thought we could help each other out. Trading and such." He jerks his head toward my mother. "Like the furs."

I try to picture myself through this man's eyes, to imagine what he sees when he looks at me, but I cannot. Everything about me is as foreign and strange to him as he is to me. I have no idea how the weapon tucked in his belt works, or what kind of animal his clothes came from. I do not know what a railroad is or why it would bring these men into our lives, and most importantly, I cannot imagine how he heard of us.

"We do not mix with outsiders," my mother says, standing taller. "We ask that you stay off our mountain and do not cross the perimeter into our territory again."

"Your mountain?" The man called A-bra-ham frowns. "I think you're a bit confused, lady. The government owns this here mountain."

"We have been here for seventy years." Elder Warrior glares up at the man like she is considering ending him now. "How long has your government been here?"

Tim scratches his beard again, but he does not blink when he says, "Never mind all that. We don't plan on causing trouble, and we aren't going to force you to trade with us if you don't want to. Just thought we could help each other out, is all. Personally, I don't care where you live or how you choose to do it as long as you don't stop me from making a life for my family."

"We have no plans to interfere with your town," my mother tells him.

"That's fine, then. Just know we're down there, and if you do want to trade, we'll be happy to. Otherwise, you can consider this matter closed."

Raven nods once, signaling the end of the conversation. "We appreciate your good will."

Tim lets out a little laugh, and the way he shakes his head makes it seem like he's confused by something. "Same here. Have a nice day."

He turns, but Abraham does not. The other man looks us over again, his eyes lingering on me, and the hair on my arms stands up under his gaze.

I believe Tim is telling the truth, but Abraham is not the same kind of man. He is the kind of man Jameson and Zachariah wanted to protect us from, the kind of man who would have taken our ancestors against their will. Who will do the same to us if we let our guard down.

"Have a nice evening, ladies." He winks before turning to follow Tim.

We stay where we are, silent and united until the men have disappeared from sight.

Then my mother turns on me. "You must control your husband."

Heat flares through me, hotter than the sun. "We will not talk about this here, Raven."

"He was wrong." She points to the trees the men disappeared through. "We did not need *men* to deal with this problem. You must learn how strong you can be. One day you will be High Elder, and you cannot lead if you let a man tell you what to do."

"Jameson does not tell me what to do. We are equals. Power does not make a person strong. I could choose to beat my husband down, but that would not make me a better leader, it would only make me a sad person."

I turn away from her, pushing past the warriors and Elders and leaving them behind.

Back in the women's village, I find Jameson pacing while Zip stares up at him from the ground. My husband rushes to my side when he sees me, his gaze moving over me like he is searching for injuries.

"I am fine," I say.

The anxious light in his eyes does not fade. "What happened?"

"The men left. I believe the one was telling the truth when he said he would stay away, but I worry the other is the kind of man you were concerned about. He had evil in his eyes."

I picture the weapons they had and do my best to describe them to Jameson. He nods as he listens, the worry in his eyes only growing more intense.

"Guns." He lets out a deep breath. "They fire little pieces of metal the way a bow fires an arrow, only much faster."

"They are dangerous?" I ask even though I know the men would not carry them if they were not.

"They are," Jameson says.

We are still talking when the rest of our party returns, and my mother looks at my husband like he is a bug she wishes to crush under her foot.

"Did Wilderness tell you we took care of the problem?" She lifts her chin and stares down her nose at him despite the fact that he is more than a head taller. "No *men*."

The way she spits out the last word makes it sound like she is talking about a pile of goat dung. It is ugly and full of hate, just like she is at this moment. I have seen my mother in many moods, and I know there is softness in her, but right now she seems harder than the rock we live on.

"Don't get overly confident," Jameson says. "They could come back. You should have the warriors keep watch."

"We will not lose sleep because of what a foundling says." She pushes past us and heads for the trees.

The other women follow, but unlike my mother, do not seem as hard or as arrogant. Hopefully, the other Elders can make her see reason. These men might never come up the mountain, or they could move in while we are asleep and destroy us.

CHAPTER TWENTY-FIVE

Jameson

THE SOUND OF WILDERNESS'S BREATHING IS HEAVY IN the darkness when I ease the door open, making me pause. It's something I've grown used to, and I can't imagine being able to sleep well without it. Not anymore. Which is why I have to do this. Why I have to risk everything to make sure those men don't come up the mountain.

Outside, the night air warms my skin, the heat of the day holding on even though the sun has set, and the utter stillness of the women's village wraps around me as I cross the walkway to a rope ladder, keeping my steps light. After what happened today, even a small creak might draw someone out to investigate.

Zip walks at my side, his nails tapping quietly against the wood. I'd leave him behind if I thought he'd let me, but I know it would only result in him whining until he woke Wilderness, and I can't let that happen. I don't want her to know I've left until morning.

The silence of the village feels ominous. It's foolish not to have at least one of the warriors on watch, but Raven is the very definition of a fool, arrogant and pigheaded. If she doesn't do something to change the course of things soon, she'll be the end of all of us. I'm sure of it.

I've started thinking of myself as a part of this village more and more every day. In the beginning, it caught me by surprise because it was something I hadn't expected. At first I just thought of myself as being with Wilderness, and then the other men worked their way into my life—and Zip, too, although I'd say he forced his way in more than anything. Now, though, I can't imagine being anywhere else, with any other group. Even the women who look at me and see a weak, pathetic man are present when I picture my future, because although I don't understand or agree with everything they do, it has all worked together to create a world I love. One I refuse to sit back and let slip away.

I find Zachariah waiting inside the forest with two bundles, and when Zip and I stop in front of him, he hands one to me. We dress without talking, me in the clothes I wore the day the warriors dragged me here, and him in another man's shirt and pants. A man who is most likely dead now. The only things we don't have are shoes, but the leather tied to my feet will be good enough. After over a year of wearing them, I barley notice the sharp rocks I step on anymore.

Once we're dressed, we move side by side through the trees, our steps swift as we descend the mountain. We don't have much time and can't afford to lose the cover of darkness, so I try to keep my pace steady. Before long, I'm panting, and at my side, Zachariah is as well, while Zip seems unaffected by the run. But we don't slow, and by the time we've made it to the halfway point, my shirt is sticking to my damp skin.

I've grown used to going bare-chested, and wearing these clothes after more than a year is confining. It's necessary, though, because I worry Wilderness was right and the men they talked to today have things on their mind other than trading. Plus, I have an unsettling suspicion about how they heard we were up here.

The trees thin and the ground flattens out, becoming softer and less rocky. We slow, and Zachariah and I work to relax our breathing while Zip pants away at my side. In the distance, the flicker of lights tells me we've found the right place.

We passed the town when the warriors brought me to the mountain more than a year ago. It was one of the many places left to rot when the plague swept the country, but it now looks like it has found new life. Not only are there lights shining in the distance, but music, too, rising above the buildings and floating up to meet the empty sky above.

"Music," Zachariah says. "Have not heard music like this in thirty years."

"Are you going to be able to do this?"

He nods but presses his lips together like he doesn't savor the idea of going back into the old world. "Have to."

We pause at the edge of the forest, and I turn to Zip. "Sit." The dog obeys, wagging his tail as he stares up at me. "You need to stay here. Okay?" He tilts his head when I take a step back. "Stay."

I take another step, and the dog drops to the ground. He lays his muzzle on his paws and stares up at me like he thinks I'm abandoning him, and I almost laugh. Damn dog. I'd take him with us, but I'm afraid a dog trotting along at my side would be too conspicuous.

"Ready?" Zachariah asks.

I turn my back on Zip. "Yeah. Let's get this over with."

He and I walk the rest of the way in silence, and the closer we get to the town, the more anxious I get. My insides feel like they're full of worms, both from the uncertainty of what we'll face here and what will happen when we return to the village. We know what we're risking by doing this, but Zachariah and I agreed it had to happen. Raven wouldn't listen to reason, but if we can see what's happening down here and get a better idea of what to expect, maybe we'll be able to convince her.

We reach the first few buildings, crumbling houses with overgrown, weed-choked yards, and pass between them so we can move deeper into the town. When we step out onto the street, the lights are brighter and the music louder, thumping through the air and pulsing against the buildings as we move, sticking to the shadows. The men who came to the mountain said they had families, but the rowdy atmosphere makes me doubt they were telling the truth. It's the middle of the night, and if there were kids living in this town, the noise would make it impossible for them to sleep.

The sound of talking and laughter breaks through the music as we reach the center of town, and next to me, Zachariah stiffens but doesn't slow. We walk down a dark alley between two buildings but look around the corner before stepping out. I can see them now, a big group of people. There's a bonfire in the middle of the street made of what looks like old furniture and books, pretty much anything they could drag from the houses and burn. There are men gathered, and women, too. They're laughing and drinking.

"What do you see?" Zachariah asks.

"Thirty people, maybe more." I squint into the darkness. "I don't see a lot of weapons. A few guns on hips, but that's about it."

"Good."

A man comes out of the house behind the group and throws something, and a second later the sound of breaking glass cuts through the noise and he yells, "Shut the hell up. I got kids!"

So, there *are* kids.

Maybe the man—Tim—was telling the truth. Doesn't mean there won't be trouble, but knowing there are at least a few people out here just trying to start over is a relief. It means we could be facing a small group.

I duck back into the shadows and kneel beside Zachariah. "There are kids, so that much is true. I want to look around a little more, though. Make sure we don't see anything suspicious."

We go back down the alley and cross over to another one, coming to the main street behind the fire. When I'm sure the coast is clear, we step out side by side, keeping our heads low as we walk, acting casual. If anyone sees us, we probably won't stand out—even with the leather strips on our feet. The people are drinking, and based on the large gathering around the fire, I'm guessing the railroad sent a big group out, meaning a few new faces won't be that noticeable.

We pass within twenty feet of the fire, but like I thought, no one seems to notice us. Beside me, Zachariah is jumpy, and even in the darkness I can see the way his eyes won't stop moving. It's like he's trying to take everything in at once.

"You okay?" I ask out of the corner of my mouth.

"Yes," he says, but he shakes his head. "I did not ever want to come back here. This world feels like a storm after being in the village."

I kind of know what he means. The people are rowdy despite being asked to stay quiet, and whatever music they're playing pulses through the air until it feels like the bass is thumping against the inside of my skull. Their laughter isn't the same as the laughter that moves through the village during our festivals, because it's too thick and aided by alcohol. The village has wine, but they don't drink to excess the way the outside world does. They stress control in all things, which is part of Raven's problem now, but typically it means they live a happy and harmonious existence.

Like Zachariah, being here is making me nervous, but I can't leave until I take a good look around, because I have a strong suspicion about something.

We reach the end of the street and go over one more, and the music and laughter fade, giving way to new sounds. Animal growls and chuckles that aren't happy, but instead angry or mad, even violent.

I stop when the sounds grow louder. The light of a second fire flickers across the surrounding buildings, fainter than the other one. The houses here are crumbling shells of what they were seventy years ago, with missing doors and windows shattered either by nature or men desperate to scavenge for supplies during the early days of the plague. Places like this are scattered all over the country, small towns where most of the original inhabitants were wiped out by the virus. Those who did survive fled to cities where refugee centers had been set up, and that's where most of the population has stayed, on the east or west coasts, near the ocean.

After the plague, the middle of the country returned to the wild. Nature took over small towns like this one, forgotten for decades. Repairing the railroad tracks wasn't even considered until five years ago, but finding people to fund the venture wasn't easy, and getting people to work in the middle of nowhere even harder. The big cities are ripe with pollution and poverty, but they're better than going out into the unknown.

The bark of a dog draws me forward, but it sounds nothing like Zip. It's savage or angry, and each step I take has my insides feeling more and more weighed down. When I draw closer, a small fire comes into view, built on what at first glance looks like a vacant lot. Upon closer inspection, I spot the remains of a chimney, the brick black and charred, and realize it's actually what's left of a foundation.

Just past the fire, a handful of men sit in a semi-circle, and in front of them are two dogs so emaciated their ribs seem on the verge of ripping through their skin. One has its back to me, but the other has his teeth bared. He growls and snaps when the first dog tries to step forward, and the men laugh and holler, their voices echoing through the air.

"Dog fight," I say, thinking of Zip. It makes me want to pull out my knife and cut the throats of every man here.

Behind me, Zachariah mutters, "Bastards."

I look over my shoulder, surprised by the curse coming out of his mouth. He's been so thoroughly fused with the village that most of the time I forget he's a foundling like me, but now, standing in the middle of this town, I'm able to see some of the old Zachariah. His icy eyes look colder than ever, and I've rarely seen him go this long without a smile on his face. I get the sense he feels like he's been transported back in time, and he doesn't like the feeling.

"I just want to get a closer look, and then we'll head home."

Zachariah nods once.

He stays where he is as I move closer. Most of the men have their backs to me, but the few facing me are too focused on the dogs to notice my figure moving through the shadows. I inch forward, watching where I put my feet so I don't alert anyone to my presence, and when I'm close enough, I crouch behind a pathetic bush that's half dead but full enough to hide me from view.

One of the dogs lunges and manages to get the second one in his jaws. A whimper of pain echoes off the surrounding houses, and the men whoop. They yell over the noise as the dogs go at it, rolling around as one of them fights to live while the other fights for whatever scraps these men are giving it. I can only see four of their faces, but none of them looks familiar. Three are too hidden by the darkness for me to make them out, and though I want to move closer, I force myself to stay where I am and be patient. I learned many things while hunting with Wilderness, one of them being that no one is ever rewarded by acting impulsively.

A dog lets out one final whimper, then silence booms through the night. The canine left standing backs away from the lifeless animal and looks around like he's waiting for his reward. Even before one of the men stands and points a gun at the dog, I know he'll get nothing.

The gunshot makes my entire body jerk and leaves a ringing behind in my ears. Even from where I sit, the acrid scent of gunpowder tickles my nostrils, but I barely register it because my gaze is too focused on the blond man who fired the gun. Eric.

Zachariah tugs on my shirt when I don't move, snapping me out of it. I scurry back a few steps before climbing to my feet.

"It's Eric," I whisper.

"The foundling who ran?" he asks even though he has to remember the man I'm referring to.

"Yes," I say. "He has to be the one who told those men about the village. I should go talk to him. Find out what he's doing here."

Zachariah eyes grow wide. "You cannot. It will give us away."

"Not if I tell him I escaped and have been living here. He'll believe me. Why wouldn't he?" I don't explain because Zachariah knows as well as I do. It would never occur to most people that someone who was abducted would choose to stay of their own free will. "It might be the only way."

He nods, but with hesitation. "Be careful."

"I will."

I take a deep breath then blow it out, working to ease my nerves. It isn't going to be easy, but I can play the part. Eric has been drinking, which should help.

I shove my hands in my pockets as I step out, trying to act natural. A part of me can't even remember how to do that wearing these clothes, because they don't feel natural to me anymore, but I do my best. A tune comes to me from out of nowhere, and I start whistling, and a few men turn my way. Eric is one of them, but I can tell by the expression on his face he doesn't recognize me. It's my hair. It's grown since I saw him and now hangs past my chin. Maybe it will give me away.

"Holy shit," I say, stopping like I'm in shock. "Eric?"

He narrows unfocused eyes on me. "Do I know you?"

"It's me, Jameson. From the railroad company and that—" I look around, acting like I don't want to say where else I know him from, but hoping he picks up on it.

"The mountain," he snarls, sounding even wilder than the dogs had a few moments ago.

"Yeah." I shake my head like I can't believe it was real, which in a way is true. "What are you doing here?"

I hold my breath, hoping he hasn't been here for long. Since the two men only came up the mountain today, I'm assuming Eric just got here and told them about the village. If he'd been running his mouth off for months, they would have come earlier.

"Came back to get some revenge." He puts the bottle he's holding to his lips and tips it back, sucking down the rest of the liquid. When it's empty, he tosses it aside. It shatters against a house, and shards of glass rain down, catching flickers of firelight as they do. "Damn women. How'd you get away?"

"Ran," I say. "Same as you. About five months ago."

"What about John? He got hurt on our way down, and I had to leave him. Did he make it?"

I shake my head, and Eric's face contorts. He looks like he's mentally cutting the throats of every woman in that village.

"They found him, but he was already dead," I lie, hoping to defuse some of his anger.

His expression doesn't change. "The others?"

"Still there when I left," I tell him. "Where'd you go? I came down and found this place and just kind of hung out. It's better than the city."

"Hitched a ride with the next company I came across and went back. I wasn't planning on staying in this godforsaken place, but I couldn't stop thinking about those women. Couldn't get them out of my head. When I got a call to sign up for this crew, I figured it was the perfect opportunity for some revenge." His hard expression finally changes, but the grin curling up his lips is even more disturbing. It makes him look evil. "Those women are looking for husbands, after all. Figured I should just bring them some."

The men gathered around the fire laugh, and I take the opportunity to look them over. They're ragged and dirty, and based on the scars they wear, none of them have had easy lives. But there are only eight of them, and if these are the only men Eric has on his side, we might be okay. Even without guns, we could take them.

"So this is the group you put together?" I say, trying to sound casual.

"Some of them." Eric shrugs. "There are about forty of us. I told the men there was plenty of pussy to go around, and they signed up without even blinking. I want to get my hands on the bitch leading the place, though. Can't wait to hear her scream."

I shudder, thinking about Raven, and Zachariah, who is only a few feet away listening to every word. Something scrapes against the ground behind me, and I hold my breath, forcing myself to keep my eyes forward like I didn't hear it. Eric looks past me into the darkness, but he doesn't seem to see anything, and a second later his eyes are on me once again.

"You in?" he asks.

"No way. I'm not going back up there," I say, taking a step back.

"Looks like we got us some pussy right here, boys." Eric spits at his feet while the men around him laugh. "Suit yourself. More for the rest of us. I'll be sure to find that little wife of yours and give her a good ride for you."

I clench my hands into fists. "You do that."

"Fucking pussy." Eric snorts and turns his back on me.

No one seems to notice when I walk away, and I have to work hard to keep my steps light because all I want to do is run. First back to the fire so I can choke the life out of Eric, and then up the mountain so I can get ready for anyone who might come into our village and try to destroy it.

When I reach Zachariah, I grab his arm and take off. We don't run down the street, but we don't walk the way we did coming in. My heart is pounding, and dread has filled my bones. I knew it would be Eric before I even set eyes on him, but I still feel like I've been sucker punched.

"Did you hear all that?" I ask Zachariah when we've made it down a couple streets and past the other fire.

We move side by side through the darkness, heading for the mountain and home. The sounds from the town fade more with each step, but the dread inside me only grows heavier.

Zachariah swears for the second time. "This is not good. Raven will want to send a party out to stop them from coming up the mountain."

"They have guns, Zachariah. We can't take forty. People will die."

"I know." He sucks in a deep breath and then lets it out. "I will try to talk to her. I will make her see reason."

I don't say what I'm thinking, that of everyone in the village, he's the only person who might be able to influence her, but even he won't be successful in this.

THE SUN IS TRYING TO COME UP WHEN ZACHARIAH, ZIP, AND I make it back, but the thick clouds clogging the sky are doing their best to beat it down. We go to the women's village, not the men's. We both know we may face punishment, but neither of us is willing to sit back and do nothing.

Only a few women are up, standing around the fire preparing the breakfast stew, and they stop when they see us. They stare, but there are no accusations in their eyes like I expected, and I find myself wondering if they disagree with Raven as much as we do.

"I will go to Raven," Zachariah says. "She must be made to listen."

I nod, but he doesn't need to go anywhere, because at that moment she calls down to us, "Zachariah, where have you been?" Her eyes are huge as she looks us over, taking in our clothes. "What have you done, *husband*?"

The way she pronounces the last word makes it sound like a curse or an accusation, or like she's trying to remind Zachariah of his place.

For once, it doesn't work, and he steps forward, looking up at her with unblinking eyes. "We went down the mountain so we could see what we are facing. It is not good, Raven. It—"

"You did not have permission to go anywhere!" Her voice echoes through the village, and several doors behind her open.

I look past Raven and see Wilderness step out of her hut, wrapped in a knee-length fur. Her hair is as wild as her name, like she's just woken up, and the shock on her face tells me she didn't realize I'd left until this very moment.

"Raven," Zachariah begins again, "you must listen. We—"

"Do not tell me what to do, husband. It is not your place." Her eyes snap to me and narrow to tiny slits. "This foundling has worked some kind of spell on you and on my daughter. He thinks he can change our ways, but we will not let an outsider tell us how to live. I have had enough of his interference. Jameson will meet his end today."

Gasps break out of the women, and on the other side of the village, high above my head, Wilderness screams, "No!"

She runs down the walkway, holding the fur close to her body as she zigzags through the trees, and by the time she reaches her mother, her cheeks are pink from exertion. She drops to her knees in front of Raven, lowering her head.

"Please, I beg you. Do not do this. He is my husband. He is only trying to help."

"You have let him change you." Raven takes a step away from her daughter, but the distance between them seems much bigger than two feet. "But I will not let him change us. We must put an end to him before he destroys everything we have built."

"It is not Jameson who is going to destroy this place," Zachariah calls out. "It is you, Raven."

Her face contorts just as a violent wind whips through the village, making the trees sway, their branches knocking together. The sun has been completely choked out by puffy gray clouds, and in the distance the sky is an ugly gray that matches the volatility simmering in Raven's eyes.

"Go to your village," she says.

"You cannot make the decision to end Jameson on your own," Zachariah tells her, not backing down. "You must meet with the Elders. And while you are there, you can talk about this. The foundling who ran from here, the one we never found, he is at the bottom of the mountain. He is the one who told others about us. If he brings them here, they will have weapons you do not understand. Weapons that put forth a boom like thunder and a strike like lightning. They can shoot a woman down on the furthest platform," he points past Raven, back toward the women who are listening in the distance, "and take down a bear with one shot. These men will do much worse than what the men in the hotel did, because they will steal this village and the life you love so much. Talk about that, Raven. Think about that."

The village is silent when Zachariah stops talking. He doesn't blink as he stares up at Raven, and she meets his gaze head on, seemingly unmoved by his words.

The other women standing around aren't as unaffected, though. There's terror on their faces, and dread. While Raven is so stubborn she can't listen to reason, the other women have no such issue. They look at Zachariah and then at one another like they're searching for answers, and hope blooms inside me that someone will be able to reason with Raven.

"Go," she tells Zachariah.

He turns away, heading toward the men's village, but I don't follow, instead moving toward the trees. Zip hops into the pulley cart, and I can feel Raven's gaze on my back as it moves up, but I refuse to acknowledge her. Wilderness is on the platform when the dog jumps off, and then I'm climbing up.

When I reach the top, she takes my hand and leads me across the walkway, past her mother and the other women, and the defiance does two things. It signals that Wilderness's hut is my home now, not the men's village, and it also lets Raven know we won't go down without a fight. I'm the husband of Wilderness, and she is my wife.

CHAPTER TWENTY-SIX

Wilderness

INSIDE ME, THE FEAR OF LOSING JAMESON WARS WITH THE fear of losing my village, competing for my attention even though they are one and the same, because both come down to my mother and her inability to accept what needs to be done.

"I'm sorry I didn't tell you I was going," my husband says once we are alone in our hut.

"I know why you did it, and I do not care. We needed to know what was going on." I motion to the bed but shake my head before he has a chance to sit. "Take those clothes off first. I do not like them on you. It makes you look like an outsider when you are not. You are one of us."

My husband pulls the shirt over his head and tosses it aside, and then removes the pants, and I go to him, wrapping him in fur. I want to do much more, but there will be time later, after the Elders have talked some sense into my mother. Her fear has blinded her, and the time has come for her to see the truth. I will not let her end my husband,

and running off and leaving the village behind is not an option. Fighting is the only solution.

Outside, the wind slams into the side of the hut, shaking it around us. There was a time when the movement would have terrified Jameson, but now he barely reacts, and it is yet another sign of how far we have come.

He sits, patting the bed, and I take my place at his side.

"The man you talked to, Tim, was telling the truth, but not all the people down there are good," Jameson says. "Life in the cities is hard. I don't think I can even explain it in a way you'd understand. The buildings are old and falling apart. People work so hard there's no time for rest, but it's never enough. You're given nothing for free, and most jobs pay so little you can't stay ahead. Drugs—medicines that make you forget—are rampant, and people use them to escape reality.

"The company fixing the railroad gives money to people desperate to get away from the city, and they come out here. That's who these people are, which means there are some good ones who only want a real life. But some are criminals who can't find work in the cities. Eric is one of them, and he's with other men who are the same. Forty of them. He wants revenge, and he'll bring men with him."

"We are more than forty," I tell my husband.

"They'll have guns. Even if we beat them, people will die in the process."

I like to think of us as strong, unable to be beaten by anything, but in this instance I must defer to my husband's opinion. Even his explanation of these weapons cannot make me understand them completely, but Jameson is from that world, and if we listen to him, we can prepare.

"What do you suggest we do?"

"I don't know." My husband stares at the floor like he is thinking.

We sit in silence, side by side, each of us lost in our own thoughts. I have no real understanding of the weapons he speaks of, but I believe him when he says they are dangerous. I believe him when he tells me people will die. But fighting is our only option, because we cannot leave. This mountain is our home. We have been here for seventy years, and starting over is impossible.

"There must be a way," Jameson mumbles.

Deep in my belly, something stirs, and I instinctively know it is our baby. My stomach is much rounder than it was, although still very small, and the child growing inside me is a constant reminder of what we stand to lose, as well as what we have to fight for. Both in the village, and outside it.

"We will find a way." I push the fur wrapped around me aside and take my husband's hand, putting his palm flat against my stomach, savoring how warm his skin feels against mine. I am not sure if the baby's movements are strong enough for him to feel, but I want to give him the chance. "We cannot give in."

"If there's a battle," he says, still staring at my stomach, "I don't want you to fight."

"You know that is not how it works here. I will fight because it is my duty. I will fight not just for our baby, but also for all the babies to come. I will fight not just for our way of life, but for the life you and I hope to have."

Jameson lets out a sigh but nods like he is thinking the same thing. His hand slides up my body to my breast, and he lifts his gaze from my stomach so he is looking me in the eye. Then he kisses me, easing me onto my back as I pull him closer and our furs fall away.

THE STORM DUMPS WATER ON THE VILLAGE FOR HOURS. IT bangs against the outside of the hut and roof, making conversation impossible, but it does not matter. My husband rests since he was up all night, and I take the time to think about what we can do. I believe him when he says Eric will come here, but we are strong people, and I know we can stop him. This cannot be the end of us.

It is late by the time someone knocks on the door, and I pull it open, expecting to see my mother, but find Grove standing outside my hut instead. The woman looks down at me with a pained expression, and I know right away something bad has happened.

"What is it?"

"Rain went down the mountain to check on the things the foundlings said, and some men found her. They tied her to a tree and took her against her will. They cut her. They carved symbols into her skin—" Grove falters like the words are too painful, swallowing before she is able to go on. "They did not kill her, but instead sent her back as a warning."

Behind me, Jameson gets to his feet. "What did they carve into her?"

Grove looks past me. "I do not know. They are symbols we do not understand. The Elders have asked for you and Zachariah."

"We will dress," I say.

Jameson is already wrapping the leather around himself when I shut the door, and we move silently like we are too afraid to speak. Zip is up, watching us with dark eyes that seem to understand much more than they should, and for the first time does not follow when we leave the hut, but instead sits on the platform and watches us go.

Jameson and I walk side by side through the rain, following Grove down the walkways. News of what happened must have spread, because women stand in the doorways despite the storm, watching us pass with worry in their eyes and fear in their hearts. I do my best to keep my shoulders back, but the dread of what I will see when we reach the healer's hut makes it difficult to stand tall.

The Elders and other warriors have gathered outside, but they step aside when we approach. Zachariah is already in the hut, kneeling next to the bed where Rain lies. Her face is a bloody mess, distorting her features so that if it not for her dark skin, she would be unrecognizable.

My mother stands beside the bed, and looking at her reminds me of a shell after a snail has died, hollow and purposeless. I have never seen her look as weak and vulnerable as she does at this moment.

The lamplight catches the tears in Raven's eyes when she turns toward us, making them shimmer. "I did not believe you."

Jameson does not look at her or say a word, but instead kneels next to Zachariah, and I am struck by how similar their expressions are. Fear and regret shimmer in their eyes, along with other things I cannot name. Things that turn my body cold with dread.

"Is it writing?" my husband asks.

Zachariah reaches for the fur covering Rain's body. It is pulled up to her chin, and he slides it down to reveal more of her flesh. She is naked, her body tortured. There are cuts on her arms and breasts, her blood bright red against her brown skin, as well as round marks that look like burns. Her wrists are chaffed from the rope they bound her with, and her neck swollen as if someone tried to choke the life out of her. The worst is on her stomach, though, where blood glistens on the symbols carved into her flesh.

My husband utters a word I do not know, and Zachariah hangs his head like he cannot bear to look at Rain's brutalized body.

"What does it mean?" I ask.

Jameson turns his gaze on me. "It says '*Send Raven.*'"

My mother closes her eyes like she is asking the Great Mother for help, and the silence in the hut is thick enough that if not for the wind and rain, I would think my hearing had been stolen from me. The evilness of this moment, of the men who would brutalize this woman, is exactly what our ancestors were running from. But it is our doing this time. This man, Eric, came here and did these things because of what we first did to him. If we had not brought him here, this would not be happening. We brought this evil upon ourselves.

"What do we do?" I ask, still looking at my husband.

Zachariah covers Rain's body and gets to his feet. "We will fight to save our village."

"No," my mother says, and then opens her eyes. "They have asked for me. I will go."

"You cannot." I take a step toward her, reaching out, but do not touch her.

There has been a valley of distance between us lately, and I fear if I get too close I may fall in. But she is still my mother, and no matter how much her actions have pained me, I cannot allow her to throw herself at the mercy of men who would do such horrible things.

"I must."

Her brown eyes bore into mine, and I am struck by how similar they are to Hawk's. How did I not see it sooner? All these years, and I never noticed how much my childhood friend looked like my mother. I should have.

"I am High Elder," Raven says. "I will protect this village."

"It's a trap." When my husband climbs to his feet, he seems to stand as tall as the trees. "He has no intention of letting you off that easy."

Pride swells inside me at the way he stands up to her. After everything my mother has said and done, he still refuses to back down. Until I met my husband, I did not know a man could be this strong.

"I must try," my mother says, and for the first time in many cycles, she does not look at him like he is evil.

Zachariah takes her hand, and even though she looks down at their entwined fingers, she does not chastise him for the touch.

"Raven, you must listen. You are strong, and you are a good leader, but you do not know when to open your ears and hear other people. In this matter, the boy is right. The foundling who ran will end you, and it will be much worse than what happened to Rain. Then he will bring his men up here anyway and do the same to us."

"What do you suggest?" my mother asks. "If I go to him, there is a chance he will leave the rest of the village alone, but if I do not, they will come up here and destroy us for sure."

"They'll do that anyway," Jameson says.

"You must listen to the men," a voice booms from the corner. "I remember the weapons they speak of, and I know the devastation they can bring. We must not be rash in making a decision." Everyone turns as Mother Elder pulls herself to her feet with great effort, waving away the healer's offer of help. "We have reached a turning point in our village, and it has brought me much pain. Not for the same reason it has pained Raven, but because Wilderness is right."

Flames lick at my cheeks when all eyes turn toward me. I focus on Mother Elder, though, who traps my gaze with her milky eyes as she hobbles forward. When she stops in front of me, her gnarled hands grasp mine, and despite her bony fingers, her grip is strong as she squeezes my hand.

"Raven told me what you said, about how we are no different than the men in that hotel. At first my anger blinded me, and I could not see the truth in your words. I was there, and I know what those men did. I was a witness to their evil. But when the anger faded, the Great Mother allowed me to see the truth. We have done so many things wrong." Her fingers tighten on mine, and I nearly cringe at the way my bones grind together. I had no idea this frail woman had the strength inside her for such a grip. "I started all this. I let the other women talk me into holding onto my fear." She pauses again, her eyes slipping closed as she takes in a deep breath, and when she opens them again, she says, "I was the woman who found out she was with child after arriving here, and when the baby was born, I was still just a child myself. I loved him, though, and he brought me joy I did not know I could have. Especially after witnessing so much evil.

"But the ghosts from the hotel would not leave me. They haunted my days and nights, and as the boy grew, I started to see the faces of those men in his expressions. In his smiles. In his laughter. In his tempers. I let the other women convince me he was evil, but he was only a child. He did not deserve what we did to him. We punished him for the mistakes his father made."

My mind spins like leaves caught on a fall wind, around and around in a circle, as I try to take in what Mother Elder is saying. One word stands out more than all the others, though. *Father*. Jameson said that word to me once, referring to Zachariah, but I did not know what it meant. Now, though, I feel as if I am beginning to understand.

I tear my gaze from Mother Elder and find the two men watching me. Jameson and Zachariah. Before coming here, they had very different lives with very different ideas for the future, but they have both found a way to fit into this world despite what we have done to them. Both bear scars on their backs that were placed there by us, but both also carry hope in their eyes that shimmers like the sun on water.

I turn back to Mother Elder and ask the question that has lived in my mind since Jameson first said the word to me more than a year ago. "What is father?"

She blinks, and a single tear rolls down her cheek, over her weathered skin. When she reaches out to pat my own cheek, her wrinkled hand is soft against my face. "We stole so much from you. It is not fair. Zachariah is a good man, the best kind. He loves you and your mother and your brothers. I see it in the way he looks at you." She takes a deep breath, and when she lets it out, she says, "Zachariah is your father. He and your mother made you together, just as you and Jameson have made the child growing in your belly. In the outside world, that means more than it does here, but that does not change love. Zachariah loves you."

The truth that has been nagging at my brain claws its way to the surface. All the things Jameson has said about what he wants to be to our baby come back, and it feels as if the sun has broken through the clouds, for the first time allowing me to see what Zachariah is to me. He is my mother's husband, and though I have always known what that meant, I have never thought about the part he played in creating me. But he did have a part, as much of a part as my mother did, only the village kept him from me in a way I could not see until now. I grew up at my mother's side, but Zachariah—my father—has always lived on the outskirts of my life.

There are others as well. I have already accepted that Hawk came from my mother the same way I did, and I remember when we were young together, but there were more after him. Two other yieldlings who stayed with us for a time, suckling at my mother's breast before going to the men's village to live. Brothers. That is what Mother Elder called them.

"I have brothers," I say, realization dawning on me.

This is what Jameson described. This is what his tears were for. A man and a woman living together, raising their children side by side. That is what he wants.

"Why did we do things this way?" I ask Mother Elder.

"Fear can make people do strange things, Wilderness. We thought this would make us stronger. We thought keeping a physical distance between us and the men would help us maintain control. We did not understand that equal is best. That family and love make people strong, not power." She looks past me to where my mother stands, tears shimmering in her eyes. "Men are not evil, people are. We saw that in Dawn, and we see the good in the men standing here now. We must change if we want to survive this. No more resisting what is to come, Raven. You will not go down the mountain to those men. You will not sacrifice yourself. We will instead work together, the men and the women, to save our village."

My mother nods as tears fall down her cheeks, and when Zachariah reaches out to take her hand, she does not pull away or chastise him or tell him he is wrong, but instead leans her head against his chest and cries.

CHAPTER TWENTY-SEVEN

Jameson

"DO YOU HAVE ANY THOUGHTS ABOUT HOW TO DO this?" Zachariah asks after we've left the women.

I shake my head and look around, taking in the huts and the trees, and the meager weapons the warriors carry. The storm has passed, but the world is soaked, and water drips from the trees above us and throughout the forest. The echo of them plopping against the wooden platforms is loud in the quiet morning. The sun has risen but is hidden behind clouds, covering the forest in darkness and making it seem like night is moving in.

Despite the turning point we came to in the hut, I'm not foolish enough to think the road ahead of us will be an easy one. Raven regrets the things she's done right now because she can see the consequences in what happened to Rain, but she isn't a woman easily swayed, and she's used to being in control. I can only hope the other Elders and warriors understand the severity of the situation and realize Zachariah and I are an asset, not a hindrance.

"I don't know," I tell him. "Despite our trip down the mountain, we don't know what's going on in that town. I'm willing to bet most of Eric's men will be armed, though, if not all of them. Guns may be pricey, but they aren't hard to come by, and I doubt he'd come up here without at least half of his men carrying guns."

The wind blows, and drops of water fall from the trees above us, landing on my head. I look up, then down. The ground is a good twenty feet below us, which very well could be our only advantage. That, and the trees. The huts have been up here for long enough that in places the branches have grown over the wood. Just a few feet away from where Zachariah and I stand, a thick branch curls around a post, the wood from the rail long ago absorbed by the tree as it grew. When the women built these huts, they weren't nearly as secluded as they are now, but after decades of living up here, many of the homes have become partially obscured by the surrounding foliage.

"We have the advantage," I say, waving to the trees. "If we can stay up here and out of sight, we might be okay. They can't shoot what they can't see."

Zachariah nods, thinking it through. "That is very true."

"How many bows do we have? Spears?"

"That is something you will have to ask the warriors."

"Can the men shoot?" Wilderness taught me how to shoot when she took me hunting, but I've been around long enough to know most women wouldn't do that. They want to be stronger in every way, so I doubt they ever took the time to teach even their own husbands how to defend themselves.

"They cannot," Zachariah says, confirming my suspicion, "but they can throw a spear."

"Then we'll need to make sure we have plenty of those." I push off the rail and head down the walkway. It swings under my feet with each step, and I stare down, trying to figure out how else we can use this height to our advantage. Dropping things on people when they get too close, like rocks. "We need to find big rocks we can throw at Eric's men."

"I will get the yieldlings on it," Zachariah says from behind me.

"We'll need everyone, men and women, to be up here so we can keep them safe. The kids and elderly should be in the huts at the back." I stop and turn to face him. "And we'll need to get all the rope ladders up except one. We'll pull that up last."

"This is good," he says, patting me on the arm. "We will be okay."

"I don't know about that. We have no idea when Eric plans on coming or how long we have to get ready. He sent us an ultimatum, which means he'll give us a day or so to respond, but I doubt he'll hold off for long. I didn't get to know him well, but he's impulsive, I know that much from when he ran."

"Then we should move fast," Zachariah says.

"Yes."

He heads for the men's village so he can send the yieldlings into the forest to gather rocks while I head back the way I just came. I need to find Grove or one of the other warriors so I can figure out what we have in the way of weapons. The women seemed pretty loaded down when they took me from the camp, but there were only eight of them, and the weapons they had won't be enough to go around. Wilderness has four bows in her hut and dozens of arrows, but she's a hunter, and I doubt all the women have such a big cache of weapons.

The women are leaving the healer's hut when I get back, and even though I want to go to Wilderness, I search the crowd for the tall warrior instead.

I call out when I spot her, and she turns. "I need to know how many weapons we have to work with."

Anger shadows her face like she thinks I'm overstepping, but it fades almost as fast as it appeared. "This way."

Silently, I follow Grove through the trees with Wilderness right behind me. It's going to take time for these women to get used to the idea of the men helping, but I think after today, assuming Raven doesn't derail our progress, we might be able to make it work. It's just too bad it had to happen like this.

I'm anxious to see what weapons we have, but I haven't forgotten the bombshell Mother Elder dropped on Wilderness today. She knows who Zachariah is now and what he should mean to her, and I have a feeling the revelation will have a big impact on who she is. She's always loved the man she thought of as her mother's husband, but now that she understands what a father is, she's going to have to deal with everything she's lost over the years.

I slow so we're walking side by side and slip my hand into hers. "Are you okay?"

"I am," she says, but her expression is thoughtful. "You tried to tell me who he was, but I did not want to hear it. It is strange, knowing he should have more meaning in my life than he has. What is the role of a father in the outside world?"

"He's supposed to be the mother's partner. They help each other. Support each other. You aren't the only one who missed out on that. Raven did, too."

"She loves Zachariah very much, but she refused to let him see it."

"Maybe she will now."

I give her hand a squeeze as Grove comes to a stop at a hut on the far end of the village. I've never been down this far, there was never any reason for it, and I'm shocked when she pulls the door open to reveal a storage hut. There are furs piled along one wall while weapons line the other side. Bows, arrows, spears, and even knives carved out of bone.

I drop Wilderness's hand and step past Grove, a surge of hope shooting through me. "There's so much."

"We are peaceful," Grove says, "but we have always lived in fear that men would come and take us back to the hotel. We wanted to be ready."

I remember the throats they slit right in front of my eyes, the crack of the whip across my back, and the screams Hawk let out during his punishment. They aren't as peaceful as they like to believe, but given the choice between these misguided women and the man who brutalized Rain, I choose the women. I can only hope once this is over they can settle into life and become the peaceful group they believe they are.

"How many women know how to shoot a bow?" I ask, turning to face Grove and Wilderness.

"All of them," the tall warrior says.

"How many men?" I ask even though the answer is obvious.

Grove shakes her head. "None."

Wilderness hangs her head, and I take comfort in knowing she at least understands what they've done to themselves.

"The men can throw these." I grab a handful of spears. "We'll get them up here now so they can practice. Zachariah sent the yieldlings out to gather rocks. We're going to use the trees to our advantage. The men down there may have guns, but we have the element of surprise. Hopefully."

CHAPTER TWENTY-EIGHT

Wilderness

WHEN MY HUSBAND AND I PART WAYS, I HEAD TO the men's village in search of Zachariah. He is there when I step through the trees, talking to a group of men, Hawk among them. Just looking at them makes my heart swell until it feels twice as big, and memories come back in a rush, slamming into me like a burst of wind. How many times has Zachariah looked at me with an expression in his eyes I did not understand? How many times have I felt like he wanted to say or do more? It all makes sense now, the looks and moments when he reached out as if wanting to touch me. How did I never realize what he should mean to me?

Because I could not know.

Zachariah is something I never knew existed. Not until Jameson came into my life and I found out I was with child did I realize the importance of my husband's role. How my mother could have spent her entire life living this way and denying a bond that should have been so obvious is something I will never understand, and something that will be very difficult to forgive. Mother Elder is right. They have stolen so much from me.

Zachariah turns like he can feel my gaze on him, and when his eyes meet mine, he smiles. It is the most genuine smile I have ever seen on his face, and the warmth radiating from it is what finally spurs me forward. He walks toward me as I cross the men's village, and we meet in the middle.

"My daughter," he says when he stops in front of me, and the word fills me with a joy I never knew existed.

"Father." My throat tightens like a snake has curled around it, and I find I can barely get the word out.

My eyes fill with tears, and I feel like a small child again. Suddenly, I remember the day I fell from a tree in the woods. I was only five at the time and had snuck away to play with Hawk even though we knew it was not allowed, but we had missed one another, which is a feeling that never really went away. In the forest, we climbed a tree, racing to see who would reach the top first. I was in the lead, but halfway up, the branch under my hand broke, and I fell.

The force of the fall had knocked the air from lungs, and I found I could not even cry out. Hawk left me there, running back to the men's village to get help, and I remember staring up into the blue sky and believing I was going to meet the Great Mother.

Zachariah seemed to appear out of nowhere, his blue eyes replacing the sky. He scooped me into his arms, but instead of taking me to my mother, he carried me to his own hut. There, he cleaned the scrapes on my arms and legs and wiped the tears from my cheeks, and it was the gentleness in his touch that finally helped me calm down.

When had finished, he knelt in front of me and said, "You are okay, Wilderness, just as you will always be as long as I am here."

His words had wrapped me in a comforting cocoon, and after that I always felt safe and protected in his presence, always felt like I could go to him if I needed anything even if he had never been anyone to me. At least not that I knew of.

"Why did you not tell me earlier?" I ask Zachariah now, blinking when tears fill my eyes, blurring his face. "I know you wanted to."

He gives me a sad smile. "You were not ready."

He is right, but it still stings to hear such a hard truth. "I should have known."

"There is no way you could have."

Tears slide down my cheeks, and Zachariah wraps his arms around me, and I lean my head against his chest so I can hug him back. There have been many times in the past when I would have liked for him to do this. After I fell out of the tree and cried, when I dragged myself back to the village after an altercation with a wild cat, bleeding and scared. At the age of six when he caught Hawk and me playing and told us we were no longer allowed to do such things. When Jameson and Hawk were whipped. When Zachariah told me he was proud of me. We have missed out on so many moments in my twenty-six years, but I pray to the Great Mother that the next twenty-six will bring plenty more, and that from here on out, things will be different.

Zachariah and I stay that way for some time, and when he finally pulls back, I find that the men in the village have stopped to watch us, Hawk among them. The brown eyes that are so much like my mother's are focused on us as if trying to understand what is happening. There is change in the air, and it feels like a warm breeze after a brutally cold winter.

"Hawk is my brother," I say, looking up into my father's eyes.

"He is." The smile that spreads across Zachariah's face is even more beautiful than all his other smiles combined. "You and Hawk grew in your mother at the same time. You are twins. That is why you feel such a strong bond."

Twins. I did not even know such a thing existed, but it makes all my memories come into better focus. The early ones, although fuzzy, all have Hawk in them, and I understand now why I could never let him go. We were together before we were ever born, and we should have stayed together instead of being ripped apart the way we have been.

"Who else?" I ask, awed and suddenly excited by the idea of the family I never knew existed. "I know my mother had other yieldlings. Who are they?"

"Ash and Talon." Zachariah pauses for a moment before saying, "Reed was another, but he died."

Reed. I remember the blond boy who was killed by the rattlesnake many seasons ago, as well as the way my mother locked herself in her hut after his death, refusing to come out for days. She said she was ill, but when I saw her, she seemed healthy. Now, I know why. She may have passed her boys off to the men, but it was not an easy thing for her to do. She may have built walls around her heart, but no matter how hard she tried to keep people out, some of them got through. Zachariah, and her sons.

"I have brothers," I say as tears fall down my cheeks for the brothers I have and the one I lost, and for the years that have slipped away. There will be more, but Mother Elder is right. So much has been stolen not just from me, but from all of us.

"You do." My father pulls me against him again, tears in his own eyes, and together we cry.

THE MEN AND BOYS RETURN TO THE WOMEN'S VILLAGE WITH Zachariah and me. All of them. I have no idea where they will sleep tonight, but we cannot risk anyone living so close to the ground when we do not know what Eric has planned for us. Soon, Jameson and I will head down the mountain to keep watch, but before that, we must be sure we are ready for anything.

We haul rocks into the trees using the pulley cart and load them into baskets along the first walkway, knowing Eric and his men will reach this section of the trees first.

"I want all the men to practice throwing spears," Jameson calls.

I watch him, marveling at the leader he has been today. It is a new thing for this village, a man taking charge, but it fills me with a sense of pride, knowing this powerful man is my husband. He has one of my bows in his hand and a sheath of arrows on his back. Unlike the other men, he is ready for what is to come because I have taken the time to teach him to shoot. But he is alone in that skill, and the determination in his eyes tells me how deeply he feels the other men's disadvantage.

Jameson crosses the walkway behind the other men as they hurl spears to the ground, and turning when he reaches the end. His back comes into view, and a pang of regret and sadness shoots through me, almost as if one of those spears has pierced my heart. His eagle tattoo is still distorted, but the scars from his punishment have faded, and next to the leather sheath they seem dark. Every time I look at those scars it feels like I am being whipped, and sometimes at night when my husband is asleep, I kiss the lines crisscrossing his back and pray to the Great Mother that I will be able to forgive myself the way he has forgiven me. It is not just me who must work to earn Jameson's forgiveness, though, but all the women. My mother especially.

We must survive this, because we have much to make up for.

Across the walkway, the men are lined up, and one by one they hurl spears to the ground, aiming for the distant trees and stumps in the clearing. Some of them miss, but most hit the mark. Their good aim only gives me a little bit of relief, though, because I find it impossible to stop thinking about the weapons Eric's men will have and how different they are from our own.

"We'll have to do our best to stay out of sight," Jameson yells as the men continue their target practice. "Their weapons are a lot more advanced than ours. They'll be able to hit us all the way up here. But if they can't see us, they can't hit us. That's why I want you to stick close to the huts and the areas where the leaves are thick."

My mother stands on the opposite platform, watching as the men hurl the spears, and despite our conversation in the hut, she wears an uneasy expression. I look the men over, trying to see what she sees. There are men everywhere, scattered throughout the walkways and platforms, hurling spears and hauling up rocks, as well as talking to the women who call them husband. It is something that has never happened before. Husbands come to huts at night, and the men join us in our village often for festivals, but we have never had them all up in the trees like this, and seeing the two groups mixed together the way they are causes hope to swell inside me, but my mother looks like the sight fills her with fear. She must know this is for the best, though. She cannot continue to resist when we are on the brink of losing so much, can she?

Raven's gaze follows Grove and Ash when they pass her, watching as the warrior gives her husband a bow. My mother's expression darkens in a way I cannot read, and then she turns away. She leaves, but I do not watch her go despite the worry swirling through me. I am too focused on Ash, the brother I did not know I had, as Grove shows him how to shoot. He is her husband and she is a warrior, and yet she has never bothered to teach him how to defend himself. Before Jameson came here, it made sense to me, because she was the woman and he was just a man, but at this moment, it seems so very wrong.

Only a few lengths down from them, Hawk stands with Blossom. Since the time Jameson and I came upon them in the forest, I have wondered about them more and more. Before today I had no hope that Blossom would ever be allowed to take a new husband, but perhaps it is possible after this. Maybe the Elders will allow it, and together they will find the same happiness Jameson and I have found.

The bundle on Blossom's back wiggles, and it hits me that this is Eric's child. He does not even know it exists, but the baby carries his blood inside her veins. Will the little girl grow up to be evil like her father, or is it possible that people are more a product of their environment than their blood? I hope that is the case, and I pray to the Great Mother that we can be a good example for this baby. That we will be able to show her a life free of violence and death.

I push through the crowd and cross the walkway to Hawk, and when I stop in front of him, he gives me a smile that is more genuine than it has been in years. It also reminds me of our father.

"I have talked to Zachariah," he says.

"You mean our father?" I ask, and he nods. "Did you know?"

"I did not. There was a time when I felt a bond with Raven, but it faded long ago. To me, she has always seemed like she is filled with ice." He lets out a deep sigh like the truth saddens him. "Zachariah, I have always cared for. I saw the special relationship the girls in the village had with their mothers, and it is how I have always felt with him. I did not know the word for it, but I imagined that if we were women, he would be my mother."

His words warm me as much as the sun shining down on my head does. Hawk had love in his life even though our mother cast him aside. Zachariah has done well here, in more ways than I ever knew.

"What about Ash and Talon?" I ask my brother.

"I knew nothing of them." This time the sigh Hawk lets out is longer, as if it comes from deep inside him. "If Raven had told Dawn the truth, things might have been different. We were happy together once. I even thought I loved her."

"Raven should have told her," I agree.

When he shakes his head, it seems to push away some of my images of having a family like the one Jameson described. It will not be easy for my brother to forgive Raven, at least not right away, but I have to cling to the hope that in time he will realize she is not as cold as he thinks she is. She has regret for the things she has done, for Dawn and for many others.

"Our mother knows she was wrong," I say, reaching out to my brother. When my hand comes to rest on his arm, he stares at it like he not sure if the touch is right or wrong. "Raven is sorry for what she has done."

"Some things are much bigger than sorry, Wilderness. This is one of them." Hawk nods to Blossom, who has been standing at his side this entire time, listening. "I must get back to training. I am not a hunter like you, and I do not know how to defend myself. Being useless is not something I enjoy."

"Go, Hawk," I tell him, allowing my hand to fall from his arm. "We have plenty of time ahead of us."

My brother gives me one last look before turning away.

The urge to reach out to him, to hug him the way I hugged our father only a short time ago, is strong, but I resist. Unlike Zachariah, Hawk has never been anything but a yieldling, and the gesture would be confusing and uncomfortable for him. To Hawk, touching a woman is wrong, and I cannot expect him to change overnight. It will take time to adjust to the new ways.

The men practice for hours, but when dinnertime draws near, Jameson and Zachariah work with the warriors to distribute the spears along the walkways and platforms so they are easily accessible. We pull up all but one of the rope ladders, and throughout the trees, people retire to huts to rest. Watching the husbands and yieldlings join the women they belong to is a beautiful moment, and it helps me picture the family Jameson described. The mother and father raising their children together, leaning on one another to make the work easier.

"This is what I wanted," he says.

His hand is resting on my stomach when the movement I felt the day before happens once again, only much stronger this time. Before, it was like a tickle inside me, or the flutter of a butterfly's wings, but now it feels as if our child has reached out and touched me.

My husband looks at my belly, an expression of awe on his face. "Is that the baby?"

"It is. It grows stronger every day."

"Do you think it's a girl or a yieldling?" he asks.

"I think it is a boy," I say as I turn to face him. "And he will be my son, and yours, too."

EVENING SETS IN, AND THE SKY ABOVE US GROWS DARKER AS patches of bright yellow and orange poke through the trees, while a small group gathers to see Jameson and me off. Some of the Elders and warriors, but my mother and father as well.

Hoping it will give us enough warning when Eric and his men come up the mountain, my husband and I are heading down to serve as lookout. Nerves prick at my insides like the beaks of birds trying to poke holes in my stomach when I think about what might happen next, but focusing on the people in front of me—women and men standing side by side, working together—helps. Being united will make us stronger. It will help us win.

"When we see the men coming, we will ride back and warn everyone," I say as I pull myself onto the horse. "Keep watch."

"The warriors will take turns standing guard," Elder Warrior assures me.

My husband climbs onto the horse in front of me, taking the lead. It is a position I am not used to, but clinging to him gives me strength, and knowing he will be at my side eases more of my worry. I am not alone in this. Together, Jameson and I can defeat anything.

Raven stands at Zachariah's side, watching us prepare to leave. She does not seem as proud or regal as she usually does, and with her gray hair and pale skin, she almost looks like all the color has been sucked from her body. It makes her seem much older than she is, and much more vulnerable.

There is fear in her brown eyes when she looks up at me, and shame. She steps forward and reaches for my hand, and I allow her to take it. "Be careful, my daughter. Do not take any risks."

"I will not," I tell her, returning the gentle squeeze she gives my hand.

She steps back, and my hand slips from hers, and Zachariah reaches out to take it. The warmth of his touch is much more welcome than my mother's, illustrating how much has already changed.

"Be safe," he says but does not release my hand when he turns to Jameson. "I know you will watch after my daughter."

My husband looks over his shoulder at me, and pride and love swell inside my chest until it feels like it will burst. "I'll die for her if I have to."

Zachariah finally releases my hand and steps back. Zip, sitting at his side, looks up at us anxiously, almost like he wants to hop onto the horse as well, but all it takes is one command from my husband for the dog to settle down.

Something flickers in my mother's eyes when she looks at Jameson, but her expression is softer than it has been for more than a season. "I have not given you enough credit," she tells him. "You loved my daughter when you did not have to. You stood by her when you could have run. You gave her a child when you could have refused, and you stood up for us when we did not want you to. You are a good man, Jameson."

"I try to be," he says, but the coldness in his tone says he has not yet forgiven her.

Raven lowers her gaze at his accusatory tone. "Please forgive me for the things I have said and done to you."

"We'll have time for that," Jameson replies then clicks his heels against the horse's flank.

I wrap my arms around his waist when we take off. The forest zooms past in a blur of green, leaves slapping against my skin and branches reaching out as if trying to pull us down. The sky grows darker with each beat of the horse's hooves, the sun moving further down in the sky until there is only a hint of light left on the horizon. At several points, the horse must slow due to the rocky terrain, but in no time we have reached the center of the mountain.

"How far should we go?" my husband asks when he has slowed the horse to nothing more than a trot.

"A little further," I tell him. "I must find a good tree to climb."

Jameson urges the horse forward while I scan the trees. They tower above me like majestic beings, their arms reaching to the sky as if begging the Great Mother to watch over us. I do the same, silently asking for protection as I search for the perfect lookout point.

When I spot a tree with thick, low branches, I signal for Jameson to stop, and when he does, I slide off, my feet hitting the ground with a soft thud. My husband follows as I study the tree in front of us, my heart pounding with a mixture of anticipation and fear.

"I will climb," I say, still staring up at the branches. "From up there, I will be able to see over the trees and down the mountain. It is dark enough now that their lights will give them away when they do decide to come."

"I'll be down here."

His voice is firm and reassuring, but before I can take even one step, he has me in his arms. His heart beats in sync with mine, almost like we are one person, and I close my eyes, letting the strength of his body seep inside me so I have the courage to get through this night.

"Be careful," he whispers.

"I am only climbing a tree," I tell him, but inside it feels like much more, and the worry in his voice says he can feel it, too.

I haul myself up, my feet gripping the branches as my arms pull me higher and higher. The bark scratches my skin while the summer air tries to suffocate me with its heat, and by the time I am halfway up, my skin is sticky with sweat, but still I push myself.

When I finally reach a point where I can see out past the tree line, I take a deep breath and work to calm my pounding heart. I find a groove on a thick branch that fits my backside perfectly and settle in, hoping the security of the spot will ease my nerves but knowing nothing can as long as the future is so uncertain.

The dark night has swallowed up my husband, but it does not matter because I know he is there, and his presence is enough to keep me alert and ready. The world grows darker, and then seems to lighten as my eyes adjust to the blackness. Above me, the sky is clear of the rainclouds that clogged it the day before, and stars twinkle down like they are winking at me. In the distance, lights flicker, but they do not move closer. They must be from the town Jameson and Zachariah visited.

Time passes, and I grow weary but refuse to allow my eyes to close. The lights disappear one by one, turning the world in front of me black. The town is asleep, but I am not foolish enough to think Eric has given up. If he does not come tonight, he will come tomorrow, and I must stay alert.

To pass the time, I pray to the Great Mother, asking for strength and survival, and for peace both inside and outside the village once this whole ordeal has finally come to an end.

By the time lights appear in the distance, my backside has gone numb. They are nothing but little specks bouncing through the darkness like fireflies, and at first I feel certain I am seeing things. Soon, though, they grow larger. Clearer. Closer.

They are coming.

I twist my body around so I can descend, moving much more carefully on the way down than I did on the way up. The lower I get, the thicker the darkness becomes, aided by the abundant leaves above my head that have effectively blocked out the light from the moon and stars. On the ground there is a scratch of movement, telling me my husband is awake and already on his feet. When I am still a man's height off the ground, he grabs me and pulls me down.

"They're coming?" he asks once my feet are on the ground.

"They are a long way off," I tell him. "But there are lights. Ten, maybe more. They are coming."

Jameson pulls himself up onto the horse's back then lends me his hand so I can climb on behind him. Once I am seated, I wrap my arms around his waist, and he takes off up the mountain, much faster than he did going down. Branches whip against my arms and legs, scratching me, but I do not cry out. My heart beats faster than the pounding of the horse's hooves, making it impossible to catch my breath. Soon Eric and his men will be in our village. Soon we will fight to save our lives and our way of life. We cannot let these men defeat us.

The forest is dark and still damp from the rain. Mist has begun to rise, making it more difficult to see, but my husband does not slow, and under me the horse's steps are steady and sure. Through the darkness, the village comes into view, so hidden by the mist and trees that I do not think I would notice it if I did not know it was there. The huts are black spots in the sky, hovering high above our heads, the ones farthest away so well concealed that they are nothing more than extensions of the trees they cling to. Hopefully, Jameson is right, and the trees give us the advantage we need.

We break through the brush and race into the clearing. Jameson urges the horse to slow, and the animal neighs, the sound echoing through the silent night, and a chill shoots through me. Even the animals in the forest are quiet, as if they know danger is on the way.

Seconds after the horse's call has faded to nothing, the echo of doors opening pierces the silence. I jump from the horse, and my husband follows, smacking the animal on its rump once he is down. It takes off, back toward the men's village and his friends, while we head for the trees.

"Up." Jameson grabs my arm and urges me toward the tree where the lone rope ladder hangs.

The fire that usually glows in the center of the village has been extinguished, and the ladder has been swallowed up by the darkness. Somehow, I manage to find it, but like a child who imagines creatures hiding in the shadows, my heart thuds faster. I scramble up with Jameson right behind me, and the second we are both on the platform, he drops to his knees so he can pull the ladder up. We have a good head start on the men, and it could still be hours before they arrive, but we do not want to leave anything to chance.

"They are coming?" a voice I recognize as Grove's says behind me.

"They are."

"How many did you see?" another woman asks.

"I saw lights in the distance. There were not many, but I do not think all the men have lanterns. Eric told Jameson he had forty men, so that is the number we should count on."

"We're in luck, though," my husband says. With the ladder safely up, he climbs to his feet and joins the warriors and me. "The darkness will make it harder for them to hit us."

I do not point out that it will also make it harder for us to hit them.

CHAPTER TWENTY-NINE

Jameson

WE'VE BEEN HUNCHED DOWN IN THIS HUT FOR hours, but there's no sign of the men. I'd wonder if Wilderness was seeing things, except I think Eric had the same realization I did. Darkness makes it harder to kill people.

"The sun will be up soon." I whisper to make sure my voice won't penetrate the walls of the hut, but it's still loud enough to rouse Zip from his restless sleep. I scratch his head as I say, "He'll come at dawn."

No one argues, but I have no delusions about these women trusting me. I'm still a foundling to most of them. Even Raven's apology doesn't make me think she's changed, especially with the uneasy way she looks at me every time I hand out orders. Everything takes time, and right now the warriors and other women crowded into this hut are wondering if they should be listening to me at all.

Wilderness slips her hand into mine and gives it a squeeze, and I try to hold onto her strength, but all it does is remind me that she's at the front lines. That she'll be in danger. As will our baby.

Light streams in through the cracked door, soft at first but soon growing brighter, and with each passing moment I get more and more tense. Zip whines, and I drop Wilderness's hand. I pull an arrow out, and around me the women shift. I know they're feeling it, too. Morning has dawned, and Eric will be on his way.

"Get ready," I say, mostly to myself, but the others nod.

The minutes pass, and my heart thumps in my ears until it's all I can hear, and for the first time since coming here, I feel as weak and useless as these women think I am. It's the powerlessness of the situation, though. Eric is out there, and he wants to destroy us, and I can't do a damn thing to stop him from coming.

When a male voice finally breaks through the quiet, it's loud and clear, and audible even over the thudding of my heart.

"Hello, there!"

No one moves.

Eric announcing his arrival wasn't something I expected, and for a moment I'm not sure how to react. I thought he'd see the ladders pulled up and search for another way into the trees. Thought he'd try to sneak in the back door. But this? Why is he making himself so vulnerable?

"What do we do?" Wilderness whispers.

Zachariah's eyes meet mine from across the hut, but all he does is shrug. Like me, he's shocked by Eric's boldness. Is the asshole that sure of his position, or is he so arrogant he's underestimating us?

"I want to see Raven. The *High Elder*." The sarcasm in Eric's voice makes me cringe.

Raven climbs to her feet, brushing Zachariah's hands away when he tries to stop her. "I should go out."

"No." I jump up, as does almost everyone else in the hut, and the look she shoots me confirms my fears. She doesn't like taking orders from a man, especially a foundling. "He'll kill you. Remember what I said. We have to keep out of range."

"He is asking for me," Raven argues. "Maybe we can reason with him."

"You cannot reason with a man like this," Zachariah says.

The stubborn gleam in Raven's eyes is back, and I can feel the tentative peace we had slipping away. Old habits die hard, and an entire day of men telling her what to do has worn on her patience and made her fear the future.

"Raven," Wilderness says, "you cannot do this."

"I am High Elder." She takes a step toward the door, her head held high. The stance used to make her seem strong, but now she just reminds me of a child who is determined to get her way. "I must do what I can to protect this village."

"You will not go out alone." Zachariah grabs Raven's arm, stopping her when her hand moves toward the door. "I will go with you."

"No—" Wilderness reaches out, but she doesn't touch either of them.

Her eyes bounce between her mother and father like a ball being tossed back and forth, and the fear in them is clearer than the sky on a cloudless day. She's terrified of losing both her parents before they've had a chance to be a family, and I understand, but I also know as well as she does that no one can tell Raven what to do.

"Raven!" Eric screams, his voice echoing off the trees above us.

She takes another step toward the door. "I must go."

The other women in the hut don't argue, and silently I curse them for their ways and their inability to relinquish control.

Raven pulls the door open, and light streams in through the gap. Until this moment, I hadn't realized how stuffy the hut had gotten, and when a burst of fresh air whooshes inside, I suck in a deep breath. There isn't a damn thing I can do to change Raven's mind, which means it's time to get ready for battle.

"Stay," I tell Zip as Raven steps out of the hut.

Zachariah is right behind her, and I move after them but keep low, hoping Eric can't see me. The railing provides no cover, but the branches around the platform are thick, and the leaves should do the job of hiding me from view. At least I hope so. I don't want to give everything away yet. Let him think we're all cowering in fear.

Wilderness follows me out, as do a few others. A warrior with a bow moves behind the hut and climbs onto the roof while the rest of the women crouch down, taking cover behind the thick branches surrounding the platform.

Raven walks forward with her head held high, and I marvel at how powerful she can make herself look, even when she's being a fool. She stops in the center of the walkway, with Zachariah at her side, and as close to her as he's standing, it almost looks like he's prepared to throw himself in front of her if necessary.

Through the leaves, I see Eric smile up at Raven, not the least bit intimidated. There are no more than twenty men on the ground, but that doesn't mean there aren't more in the forest. Every visible man is armed, and they all look as brutal as their leader. Dirty, ripped clothes, and eyes that gleam as they look Raven over. A few smile, sending a shiver down my spine, but most don't even blink. I'm not sure which is worse, the sick look in some of the men's eyes, or the lack of emotion in others.

Raven looks at Eric like he's a speck of dust. "What do you want, foundling?"

The door to the hut on the other side of the walkway opens, and women crawl out. Like us, they stay low, keeping themselves hidden.

"I gave you a chance to stop this." Eric glares up at Raven. "You could've come, and I woulda been happy to have just you. Remember that while you watch your people get butchered."

"The only butchering that happens today will be your men," she calls out, her voice rising above the trees.

On the other platform, Grove gets to her knees and raises her bow. The other warriors follow suit, and the women around me do the same, positioning themselves so they're taking aim through the branches. I start to lift my own bow, but my shaking hands tell me something is off. Then I see it. Eric's finger is on the trigger of his gun. He's ready to fire. He wants to fire.

If anyone up here releases an arrow, he'll shoot Raven, maybe even Zachariah as well. They're sitting ducks where they are, out in the middle of the walkway, and for the millionth time I curse Raven and her pigheadedness. She should have stayed on the platform and not gone out into the middle of the walkway. Here she could duck down and slip from view, but out there she can't do a damn thing. She has a bow, but she hasn't even taken an arrow out of the sheath on her back. Even Eric's arrogance doesn't match hers, because he wasn't fool enough to come here without backup, but she's put her life on the line, thinking her position as High Elder can save her from anything.

"Don't shoot," I hiss to the women around me.

I scoot forward and peer down, trying to get a better look at the men on the ground. Everyone around Eric is armed with guns, but they aren't all as ready as he is. Some have their weapons out, but others still have them tucked away in their belts. They underestimate these women, but Raven is also underestimating Eric.

Wilderness nudges me and motions to the forest at the men's backs. Past them and almost concealed by the trees, a hint of movement catches my eye. Not only in one place, either, but in several. Wilderness is a good hunter, so I'm not surprised she saw it. I just hope the other women see it, too.

Like she's reading my thoughts, Raven reaches back and pulls out an arrow, and the men on the ground respond by pulling out more guns.

"Shit," I mutter, taking a deep breath.

The situation is spiraling out of control much faster than I anticipated, and the only thing I can think to do is jump to my feet and lift my arms. "Eric."

He turns his gun on me, and his upper lip curls. "Thought you ran off." He spits on the ground like he's imagining it's my face. "Guess she pulled some kind of pussy voodoo on you after all, just like that sick fuck there." I don't need him to wave toward Zachariah to know who he's talking about, but he does anyway.

"Tell us why you have come," Raven calls.

I want to tell her to shut up, but I can't because I'm a man and she's liable to fire just to spite me.

Eric's finger twitches above the trigger, and my heart pounds. I take a step closer to the walkway, and Wilderness reaches out, trying to grab my leg, but I move further from her.

"You know why," Eric calls. "That pussy whipped son of a bitch told you all about it."

Raven raises her bow, arrow nocked and ready, and aims it at Eric. "You will leave."

He raises his hands, the gun in the right one, and grins up at her. "We can still end this. All I want is you and that bitch who called me her husband." The men around him mumble in protest, but Eric waves them off. "Shut up."

"You would like to see Blossom?" Raven calls. "Very well."

I've taken couple steps toward the walkway when the click of a door echoes through the silence. Footsteps follow, and behind me the women shift. On the other platform, they're ready and waiting, but I'm not sure who they're looking to for a signal. Before this, I would have said me, but Raven has once again taken control.

The sneer doesn't disappear from Eric's face, but he takes his eyes off Raven so he can search the trees for Blossom. I can tell when she comes into view, because his upper lip curls even more.

"That my baby?"

"It is," Blossom calls out.

Eric shakes his head twice. "Wrong."

He turns his gun on her so fast I don't even have time to register what's happened. The crack of the gunshot makes several women cry out, and instead of releasing their arrows, most of them freeze, too shocked and frightened to do anything. A few do fire into the men, though, and on the ground, one goes down, screaming as the tip of an arrow pierces his shoulder. Another gets an arrow in the gut and falls to his knees. A third man is hit in the leg. He screams as he fires off a shot of his own, aiming for the trees.

Shots ring out all around me, and more arrows fly through the air, and behind us men rush out of the huts with spears and hurl them down at Eric and his men.

"Run!" I call to Zachariah, who has curled his body around Raven in an attempt to protect her.

Behind me, a woman steps from the cover of the trees and raises her bow, but before she's had the chance to release an arrow, a bullet hits her in the chest. She cries out, dropping her weapon, and her body droops forward, bending over the railing. I reach for her too late, my fingers brushing fur as she topples forward, and I watch in horror as she falls to the ground.

That's when I realize Wilderness is now on her feet, shooting at the men.

I grab her and pull her down, calling out, "Keep low!"

All around us, women fire arrows while men hurl spears and rocks. Zachariah and Raven are no longer on the walkway, but are once again hidden by the trees on the platform across from us. Bodies are sprawled out on the ground, and a surge of victory goes through me despite the blood, because most of them are Eric's men.

But more men pour out of the forest and fire into the trees, and splinters hit my face when a bullet pings off the wood in front of me. I shove Wilderness down then stand with my bow raised, searching for Eric, ready to end this. He's huddled behind a fallen tree, but I won't be able to get to him from my position, so I step onto the walkway, hoping to get a better shot. He isn't watching me, and he doesn't notice when I pull the string on my bow back. I take aim, letting out a deep breath the way Wilderness taught me to, and I release the arrow just as a splintering pain bursts through my side.

CHAPTER THIRTY

Wilderness

JAMESON STANDS OVER ME WITH HIS BOW RAISED. HE forced me down, and though I do not want to stay here, I find I cannot move. The crack of the men's weapons makes it difficult to think straight, and I do not know what to do or who has gotten hurt or even killed. All I know is we are no match for these weapons, and my mother has once again proven herself to be a fool.

Above me, my husband cries out, and everything freezes as blood bursts across his side. At first I cannot figure out what happened. Not even when he falls at the edge of the platform. Then another crack breaks through the air, jolting me out of my stupor, and I realize Jameson has been injured.

I want to dive for him, but I stay low as I drag myself to his side. There is blood everywhere, on his side and back, and puddled on the wood beneath him.

"Jameson," I gasp, his name getting tangled with my sob.

"I'm okay," he grunts, but when he holds his hand against his side, blood gushes between his fingers. "Help me to the hut."

I help him to his feet and put my arm around him. Trying to keep our bodies low is a challenge, especially with him injured and leaning against me, making every step difficult, but somehow we manage to make it into the hut where he slumps against the wall. Zip is at his side in a blink, whining as he sniffs Jameson while I grab a fur off the floor so I can press it against the wound. There is so much blood, but it is all I can do is try to stop the flow. It will not be enough, and I know it. Jameson needs the healer, and soon. Only she is across the walkway in the other hut, and between us lies death.

"Shit," my husband gasps out. "That hurts." He takes a deep breath and touches his back, gasping in pain once again. "The bullet went all the way through. That's good. I'll be okay."

Someone screams, and I tear my gaze from my bleeding husband. Across the walkway, on the other platform, lies Blossom's body. She has met her end, but the baby is gone, and I pray someone has taken the child into the hut. Below us, scattered across the dirt, are the bodies of Eric's men, but there are others as well. Women from our village. Women who have been with me since birth. Women who are family. Women who only wanted to live a life of peace.

If this does not stop soon, more of us will meet our end. I have to do something.

I focus on Eric and the men with him, hiding behind trees and logs, keeping low until they are ready to fire. The men who have come up the mountain with Eric have no issue with us. They are only here because of him. If I take out Eric, the others will run. I am sure of it.

I grab my bow and stand, brushing my husband's hand away when he reaches for me. "I will not let more people meet their end today," I tell him. "I will not let you meet yours."

Jameson calls out to me before I have gone too far, "Wilderness." I turn. "Shoot straight."

"I do not know any other way," I tell him and step out of the hut.

Once again, I keep low as I look around, trying to find the best approach. Across the village on various platforms, women crouch, each of them holding bows while at their sides, men kneel with spears. Below us, I can see the top of Eric's head. Like the other men, he is huddled behind a log and mostly hidden by brush. He looks up every few seconds and fires toward the trees, but he does not take his time, and he hits nothing. Jameson was right. Eric is impulsive. It is another advantage we have over him. Two men crouch at his side, but it seems like most of those who came with him have fled or have already met their own ends.

Eric will not be far behind.

I sling my bow over my shoulder and move behind the hut. Here, the branches are thick where they have long ago grown around the building, and I use them as footfalls to pull myself onto the roof. The wood groans under my weight as I position myself in the center, keeping my body low in hopes of distributing my weight. From up here, I have a good view of Eric, and as long as he does not move, I should be able to hit him with no problem.

My hands are steady when I wrench my bow from my back and nock an arrow. I pull back on the string and take a deep breath, blowing it out so my body does not tense up. I have Eric in my sights, his head lined up with the tip of the arrow.

His end will come very soon.

Just as I am about to let my arrow fly, he moves forward, leaning over the log so he can take a shot. I relax my arms and breathe in and out. Slowly. Keeping my body steady and my nerves at bay. A few beats pass, and Eric has again settled onto the ground, and I raise my bow for the second time and pull the string back. My arms are steady and strong, but I take my time. I cannot rush this.

When he does not move again, I ask the Great Mother to guide my arrow, then blow the air out of my lungs one more time before releasing the string. My arrow whirls through the air, and the point sinks into Eric's eye, the impact making his head jerk back. His body slides down, his head coming to rest against the log he was using as a shield, and then he is still.

The men at his side let out shouts of surprise as they jump to their feet and run for the forest, but I already have an arrow ready. I let it go, and the arrow hits the man closest to Eric in the back, sending him to the ground. I reach behind me, ready to shoot again, but the third man is down before I can wrap my fingers around another arrow, and I glance toward the opposite platform just as Grove lowers her bow.

When I look back, I discover that the other men have fled with Eric's death, and the clearing is now empty. It is over. We have won.

There is no time for celebration, though. Not with Jameson hurt.

I scoot backward and climb down from the roof, my feet finding the branches instinctively. Once I have reached the platform, I hurry to the hut where my husband lies bleeding. He is not the only injury, and I know many people I love have met their ends today, but right now I can think only of Jameson.

"Are you okay?" I ask when I drop to my knees at his side.

He wears a twisted expression on his face as he presses the bloodied fur against his wound. "I'm fine. Is it over?"

"Eric has met his end." There is so much blood, and Jameson's skin appears pale next to the red streaked across his stomach and chest. "The rest of his men have run."

"They're cowards," my husband says. "Another advantage we had over them."

He winces when I put my hand on top of his, pressing the fur harder against his wound, and Zip whines again.

"We must get you to the healer."

I expect him to argue, to tell me the injury is not as bad as it looks, but he does not, and that scares me more than even the blood pooled beneath him on the floor.

Jameson needs help getting to his feet and once again has to lean on me for support when we head out of the hut. Zip trails after us, and I have to force myself not to look at the bodies spread across the ground as we walk. There are too many, and right now my focus must be on saving my husband.

Blossom's empty eyes stare at up at us when we reach the other platform, but there is no sign of the baby as I pull Jameson past her and into the hut. Again, I try not to focus on it. Jameson is all I can worry about right now.

"He needs help!"

He grunts when I ease him to the floor, and Zip hurries to his side. The dog's panic is echoed in my own body as I spin around in search of the healer, but the scene I am met with pushes my concern for Jameson away like nothing else has been able to.

My mother lies on the floor, her head in Zachariah's lap and her skin as pale as snow, while splatters of red dot her lips. Below her, the floor shimmers red, but the fur she wears is so dark it takes a moment for me to figure out where the blood is coming from. Then I see the wound. It is her chest.

"No." I drop to my knees at my mother's side.

Jameson grunts, and I reach for him, and then for my mother, caught between them yet again and at a loss as to what I should do or who needs my attention the most. They are both pale, and my instinct is to go to my husband. We have a child on the way, and my baby will need a father in the new life I hope to forge in our village. Then my gaze meets Zachariah's. His pale eyes are shimmering with unshed tears and more tortured than I have ever seen them, and all the air leaves my body.

"Nothing can be done." He blinks, and the tears run down his cheeks, cutting trails of misery through the dirt on his face. "The healer can do nothing."

"No," I gasp again, moving closer as all thoughts of Jameson and our baby fade from my mind. This cannot be the end. Raven is too strong, too big. We need her here.

"Wilderness," my mother says, holding her hand out. While Zachariah's expression is one of devastation, hers is serene. "It is okay. This was meant to be. The village is changing—" She coughs, and blood sprays from her lips, dotting her pale skin with more droplets of red. "They need a new leader. They need you. And Jameson."

"No." I grasp her hand and shake my head, tears spilling from my eyes. "No." It is all I can say. That one word. That one useless word.

"Yes, my child. The Great Mother is calling me to Paradise, and I must go. I have made too many mistakes. Cost the village too much." She lets out a deep breath, the sound raspy and painful, and her face contorts, but only for a second. Then the serene expression is back. "I did not want this to happen, but I caused it all the same. You must learn from my mistakes, Wilderness. You are so much stronger than I am."

Her hand tightens on mine, and my eyes fill with tears, falling when I lean forward and rest my head on her shoulder. "I am not strong enough to lead. Not yet. We need you here."

My mother runs her hand down my head, smoothing my hair back. "You are much stronger than I gave you credit for. Stronger than me. You will do well, Wilderness."

She coughs again, and I look up to find her gaze on Zachariah, who is crying openly now, his shoulders shaking from the powerful sobs. Raven pulls her hand from mine, and my heart sinks like a rock in a pond. I cannot move, not even to focus on Jameson, but my mother does not look at me again. She only has eyes for Zachariah.

"My husband." She touches his cheek, wiping a tear away and leaving a trail of blood in its wake. "How I have loved you. From the moment I saw you at the Gleaning, I knew you had been made for me. I am sorry I did not say it earlier. Sorry I did not give you more of myself." She lets out a wet, raspy breath. "You will help them. Be there to show them the way."

"Do not leave me, Raven." Zachariah leans down and presses his lips against her cheek. "Do not go."

My mother coughs, and when she sucks in a breath, it rattles in her chest. "I do not have a choice. If I could stay for anyone, it would be you."

Raven threads her fingers through Zachariah's short hair, pulling his face closer to hers. Each breath she lets out seems to hurt more than the one before, until one final gasp escapes her lips and her body goes still. Her hands slide from Zachariah's head and drop to the ground with a thud that shakes my body, but he does not move. He keeps his face pressed against hers as he cries, his sobs coming harder than ever, so hard it would not surprise me if they shook the entire hut.

"Wilderness," someone behind me says, and I turn to find the sad eyes of the healer focused on me. "I need your assistance."

Pushing my sorrow aside for the time being, I return my focus to my husband. Zip is already with him, curled up beside Jameson like he knows what has happened, while the healer kneels on his other side. She presses a green bundle against Jameson's wound, making his face scrunch up in pain. Thanks to my many cuts and injuries, I am more than familiar with the fuzzy green leaves, only I cannot imagine them working on such a big wound.

"Will this work?" I ask the healer when she motions for me to move forward.

"Yarrow is all we have." She nods toward Jameson. "You must press it to the wound and hold it there."

I do as I'm told, replacing the healer's hands and pressing the plant against the wound on my husband's back and another handful against the one on his front. He winces and grunts, but I do not ease up, knowing the pressure and the plant will work together to slow the bleeding.

The healer pats my shoulder before hurrying away to other patients, and I can only pray her rush to leave my husband means he is not in any grave danger.

"Raven has met her end," I say when we are alone.

Jameson places his hand over mine. "I know. I'm sorry, Wilderness."

"She said we are to lead. I do not know if I can do that, Jameson. I am a hunter, not a leader like my mother. I am not ready."

He sucks in a deep breath as if he cannot bear the pain then says, "You're ready. I believe in you, and so did she."

I say nothing, but instead look toward the other side of the hut where Zachariah still sits leaning against the wall. He is no longer crying, but he acts like he does not know what is going on around him. Never before I have seen my father look so lost. He stayed here because of Raven, and now she is gone. Hopefully, my brothers and I are enough for him, and he can find a place in our village even though he is no longer a husband, because I am not ready to lose the father I just found. There is too much ahead of us to look forward to.

JAMESON'S BLEEDING STOPS, BUT HE IS WEAK FROM LOSING SO much blood, and I have to help him back to my hut to rest. When he lies down, he closes his eyes, and the pallor of his skin reminds me of the way the color drained from my mother's face after she left her body, headed for Paradise.

"This is not your end," I say, kneeling at his side.

When he opens his eyes, the smile he gives me is small. "I'm not leaving you."

Despite his confident words, he closes his eyes and lets out a deep breath like he has no energy, and as if thinking the same thing, Zip jumps up on the bed uninvited and curls up at my husband's side. Having the dog with him is a comfort to me. I do not want to leave Jameson, but sitting next to his bed while he sleeps will help no one, and there is much to do. We have lost a lot today, and if I am to lead as my mother requested, I must put others first. Even with my husband injured.

"I must go," I tell him. "I must find out who else we have lost."

Jameson opens his eyes, and he swallows before he can find his voice. "I'll be fine. Zip will keep me company."

The dog lifts his head at the sound of his name, and I scratch him behind the ear the way I have seen Jameson do a hundred times.

"Rest," I say and press my lips to his forehead.

He nods, and his eyes slide closed once again.

Zip scoots closer to him, resting his muzzle on Jameson's stomach. My husband's ghostly complexion pierces my heart, and before I turn to leave, I ask the Great Mother to keep him safe and make him strong.

It is only afternoon, but after what happened, it feels like it should be much later. People move as if in shock, but the sight of it is almost pleasant, because for once we are together. Two platforms over, a father holds a little girl, and beyond that, a man and a woman stand with their arms wrapped around each other in an embrace. Below me, another woman works with the teen yieldlings to move the bodies of Eric's men, while Grove and Ash gather our fallen. The camaraderie in the air gives me hope that we can be something more than what we have been for the past seventy years. If we allow it, this can be a new beginning for us.

I toss a rope ladder down so I can descend, and then head over to where I saw Ash and Grove. At their feet are four bodies, all women, but I know we have lost more than this.

"How many have met their end?" I ask when I stop next to them.

"Nine." Grove turns so she can look me in the eye. "Including Raven."

"I know." The pain in my heart matches the worry weighing me down on the inside.

My mother and I had grown distant, but I will still miss her, as will many others. For the past twenty-six years, all I wanted was to be as strong as Raven, but I now realize I need to be more. I must be stronger than she was, both for my children, and for the village.

"She said I am to lead with Jameson," I tell Grove and Ash. "How can I do that?"

"By being yourself, Wilderness," she says. "You were right. Not just about the foundling, but about the men." Her gaze moves to Ash, and the sadness in her eyes looks out of place on such a great warrior. "I have a son I have not touched in two years. I gave him up like I was supposed to, but it was not what I wanted. He is my flesh. We should be together."

I stare at her in wordless wonder. How many other women feel this way? Did my mother? I remember how she locked herself in her hut after Reed met his end, and I realize she must have. Yet she gave her boys up anyway because she thought it was right. Just like I stood up for my husband because I could see the error of the old ways.

"Do you think the other women will see it that way?" I ask Grove.

"I think it will be a struggle for some, but not for the younger ones. Mother Elder will be on your side, though, and that will help."

I let out a deep sigh and look down at the dead women in front of me. Blossom, Willow, Summer, and Autumn. They were all my family, and they have all met their end because of what we did to Eric. He was evil, but he was not wrong to be angry.

But I find I cannot regret what has happened, because it has led us here. We have made mistakes and wronged people, but it is what brought Jameson to me, and without him, I would not have been able to see the truth the way I see it now. Like a rainbow after a horrible storm, I can picture a future full of hope and happiness.

"We will figure it out together," I say to Grove and Ash, and they nod in agreement.

WE BURY ERIC AND HIS MEN IN THE FOREST JUST PAST THE men's village, marking their graves with stones as a reminder that we must not repeat our mistakes. Our family, the nine men and women who met their ends and have passed into Paradise, we take to the clearing. My mother included.

Jameson, still too weak from blood loss, does not go, but Zachariah stands at my side as we lay the bodies to rest together. It is how it should be, how it should have been all along—the men and women resting side by side. I braided Raven's long hair before they brought her out here, weaving flowers through it as she did for me when I was a child. Her skin, which has always been fair, now looks as white as snow against the dark earth.

"She was the most beautiful woman I have ever known," Zachariah says.

I put my arm around my father's waist and lean my head against his chest. "She was the strongest woman I have ever known."

When they begin tossing dirt into the hole, I turn away, but Zachariah stays. Moving on will be hard for him, but like my mother, he is strong, and I know he will get through it, especially now that he has his children to cling to.

On the way back to the village, I spy Ivy, carrying Blossom's baby in her arms, the girl's blond hair reminding me of her father, but also of what I must do. I must teach not just this child, but all the children to come what it means to love.

Hawk walks ahead of me, his gaze on the ground, and my heart goes out to him, knowing he was not prepared for the blow Blossom's death brought. Moving faster, I fall in beside my brother, wanting to reach out and give his hand a squeeze, but holding back.

Instead, I ask, "Will you be able to move on?"

He lifts his gaze from the ground, his brown eyes focusing on me, and nods, causing his blond hair to flop across his forehead. "I have lost two women, but this one was harder because I chose her for myself. Maybe there will be another for me, but I do not know."

"At least men are no longer forced to leave," I say, thinking of the women who met their ends today. Most of them left husbands behind, but for once it does not mean they must wander the wilderness in search of their own end. "We can move on together."

This time when the urge to slip my arm around Hawk comes over me, I do not hold back. He tenses like he is not sure he likes it, but after a couple more steps, he stops and turns to face me, and as I study his features, I'm able to see both my mother and father in him for the first time. I have never seen myself other than brief glimpses of my reflection in the water, and I cannot help wondering if Hawk and I resemble each other. Do I have my mother's nose as well? My father's forehead? His smile?

"Do I look like her?" I ask my brother.

Hawk somehow finds it in himself to smile. It is small, but it is a start, and it warms me more than the sun shining down on my head. "You do, but also like him."

"Good. I like knowing she is still here."

"You are better than she was, Wilderness. You got the best parts of both of them. That is what will make you a good leader."

"Thank you, brother," I say, blinking away tears.

"You are welcome, sister," he replies, saying the new word hesitantly, almost like he is not sure how voicing it will change things.

Back in the privacy of my hut, I cry for the loss of my mother while Jameson's hand rests on my stomach. It is fitting, focusing on a new beginning instead of an end. This child is half me, but it is also half Jameson, and it will know all the things we have learned and the peacefulness of this village, but will also start its life with a family. With a mother and a father, and if the Great Mother chooses to bless us even more, brothers and sisters. And what Jameson tells me is called a grandfather.

"If it is a girl," I say, putting my hand over Jameson's, "I want to name her Raven."

"And if it's a boy?" he asks.

"Zachariah."

He smiles and laces his fingers through mine. "I couldn't think of better names."

I stare at our hands, fingers entwined on top of my stomach, and dream about the future. The vision Jameson brought to our village has made it perfect, and I look forward to the years ahead of us.

EPILOGUE

Jameson

WE RIDE DOWN THE MOUNTAIN AS A GROUP. Wilderness is behind me on the horse, sitting sidesaddle to accommodate her growing stomach, and Zip trots along at my side as usual. The trees have begun to change, their leaves now more brown and yellow than green, and the air has cooled enough that I had to wrap a fur around me when we left the hut this morning. Grove rides the horse next to mine, with Ash on the other side of her, while Zachariah takes up the rear, and even though his smile seems to have been permanently erased, he wears an expression of tranquility.

The town is still a good way off, but even from here I can see the crowds milling around. When the train started working, it brought more people to the area, and for the first time in over seventy years, the town of Mountain Pass is bustling with life. Smoke billows from chimneys as the whistle of the train echoes through the open space, signaling its approach, and Wilderness tightens her grip on my waist. Like the other villagers, she isn't used to civilization yet, even after months of trading with the people down here.

Men and women turn to stare when we ride into town, just like they always do, but it doesn't bother me. I realize to them we seem backward and savage, but I've lived both lives, and I know the truth. There's savagery and evil in everyone, just as there is goodness, and choosing a more peaceful existence where the people are at least trying to fix their mistakes only makes sense.

We reach the center of town and come to a stop as the train rolls into the depot, steam rising around it as it slows to a stop, and like migrating geese, people get off while more climb on. The passage of visitors to this town seems never-ending, and I know this place isn't alone. All up and down the tracks, other towns have sprung up, bringing more and more people to the center of the country. It's why we decided to come down the mountain in the first place. We knew it was only a matter of time before someone got curious and came looking for us, and making our presence known seemed like the smartest approach. We can't force people to stay away, but we can let them know we aren't a threat.

I slide off the horse then turn to help my wife down. Wilderness smiles, but it's shaky. Like the others, being here makes her nervous.

"Jameson!" Tim calls, waving from the door of the store he opened only two months ago. "I was hoping to see you today."

Zip drops to the ground beside the horses while I head Tim's way, holding my wife's hand, and Zachariah and Ash follow, their arms loaded down with furs. Grove takes up the rear, and like the true warrior she is, she towers over everyone in both stature and presence, her expression alone enough to deter anyone from messing with us. We're still a novelty in this town, despite the peaceful agreement we've made with Tim and a handful of other merchants, and it isn't just curiosity thrown our way when we come down to trade. Suspicion and hostility run as rampant in the looks people give us.

Inside the store, we find bolts of cloth and rope and buttons, and once again I marvel at how lucky we got when we met Tim. His wife is a seamstress who toiled in a hot factory for ten hours a day when they lived in the city, and they came out here to not only start a new life, but also a new business. She's as welcoming as her husband and has been more than thrilled with the leather and pelts we bring her.

"I got this yesterday when the train came in, and I thought of you." Tim pulls a box out from under the counter and holds it out, and the way his gaze moves to Wilderness leaves no doubt in my mind what's inside.

I remove the lid to find a snowy white baby outfit. The fabric is soft and thick, and it has a hood to pull up over the baby's head. Wilderness is due in December, and the cold has worried me more and more as the time draws near, something I mentioned to Tim's wife, Yvette, last time we were here.

"It is beautiful." Wilderness reaches out to touch the fabric, her brown eyes growing wide at how soft it is. "What kind of animal is this?"

"No animal," Tim says with a chuckle. "Just plain old cotton."

My wife shakes her head like she doesn't understand. "We cannot take this. We did not bring enough to trade."

"It's a gift from Yvette and me." Tim pushes the box toward her. "Please."

She smiles when she looks at me. I'm wearing the wolf pelt she gave me more than a year ago, while the sapphire I gave her hangs around her neck. The gifts touched us both when we were still trying to find our way with one another, and because of that, I know she'll accept the baby outfit. She understands the importance of a gesture like this.

"Thank you," she says, taking the box from him. The way she wraps her arms around it tells me it will be a precious possession. Just like the wolf pelt once was. "Tell Yvette we are grateful."

Tim returns her smile, amusement shimmering in his eyes. "I know she'll be sad she missed you today, but she's at home tending to a sick kid. I'll let her know you liked it."

"Very much," Wilderness murmurs.

We deliver the fur to Tim, who gives us money in exchange, and with it we visit the other shops in town whose owners we've also made arrangements with. Some of them still look at us with suspicion, but most welcome our business and even put things aside for us. It's a nice deal for everyone involved.

The forest provides us with almost everything we need, but this has made it easier to do certain things. It's given us new nails to repair huts and walkways, and rope to reinforce old bridges, as well as medicine like antibiotics. The forest is ripe with homeopathic remedies, but the knowledge that some illnesses need actual drugs has weighed on me, especially after Oak, the simple-minded boy who loves sitting by the fire so much, almost died of a fever over the summer. No matter what the healer tried, he didn't get better, and if I hadn't been able to come down the mountain and trade for medicine, he wouldn't have made it. Which had me thinking about Talon and the limp he will have for the rest of his life, thanks to a poorly set break, and of Reed who died from a rattlesnake bite, and of my own child and what the future holds.

We gather the necessities we came down to get, but before we leave, I splurge and buy a bag of peppermint candies. The children in the village, who have never had sweets, will no doubt think I'm a hero, and I can't help hoping the gesture will even touch some of the women who still haven't warmed to me. There are only a handful, but the ones who haven't embraced the changes are the harshest critics, and anything to make life easier is welcome.

When we've finished in town, we head back the way we came. Stares follow our progress once again, and I find I'm more than happy to leave the real world behind and head back into the forest. The home we've created is still a work in progress, but it's better. Most of the men now live in the trees with their wives and children. The word yieldling hasn't slipped away, but I've heard people use it to refer to baby girls as well, giving me hope that one day there will be no difference between the two. The women still hunt and provide, but they're teaching the men to shoot as well, and we're working on becoming equals.

That night, back in our hut, Wilderness pulls out the little outfit and rubs her hand over the soft fabric. "Our baby will be the first to know this new life."

I lay my hand on her round stomach, right over a hard knot that I imagine is an elbow or knee. "It's a good life."

"It is."

"Are you still happy we started trading with the town?"

"Yes. I think it was right. The people there do not understand us, but the more we go down, the more they will realize we are not a threat to them." She lets out a deep breath. "I only fear they are a threat to us. Not because I think they will come up here, but because I worry the children in our village will be tempted to go down there. That they will taste the sweets and see the ease of everything those people have and want to leave."

"Was I wrong to buy the peppermints?"

She smiles and puts her hand over mine. "No. You have a good heart, and that is why you did it. We cannot hide from the world forever, no matter how much we wanted to. Eventually, it was bound to find us. If children leave, it is their right. I will not hold people hostage anymore."

The days pass, leaving fall behind and bringing winter and snow. My wife's belly grows until she has trouble climbing the rope ladder, and I have to help her into the pulley cart to get her up and down. A change Zip doesn't seem to appreciate.

It's the middle of the night when her time finally comes. The walkways are covered in snow, and more flakes fall on my head as I hurry across the village. By the time I make it back to our hut with the midwife, Wilderness is barely able to breathe through her contractions.

I stay by her side, holding her hand the entire time, and just before dawn, our son comes into the world screaming. He's the most beautiful thing I've ever seen, with dark hair and blue eyes as pale as his grandfather's.

Later that day, the man himself makes an appearance, dragging snow into the hut and giving us a genuinely wholehearted smile for the first time since Raven died. When Wilderness slips the baby into his arms, he stares down at the bundle like he's never seen anything so beautiful, and I understand exactly how he feels.

"Is it a boy?" he asks.

"It is," Wilderness says. "He will be called Zachariah."

Zachariah looks up, his blue eyes shimmering with tears, but he seems too choked up to utter a word. Instead, he stares at his daughter as he holds his grandson, and the moment is the most perfect thing I've ever seen. It's full of love and family and peace, things I never knew I could have, and things Zachariah never thought he would get.

Neither of us came to this village by choice. Like me, he probably saw the women who dragged him here as savages. In many ways they were, but in other ways they saved my life. They gave me a woman who is braver than anyone I've ever met, who stood up for me, who loved me, who would die for me if she had to. They gave me a family and a home that still feels like a different world, but in a good way. A magical way I never could have imagined existed.

I sit at my wife's side while Zachariah paces the room, whispering to the baby, and when she slips her hand into mine, I bring it to my lips, reveling in the fact that I can touch her whenever I want.

"I love you," I whisper.

She turns her eyes on me, and they shimmer in the soft glow of the lantern. "I love you, Jameson."

It's a moment more perfect than anything I could have ever imagined, more perfect than I would have dared dream. Sitting in a hut in the middle of nowhere with my wife at my side and my baby in the arms of my father-in-law, I find that I'm at peace. Not just with where I am, but with how I got here. It was a rough road to travel, but every second of it was worth it because it brought me to Wilderness.

THE END

ACKNOWLEDGEMENTS

First of all, I want to take a moment to wholeheartedly thank my agent, Stacey Donaghy, who tried so hard to sell *Tribe of Daughters*. Without the combined efforts of Stacey Donaghy and Sue Miller, another agent at Donaghy Literary Group, this book wouldn't be what it is. They not only helped me find a new and better title, but also dug into the manuscript and made notes so I was able to revise it, making the story much stronger. Their overwhelming support and enthusiasm for this novel kept me going during those long months of negative responses, and Stacey in general has been the best cheerleader a person could ask for while trying to navigate the disheartening world of publishing. No, we didn't find a home for it, but hopefully publishing it on my own will at least mean we're able to find an audience.

The idea for this story came to me after learning about the Mosuo people, who are believed to be China's last matrilineal society. I learned about this group after hearing references to their culture twice in a short period of time, once while listening to an audiobook and a second time while watching TV.

After the second time, I decided to look them up, and reading about their culture gave me an idea, which led to this book. While my group is very different from the Mosuo, it was the concept of "walking marriages," as well as the role the men play in their culture—according to some, men have no responsibility in Mosuo society and no jobs, but instead rest all day and conserve their strength for nighttime visits—that really inspired me to create this world. No, they do not capture men and drag them to their village, or punish them—as far as I know. That part of the story was my idea completely and in no way reflects the values of the Mosuo people.

I wrote the first draft of this novel in a week. Never before has a story come to me so clearly or been so vivid, and once I got started, I had a hard time focusing on anything else. This, by all accounts, is my favorite book I've written, and I hope readers enjoy it as much as I have.

To my first readers: Erin Rose, Rebekah Caillouet, Diana Gardin, Carey Monroe, Laura Johnsen, Julie Dewey, and Jan Strohecker. Thank you for reading, cheering me on, searching for typos, and giving me feedback. As always, it's an honor to have such an amazing group of dedicated readers.

To the NAC, my first big support group and one of the places I always turn when I need a sympathetic ear, a huge thank you! Marnee Blake, Diana Gardin, Ara Grigorian, Amanda Heger, Sophia Henry, Jamie Howard, Marie Meyer, Jessica Ruddick, Annika Sharma, Laura Steven, Meredith Tate, and Tegan Wren.

To my Apocalyptic Authors Group, who knows the woes of trying to get any traditional publisher to pay attention to an apocalyptic story: Michelle Bryan, Dia Cole, Eli Constant, and Claire Riley. Thanks for listening to me bitch and moan!

Thank you, as always, to Lori Whitwam for her editing skills and for being a friend, for working with me on adding weeks and canceling weeks, and for being a fan as well. I'm so glad we get to work together.

To Amber Garcia and her PR expertise, thanks for all the tours and shares, and for the multiple times you remind me to send teasers and excerpts, and all the other things I forget to attach to my emails.

To my readers, yes, that's you. If not for the fans who leave reviews, send messages and emails, or post on Facebook, I don't think staying positive would be as easy as it has been, and if not for the readers who decided to take a chance on a new author four years ago, I wouldn't be where I am. Thank you so much for reading and loving my stories, but also for supporting me the way you have.

A special thanks also has to go to the editorial staff at Sourcebooks, who tried so hard to find a place for TRIBE. Even though they ultimately decided the book just didn't fit their current catalogue, they took the time to make notes and give feedback in hopes that I would be able to make the book stronger and find a home for it at another publisher. While that didn't happen, I still appreciate the fact that someone out there was able to read this book and see it for how great it is.

To my husband, who is always there for me, who listens when I complain about the difficulties of the traditional publishing world and has supported me at every turn, thank you. He may not read my books most of the time, but he brags about me more than I brag about myself, and is definitely one of my biggest supports. And to my kids, who are always enthusiastic when it comes to my career, telling teachers and friends about my writing and leaving me alone when I need some peace and quiet. I have the best family in the world.

ABOUT THE AUTHOR

Kate L. Mary is an award-winning author of Adult, New Adult, and Young Adult fiction, ranging from Post-apocalyptic tales of the undead, to Speculative Fiction and Contemporary Romance. Her Young Adult book, *When We Were Human*, was a 2015 Moonbeam Children's Book Awards Silver Medal winner for Young Adult Fantasy/Sci-Fi Fiction, and a 2016 Readers' Favorite Gold Medal winner for Young Adult Science Fiction, and her Dystopian novel, *Outliers*, was a Top 10 Finalist in the 2018 Author Academy Awards and the First Place Winner in the 2018 Kindle Book Awards for Sci-Fi-Fantasy Fiction. Don't miss out on the *Broken World* series, an Amazon bestseller and fan favorite.

For more information about Kate, check out her website: www.KateLMary.com

CPSIA information can be obtained
at www.ICGtesting.com
Printed in the USA
LVHW012107220519
618750LV00015B/1037/P